Thomas Hood

Tales, Romances, and Extravaganzas

Thomas Hood

Tales, Romances, and Extravaganzas

ISBN/EAN: 9783744775755

Printed in Europe, USA, Canada, Australia, Japan

Cover: Foto ©Andreas Hilbeck / pixelio.de

More available books at **www.hansebooks.com**

TALES, ROMANCES,

AND

EXTRAVAGANZAS.

BY

THOMAS HOOD.

INCLUDING:

OUR FAMILY. — A DOMESTIC NOVEL.
MR. WITHERING'S CONSUMPTION AND ITS CURE. — A DOMESTIC
EXTRAVAGANZA.
THE CAMBERWELL BEAUTY. — A CITY ROMANCE.
THE CONFESSIONS OF A PHŒNIX.
MRS. BURRAGE. — A TEMPERANCE ROMANCE.
MRS. PECK'S PUDDING. — A CHRISTMAS ROMANCE.
THE SCHOOLMISTRESS ABROAD.
THE TOWER OF LAHNECK.
MRS. GARDINER. — A HORTICULTURAL ROMANCE.
MR. CHUBB. — A PISCATORY ROMANCE.

NEW YORK:

G. P. PUTNAM; HURD AND HOUGHTON.

401 BROADWAY, CORNER OF WALKER ST.

1866.

RIVERSIDE, CAMBRIDGE:
PRINTED BY H. O. HOUGHTON AND COMPANY.

ADVERTISEMENT.

THIS volume is chiefly composed of the later prose writings of its author, — his contributions to the "New Monthly" and to "Hood's Magazine," — and includes some of his favorite productions. Among these is, "Mrs. Gardiner. — A Horticultural Romance" — which his son, who inherits no little of the father's humorous and poetical power, regards as his most humorous work. It was dictated to his wife from a sick-bed, in the presence of his two children, and amid the irrepressible bursts of laughter of the whole family. The sadness mingled in this mirth renders the scene one of the most remarkable in literary history. "Mrs. Peck's Pudding" was published in the last Christmas number of his magazine, and, as his children say in their most interesting Memorials, afforded seasonable amusement at all firesides but its author's. We trust that both these stories, with the many others equally entertaining in this collection, will furnish to many generations of readers not merely Christmas amusement, but amusement for all the year round.

CONTENTS.

CONTENTS.

PAGE

OUR FAMILY:

A DOMESTIC NOVEL.

OUR FAMILY.

A DOMESTIC NOVEL.

CHAPTER I.

WE ARE BORN.

THE clock struck seven —

But the clock was a story-teller; for the true time was One, as marked by the short hand on the dial. The truth was, our family clock — an old-fashioned machine, in a tall mahogany case, and surmounted by three golden balls, as if it had belonged to the Lombards — was apt to chime very capriciously.

However, it struck seven just as my father came down stairs from the bedroom, rubbing his hands, and whistling in a whisper, as his custom was when he was well pleased, and walking along the passage somewhat more than usual on his tiptoes, with a jaunty gait, he stepped into the sitting-room to communicate the good news. But there was nobody in the parlor except the little fairy-like gentleman, who walked jauntily to meet him, rubbing his hands, and silently whistling, in the old mirror, — a large circular one, presided over by some bronze bird, sacred perhaps to Esculapius, and therefore carrying a gilt bolus, attached by a chain to his beak.

From the parlor my father went to the surgery: but there was nobody there; so he repaired, perforce, for sympathy into the kitchen, where he found the maid, Kezia, sitting on a wooden chair, backed close against the whitewashed wall, her hands clasped in her lap, and her apron thrown over her head, apparently asleep and snoring, but in reality praying half aloud.

1

"Well, Kizzy, it's all happily over."

Kezia jumped up on her legs, and having acknowledged, by a bob, her master's presence, inquired eagerly "which sect?"

"Doublets, Kizzy, doublets. A brace of boys!"

"What, twins! O, gimini!" exclaimed the overjoyed Kezia, her checks for a while glowing both of the same color. "And all doing well, missis and babes?"

"Bravely — famously — mother and all!"

"The Lord preserve her!" said Kezia, with emphatic fervor — "the Lord preserve her and her progeny," pronouncing the last word so that it would have rhymed with mahogany.

"Progeny — with a soft *g*," muttered my father, who had once been a schoolmaster, and had acquired the habit of correcting "cake-ology."

"Well, prodge, then," murmured Kezia. her checks again looking, but only for a moment, both of a color. For, by a freak of nature, one side of her face, from her eye to the corner of her mouth, was blotched with what is called a claret-mark — a large irregular patch of deep crimson, which my father, fond of odd coincidences, declared was of the exact shape of *Florida* in the map. Be that as it might, her face, except when she blushed, exhibited a diversity of color quite allegorical, one side as sanguine as Hope, and the other as pallid as Fear.

Now, a claret-mark is generally supposed to be "born with the individual;" whereas Kezia attributed her disfigurement to a juvenile face-ache, to relieve which she had applied to the part a hot cabbage-leaf, but gathered unluckily from the red pickling brassica instead of the green one, and so by sleeping all night on it, her cheek had extracted the color. An explanation, offered in perfect good faith; for Kezia had no personal vanity to propitiate. She had no more charms, she knew, than a cat — not any cat, but our own old shabby tabby, with her scrubby skin, a wall eye, and a docked tail. But in moral Beauty — if ever there had been an annual Book of it — Kezia might have had her portrait at full length.

Her figure and face were of the commonest human clay, cast in the plainest mould. Her clumsy feet and legs, her coarse red arms and hands, and dumpy fingers, her ungainly trunk, and hard features, were admirably adapted for that rough drudgery to which she unsparingly devoted them, as if only fit to be scratched, chapped, burnt, sodden, sprained, frostbitten, and stuck with splinters. And if sometimes her joints stiffened, her back ached, and her limbs flagged under the severity of her labors, was it not all for the good of that family to which she sacrificed herself with the feudal devotion of a Highlander to his clan? In short, she combined in one ungainly bundle of household virtues, all the best qualities of our domestic animals and beasts of burden — loving and faithful as the dog, strong as a horse, patient as an ass, and temperate as a camel. At nineteen years of age she had engaged herself to my mother as Servant of All Work; and truly, from that hour, no kind of labor, hot or cold, wet or dry, clean or dirty, had she shunned: never inquiring whether it belonged to her place, but toiling, a voluntary Slave, in all departments; nay, as if her daily work were not enough, sleep-walking by night into parlor and kitchen, to clean knives, wash up crockery, dust chairs, or polish tables!

To female servants in general, and to those in particular who advertise for small families, where a footman is kept, the advent of two more children would have been an unwelcome event: perhaps equivalent to a warning. Not so with Kezia. Could one have looked through her homely bosom into her heart, or through her plain forehead into her brain, they would have been found rejoicing beforehand in the double, double toil and trouble of attending on the twins. My father's thoughts were turned in the same direction, but with a gravity that put an end to his sub-whistling, and led him, half in jest and half in earnest, to moralize aloud.

"Two at once, Kizzy, two at once — there will be sharp work for us all. Two to nurse — two to suckle — two to wean — two to vaccinate (he was sure not to forget that!) — two to put to their feet — "

"Bless them!" ejaculated Kezia.

"Two to cut their teeth — two to have measles, and hooping-cough — "

"Poor things!" murmured Kezia.

"Ay, and what's worse, two more backs to clothe; and two more bellies to fill — and I can't ride on two horses, and pay two visits at once."

"You must double your fees, master."

"No, no, Kizzy, that won't do. My patients grumble at them already."

"Then I'd double their physicking, and order two draughts, and two powders, and two boxes of pills, instead of one."

"But how will they like such double drugging, Kizzy — supposing that their constitutions are strong enough to stand it?"

Kezia was silent. She had thrown out her suggestion for the benefit of the family; and beyond that limited circle her mind never revolved. Her sympathies began, and, like Domestic Charity, ended at home. Society, and the large family of human kind in general, she left to shift for themselves.

The conversation having thus dropped, my father crept up stairs again, to see how matters were going on overhead; whilst the maid proceeded to answer a muffled knock at the front-door, followed by an attempt to ring the night-bell, but which had been completely dumbfounded by Kezia with paper and rag. The appellant was Mr. Postle, the medical assistant.

"A nice night for a ride through the Fens," grumbled the deputy-doctor, shaking himself in his great coat like a wet water-dog, before he followed the maid into the kitchen, where he seated himself in his steaming clothes before the fire.

"Mr. Postle!"

Mr. Postle looked up at the speaker, and saw her hard features convulsively struggling into what bore some distant resemblance to a smile.

"Mr. Postle!" and her voice broke into a sort of hysterical chuckle. "You don't ask the news?"

"What news?"

"What! Why, there's an increase of the family!" said Kezia, her face crimson on both sides with the domestic triumph. "We've got twins!"

"Humph!" grunted Mr. Postle. "Better one strong one, than two weakly ones."

"Weakly!" exclaimed Kezia; "why, they're little Herculuses! Our babbies always are."

A suppressed laugh caused the assistant and Kezia to look round, and they beheld, close beside them, the nurse, Mrs.

Prideaux. It was one of her peculiarities that she never shuffled about slipshod, or in creaking leather; but crept along noiselessly as a ghost, in a pair of list moccasons; and thus taking advantage of my father's visit to the bedchamber, she had descended for a little change to the kitchen.

A very superior woman was Mrs. Prideaux: quite the attendant for an aristocratic invalid, lying in down, beneath an embroidered quilt, and on a laced pillow. She was never seen in that slovenly dishabille, so characteristic of females of her profession; no, you never saw *her* in a slatternly colored cotton gown drawn up through the pocket-holes, and disclosing a greasy nankeen petticoat with ticking pockets — nor in a yellow nightcap, tied over the head and under the chin with a blue and white bird's-eye handkerchief — looking like a Hybrid, between a washerwoman and a watchman. A pure white dimity robe, tied with pale-green ribbons, was her undress. Her personal advantages were very great. Her figure was tall and genteel; her features were small and regular — so different to those dowdy Dodo-like creatures, bloated, and ugly as sin, who are commonly called " nusses." Then she did not take snuff; nor ever drank gin or rum, neat or diluted: a glass of foreign wine or liqueur, or brandy, if genuine Cognac, she would accept; but beer, never. No one ever heard her sniff, or saw her spit, or trim the candle-snuff with her fingers. And if ever she dozed in her chair, as nurses sometimes must, she never snored : but was lady-like even in her sleep. Her language was not only free from vulgarisms and provincialisms, but so choice as to be generally described as " book English." You never heard Mrs. Prideaux blessing her stars, or invoking Goody Gracious, or asking Lawk to have mercy on her, or asseverating by Jingo. She would have died ere she would have complained of her lines, her rheumatiz, her lumbargo, or the molligrubs. Such broad, coarse words could never pass those thin, compressed lips. But perhaps the best test of her refined phraseology was, that though the word was so current with mothers, fathers, sisters, brothers, gossips, and servants of both sexes, that it rang in her ears, at least once in every five minutes, she never said — babby.

In nothing, however, was Mrs. Prideaux more distinguished from the sisterhood, than the tone of her manners : so affable, yet so dignified — and above all, that serene self-possession under any circumstances, supposed to accompany high breeding and noble birth. Thus, nobody ever saw her flustered, or non-plushed, or at her wit's ends, or all in a twitter, or narvous, or ready to jump out of her skin; but always calm, cool, and correct. She hinted, indeed, that she was a reduced gentlewoman, deterred by an independent spirit from accepting the assistance of wealthy and titled connections. In short, she was a superior woman, so superior, that many a calculating visiter who would have tipped another nurse with a shilling, felt compelled to present a half-crown, if not a whole one, to Mrs. Prideaux, and even then with some anxiety as to her reception of the offering.

Such was the prepossessing person, whose presence notwithstanding was so unwelcome to the medical assistant, that her appearance in the kitchen seemed the signal for his departure. He rose up instantly from his chair, but halted a moment to ask Kezia if there had been any applications at the surgery in his absence.

"Yes, the boy from the curate's, for some more of the paradoxical lozenges: he says he can't preach without 'em."

"Paregorical. Well?"

"And Widow Wakeman with a complaint —"

"Ah! in her hip."

"No, in her mouth, that she have tried the Scouring Drops, and they won't clean marble."

"I should think not — they're for sheep. Well?"

"Only a prescription to make up. Pulv. something — aqua, something — summoned, and cockleary."

"Anything else?"

"O yes, a message from the great house about the Brazen monkey."

"Curse the Brazil monkey!" and snatching up a candle, Mr. Postle yawned a good-night apiece to the females, and with half-closed eyes stumbled off to bed.

"A quick-tempered person," observed Mrs. Prideaux, as soon as the subject of her comment was beyond earshot.

"Yes, rather caloric," she meant choleric. As an exception to her simple habits Kezia was fond of hard words, perhaps because they were hard, just as she liked hard work.

"Well, Kezia, you observed the clock?"

" The clock, ma'am ? "

" Yes. The precise date of birth is of vast importance to human destiny."

" O, for their fortune-telling ! I never thought of it — never ! " And the shocked Kezia began to heap on herself, and her sieve of a head, the most bitter reproaches.

" No matter," said the nurse. " I *did* mark the time exactly." And as she spoke she drew from her bosom, and gazed at a handsome enamelled watch, with a gold dial, and a hand that marked the seconds.

" You are aware that one of the twin infants was born before, and the other after, the hour of midnight ? "

" No, really ! " exclaimed Kezia, her dull eyes brightening at the prospect of a double festival. " Why, then, there will be two celebrated birthdays ! "

" The natal hour involves matters of much deeper importance than the keeping of birthdays," replied the nurse, with a startling solemnity of tone and manner. " Look here, Kezia," and returning the watch to her bosom, she drew forth a little blue morocco pocketbook, from which she extracted a paper inscribed with various signs and a diagram. " Do you know what this is ? "

" I suppose," said Kezia, turning the paper upside down, after having looked at it in every other direction, " it is some of Harry O'Griffis's characters."

" Not precisely hieroglyphics," said the nurse. " It is a scheme for casting nativities. See, here are the Twelve Houses, — the first, the House of Life : the second, of Riches ; the third, of Brethren ; the fourth, of Parents ; the fifth, of Children ; the sixth, of Health ; the seventh, of Marriage ; the eighth, of Death ; the ninth, of Religion ; the tenth, of Dignities ; the eleventh, of Friends ; and the twelfth, of Enemies."

" And in which of those houses were our two dear babbies born ? " eagerly asked Kezia.

Mrs. Prideaux looked grave, sighed, and shook her head so ominously, that Kezia turned as pale as marble, her very claret-mark fading into a scarcely perceptible tinge of pink.

" Don't say it — don't say it ! " she stammered, while the big tears gathered in her eyes : " What ! cut off precockshiously like blighted spring buds ! "

"I did not say death," replied the nurse. But there are other malignant signs and sinister aspects, that foretell misfortunes of another kind — for instance, poverty. But hush —" and she held up a warning forefinger whilst her voice subsided into a whisper.

"I hear your master. Leave your door ajar, and I will come to you presently in your own room." So saying, she rose and glided spectre-like from the kitchen — where she left Kezia staring through a haze, damp as a Scotch mist, at a vision of two little half-naked and half-famished babes turning away, loathingly, from a dose of parish gruel, administered by a pauper nurse, with a workhouse spoon.

CHAPTER II.

OUR HOROSCOPE.

A LONG hour had worn away, and still Kezia sat in her attic with the door ajar, anxiously expecting the promised visit from the mysterious nurse. Too excited to sleep, she had not undressed, but setting up a rushlight, seated herself on the bed, and gave full scope to her foreboding fancies, till all the round bright spots, projected from the night shade on the walls and ceiling, appeared like so many evil planets portending misfortunes to the new-born. From these reveries she was roused by a very low, but very audible whisper, every syllable clear and distinct as the sound of a bell.

"Whose room is that in front?"

"Mr. Postle's."

"Can he overhear us through the partition?"

"No, not a word."

"You are certain of it?"

"Yes, I have tried it."

"Very good." And Mrs. Prideaux having first carefully closed the door, seated herself beside the other female on the bed. "I have left the mother and her lovely twins in a sound sleep."

"The little cherubs!" exclaimed Kezia. "And must they,

will they, sink so low in the world, poor things! Are they unrevocably marked out for such unprosperous fortunes in life?"

"They must — they will — they are. Listen, Kezia! I have not been many days, not many hours under this roof; but my art tells me that the wolf already has more than looked in at the door — that the master of this house knows, by experience, the bitter trials of a poor professional man — the difficulties, the cruel difficulties, of one who has to keep up a respectable appearance with very limited means."

"The Lord knows we have!" exclaimed Kezia, quite thrown off her guard. "The struggles we have had to keep up our genteelity! The shifts we have been obligated to make — as well as our neighbors," she added hastily, and not without a twinge of mortification at having let down the family by her disclosures.

"I understand you," said Mrs. Prideaux, with a series of significant little nods. "Harassed, worried to death, for the means to meet the tradesmen's bills, or to take up overdue acceptances. I know it all. The best china, and linen parted with to help to make up a sum (Kezia uttered a low inward groan), the plate in pledge (another moan from Kezia), and the head of the family even obliged to absent himself, to avoid personal arrest."

"She is a witch, sure enough," said Kezia to herself. "She knows about the baileys."

"Yes — there have been sheriff's officers in this very house," continued the nurse, as if reading the secret thought of the other. "Nor are the circumstances of your master much mended even at the present time," — and she fixed her dark eyes on the pale-blue ones, that seemed to contract under their gaze like the feline organ under excess of light — "at this moment, when there are not six bottles of what, by courtesy, we will call sherry, in his cellar, nor as many guineas in his bureau."

"Why, as to the wine," stammered Kezia, "we have had company lately, and I would not answer for a whole dozen; but as regards the pecuniery, I feel sure — I know — I'm positive there's nigh a score of golden guineas in the house, at this blessed moment — let alone the silver and the copper."

"Your own, perhaps?"

Kezia's face seemed suddenly suffused all over with claret, and felt as hot too as if the wine had been mulled, at being thus caught out in an equivocation, invented purely for the credit of the family.

"In a word," said the nurse, "your master is a needy man; and the addition of two children to his burdens will hardly improve his finances."

"But our practice may increase," said Kezia. "We may have money left to us in a legacy — or win a grand prize in the lottery."

"I wish it was on the horoscope," said Mrs. Prideaux, looking up at the ceiling, as if appealing through it to the planetary bodies. "But the stars say otherwise. Rash speculations — heavy losses by bad debts — and a ruinous Chancery suit, as indicated by the presence of Saturn in the twelfth house."

"Satan!" ejaculated Kezia, with a visible shudder. "If *he*'s in the house, there'll be chancery suits no doubt, for he is in league they say with all the lawyers, from the judges down to the 'turneys."

"And with litigation," said the nurse, "will come rags and poverty, ay, down to the second and third generations."

"What, common begging — from door to door?"

"Alas, yes — mendicity and pauperism."

"Never!" said Kezia, with energy, starting up from the bed, and holding forth her clumsy coarse hands, with their ruddy digits, like two bunches of radishes to tempt a purchaser, — "never! whilst I can work with these ten fingers!"

"Of course not, my worthy creature, only don't be quite so vehement — of course not. And, as far as my own humble means extend, you shall not want my poor co-operation. I have already devoted my nursing-fee and perquisites, whatever may be the amount, towards a scheme that will help to secure the little innocents from absolute want. There is a society, a sort of masonic society of benevolent individuals, privately established for the endowment of such unfortunate little mortals. For a small sum at the birth of a child, they undertake to pay him, after a certain age, a yearly annuity in proportion to the original deposit — a heavenly plan, devised by a few real practical Christians, who delight in doing good by stealth ; and especially to such forlorn beings as are born under the influence of a malignant star. Now the year that threatens our dear darling twins is the seventh ; a tender age, Kezia, to be left to the charity of the wide world !"

Poor Kezia turned as white as ashes ; and for some minutes sat speechless, writhing her body and wringing her hands, as if to wring tears out of her finger-ends. At last, in a faltering voice, she inquired how much seventeen guineas would grow into, per annum, in seven years.

" Why, let me see ; " and Mrs. Prideaux began to calculate by the help of a massive silver pencil-case and her tablets ; " seventeen guineas, for seven years, with interest — and interest upon interest — simple and compound — with the bonus, added by the society — why, it would positively be a little fortune — a good twenty pounds a year — enough at any rate to secure one, or even two persons, from absolute starvation."

Kezia made no reply, but darted off to a large iron-bound trunk which she unlocked, and then drew from it a little round wooden box, the construction of which, every one who has swallowed Ching's worm medicine, so celebrated some thirty or forty years ago, will very readily remember. Unscrewing one half of this box with a shrill screeching sound, that jarred the nerves of Mrs. Prideaux, and set all her small white teeth on edge, Kezia poured into her own lap, from a compartment formerly occupied by oval white lozenges, ten full weight guineas of the coinage of King George the Third ; then turning the box, and opening the opposite half, with a similar *skreek*, and a fresh shock to the nerves and teeth of the genteel nurse, she emptied from the division, once filled with oval brown lozenges, eight half-guineas, and nine seven-shilling pieces ; in all, seventeen guineas, the sum total of her hoarded savings since she had been at service.

" Then, take them," she said, holding out her apron by the corners, with the precious glittering contents towards the nurse.

" Bless you — bless you for a true Samaritan !" replied Mrs. Prideaux, passing her hand lightly across her eyelashes — whilst something like a tear glistened upon one of her fingers, but the radiance came from a brilliant ring. " I will add this bauble to the stock," said the nurse, drawing it off, and throwing it into Kezia's apron. " But, my good girl, I am afraid you have contributed your all. You ought to consider yourself a little — you may be ill — or out of place. At any rate, reserve a trifle against a rainy day."

"No, no — don't consider me — take it all — all, every penny of it," sobbed Kezia. "The poor dear innocents! they are as welcome to it as my own little ones — at least, if I had any."

"To be sure it is for *them*, — one two, three," said the nurse, counting the pieces separately into a stout green-silk purse with gilt rings: "seventeen guineas exactly. With my own poor mite, and the ring, say twenty, or five-and-twenty, to be invested for the dear twins in the Benevolent Endowment Society. for children born under Malignant Planets."

"O, I do wish," exclaimed Kezia, with the abruptness of a sudden inspiration, "I do wish I knew the fortune-teller that prophesies for Moore's Almanac!"

The nurse turned her keen dark eyes on the speaker, and for a minute regarded her, as if, in the popular phrase, she would have looked her through and through. But the scrutiny satisfied her; for she said in a calm tone, that the name in question was very well known, as Francis Moore, physician.

"But people say," objected Kezia, "that Francis Moore is only his alibi," she meant alias.

"It is *not her* name," replied Mrs. Prideaux, with a marked staccato emphasis on the negative and the pronoun. "But that is a secret. And now, mark me, Kezia — not a syllable of this matter to any one, and least of all to the parents. The troubles we know are burdensome enough to bear, without an insight into futurity. And to foresee such a melancholy prospect predestined to the offspring of their own loins."

"O, not for the world!" exclaimed Kezia, clasping her hands together. "It would kill them outright — it would break both their hearts! As for me, it don't signify. I'm used to fretting. O, if you knew the wretched sleepless hours I've enjoyed, night after night, when master was in his commercial crisuses, with unaccommodating bills — he'd have had that money long and long ago, if I had had the courage to offer it to him, but he's as proud on some points as Lucifer. And, to be sure, we've not been reduced more than our betters, perhaps, at a chance time, when they could not get in their rents — or the steward absconded with them — or the stocks fell suddenly — or the bank was short of cash for the dividends, or the key of the bureau —"

She stopped short, for Mrs. Prideaux had vanished. So after an exclamation of surprise, and a thoughtful turn or two up and down her chamber, the devoted Kezia threw herself on her knees beside the bed, and prayed fervently for her master, her mistress, and the dear little progeny, till in that devout posture she fell asleep.

CHAPTER III.

WE ARE NAMED.

It is assuredly a mercy for humankind that we are born into this world of folly as we are, mere purblind, sprawling, oysterly squabs, with no more *nous* than a polypus, instead of coming into it with our wits ready sharpened, and wide awake as young weasels! Above all, it is providential that we are so much more accessible to lachrymose than ludicrous impressions; more prone to tears, squallings, sobs, sighs, and blubberings, than to broad grins or crowing like chanticleer. For, while at a royal or imperial establishment, one Fool has generally been deemed sufficient; at the court of a Lilliputian Infant or Infanta, it seems to be held indispensable that every person who enters the presence must play the zany or buffoon, and act, talk, sing, cut, and pull, such antics, gibberish, nonsense, capers, and grimaces, that nine tenths of the breed of babies, if their fancies were at all ticklesome, must needs die of ruptured spleen, bursten bloodvessels, split sides, or shattered diaphragms. Yes, nine tenths of the species would go off in a guffaw, like the ancient who lost his breath in a cachinnation, at seeing an ass eating figs. For truly that donkey was nothing to the donkeys, nor his freak worth one of his figs, compared to the farcicalities exhibited by those he and she animals who congregate around the cots and cradles of the nursery.

Thus, had our own little vacant goggle-eyes at all appreciated, or our ignorant sealed ears at all comprehended, the absurdities that were perpetrated, said and sung, daily and hourly, before and around us, my Twin-Brother and myself must inevitably, in the first week, have choked in our pap, and died, strangled in convulsion fits of inextinguishable laughter, or perhaps jaw-locked by a collapse of the overstrained risible muscles.

It would have been quite enough to shatter the tender lungs and midriff of a precocious humorist, to have only seen that ungainly figure which so constantly hung over us, with that strange variegated face, grotesquely puckering, twisting, screwing its refractory features to produce such indescribable cacklings, chucklings, and chirruppings;—to have heard her drilling that impracticable peacocky voice, with its rebellious falsetto, and all its mazy wanderings, from nasal to guttural, from guttural to pectoral, and even to ventral, with all its involuntary quaverings, gugglings, and gratings, — into a soothing lullaby, or cradle-hymn. It must have asphyxiated an infant, with any turn for the comic, to have seen and heard that Iö-like creature with her pied red and white face, lowing —

> " There 's no ox a-near thy bed; "

or that astounding flourish of tune, accompanied by an appropriate brandishing of the mottled upper limbs, with which she warbled —

> " 'Tis thy Kizzy sits beside thee,
>   And her harms shall be thy guard."

It was ten thousand mercies, I say, that the stolid gravity of babyhood was proof against such sounds and spectacles: not to forget that domestic conclave, with its notable debate as to the names to be given to us in our baptism.

" For my own part," said my mother, enthroned in a huge dimity covered easy-chair, " I should like some sort of names we are accustomed to couple together, so as to make them out for a pair of twins."

" Nothing more easy," said my father. " There's Castor and Pollux."

" Was Castor the inventor of castor-oil?" inquired my mother, in the very simplicity of her heart.

"Why, not exactly," replied my father, suddenly rubbing his nose as if something had tickled him. "He was invented himself." An answer, by the way, which served my other parent as a riddle for the rest of the day.

"And what was their persuasion?"

"Heathen, of course."

"Then they shall never stand sponsors for children of mine," said my mother, whose religious sentiments were strictly orthodox. "But are there no other twin brothers celebrated in history?"

"Yes," replied my father. "Valentine and Orson."

"Why, one—one—one of them," exclaimed Kezia, stuttering in her eagerness—"one of them was a savage, like Peter the Wild Boy, and sucked a she-bear!"

"Then *they* won't do," said my mother, in a tone of great decision.

"And Romulus and Remus are equally ineligible," said my father, "for they were suckled by a she-wolf."

"Bless me!" exclaimed my mother, lifting up her hands, "the ferocious beasts in those days must have been much tamer and gentler than in ours. I should be sorry to trust flesh and blood of mine to such succedaneums for wet-nurses."

"And what would be your choice, Kizzy?" inquired my father, turning towards the maid of all work, who, by way of employing both hands and feet, had volunteered to rock the cradle, whilst she worked at the duplicate baby-linen, so unexpectedly required.

"Why then," said Kezia, rising up to give more weight to the recommendation, "if that precious pair of infants was mine, I'd christen them Jachin and Boaz."

"The pillars of the temple"—said my father. "But suppose, Kizzy, the boys chose to go into the army or navy?"

"They would fight none the worse," said Kezia, reddening, "for having Bible names!"

"Nor better," said my father, *sotto voce*. "And now, perhaps, Mrs. Prideaux will favor us with her opinion?"

But the genteel nurse, with a sweet smile, and in her silvery voice, declined advising in such a delicate matter; only hinting, as regarded her private taste, that she preferred the select and euphonious, as a prefix. Her own son was named Algernon Marmaduke Prideaux.

" Perhaps," said my father, leaning his head thoughtfully on one side, and scratching his ear, — "perhaps Postle could suggest something. His head 's like an Encyclopædia."

" He have," said Kezia, suspending for a moment her needlework and the rocking of the cradle. " He 's for Demon and Pithy."

" For what ! ! !" exclaimed my mother.

" Demon and Pithy.'

" Phoo, phoo — Damon and Pythias," said my father, " famous for their friendship, like David and Jonathan, in the classical times."

" Then they 're heathens, too," said my mother, "and won't do for godfathers to little Christians."

A dead pause ensued for some minutes, during which nothing was audible but my father's ghost of a whistle, and the gentle creak, creak, of the wicker cradle. The expression of my mother's face, in the mean time, changed every moment for the worse ; from puzzled to anxious, from anxious to fretful.

" Well, I do wish," she exclaimed at last, just at the tail of a long sigh. — " I do wish, George, that you would think of some name for our twins. For, of course, you don't wish them to grow up anonymous like Tobit's dog !"

" Of course not," replied my father. " But I can hit on only one more suggestion. Supposing the infants to be remarkably fine ones — "

" And so they are !" put in Kezia.

" And of an uncommon size for twins — "

" They 're perfect Herculuses," cried Kezia.

" What think you of Gog and Magog ? "

" Fiddle and fiddlestick !" exclaimed my mother, in great indignation. " But I believe you would joke on your deathbed."

"Rabelais did," said my father. " But come," he added, in his genuine serious voice, for he had two, a real and a sham Abraham one, " it is my decided opinion that we could not do better than to name the children after your brother. He is wealthy, and a bachelor ; and it might be to the advantage of the boys to pay him the compliment."

"I have thought of that too," said my mother. "But my brother does n't shorten well. Jinkins Rumbold is well enough ; but you would n't like to hear me, when I wanted the children. calling for Jin and Rum."

"Pshaw !" said my father, "I am philosopher enough to bear that for the chance of a thumping legacy to our sons."

The genteel nurse, Mrs. Prideaux, backing this worldly policy of my father's with a few emphatic words, my mother concurred ; and, accordingly, it was decided that we should be called after Jinkins Rumbold ; the Jinkins being assigned to my twin brother, the first-born, and the Rumbold to my "crying self."

It is usual. however, in dedicating works, whether of Art or Nature, in one or two volumes, to ask previously the permission of the dedicatee. To obtain this consent, it was necessary to write to our Godfather Elect : and accordingly my father retired to the parlor, and seated himself, on epistolary deeds intent, at the old escrutoire. But my parent was an indifferent letter-writer at the best ; and the task was even more perplexing than such labors usually are. His brother-in-law was a formalist of the old school ; an antiquarian in dress, speech, manners, sentiments, and prejudices, whom it would not be prudent to address in the current and familiar style of the day. The request, besides, involved delicate considerations, as difficult to touch safely, as impossible to avoid. In this extremity, after spoiling a dozen sheets of paper and as many pens, my father had recourse, as usual, to Mr. Postle, who came, characteristically at his summons, with a graduated glass in one hand. and a bottle of vitriolic acid in the other. It was indeed one of his merits, that he identified himself, soul and body, with his business : so much so, that he was reported to have gone to an evening party with his handkerchief scented with spirits of camphor.

"Mr. Postle," said my father, "I want your opinion on a new case. Suppose a rich old hunks of a bachelor uncle, whom you wished to stand godfather to your twins, what would be your mode of treatment, by way of application to him !"

The assistant, thus called in to consultation, at once addressed himself, seriously, to the consideration of the case. But in vain he stared at the Esculapian bronze bird with the gilt bolus suspended from its beak, and from the bird, at the framed sampler, and thence to the water-color view of some landscape in Wales, and then at the stuffed woodpecker, and in turn at each of the black profiles that flanked the mirror. There was no inspiration in any of them. At last he spoke.

"If it's all the same to you, sir, I think if we were to adjourn to the surgery, I could make up my mind on the subject. Like the authors, who write best, as I have heard, in their libraries, with their books about them, my ideas are always most confluent, when, in looking for them, my eyes rest on the drawers, and bottles, and gallipots. It's an idiosyncrasy, I believe, but so it is."

"So be it," said my father, gathering up his rough composing drafts, and hurrying, with Postle at his heels, into the surgery, where he established himself at the desk. The assistant in the mean time took a deliberate survey of all the wooden earthenware, and glass repositories for drugs, acid, salt, bitter, or saccharine; liquid, solid, or in powder.

"Now then, Postle," said my father, "how would you set to work to ask a rich old curmudgeon to stand sponsor to your children?"

"Why, then, sir," replied Postle, "in the first place, I would disclaim all idea of drawing upon him"—(and he glanced at a great bottle apparently filled with green tinsel, but marked "cantharides")—"or of bleeding him. Next I would throw in gentle stimulants, such as an appeal to family pride, and reminding him of your matrimonial mixture. Then I would exhibit the babies—in as pleasant a vehicle as possible—flavored, as it were, with cinnamon"—(he looked hard at a particular drawer)—"and scented with rose-water. As sweet as honey"—(he got that hint from a large white jar)—"and as lively as leeches." (He owed that comparison to a great fact on the counter.)

"Very good," said my father.

"After that," continued Mr. Postle, "I would recommend change of air and exercise, namely, by coming down to the christening: with an unrestricted diet. I would also promise to make up a spare bed for him, according to the best prescriptions; with a draught of something comforting to be taken the last thing at night. Say, diluted alcohol, sweetened with sugar. Add a little essential oil of flummery; and in case of refusal, hint at a mortification."

"Capital!—Excellent!" exclaimed my father. And on this medical model he actually constructed a letter, before dinner-time, which might otherwise have puzzled him for a week!

CHAPTER IV.

THE bed in the spare bedroom had been aired for my father: who, between his attendance on my mother, and another lady in the same predicament, had never been out of his clothes for three successive nights. But the time for repose had arrived at last; he undressed hastily, and was standing in his nightgown and nightcap, his hand, with the extinguisher just hovering over the candle, when he heard, or thought he heard, his name called from without. He stopped his hand and listened—not a sound. It had been only the moaning of the wind, or the creaking of the great poplar at the end of the house; and the hollow cone was again descending over the flame when his name was shouted out in a peremptory tone by somebody close under the window. There could be no mistake. With a deep sigh he put down the extinguisher—opened the casement, and put forth his head. Through the gloom he could just perceive the dark figure of a man on horseback.

"Who is there?"

"Why the devil," grumbled the fellow, "have you muffled the night-bell? I've rung a dozen times."

"Why?"—replied my father—"why, because my mistress is confined."

"I wish mine was," growled the man, "in a madhouse. You're wanted."

"To-night?"

"Yes: I'm sent express for you. You're to come directly."

"Where?"

"At the great house, to be sure."

" Well, I'll come — or at any rate Mr. Postle — "

" No — you must come yourself."

My father groaned in spirit, and shuddered as if suddenly struck to the lungs by the night-air.

" Who is ill ?" he asked ; "is it Prince George ?"

" No — it's the little " — the rest was lost in the sound of the horse's heels as the messenger turned and rode off.

My father closed the casement with a slam that nearly broke the jingling glass ; and for some minutes stood ruefully looking from the candle to the bed, and from the bed to the chair with his clothes. But there was no remedy : with his rapidly increasing family he could not afford to slight a patient at the great house. So he plucked off his nightcap, threw it on the floor, and with both hands harrowed and raked at his hair, till every drowsy organ under it was thoroughly wakened up ; then he dressed hastily, crept down stairs, wisped a bandana round his throat, struggled into his great-coat, thrust on his worst hat, and, pocketing the door-key, stepped forth into the dark, damp, chill air. He thought he never felt so uncomfortable a night in his life, or encountered worse weather ; but he thought a mistake. He had met with inferior qualities by fifty degrees. However there were disagreeables enough, wind and fog, and his road lay for half a mile on the border of a Lincolnshire river, and through a dreary neighborhood, — for out of Holland or Flanders, there was not such another village, so low and flat, with so much water, running and stagnant, in canals and ditches, amidst swampy fields growing the plant cannabis, or hemp — or with so many windmills, and bulrushes, and long rows of stunted willows, relieved here and there by an aspen that seemed shivering with the ague. On he went, yawning and stumbling, past the lock, and over the bridge, and along by the row of low cottages, all as dark as death except one, and that was as dark as death too, in spite of its solitary bright window. For the doctor stopped as he went by to peep in at the narrow panes, and saw one of those sights of misery, that the eye of Providence, a parish doctor, a clergyman occasionally, and a parliamentary commissioner still more rarely, have to look upon. On the bed, if bed it might be called, for it was a mere heap of straw, matting, rushes, and rags, covered by a tattered rug, sat the mother, rocking herself to and fro, over the dead child, wasted to a skeleton, that was lying stark across her lap. Beside her sat her husband, staring steadfastly, stupid with grief at the flame of the rushlight, his hollow cheeks showing yellow, even by the candle-light, from recent jaundice. Neither moved their lips. On the floor lay an empty vial, with the untasted medicine beside it in a broken teacup; there was a little green rush basket near the mother's feet, with a few faded buttercups — the last toys. My father saw no more, for the light that had been flickering, suddenly went out, and added Darkness to Sorrow and Silence.

In spite of his medical acquaintance with similar scenes of wretchedness, he was shocked at this startling increase of desolation ; and for a moment was tempted to step in and offer a few words of consolation to the afflicted couple. But before his hand touched the latch, reflection reminded him from his experience, how inefficacious such verbal comfort had ever been with the poor, except from sympathizers of their own condition. In the emphatic words of one of his pauper patients, " When a poor man or woman, as low down in life as myself, talks to me about heaven above, it sounds as sweetlike as a promise of going back some day to my birthplace, and my father's house, the home of my childhood ; but when rich people speak to me of heaven, it sounds like saying, now you 're old and worn out, and sick, and past work, and come to rags, and beggary, and starvation, there 's heaven for you — just as they say to one, at the last pinch of poverty — by way of comforting — there 's the parish."

So my father sighed and walked on : those two wretched, sickly, sorrow-stricken faces, and the dead one, seeming to flash fitfully upon him out of the darkness, as they had appeared and vanished again by the light of the flickering candle. And with this picture of human misery in his mind's eye he arrived at the Great House : and still carrying the dolorous images on his retina, across the marble hall, and up the painted staircase, and through the handsome antechamber, stepped with it, still vivid, into the luxurious drawing-room, that presented a new and very different scene of distress.

On her knees, beside the superb sofa, was the weeping lady of the mansion, bending over the little creature that lay shivering on the chintz cushion, with its arms hugging its own diminutive body, and the knees drawn up to the chest. Its dark almond-shaped eyes rolled restlessly to and fro: its tiny mouth seemed puckered up by suffering, and its cheeks and forehead were deeply wrinkled, as if by premature old age. The nurse, a young woman, was in attendance, so exhausted by watching that she was dosing on her feet.

As my father advanced into the room, he could distinguish the low moaning of the afflicted lady, intermixed with all those fond doting epithets which a devoted mother lavishes on her sick child. The moment she became aware of his presence she sprang up, with a slight hysterical shriek, and running to meet him, exclaimed,

"O doctor, I am so glad you are come! I have been in agonies! My poor dear darling, Florio, is ill — going — dying!" and she sobbed aloud, and buried her face in her handkerchief.

My father hastily stepped past her, to the sofa, to look at the patient: and at the risk of bursting, suppressed an oath that tingled at the very tip of his tongue. A single glance had filled up the hiatus in the groom's communication — the sufferer was a little Brazilian monkey.

My father's surprise was equal to his disgust, aggravated as it was by a vivid remembrance of the domestic distress he had so recently witnessed through the cottage-window. His head filled with that human bereavement, he had totally forgotten the circumstance that once before he had been summoned to the Great House on a similar errand — to prescribe for a sick lapdog, named after an illustrious personage, at that time very popular, as Prince George. But the whispers of Prudence stifled the promptings of Indignation, reminding him, just in time, that he was a poor country practitioner, the father within the last eight and forty hours of a pair of twins. Accordingly he proceeded with all gravity to feel the pulse and examine the skin of the dwarf animal; laying his hand on the chest to estimate the action of the heart; and even ascertaining, at the expense of a small bite, the state of the tongue.

The weeping lady in the mean time looked on with intense anxiety, uttering incoherent ejaculations, and putting questions with unanswerable rapidity. "O the darling! — my precious pet! — is he hot — is he feverish? My little beauty! — Is n't he very ill? He don't eat, doctor — he don't drink —

he don't sleep — he don't do anything — poor dear! Look how he shivers! Can you — can you — do anything for him — my little love of loves! If he dies I shall go distracted — I know I shall — but you 'll save him — you will, won't you? O do, do, do prescribe — there 's a dear good doctor! What *do* you think of him — my suffering sweet one? — tell me, tell me, pray tell me — let me know the worst — but don't say he 'll die! He'll get over it, won't he — with a strong constitution? — say it 's a strong constitution. O, mercy! look how he twists about! — my own, poor, dear, darling little Flora!"

My father, during this farrago, felt horribly vexed and annoyed, and even looked so in spite of himself: but the contrast was too great between the silent, still, deep sorrow — still waters are deep — for a lost child, and these garrulous lamentations over a sick brute. But the hard, cold, severe expression of his face gradually thawed into a milder one, as the idea dawned upon him of a mode of extracting good out of evil, which he immediately began to put in practice.

"This little animal," — he intended to have said my little patient, but it stuck in his throat — "this little animal has no disease at present, whatever affection may hereafter be established, unless taken in time. It is suffering solely from cold and change of climate. The habitat of the species is the Brazils; and he misses the heat of a tropical sun."

"Of course he does — poor thing!" exclaimed the lady. "But it is not my fault — I thought the Brazils were in France. He shall have a fire in his bedroom."

"It will do no harm, madam," said the Doctor. "But he would derive infinitely more benefit from animal heat — the warmth of the human body."

"He shall sleep with Cradock!" exclaimed the lady, looking towards the drowsy young woman, who bit her lips and pouted: "and mind, Cradock, you cuddle him."

"I should rather recommend, madam," said my father, "a much younger bedfellow. There is something in the natural glow of a young child peculiarly restorative to the elderly or infirm who suffer from a defect of the animal warmth — a fact well-known to the faculty: and some aged persons even are selfish enough to sleep with their grandchildren, on that very account. I say selfish, for the benefit they derive is at the expense of the juvenile constitution, which suffers in proportion."

"But where is one to get a child for him?" inquired the lady, perfectly willing to sacrifice the health of a human little one to that of her pet brute.

"I think I can manage it, madam," said my father, "amongst my pauper patients with large families. Indeed, I have a little girl in my eye."

" Can she come to-night?" asked the lady.

"I fear not," said my father. "But to-morrow, ma'am, as early as you please."

"Then for to-night, poor dear, he must make shift with Cradock," said the lady, " with a good tropical fire in the room, and heaps of warm blankets."

(Poor Cradock looked hot, at the very thought of it.)

"And about his diet?" asked the lady — "it's heart-breaking to see his appetite is so delicate. He don't eat for days together."

"Perhaps he will eat," said my father, "for monkeys, you know, madam, are very imitative, when the child sets him the example."

"I'll stuff her!" said the lady.

"It can do her no harm," said my father; "on the contrary, good living will tend to keep up her temperature. And as her animal warmth is the desideratum, she must be carefully guarded against any chill."

"I'll clothe her with warm things," said the lady, "from head to foot."

"And make her take exercise, madam," added my father: "exercise in the open air, in fine weather, to promote the circulation of the blood, and a fine glow on the skin."

" Cradock shall play with her in the garden," said the lady; "they shall both have skipping-ropes."

"I can think of nothing else," said my father; "and if such careful treatment and tender nursing will not cure and preserve her, I do not know what will."

"O, it must, it will, it shall cure her, the darling precious!" exclaimed the delighted lady, clapping her jewelled hands. " What a nice clever doctor you are! A hundred, thousand, million thanks! I can never, never, never repay you; but, in the mean time, accept a slight token of my gratitude," and she thrust her purse into my father's hand.

For an instant he hesitated ; but, on second thoughts, he pocketed her bounty, and with due thanks took his leave. " After all," he thought, as he stepped through the antechamber, " I am glad I was called in. The monkey may live or die : but, at any rate, poor little Betty Hopkins is provided for one while with a roof over her, and food, and raiment."

The night was finer ; the weather, as he stepped into it, was wonderfully improved : at least he thought so, which was the same thing. With a light, brisk step he walked homewards, whistling much above his usual pitch, till he came abreast of the cottage of mourning. There he stopped, and his sibilation sunk into silence, as the three melancholy faces, the yellow, the pale, and the little white one, again flashed on his memory. Then came the faces of his own twin children, but fainter, and soon vanishing. His hand groped wearily for the latch, his thumb stealthily pressed it down ; the door was softly pushed a little ajar, and the next instant, something fell inside with a chinking sound on the cottage floor. The door silently closed again, the latch quietly sunk into the catch ; and my father set off again, walking twice as fast and whistling thrice as loud as before. A happy man was he, for all his poverty, as he let himself in with the house-key to his own home, and remembered that he had under its roof two living children, instead of one dead one. Quickly, quickly he undressed and got into bed : and, oh ! how soundly he slept, and how richly he deserved to sleep so, with that delicious dream that visited him in his slumbers, and gave him a foretaste of the joys of heaven !

CHAPTER V.

A DILEMMA.

THE sun was high in heaven ere my father awoke the next morning, roused from his Elysian dreams by the swallows which first twittered at the eaves above the window, and then, after wheeling round the gable, went skimming along the surface of the glittering river in front of the house : contriving, temperate creatures though they be, to *moisten their clay* in the passage. The good Doctor sprang from his bed, threw open his casement, and looking cheerfully out in the fresh bright air, began whistling, in his old quiet way, the White Cockade. In the language of the professional bulletins, he had passed a good night: whereas my mother's had been a bad one. On paying his morning visit, he found her weak and languid; her face faded to a dull white, that, with its solid, settled gravity, reminded him of cold suet dumpling.

"Your mistress seems poorly this morning," said my father, addressing himself to Mrs. Prideaux, who had just entered the bedroom, dressed in a morning costume of peculiar neatness.

"I have certainly had the pleasure of seeing your lady look better," answered the nurse, "but she has been watchful, and giving way to mental solicitude."

"Solicitude! — about what?"

"It's about the christening." said my mother, with a sigh of exhaustion. "I have hardly slept a wink all night for thinking of it — and cannot yet make up my mind."

"As to what?"

"Why, whether we should have two godfathers or four."

"Four godfathers!"

"Yes — four," said my mother. "Kezia says, as there are twins to baptize, there must be a double set of sponsors. And certainly, according to the Book of Common Prayer, she is right. Here it is — " and she pulled the authority from under her pillow — "The Ministration of Public Baptism of Infants, to be used in the Church. *And note, that there shall be for every male child to be baptized two godfathers and one godmother.*"

"Humph!" said my father. "The rule seems plain enough. But will not the same pair of sponsors serve over again for the second child?"

"That is the very point," said my mother. "I have been turning it over and over, all night long, till my poor head is in a whirl with it; but am none the nearer. What is your own impression about it?"

"The duties of a godfather are rather serious," said my father, "and if duly fulfilled would be somewhat onerous. But as they are commonly performed, or rather compounded for, by some trifling gift, a spoon, a mug, or a coral — "

" And some godfathers," exclaimed my mother, " neglect even that! There was old Mackworth, who stood for little Tomkins, and rich as he is, never gave his godson so much as a salt-spoon ! "

" Such being the case," said my father, putting on his gravest face, " I really think that a couple of able-bodied men might stand sponsors, not merely for two babies, but for a whole regiment of infantry."

" It depends on the canons," said my mother, unconsciously supplying the infantry of my father's equivoque with appropriate artillery.

" On the what ? "

" On the canons of the church," said my mother ; " and I do wish that in your rounds you would look in on the Curate and obtain his dictum on the subject."

" Perhaps Mrs. Prideaux can enlighten us," said my father, turning towards that lady-like personage, who was hushing my brother on her lap, with a lullaby refined enough to have been of her own composition.

" No, I have asked Mrs. Prideaux," interposed my mother ; " but she has never nursed twins before, she says, and therefore cannot furnish a precedent."

" And if the Curate has never baptized twins before," said my father, " he will be in the same predicament."

" Of course he will," said my mother, looking as blank as if the clergyman in question had already declared himself at the supposed nonplus. " I'm quite troubled about it, and have been sleepless all night. It would break my heart to find hereafter that the dear infants had only been half Christianized through any departure from the orthodox rules."

" I'll tell you what," said my father, starting up from a brief reverie, during which he had assumed his usual air and attitude, at the consideration of an intricate case. I'll ask Postle."

" Kezia has asked him," said my mother.

" Well ? "

" Why, he said that two godfathers are the proper dose for a male child, but whether it ought to be repeated for twins, was more than he could say, and advised a consulting clergyman to be called in."

" Precisely so — it is a clerical case."

"For my part," continued my mother, "I am at my wit's ends about it ; for four sponsors, if there must be four, are not to be looked up in a hurry — "

"There's no need of four," exclaimed a voice, and in another moment the face of Kezia became visible between the foot-curtains of the bed, her claret-mark mulled by heat and haste to a rich purple, and the other cheek vying with it in color through triumph and excitement. "There's no need for four ! Two godfathers will be enough for both twins ; here it is under the Church's own hand ;" and she held out an open letter to her mistress.

That invaluable Kezia ! At the first hint of the dilemma, from my mother — having previously teased, and tried to unpick the difficulty, in her own mind, she had carried it down stairs, to where all mysteries and doubts were taken for analysis and solution — the surgery. But Mr. Postle, as already stated, was unable to decide the question. In this extremity, it occurred to her that there was a certain channel, through which she might obtain the requisite information : one Mrs. Yardly, whose husband, the parish clerk, would be as competent an authority as to the baptismal ceremonial as the curate himself. The acquaintance, it was true, was a very slight one : but where the good of the family was concerned, the faithful maid of all work was accustomed to get over far more formidable fences. Accordingly she at once composed and despatched a missive, of which the following is a correct copy, to the Amen Corner of our village.

"DEAR MADDAM, —

"Hopping you will xcuse the Libberty from allmost a purfeet Strainger havin but wunce xchanged speach with you in the Surgary, about a Pot of Lennitive Electricity. But our hole Fammily being uncommon anxous respectin the Cristnin of Hinfants. About witch we are all in a Parradox thro havin Twinns. The sweatest, finest thrivingest littel Cherrubs you ever saw. As lick as too pees And a purfeet plesure to nus only raythcr hoarse and roopy with singin dubblikit lullabis and so much Cradle Him. Not to menshun a xtra sett of Babby linnin to be made at a short notis for the Supper nummery And all the housold wurk besides. But its impossible to help slavin wuns self to Deth for such a pare of dear luvable littel hinnocents, and I allmost wish I was ded to be a Gardian Angle for their sacks being purfectly misrable wen I think wat Croops and Convulshuns and Blites beset such yung toothless Buds. And half crazy besides with divided oppinions between Small Pock and Cow Pock witch by report runs sum times into horns and Hoofs. Lord preserve the dear littel Soles from such a trans moggrificashun. But lettin alone Waxynation our present hobject bein to make them Hares of Grace. And as such how menny must stand Sponsers for them at the Fount? The Prayer Book says two god fathers for evvery Mail, but the Pint is wether the same two cannot anser or not for boath. As yet only two have been providid, namely their unkel Mr. Rumbold the Dry Salter and a Mister Sumboddy, a Proxy in Docters Commons. So that if so be Fore Fathers is necessery for Twinns we shall be at a Non Plush. The nus Mrs. Priddo never havin nust Twinns afore cant find a President. And Mister Postle say it is out of his line of practis. But yure Husbund Mister Y bein a clisiasticle Caracter of course knows wat is propper and ortherdoxical and an erly Line from ether him or you to that effect would grately obleege and releave all our minds. For as you may supose we are anxous for the dear Hinfants to have a reglar Babe teasing. And shud be shockt arterwards to find they had been skrimpt in their Spirritual rites. Witch is a matter in witch wun would prefer their Babbies to be rayther over then under dun. Bless, bless, their preshus littel harts. With witch I remane dear Maddam

" Yours &c.

" KEZIA JENKS."

The answer to this epistle had just arrived; and after a hasty perusal by Kezia, was thrust open into her mistress's hand.

" Here, take it George," said my mother, " and read it aloud."

My father took the document, and began to read — the owner of the letter lending her ears as intently, as if she learned the sense of the writing for the first time.

" MADAM, —

" In reply to your epistolary favor to my Wife beg to say you are quite wellcome gratis to any experience or information in my Power, parochial, ecclesiastical, or scholastic — Copies of Births, Deaths, or Marriage Certificates excepted, and searching the Register, which is charged for according to time and trouble.

" As regards the Sacrament of Baptism, the quotation from the Prayer Book is ceremoniously correct. Whereby, according to Rule of Three, if one Male Infant require two Godfathers how many will two require? Answer, Four. But in Practise two are religiously sufficient for twin juveniles. Our fees in any case being the same. Not that the Church object to the full sponsorial complement if parental parties think proper to indulge in the same; whether for the sake of a greater Shew, or with a view to the multiplication of customary Presents. Exempli Gratia, Mrs. Fordige with the extraordinary number of Four Twin Sons at a Birth, who were named after the Holy Evangelists, videlicet, Matthew, Mark, Luke, and John, when it was thought proper to have the full number of Godfathers, $4 \times 2 = 8$, and which I well remember walking up the aisle two and two, with Nosegays, like the team of a Stage Waggon. As was considered an interesting spectacle, especially by the Female part of the congregation. And profitable, besides, to parents, the eight Godfathers having agreed amongst themselves, and the four Godmothers likewise — Sum Total, twelve — to present Plate of the same pattern.

"In conclusion, my matrimonial Partner desires her compliments, and trusts to be excused answering the domestic details in your Letter for the present, hoping shortly to enjoy the pleasure of a Call, and to enter into the dear little innocents in person.

"I am, Madam,

"Your very humble Servant,

"REUBEN YARDLEY, P. C."

"There!" said my father, returning the letter to Kezia; and then gayly addressing mother, "our perplexities are at an end! We may drive our christening coach with a pair of godfathers, or four in hand, at our own option. For which do you vote?"

"O, for only a pair, of course," replied my mother. "The four would be so hard to collect," she added in a tone which showed that she lamented the difficulty. She was proud of her twins, and would have liked to have seen them attended up the church aisle by a double set of sponsors, walking two and two, with nosegays, and forming, as the learned clerk said, an interesting spectacle to the female spectators. For a minute or so, closing her eyes, she had even enjoyed, in a day-dream, a sort of rehearsal of such a procession: but there were too many obstacles in the way of its realization; and she reluctantly gave up the scheme.

"That's settled then!" exclaimed my father, rubbing his hands together in a most high and palmy state of satisfaction.

"Not quite," said my other parent; who from stewing had only subsided into a simmering. "There's the godmother. I have gone through every female name in the place, without hitting on anybody likely to undertake the office."

" Phoo, phoo, it's a mere form."

" I beg your pardon," said my mother, rather hastily. "Some persons think it a very responsible office, and refuse to be godmothers at all on that account. Others, again, profess a deep sense of its duties, and insist on acting up to the character."

" And is there any harm in that?" asked my father.

" There might be a world of trouble and annoyance in it," said my mother. " There 's Mrs. Pritchard, whom I sounded on the subject, when she called yesterday. 'I'm agreeable to stand,' said she, 'if I'm asked, but, mind, I shall stand on conscientious grounds. I'm not going to be a nominal godmother, like some people : — not a mere automaton, or a figure in waxwork. If I become one of their religious sureties, I'll act up to it, and do my duty as regards their spiritual bringing up;' which is all very well, but might be made a pretext, you know, for interfering in the children's education, and everything."

" No doubt of it," said my father. "And from the perseverance with which Mrs. Pritchard meddles in the temporal concerns of her neighbors, she would unquestionably be a rank nuisance where she had any pretence for busying herself with their spiritual ones. But there 's Mrs. Hewley."

" She 's in favor of Adult Baptism," replied my mother.

" Or Mrs. Trent?"

" She 's for total immersion, or dipping in running streams."

" Mrs. Cobley, then?"

" Why, she 's a Papist!"

Poor Kezia! Her variegated York and Lancaster face nad undergone, during the discussion, a dozen changes — from red and white to all red, and then back again, — her lips twitching, her brows knitting, her eyes twinkling and moistening. What would she not have give to have been in a station that would have entitled her to volunteer the godmothering of those evangelical twin babes — to have undertaken the care of their precious little souls, as well as of their dear little bodies! — to have stood for them at the font, as well as at the fire, the dresser, the tub, and the ironing-board — slaving for their spiritual welfare as well as their temporal comfort! How heartily she would have pledged herself to teach them the

Creed and the Commandments, and the Catechism, in the vulgar tongue, and "all that a Christian ought to know," if she learned some branches of education herself for the purpose! But she had, alas! no chance of enjoying such drudgery.

"There's Mrs. Spencer," suggested my father.

"She's confined," said my mother.

"Well, well," said my father, smiling, "if it comes to the worst, there's the pew-opener."

"The Lord forbid!" exclaimed Kezia, lifting up her hands and her eyes at the proposition. "What, Mrs. Pegge! Why, she stands for all the naturalized children in the parish."

"As mine are, I hope," said my father, with due gravity.

Kezia turned indignantly away; she felt sure that her master must be joking, but the subject was too serious for such treatment. What, — those beautiful twin babes — both in one cradle — both on one pillow — both under one blanket! "Bless them," she ejaculated aloud, "bless them, bless them, the dear little cherubims — I've boiled their tops and bottoms!"

The last announcement was aimed at the nurse, but it evidently hit my father also, and in some ticklesome place, for he rubbed his nose as smartly as if a fly had settled on it, and then setting up his whisper of a whistle, stepped briskly out of the bedchamber and down the stairs into the surgery. Why he stopped his music, to laugh out at about the middle of the flight, was known only to himself.

<hr>

CHAPTER VI.

CATECHISM JACK.

My father was the parish doctor; and when he entered the surgery, Mr. Postle was making up a parish prescription. A poor, shabbily-dressed woman was waiting for the medicine, and a tall, foolish-looking lad was waiting for the poor woman. She was a widow, as it is called, without encumbrance, and had a cottage and some small means of her own, which she eked out, with the stipend allowed to her by the overseers for taking charge of some infirm or imbecile pauper. The half-witted boy was her present ward.

"It's for Jacobs," said the woman, as my father glanced over the shoulder of his assistant at the prescription. "He gets wus and wus."

"Of course he does," said my father; "and will, whilst he takes those opium pills."

"So I tell him," said the woman; "with his ague, and in a flat, marshy country like this, with water enough about to give any one the hydraulics."

"Hydroptics."

"Well — droptics. You want stimulusses, says I, and not nar—nar—cis — "

"Narcotics."

"Well — coties. But the poor people all take it. If it's their last penny, it goes for a pennorth of opie, as they call it, at Doctor Shackle's."

"I wonder he sells it," said my father.

"And asking your pardon, doctor," said the woman, "I wonder you don't. They say he makes a mint of money by it."

"Never!" said my father, with unusual emphasis, — "never, if I want a shilling."

"Talking of money," said the woman, "there's a report about goolden guineas, chucked last night by nobody knows who — for it was done in the dark — into the Hobbes's cottage. They have just lost their only child, you know."

The assistant suddenly checked the pestle with which he was pounding, and looked inquisitively at his principal, who fixed his eyes on the idiot boy.

"Well, my lad, and who are you?" inquired my father. "What's your name?"

"M. or N.," answered the boy, slowly dragging the wet fore-finger, which he had withdrawn from his mouth, with a long snail-like trail along the counter.

"Fiddlesticks," exclaimed the woman, giving her charge a good shaking by the shoulder. "You've got another name besides that."

"Yes," drawled the boy, "some call me Catechism Jack."

"Ah! — that's an odd name!" said my father. "Who gave it you?"

"My godfathers and godmothers in my baptism," said Jack.

"No such thing, sir," said the woman; "it was the idle boys of the village, because he was always repeating on it; and, indeed, poor fellow, he can repeat nothing else."

"Then how did he get that?"

"Why you see, sir," said the woman, "between ourselves it was all along of his godmother."

"Ah!—indeed!" exclaimed my father, pricking up his ears at such an appendix to the recent discussion in the bed-room. "His godmother, eh?"

"Yes, Mrs. Tozer as was, for she's dead now, as well as his own mother; and that's how he came into my care. His mother went first, while he was in petticoats, and so Mrs. Tozer took charge of him, and sent him to the infant day-school. She was a very strict woman in her religious principles, and so was the schoolmistress; and both made it a great pint for the children to be taught accordingly, which they was. Well, one day there they were, all in the school-room up one pair, and little Jack amongst the rest, the last of the row, a-setting on the very end of a long form close to the open door. Well, by and by the children were all called up to say Catechism; so up they all got at once, except Jack, who had been playing instead of getting his task by rote, which made him backwarder to rise than the rest,—when, lo! and behold! up tilts the form, like a rearing horse, and pitches Jack, heels over head, through the door and down the whole stone flight, where he was picked up at the bottom perfectly unsensible."

"Ah!—with a concussion of the brain," said my father.

"A contusion of the occiput," added Mr. Postle; "the spinal vertebræ excoriated, of course, and bruises on both patellæ."

"I don't know about that," said the woman, "but he had a lump on the back of his head as big as an egg; the nubbles of his back were rubbed raw, and his two kneepans were as black as a coal. It was thought, too, that his intellex were shook up into a muddle."

"No doubt of it," said my father.

"Well, to go on with Jack. At long and at last he came to, sore enough and smarting, as you may suppose, for he had been carried home to his godmother, and she had rubbed his

wounds with sperrits and salt, which had got into the cuts.
And now, Jack, says she, mark my words, and let them be a
warning.　It's a judgment of God upon you, says she, for not
knowing your Catechism ; for if so be you had got it by heart,
you would have riz with the rest, and then all this would
never have happened.　But it's a judgment upon you, says
she, and the schoolmistress said the same thing ; till between
both the poor thing was so scared, he set to work, he did, at
his Catechism, and never rested, day or night, till he had got
it by heart, as he has now, so thoroughly, you may dodge him,
any how, backward or forward, and he won't miss a syllable.
And that's how he come by it, sir, as well as the nickname :
for except Catechism, which his head is too full of, I suppose, to hold anything else, he don't know a thing in the
world."

"Poor fellow !" said my father, opening one of the surgery
drawers.　"Here, Jack, will you have a lozenge ?"

"Yes, verily, and by God's help, so I will.　And I heartily
thank —"

"There, there, hush ! go along with you," said the woman,
giving her *protégé* a push towards the outer door, and then,
taking up the medicine, with a nod of acknowledgment to Mr.
Postle, and a courtsey to my father, she departed, her forlorn
charge clinging to her garments, and muttering scraps of that
formula which had procured for him the *sobriquet* of Catechism
Jack.

CHAPTER VII.

A PATIENT.

"Poor creature !" muttered my father, carefully fishing a
drowning fly out of the inkstand with the feather end of a
pen, and then laying the draggled insect to dry itself on the
blotting-paper ; "poor, harmless, helpless creature !"

The assistant stopped his pounding, and looked inquisitively,
first at the speaker and then at the supposed object of his
sympathy.

"I wonder," continued my father, still talking to himself, "if he would like to carry out the medicine?"

Mr. Postle hastily resumed his mortar-practice, with an interjectional "Oh!"

"Job is gone, I suppose?"

Mr. Postle pounded like mad.

"Job is gone, is n't he?" repeated my father.

"Yes, with the best livery."

"In that case," said my father, heedless of the best blue and drab, "we shall want another boy. And I am thinking, Postle, that yonder half-witted fellow might, perhaps, carry the basket as well as another."

"What, the Catechism chap? Why, he 's an idiot!"

"Or nearly so," said my father; "and, as such, shut out from the majority of the occupations by which lads of his rank in life obtain a livelihood. The greater the obligation, therefore, to prefer him to one of the few employments adapted to his twilight intelligence."

"What — to carry out the physic?"

"And why not?"

"Nothing," said Mr. Postle, but plying the pestle as if he would have pounded the mortar itself into a powder, "nothing at all. Only when an idiot carries out the physic, it 's time to have a lunatic to make it up."

"Phoo! phoo!" said my father, "the boy has arms and legs, and quite headpiece enough for such simple work. At a verbal message, no doubt, he would blunder."

"Yes — would n't he?" said Mr. Postle. "Take of compliments and Catechism, each a dram, mix — shake well up — and administer."

"Like enough," said my father, "if one intrusted any verbal directions to his memory. But he goes on parish errands, and knows every house in the place; and might surely deliver a written label at the right door, as well as a printed notice."

"I wish," said Mr. Postle, gloomily, "there may be any to deliver. Our drugs *are* drugs! We hardly do a powder a day. The business is in a rapid decline, and in another month won't be worth a pinch of magnesia. There 's the Great House gone already — and next we shall lose the parish."

"How! — the Great House!" exclaimed my father, with

more anxiety and alarm than he had betrayed before about his simious patient. "Is the monkey dead, then?"

"Yes — of bronchitis."

"Poor child!" ejaculated my father.

"I should like to open him," said Mr. Postle.

"I hoped she was provided for," said my father, with a sigh.

"If you mean little Betty," said the assistant, "it is no loss to her, — at least to judge by Mother Hopkins's language."

"Why, what does she say?" asked my father, with a tone and look of unmitigated surprise.

"Only all that is bitter and acid. The ungrateful old hag! I should like to stop her mouth with a pitch-plaster!"

"Hush, hush!" whispered my father; and Postle did hush, for, confirming an old proverb, Mother Hopkins herself hobbled into the surgery, with foul weather on her face. Her lips were compressed — there was a red angry spot in the middle of each sallow cheek, and anger glimmered in her dark black eye, like a spark in a tinder-box. She spoke harshly, and abruptly.

"I 'm come to return the bottles."

"Very good!" said my father, receiving vial after vial from the cankered woman, with as much courtesy and humility as if he had been honored and obliged by her custom. "I hope the medicine has done you good. How is your lameness?"

"As bad as ever."

"I am sorry to hear it," said my father; "but your complaint is chronic, and requires time for its treatment. By and by we shall see an amendment."

"We shall see no such thing," said the Shrew. "I arn't going to take any more physic."

"No!"

"No. It 's good for nothing, or you would n't give it away gratis."

My father's face flushed slightly — as whose would not? — with so much physic thrown into it, though but metaphorically — all the draughts and embrocations he had supplied her with for the last six months! But the angry hue passed away long ere one could have washed off a splash of rose-water. It was hard for him to be long angry with any one, — impossible, with a decrepit woman, so poor, so sickly, and so ragged. One glance at her cooled the transient heat in an instant. As to speaking harshly to so much wretchedness, he would as soon have poured vitriol on her tatters. His words were still kind, his voice cordial, his smile genial.

"Well! and how is little Betty?"

"Little Betty's at home," replied the woman, with a short, sharp twang in her tone that showed the very chord most out of tune had been struck upon. "She might have been at the Great House;—but, thank God, she isn't. She's not an animal!"

"You mean a beast!" suggested my father.

"I say she's not an animal,—nor shan't sleep with one. And a monkey, too — a nasty, filthy, basilicon monkey!"

"Brazilian," muttered my father — "Brazilian."

"Well, Brazilian — an ugly, foreign, outlandish varment!"

"Ah," exclaimed my father, "there's the prejudice! If the creature had been a little dog, now, or a kitten, or a squirrel, you would never have objected to it."

"Squirrels and kittens be hanged!" cried the old woman, waxing in wrath. "It an't the sort of creature — it an't the species; but the detriment to the juvenile constitution. A doctor might know better the vally of the natural warmth of the human body than to have it extracted by a brute beast."

My father was dumbfounded. The charge was so plausible, and couched in such set phrase, that he did not know what to think of it; but appealed, by a perplexed look, to his assistant.

"Prompted — put up to it," muttered Mr. Postle, in a characteristic *aside*. He had turned his back to the counter, and was apparently reading aloud the label on one of the drawers. The woman, in the mean time, thrust the last vial into the Doctor's hand as hastily as if it burnt her fingers.

"That's all the bottles," she said; "and there," throwing a paper bag on the counter — "there's the corks."

O Ingratitude! — marble-hearted fiend! — how hadst thou possessed that thankless woman with a demon, fit only, like those of old, to inhabit a swine. Weekly, daily, recalling the better times she had known, she had bemoaned her inability to fee a physician, or pay an apothecary; daily, almost hourly, she had lamented the delicate constitution of her little Betty, and the impossibility of furnishing her with a better bed, more generous diet, and warmer garments, — wants for which, by will and deed, her benefactor had endeavored to provide ; and to throw, in his very teeth, all his charitable unguents, lotions, composing draughts, and tonic mixtures, bottles and corks included, and then, in return, to pour on his benevolent head the full vials of her wrath, bitter as the waters of Marah, and corrosive as aqua fortis ! It might have moved a saint ! But there was in my father's nature so much of the milk of human kindness, and in that milk such a sweet butterish principle, that stirring his temper the wrong way seemed merely to oil it. Thus, when he responded again to the querulous ingrate, it was as the music of an Æolian harp in the parlor-window to a hurdy-gurdy at the area rails.

"Well, well. — we need not quarrel, Mrs. Hopkins. The monkey is dead, and so there is no harm done. I meant all for the best, and hoped to do you a service. Little Betty would have been comfortably lodged, and well fed, and was to be warmly clothed from head to foot."

"Thank ye for nothing !" retorted the snappish one. "I can clothe little Betty myself : and when she famishes for victuals and drink, and not afore, she shall sleep with apes, baboons, and orange outangs."

"Orang," said my father, *sotto voce* — "o—rang."

"Well — horang. I should like to see your own twins, I should, with a great Wild Man of the Woods in their cradle !"

My father's lips moved to reply ; but before he could utter a syllable he was forestalled by a noise like the groan of execration which is sometimes heard at a public meeting. All eyes turned in the direction of the sound ; and lo ! there stood Kezia, her mouth still open and round as that of a cannon, her eyes staring, her cheeks both of a crimson, her arms uplifted, and her hands clenched, with utter indignation. One of her many errands to the surgery had brought her just in time to overhear the atrocious wish that converted her, *pro tempore*, into a she-dragon. In another moment she confronted the cantankerous Mrs. Hopkins, who assumed an attitude of defiance, and plainly showed that if the flesh was weak the spirit was willing enough for the encounter. My father would fain have interfered, but was entreated, by signs and in a whisper, by Postle, not to "check the effervescence."

But the combatants shall have a chapter to themselves.

CHAPTER VIII.

THE ALTERCATION.

THOSE two angry females — just imagine them, ripe for their verbal duel! — Mrs. Hopkins fierce, resolute, and pale as the mask in marble of an ancient Fury; Kezia, with her homely person, coarse limbs, scrubby head, staring eyes, and that violent red blotch on her cheek, not unlike the ill-painted figure-head of the Bellona, or some such termagant ship of war.

"O you wretch!" began Kezia, panting for utterance.

"Wretch yourself!" returned the woman. "Who gave you leave to meddle?"

"Those babes — those blessed babes!" exclaimed Kezia; "to want them devoured in their innocent cradle by a wild man of the woods! Babes only fit to devour with kisses — and such as would soften any heart but a stone one, that nothing will touch, except the fizzling stuff as cleans marble!"

"Say, muriatic acid," suggested Mr. Postle.

"Twin babes, too!" continued Kezia, "the very pictures of heavenly innocence — and might sit to a painter for a pair of Cherubims! — and to abuse them so — it's almost blasphemy — it's next to irreligious!"

"Heyday!" exclaimed Mrs. Hopkins; "here's a fuss, indeed, about babies! — As if there was no more of them in the world! Prize ones, no doubt. I should like to see them soaped and scrambled for!"

"You would!" cried Kezia, almost in a scream; "you would! O you wicked, wicked monster!"

"Monsters are for caravans," said the woman; "and if I was you, before I talked of monsters, I would go to some quack doctor," — and she glanced viciously at my father — "for a cosmetical wash, to make both my cheeks of a color."

"My cheeks are as God made them," said Kezia; "so it's Providence's face that you're flying into, and not mine. But I don't mind personals. It's your cruel ill-wishing to those precious infants; and which to look at would convert a she-ogress into a maternal character. Do you call yourself a mother?"

"Do *you*?" asked the woman, with a spiteful significance.

"No I don't," answered Kezia, "and not fit I should. I'm a single spinster, I know, and therefore not a mothery character; but I may stand up, I hope, without committing matrimony, for two helpless innocent babes. Dear little infants, too, as I've washed and worked for and fed with my own hands; and nussed on my own lap; and lulled on my own buzzum; and as such I don't mind saying, whomever attacks them, I'm a Loness with her yelps."

"Whelps, Kizzy, whelps;" but Kizzy was too angry to notice the correction.

"A rampant lioness, sure enough! And if I was your keeper," said Mrs. Hopkins, with a malicious glance at my father, "I'd keep you to your own den. The business hasn't improved so much, I believe, as to require another assistant."

The wrath of Kezia was at its climax. Next to an attack on the family, a sneer at the business was a sure provocative. "I know my place," she said, "and my provinces. It's the kitchen, and the back-kitchen, and the washus, and the nussery; and if I did come into the surgery, it was to beg a little lunatic caustic to burn off a wart. As for our practice, Mr. Postle must answer for himself. All I know is, he can hardly get his meals for making up the prescriptions; what with mixing draughts, and rolling pills and boluses, and spreading blisters and Bergamy pitch plasters, and pounding up drugs into improbable powders."

"Inpalpable," said my father.

"Well, impalpable. Not to name the operations, such as cupping, and flea botany, and distracting decayed teeth."

"*Extracting*," said my father, "the other would be a work of supererogation."

"Well, extracting — and the vaccinating besides, — and all the visiting on horseback and on foot, — private and parishional, — including the workus. Then there's Master himself," continued Kezia, dropping a sort of half courtesy to him, as an apology for the liberty of the reference, — "if he gets two nights' rest in a week, it's as much as he does, what with confinements, and nocturnal attacks, and sudden accidents, — it's enough to wear out the Night Bell! There was this very morning, between one and two, he was called up out of his warm bed, to the Wheel of Fortune, to sow up a juggler."

"Jugular," said my father.

"Well, jugular. And the night before, routed out of his first sleep by a fractious rib. I only wonder we don't advertise in the papers for a partner, for there's work enough for a firm. First there's a put-out shoulder to be put in again, — then a broken limb to set, — and next a cracked penny cranium to be japanned — "

She meant trepanned, and the correction was on my father's lips, but was smothered in the utterance by the vehement Mrs. Hopkins. "Japan a fiddlestick!" she cried, impatiently rolling her head from side to side, and waving her hands about, as if battling with a swarm of imaginary gadflies. "What do I care for all this medical rigmarole?"

"O, of course not!" said Kezia, "not a brass button. Only when people affront our practice, and insinuate that we have a failing business, it's time to prove the reverse. But perhaps you're incredible. There was no such thing, I suppose, as the pisoned charity-boy, with his head as big as two, and his eyes a squeezing out of it, because of eating a large red toad-stool, like a music-stool, in loo of a mushroom."

"There might, and there might not," said Mrs. Hopkins.

"I thought as much!" exclaimed Kezia, "and in course you never heard of the drowned female who was dragged out of the canal, a perfect sop! and was shocked into life again, by our galvanic battering?"

"I never did," replied Mrs. Hopkins.

"O no — not you!" said Kezia, bitterly. "Nor the stabbed Irishman, as was carried into this very surgery, all in a gore of blood, and pale, and fainting away, and in a very doubtful state indeed, till Master applied a skeptic."

"A styptic," said my father, "a styptic."

"Well, a styptic. And may be you've not heard neither of the scalded child — from pulling a kettle of boiling water over her poor face and neck, — and which was basted with sweet oil, and drudged with flour, and was so lucky as to heal up without leaving a cockatrice."

"If I was you," said Mrs. Hopkins, "I would say a cicatrix."

"Well, perhaps I ought," said Kezia. "Howsomever there was n't a scar or a seam on her skin, — so that 's a cure at any rate. Then there 's the Squire. — But, maybe, nobody has seen his groom come galloping, like life or death, to fetch Master to a consulting of the faculty — no, nor the messenger from the Rectory — nor the Curate himself dropping in here for medical advice, — quite out of sorts, he said, and as hoarse as a raven with a guitar."

"A catarrh," said my father, "a catarrh !"

"Well, catarrh — and could n't swallow for an enlarged tonsor in his throat."

It is uncertain how much further Kezia might have "carried on the business," and improved it, but for an importunate voice which began calling in a stage whisper for Mrs. H. Mrs. Hopkins looked towards the road, where a shadow had for some time been fluttering on the threshold, whilst part of the skirt of a female garment dodged about the door-post, and a bobbing head now and then intercepted the sunshine, and uttered its subdued summons. But as Mrs. H. did not seem inclined to obey the call, the Unknown stepped or rather stumbled, into the surgery, for she was purblind from a complaint in her eyes, and therefore wore a green shade, so deep that it shadowed her crimson nose, like a penthouse over a pet carnation. The two females were obviously confederates, for the new-comer took up a position beside her predecessor, with a determined air and attitude which showed that the broadside of the Tartar would be supported by a volley from the Vixen. Kezia, who would have engaged a fleet of shrews in the same cause, maintained as bold a front, and there wanted but the first shot to bring on a general action, when my father interposed, and suspended hostilities by a friendly salute.

"Glad to see you, Mrs. Pegge."

"That 's as may turn out," replied Mrs. Pegge, throwing back her head, with her chin up in the air, and looking along her nose, at the Doctor, in a posture, as it seemed, of the most ineffable disdain.

"Your sight must be better at any rate," said my father, "to let you come out so far without a guide."

"Well, it is better," said Mrs. Pegge ; and then turning as on a pivot to her ally, "No thanks to nobody, eh, Mrs. H.?"

"Certainly not," said Mrs. Hopkins.

"I didn't follow the Doctor's directions, — did I, Mrs. H.?"

"Certainly not."

"And should have been no better if I had — eh, Mrs. H.?"

"Not a tittle," said Mrs. Hopkins, "but quite the reverse."

"It isn't the hopthalmy at all, — is it, Mrs. H.?"

"By no manner of means."

"Nor gutty sereny — it don't come from the stomach — do it. Mrs. H.?"

"Not in the least."

"I never said that it did," put in my father, more tickled than hurt by the attack on his medical skill.

"Of course not," said Mrs. Pegge ; "you'd have been wrong if you had, — for it's Amor Rosis — eh, Mrs. H.?"

"Exactly so — the very name," said Mrs. Hopkins.

"I can guess where they got that," muttered Mr. Postle, just loud enough to be heard by his principal ; but my father was in too good a humor, and rubbing his nose too briskly to be accessible to sinister suspicions.

"Well, well," he said, with a tone and smile of conciliation enough to have smoothed a pair of ruffles into Quakerly wristbands. "Amor, in the eye, is a very common affection amongst females, and so you may be right. And in spite of all that has passed, should you or Mrs. Hopkins wish at any time for medical advice or medicaments — "

"O no, no, no!" exclaimed Mrs. Pegge, tossing her head like a horse at the hay-rack. "We are poor, — but we won't be experimented on any longer — eh, Mrs. H.?"

"The Lord forbid!" cried Mrs. H. "We've been too much experimented upon already!"

"Perhaps," said Mr. Postle, determined to test his secret suspicions, "you had better seek other advice."

"Eh, what?" asked Mrs. Pegge, wheeling about with her green verandah, till she brought her red ferret-like eyes to bear on the assistant. " What might you say, young man ? "

" I said, that perhaps you had better seek other advice."

" Perhaps *we have*," replied Mrs. Pegge, with a suppressed chuckle, and the usual appeal for confirmation to Mrs. H.

" We certainly did," said Mrs. Hopkins.

" And whatever was advised," said Mrs. Pegge, " there was one thing not recommended, namely, for a young child to sleep in an apiary — eh, Mrs. H. ? "

" If you mean with a monkey," said Mrs. Hopkins, " most decidedly not."

" O no," said Mrs. Pegge, " Doctor Shackle knows better than that — eh, Mrs. H. ? "

" I said so ! " exclaimed Mr. Postle, with a slap of his hand on the desk that would have crushed a beetle into a dead flat.

" Hush, hush," whispered my father. " Dear me, you have killed the poor inky fly ! "

" Curse the fly ! " cried Mr. Postle, fairly beside himself with vexation. " I wish they had both been in its skin, — a couple of ungrateful old Jezebels ! "

" He ! he ! he ! " tittered Mrs. Pegge. " Some people will want one of their own cooling draughts ! "

" Why you ungrateful creature ! " cried Kezia, whose face had been purpling and swelling with indignation, till it seemed ready to burst like an over-ripe gooseberry. " I wonder you can name a 'fevervescing draught, for fear of its flying in your face ! "

" Hoity toity ! " said Mrs. Pegge, turning on Kezia, with her green shade over her glistening red eyes, like an angry Hooded Snake. " What have we here ? — A Hen Doctor — a 'pothecary in petticoats ? "

" I don't mind names," answered Kezia, " so you may be as scrofulous as you please."

" Scurrilous," said my father.

" Well, scurrilous. I don't mind that," continued Kezia. " It 's your base return for our pharmacy, and your sneers at our practice. Such shocking unthankfulness ! And to think of all the good physic you have enjoyed gratis ! "

" Physic ! " retorted Mrs. Pegge, with a sneer of unutterable contempt. " Physic, indeed ! such physic ! If it 's so good, why don't you enjoy it yourself ? I 'm sure we don't want to rob you of it. If it was worth anything it would n't be given away — eh, Mrs. H. ? "

" My own words," replied Mrs. Hopkins, " to a syllable."

" It 's not physic at all ! " said Mrs. Pegge.

" No ! " exclaimed my father : " what then ? "

" It 's the grouts of other people's," said Mrs. Pegge, " and that 's how we get it in charity. But come, Mrs. H., we have been long enough here."

" Quite," said Mrs. Hopkins.

" And it will be long enough before we come here again, — eh, Mrs. H. ? "

" Ages," said Mrs. Hopkins ; and drawing the arm of her purblind confederate under her own, she led her towards the door, through which — the one stumbling and the other limping — the two ingrates groped and hobbled away, and were seen no more.

" Say I told you so ! " exclaimed Mr. Postle, desperately snatching up the pestle, but grinding nothing, except some inarticulate execrations between his teeth. My father even looked a little grave ; and as for Kezia, she could only stare up at the ceiling, flap her hands about, and ejaculate, " O, I never ! "

" Yes, Shackle 's at the bottom of it all." muttered Mr. Postle, shrewdly adopting my father's own mode of thinking aloud as a vehicle for administering his private sentiments. " Those two beldams have been prompted by him, that 's certain — and he has been called in at the Great House."

" He has ? " said my father.

Postle, however, took no notice of the interrogation, but shook his head despondingly, and proceeded. " That infernal little monkey has done for us ! We shall never be sent for again, master or mate. No, no, a doctor who could n't save such a little creature would never preserve so great a lady ! So there is our best patient gone — gone — gone ! And the Parish will go next, for Shackle has got the Board by the ear."

" Not he," said my father.

" Then he sells opium, and we don't, and that gives him the village. The more fools we ; " and Postle shrugged his shoulders and elevated his eyebrows. " We 're unpopular with rich and poor. I should not wonder, some day, if we were even to be hung or burnt in effigy ! "

My father smiled, and rubbed his nose, and none the less that Kezia clasped her hands and groaned aloud at the imaginary picture. But he repented of his mirth, when he saw her eyes swimming in tears, fixed alternately on himself and the assistant, as if they were already swinging like Guys over the opprobrious bonfire.

"Postle — Mr. Postle," he began; but the assistant continued his soliloquy.

"There's Widow Warner's child in one of her old convulsions —"

"Poor thing!" cried my father, "I will go and look to her directly!"

"But there has been no message," said Mr. Postle, suddenly waking up from his pretended fit of abstraction. "We're not sent for."

"No matter," said my father; and snatching up his hat, and clapping it on the wrong side before, was about to hurry out of the surgery, when he was choked by an exclamation from Kezia.

"Gracious! The yellow lamp is broke again!"

"Yes — last night — for the fifth time," said Mr. Postle.

"It is very strange," said my father, looking up at the gap in the fanlight, where there ought to have been a glass globe, filled with a certain yellow fluid; and which nightly, by the help of a lamp behind it, cast a flaring advertisement over a post, across the road, and partly up a poplar-tree on the opposite side of the way. "It is very strange — there must be some cause for it."

"Nobody breaks Shackle's green lamp," observed Mr. Postle.

My father made no reply; but, stepping hastily out of the surgery, set off — at what Postle called his acute pace, in opposition to his slower, or chronic one — towards the Widow Warner's Cottage.

CHAPTER IX.

OUR CARVER.

Amongst my father's little vanities — and in him it was
partly professional — he rather piqued himself on his dexterity
in dividing a fowl or cutting up a joint of meat. The performance, nevertheless, was generally a slovenly one, — not
for want of skill in the operator, but through the fault of the
carver, which was as blunt as any *messer* in Germany.

Every family has some standing nuisance of the kind, — a
smoky chimney, a creaking door, a bad lock, a stiff hinge, or
a wayward clock, which, in spite of a thousand threats and
promises, never gets Rumfordized, oiled, mended, eased, rectified, or regulated. Our stock grievance was the carver. In
vain Kezia, who never grudged what she called elbow-grease,
rubbed the steel to and fro, and round and round, and labored
by the hour to sharpen the obstinate instrument; wherever
the fault lay, in her manipulation, the metal, the knife-board,
or the Flanders brick, the thing remained as dull as ever.
My father daily hacked and haggled, looked at the edge, then
at the back of the blade, and passed his finger along both, as
if in doubt which was which, — pshawed — blessed his soul —
wondered who could cut with such a thing — and swore, for
the hundredth time, that the carver must and should go to the
cutler's. Perhaps, as he said this so positively, it was expected
that the carver would go of itself to the grindstone : however,
it never went ; but Kezia and the knife rubbed on till the
board and the brick, and my father's patience were nearly
worn out together. The dinner-tool was still as blunt as a
spade ; and might have remained so till Doomsday, but for
the extraordinary preparations for the Christening, when, every
other household article having undergone a furbishing, the eye
of our maid-of-all-work fell on the refractory knife, which she
declared — please the pigs — should go forthwith to be set
and ground by Mr. Weldon the smith.

Luckily there was an errand due in the same direction ; so
huddling herself into her drab shawl, and flinging on her black
bonnet, without tying the strings — for there was no time for

nicety — away went Kezia through the village at her best pace, — a yellow earthenware basin in one hand, and the naked carving-knife in the other; a combination, be it said, ratherly butcherly, and to a country-bred mind inevitably suggestive of pig-sticking, and catching the blood for black puddings: but the plain, homely Kezia, who seldom studied appearances, or an ideal picture of her own person, held sturdily on her way, with striding legs and swinging arms, the domestic weapon flashing to the sunshine in her red right hand.   How her thoughts were occupied, may be guessed, — that the usual speculations of menials had no place in her brain.   Instead of thinking of sweethearts, fairings, ribbons, new bonnets, cast-off gowns, tea and sugar, the kitchen stuff, vails, perquisites, windfalls, petty peculations, warnings, raised wages, and what did or did not belong to her place, her mind was busy with the Baptism, the dear babes, Mrs. Prideaux, her master, mistress, and Mr. Postle, and generally all those household interests in which her own were as completely merged and lost as water is in water.   Amongst these the medical interest of course held a prominent place and induced in her, not only a particular attention to the practice and the patients, but a general observance — which became habitual — of looks and symptoms, with a strong tendency, moreover, to exhibit what she called her physical knowledge.   This propensity she was enabled to indulge in her passage along "the Street," a long straggling row of one-storied cottages, mud-built and thatched, and only separated by the road in front from the sluggish river, which added its unwholesome damps to the noxious effluvia from mouldy furniture, musty garments, and perhaps rancid provisions, and sluttish accumulations of dust and dirt, in dark, ill-ventilated rooms.   At the back, dotted with stunted willow-pollards, and windmills, and intersected by broad ditches, lay the Fens, a dreary expanse, flat as a map, and as diversely colored by black and brown bogs, water, purple heath, green moss, and various crops, blue, red, and yellow, including patches of hemp and flax, which at certain seasons were harvested and placed to steep in stagnant ponds, whence the rotting vegetable matter exhaled a pestilential malaria as fetid in its stench as deadly in its influence on the springs of health and life.   The eyes of Kezia rested, therefore, on many a sickly, sallow face and emaciated frame amongst the men and

women who lounged or worked beside the open windows, and
even in some of the children that played round the thresholds,
biting monstrous cantles out of slices of bread and butter, or
nursing baby brothers and sisters only half a size smaller than
themselves.   With all these people, big and little, Kezia exchanged familiar greetings, and nods and smiles of recognition,
occasionally halting for a brief conference, — for example, to
recommend " scurvy treatment " for little Bratby, to prescribe
a dose of " globular salts " for the younger Modley, or to hint
to Mrs. Pincott, whose infant was suffering from dentition,
that its gums wanted " punctuation " with the lancet.   But at
one house she paused to deliver an especial salute ; for on the
door-step sat little Sally Warner, cuddling her arms in her
pinafore, and upturning a cheerful chubby face, with a fair
brow, bright blue eyes, and rosy cheeks, but sadly disfigured
between the snubby nose and dimpled chin, and all round the
pretty mouth, by an eruption which might have been averted
by a timely dose of brimstone and treacle, — a spectacle Kezia
no sooner observed, than, abruptly stopping for an instant with
a certain gesture, she pronounced certain ambiguous words, so
appalling, in one sense, that the scared child immediately fled
indoors to her widowed mother, on whose lap, after a paroxysm of grief and terror, she went off into one of those con-
stitutional fits to which she had been subject from her cradle.

Poor Kezia !   How little she dreamt that, by merely pointing at a child with a carving-knife, and saying, " You want
opening ! " she was seriously endangering a young life !   How
little she thought that she was preparing for her dear master
another of those mortifications which were beginning to throng
round him so thickly as to justify the old proverb, that misfortunes never come single, but are gregarious in mischief, and
hunt in packs like wolves.

In the mean time my father, good easy man ! walked on
quite unconscious of the impending annoyance ; for the inci-
dent of the carving-knife, which furnished this little episode,
occurred prior to the scene in the surgery recorded in the last
chapter.

CHAPTER X.

THE VISIT; AND THE VISITATION.

A GOOD man, of kindly impulses, and contented with their gratification, is not apt to resent very violently the ungracious reception of his benefits; but, however indifferent on his own account, he cannot help feeling some vexation, partly for the sake of the ingrate himself, and partly on behalf of mankind in general. There is a wrong done to the species; a slur cast on human nature; and his cheek flushes, if not with personal indignation, with shame for his race. Thus, there are men whom a series of injuries, readily forgiven, have failed to convert into misanthropes; but have inspired, nevertheless, with a profound melancholy.

Something of this depression probably weighed down my father's spirits, seeing that he walked without his usual music, the whisper of a whistle, and looking earthwards besides — as if out of tune for sunshiny thoughts — into his own shadow — heedless alike of the sparrow's taking a dust-bath in the road, and the wagtail that kept just ahead of him by a series of short, swift runs, its delicate legs almost invisible from the rapidity of their motion, and its tail, at every halt, balancing with that peculiar vibration from which the bird derives its name.

And yet the scene was much brighter than when he had last paced the same road: the day was fine, and the landscape as lovely and cheerful as its "capabilities" allowed. The river glittered in the sun; the bleak rose at the flies, making numberless rings and dimples in the surface; and myriads of minnows and stickle-backs — for which the water was famous — wheeled and manœuvred in dark shoals, like liquid clouds, amidst the shallows; while larger fish skulked in the eddies round the lock-gates, or glistened silverly through the intricate golden arabesques that sparkled in the rippled water, and thence reflected, danced on the piles of the dam, and the supports of the Dutch-looking swing-bridge. For a swarm of expatriated Flemings had settled aforetime in the neighborhood; and by the style of such erections had made the country, in its artificial features, as well as in its natural aspect, very similar to their own.

On the other hand lay the broad ditch; here and there widening into a little pool, that bristled with rushes and flags, amidst patches of brown water, and green scum, and aquatic weeds, enlivened by numerous yellow blossoms, like bathing buttercups, over which the red, blue, or green dragon-flies, all head and tail — like glorified tadpoles — darted about on their gauzy wings; or with a dipping motion, regular as a pulsation, deposited their eggs in the stagnant fluid; or settled, and clung motionless to some reedy stem. In the clear spaces, the water-spider, skating without ice, performed its eccentric evolutions on the surface; whilst clouds of gnats pertinaciously hovered over some favorite spot, though dissipated again and again by the flutter of the fly-bird, hawking at insects, and returning after each short flight to perch on the same dead twig of the alder. The bank was gay with flowering weed, and covered with tangled verdure — plants, shrubby, pyramidal, and pendulous, interlaced and festooned by straggling creepers and parasites, out of which, at intervals, struggled the trunk of the pollard willow, still clasped by the glossy ivy, and embossed with golden or emerald moss — or the silvery stem of the aspen, up-turning at every breath the hoary side of its twinkling leaves, and changing its foliage from green to gray, and from gray to green, with the variable shades of the summer sea. The very slime oozing round the muddy margin of the pool, and filling the holes poached by the feet of horses and cattle, assumed prismatic tints; whilst the fresh plashes, running up into the road-ruts, glanced alternate blue and white with the shifting sky: in short, there was all the beauty that color, change, light and shade, life and motion, can give to even commonplace objects; and on which, generally, my father, a lover of nature, would not have turned a careless eye, no more than he would have let the sedge-bird warble, as unheard as invisible, among the waving reeds.

But his mind was preoccupied. In spite of himself the harsh voice of Mrs. Hopkins still echoed in his ear; he still saw the red and black eyes of Mrs. Pegge glimmering, like live charcoal, under their green shade. With every step, however, the image and the sounds became fainter, and the cloud passed away from his soul.

" Pshaw," he said to himself, " I am as unreasonable as the old women! Poor creatures, that have hardly daily bread enough to justify a thanksgiving — and to expect from them a grace before and after a dose of physic! To be sure they might have been more civil — and yet, poor, ragged, infirm, disappointed in life, and diseased — the one half-blind and the other a cripple — what worldly sugar have they in their cup to sweeten their dispositions? What cream of comfort, or soothing syrup, to make them mild, affable, and good-humored? And besides, what do they meet with themselves from society at large but practical rudeness? Scorned and shunned because penniless and shabby; oppressed, snubbed, and wronged, because weak and powerless; neglected and insulted, because old and ugly; and unceremoniously packed off at last, as no longer ornamental, useful, or profitable, to that human lumber-hole, the workhouse! Accustomed to endure poverty without pity, age without reverence, want without succor, pain without sympathy, — what wonder if their minds get warped with their frames, and as sensitive to slights and affronts as their bodies to damp and cold winds, — if their judgments become as harsh as their voices, or if their tempers sharpen with their features? What wonder if their prejudices stiffen with their limbs — their whims increase with their wrinkles — their repinings with their infirmities — nay, if their very hearts harden with their fates, or their patience fails utterly under the tedious suffering of some chronic disease, which Art can only palliate, whilst Hope perhaps promised a cure? No, no, we must not expect too much from human nature under such trials, and so many privations! — And so let them enjoy their discontents," said my father, raising his voice : " the worse for them, poor souls, that they are past other pleasure! — and if grumbling be a comfort, who would grudge it, any more than their solitary luxury — a pinch of snuff? "

" Or a drop of lodnum," grumbled a surly voice.

My father looked up, and recognized the speaker ; but the man, gazing straight before him, as if suddenly seized with a stiff neck, passed hastily by, to escape the words which pursued him.

" Yes, yes, Roger Heap, or a dram of oxalic acid, which I would as soon sell you as the other. It's the curse of the county, what with their laudanum drops — and opic pills —

and syruping the infants — and if ever I saw a flower like a well-frilled last nightcap it's the White Poppy!"

My father stopped, for he had reached the widow's pretty cottage, and stepping through the open front-door, walked into the parlor. It was a small room, neatly but tastily furnished; for Mrs. Warner had been left in easy circumstances by her late husband, a farmer, in those prosperous war times when farmers reaped golden harvests; and long before the distressed agriculturist learned to cry "*Ichaboe!* My glory is departed from me! and I am dependent for profitable crops on a species of foreign Penguin, of dirty habits!" His competence, indeed, was rapidly growing into a fortune, when he perished suddenly after a market-dinner by an accident which, communicated too abruptly to the widow, made her, prematurely, the mother of an infant, afflicted from its ill-starred birth with convulsions. A black profile of the father hung over the mantelpiece, beside the old-fashioned mirror; and in his vacant elbow-chair, beside the fireplace, reposed his favorite terrier, blind with age, and asthmatic, from the pampering of his mistress, whose whole affections were divided, though in unequal portions, between her little Sally and the dog. At the sound of a strange foot the wheezy animal uttered a creaking growl, but quickly began to thump the damask seat with his tail on recognizing my father, already met, or rather intercepted, by the widow, who, omitting her usual courtesy, placed herself directly before him, so as to bar his passage to the inner room.

"Well, and how is Sally?" asked my father, kindly looking down at the diminutive widow, for she was the smallest woman, to use the popular description, "that ever stood in shoe-leather, not to be an absolute dwarft." Besides which, since Master Warner's death, she had pined and wasted away to a perfect atomy, and looked even less than she really was in that pinched cap and the black dress which reduced her figure. Not that she fretted visibly, or wept: her eyes shed no more tears than those of the peacock plumes over the old mirror; but if grief has a *dry rot* of its own, by that decay she had crumbled away till her whole widowed body, as my father said, contained but just clay enough to make one little lachrymatory urn. In truth, she was singularly withered and shrivelled, and, in the common belief, still shrank so rapidly as to beget a notion amongst the more imaginative of the village

children, that she would eventually dwindle to the fairy standard, and then disappear.

"Well, how is Sally?" asked my father: "I hear she has
had a fit."

"She has," answered the tiny widow. Her very voice
seemed smaller than usual, and to come, a mere sibilant murmur, through her thin, compressed lips and closed teeth.

"Poor thing! I'll go in and look at her," said my father,
making one step sideways, and then another forward.

"There is no need," said the widow, stepping one pace
backward, and then another sideways, so as to still keep in his
front.

"Is she well, then?"

"No."

"I had better see her, then," said my father.

"Doctor Shackle has seen her," said the widow.

"Quite right — he was the nearest," replied my father,
who was as free from the professional as from any other species of jealousy. "Quite right! then I am easy about her —
for she is in good hands."

Just as my father pronounced this eulogium the object of it
issued from the inner room; and the little widow, stepping
apart, left the rival doctors — if there can be rivalry all on
one side — standing face to face. What a contrast it was!
my father, plump, rosy as a redstreak, and bright-eyed — one
of those men of the old school who looked handsome in hair-
powder; the other a tall, bony personage, sandy haired, with
large yellow whiskers, stony light gray eyes, a straight, sharp
nose, high cheekbones, colorless cheeks, and thin lips, parted
in a perpetual smile that resulted less from good temper than
good teeth — a proper enough personification of Lent, reminding one of the hard, sordid dryness of the stockfish, and the
complexion of the parsnip. Then his manners were cold and
reserved, his voice uniform in its tone — his words few and
sarcastic, and often marked in *italics*, by a sneering curl of the
lip — one of those men from whose veins, if pricked, you would
expect not blood, but milk — not milk warm and sweet, but
acrid like that of the dandelion — men whose livers, you feel
sure, are white; their hearts of the palest flesh-color, and always on the wrong side; their brains a stinging jelly, like the
sea-nettle. That my father, one of the warmest of the warm-

blooded animals, could endure such a polypus — that they could meet without his instinctively antipathizing and flying off, was proof of his easy disposition, his exquisite temper, his child-like simplicity, large faith in human goodness, and catholic attraction towards all his race.

"Well, Doctor," said my father, "how is the little patient?"

"All safe now," answered Shackle. "But a terrible shock to the system — tremendous fit — brought on by a fright."

"A fright?"

"Yes · some fool or other, with a knife, or magical instrument, or something — threatened to rip her up."

"The brute deserved a flogging!" exclaimed my father.

"I think so too," said Shackle, with a glance aside at the mother.

"Why, the brute, as you call her," began the widow, but was checked by Shackle, who placed his finger on his lip, and, stooping down to her ear, whispered:

"Assumed ignorance!"

"Poor child!" said my father; "I have been quite anxious about her."

"You must have been," said Shackle; "you came so quickly!" — a sarcasm my father, in the innocence of his heart, mistook for a civility.

"It happened hours ago," remarked the little widow.

"Is it possible!" cried my father. "But I knew nothing of it — not a syllable."

Shackle said nothing, but looked incredulously at the widow, who replied, by an almost imperceptible shake of the head.

"Postle only told me," said my father, "about ten minutes since."

"O, that Postle!" exclaimed Shackle, "what a treasure he must be!"

"He is, indeed," said my father, quite unconscious of the intended sneer.

"And that — what's her name? — Kezia?" cried Shackle, "taking such a family interest in everything — even to the medical practice!"

At the mention of Kezia and medical practice, the figure of the little widow appeared to dilate; her eyes flashed, and her tiny tongue began rapidly to moisten her thin lips; but,

before she could speak, Shackle broke in with some directions
about the sick child; and then seizing my father by the arm,
hurried him out of the cottage. "I have another case to
attend," he said, "and a very urgent one."

"I hope the present one," said my father, "is going on
favorably."

"O, quite; she is all right," answered Shackle. "By
the by, I hope I am excused. There is a certain etiquette
between medical men,— and I ought to apologize for interfering with one of your patients."

"Not at all! not at all!" cried my father. "We are both
of us engaged in the same great mission — co-operators in the
good work of alleviating human suffering."

"Exactly so — of the same order of *charity*," said Shackle,
with a sneering emphasis on the last word, intended secretly
for my father's gratuitous practice. "Yes, both of us are of
one fraternity, or, as we should be called abroad, Brothers of
Mercy." — a phrase which so delighted my father, that, seizing
Shackle's hand between both his own, he warmly urged a request conceived some minutes before.

"With the utmost pleasure," replied Shackle, bowing, and
returning the squeeze with apparent cordiality; and then the
two doctors parted — one with an ivory smile on his face, that
vanished the moment he turned his back; the other with a
kindly glow on his countenance which promised to endure till
the next meeting.

My father, however, instead of turning homewards, guided
by some vague impulse, bent his steps towards the dwelling of
the Hobbeses. — To see, after so many disappointments, how
his kind intentions had thriven in that quarter? Perhaps so.
Meanwhile little Sally was safe, and his whistle was resumed.
He was conscious of the warmth and glory of the sunshine;
heard and enjoyed the carol of the lark; observed the gray
goose leading her callow yellow gulls across the road to the
river; and laughed at the consequential airs of the hissing
gander, as he sailed on, with raised stern, and one broken
wing hanging down at his side, like the weather-board of a
Dutch yacht. But a stranger spectacle was in store for him
— a low mud cottage, rudely thatched with brown mossy straw
and reeds — the broken panes of its one window stopped with
dingy rags —and two men, in the livery of the magpie, but re-

pudiating its loquacity, in short, two Mutes, in black and white, standing one on each side of the humble door! My father stopped and rubbed his eyes like a man "drowned in a dream." But no, there they were, the two mummers, with their paraphernalia in their hands, surrounded by an undress circle of the village children, backed by an outer ring of men and women, who stared over their black, white, brown, red, yellow, cropped or curly little heads.

In another minute there was a stir and murmur of expectation amongst the crowd,—and first a black and white hat, and then a man in black with a white scarf, came stooping through the low door; followed by two other men in sables, carrying a little coffin, covered with French gray cloth, and studded with silvered nails. After a pause, as if to afford time for the spectators to gaze and comment on the handsome coffin and its ornaments, another attendant threw over it a black velvet pall with a white border; and then came forth the mourners, stumbling over the threshold, the Mother with a white handkerchief at her eyes; but the Father with his grief, all unveiled, writhing in his hard-featured, yellow face. The silk hood and scarf but partially concealed the shabby, ragged clothing of the poor woman; and the funeral-mantle was far too short for the tall man, whose mud-stained corduroys were visible a foot below its skirt; whilst one half of his best and worst beaver, brown in color and of no particular shape, bulged out roughly above the sleek hatband which encircled it, and thence flowed down his nape, and with a full convex curve over his high round shoulders. There was a moan from the crowd as the mourners appeared, and then a hush, only broken by the sobs of the bereaved parents, whereat the tender-hearted of the circle looked tearfully at each other, and clasped their hands. At last the man in black with the white scarf—composing his face, as it were, to some inaudible Dead March—solemnly took three steps forward, and then suddenly wheeling about, walked six steps backwards, with his eyes steadfastly fixed on the moving pall which followed him —and then three more steps backwards, but on his tiptoes, to look over the pall at the mourners—when all being right, he turned round again, and walked on, as slowly as he could pace, to eke out the very short distance between the hut of mourning and the church. The crowd, which had opened to the procession, closed again, and followed in its wake — men, women, boys, and girls, all seriously or curiously interested in Death, except the vacant baby faces, which leaning chubbily on the mothers' shoulders, looked quite the other way.

"A foolish job, bean't it?" said an old woman, leaning on a crutch — quite too lame to follow the funeral. "To chuck away money that way! Quite a waste, bean't it?" — and she put up a tin ear-trumpet, and turned its broad end towards my father.

"It is, indeed!" cried my father, surprised by such an echo of his own reflections.

"Ay, bean't it?" repeated the old deaf woman. "And such poor paupers as them too — as might have had a burying by the parish!"

My father hesitated to answer. He knew the poor well; their intense abhorrence of a parish funeral; and the extreme sacrifices they would make to subscribe to a burial society, and secure a decent interment. But he thought it best to chime in with the old woman's humor.

"Of course they might," he said. "The Hobbeses are on the parish books already, and the overseer would, no doubt, have given them an order on the parish undertaker."

"Who will take her?" asked the deaf woman.

My father loudly repeated his words.

"Ay — an order for a common deal-box," screamed the old woman, in a voice so different to her former one, that my father looked round for another speaker. "A rough wooden thing, only fit for soap and candles! Look there!" and she pointed with her crutch — "I'd sooner bury a child o' mine, wi' a brickbat in yonder pool! But anything is good enow for the like of us to be packed into. Ay, an old tea-chest, or a forrin fruit chest, with our pauper corpses a bulgin out the sides, and showin, like the orangers, thro the cracks!"

"No, no, no!" shouted my father.

"But I say yes, yes," cried the old woman. "Screwed down in a common box, and jolted off, full trot, to be chucked into the parish pit-hole — and a good riddance of old rubbidge! And better that than to be made a gift of, privily, to the parish doctor! Ay, you! you! you!" she screamed, shaking her crutch in my father's face — "with your surgical cuttings, and carvings, and 'natomizings! And can hardly have patience to wait till people are dead!"

"If I know what you mean," bawled my father, "I'll be 'natomized myself!"

"O, not you, forsooth!" answered the old woman, who had imperfectly heard the anecdote of Kezia and the carving-knife, and, like other deaf people, had made her own blundering version of the story. "But you long, you know you do, to cut open little Sally Warner, and to look in her inside for the cause of her fits!"

My father winced — it would have vexed Job himself.

"Plague take it!" he said, as much rumpled as it was possible for him to be in his temper. "I do believe some dog has run mad, and bitten all the old women in the village!"

"Ay, that comes home to you," cried the crabbed cripple. "And mind Death don't come home too — to your own twin babies. To begrudge poor Sukey Hobbes her funeral! Suppose it was even a hearse and six, with ostrich plumage — and why not? An only child, quite a doting-piece, and begrudged nothing in life, by fond parents, if it cost the last penny, and why should she be begrudged by them in death — and gold and silver in the house? And which some say was flung in, by night through the window by Doctor Shackle, and that he owns to it, or leastways don't deny it — but I say, chucked down the chimbly by a Guardian Angel, in the shape of a white pigeon, as was seen sitting on the roof."

"No doubt of it," shouted my father, rubbing his nose, and quite restored to good-humor by his new metamorphosis. "There was a guardian angel seen lately sitting on a rock in America — only" — and he dropped his voice — "it turned out to be an exciseman tarred and feathered."

"That's true, then," said the old woman. "But the funeral will be coming back, and I must speak a condoling word to the Hobbeses. Poor souls! I know myself what it is to be childless — but it will be an everlasting blessed comfort and consoling to them to reflect they have given her such a genteel burying as was never seen afore in their spheres of life." And the old crone hobbled off on her crutch, leaving my father to whistle or talk to himself as he pleased. He did the last.

"Yes, the old deaf body is right. The money was intended for the comfort and consolation of the bereaved couple; and they were justified in seeking for them in the mode most congenial to their own feelings. An odd mode, to be sure, considering their usual habits and rank in life ! And yet, why should not the poor have their whims and prejudices as well as the rich ? Grief is grief, in high or low, and, like other morbid conditions, is apt to indulge in strange fancies. So let the guineas go — there are worse lavishings in this world than on the obsequies of an only child ! And after all, if the money went foolishly, it came quite as absurdly — for medical attendance on a sick monkey !"

CHAPTER XI.

OUR DOCTOR'S BOY.

THE surgery was quiet — the assistant leisurely making up some sort of medical swan-shot — when my father entered, and hung up his hat.

"Well, I have met Doctor Shackle at last : — he was at Mrs. Warner's — and the child is better."

" I should like to meet him too," observed Mr. Postle, very calmly in tone, but squeezing his finger and thumb together so energetically, that the bolus which was between them — instead of a nose — was flattened into a lozenge.

"Then you will soon have that pleasure," said my father, " for I have asked him to the christening."

Mr. Postle turned faint, sick, red, and then white, with disgust : symptoms the Doctor must have observed, but that his attention was absorded by a phenomenon elsewhere.

It was Catechism Jack, — who after a preliminary peep or two from behind the door-post, at last crept, with a sidling gait and a sheepish air, into the surgery, where by eccentric approaches, like those of a shy bird, he gradually placed himself at the counter.

" Well, Jack," said my father, " what do you want ? "

Jack made no reply ; but dropping his head on his right shoulder, with a leer askance at my father, plucked his sodden finger out of his mouth, and pointed with it to one of the drawers.

"You see," said my father, in an aside to Postle, "the fellow is not quite a fool. He remembers where the lozenge came from."

"Mere animal instinct," answered Postle, in the same under tone: "a monkey would do as much, and remember the canister where he got a lump of sugar."

"I will try him further," said my father, putting his hand in the drawer for a lozenge, which he held out between his finger and thumb. "Well, Jack, what will you do if I give you this?" Jack eyed the lozenge — grinned — looked at my father; and then drawled out his answer.

"I 'll say my Catechism."

"No, no, Jack," cried my father, "we don 't want that. But will you be a good boy?"

"Yes," said Jack, his head suddenly drooping again, while a cloud passed over his face. "Yes, I will, — and not tumble down stairs."

"Poor fellow!" said my father. "They made a fault of his misfortune. I have a great mind to take him. Should you like, Jack, to get your own living?"

"Yes," answered Jack with alacrity, for my father had unconsciously given him a familiar cue — "to learn and labor truly to get my own living, and to do my duty in that state of life to which it may please God to call me."

"Catechism again!" whispered Mr. Postle.

"Yes, but aptly quoted and applied," answered my father. "Do you know, Jack, what physic is?"

Jack nodded, and pantomimically expressed his acquaintance with medicine by making a horrible grimace.

"Well, but speak out, Jack," said my father. "Use your tongue. Let us hear what you know about it. What's physic?"

"Nasty stuff," said Jack, "in a spoon."

"Yes," said my father, "or in a wine-glass, Jack, or in a cup. Very good. And do you remember my foot-boy, Job, who used to carry out the physic in a basket?"

Jack nodded again.

"Should you like to take his place, and carry out the medicine in the same way?"

"I — don 't — know," drawled Jack, sympathetically sucking his finger, while he ogled the little oval confection, which my father still retained in its old position.

" Do you think you could do it ? "

Jack was silent.

" Would you try to learn ? "

" I learn two things," mumbled Jack, " my duty towards God, and my duty towards my neighbor."

" Not very apposite that," muttered Mr. Postle.

" Not much either way," answered my father; and he resumed the examination.

" Well, Jack, suppose I were to take you into my service, and feed and clothe you — should you like a smart new livery ? "

" Yes."

" And a new hat ? "

" Yes."

" And if I were to give you a pair of new shoes, would you take care of them ? "

" Yes," answered Jack, " and walk in the same all the days of my life."

" There ! " said my father, giving Postle a nudge with his elbow ; " what do you think of that ? "

" A mere random-shot," answered Mr. Postle.

" Not at all," said my father, turning again to his *protégé*. " Well, Jack, I have a great mind to give you a trial. If I take you into the house, and find you in a good bed, and comfortable meals, and a suit of clothes, and provide for you altogether, would you promise to behave yourself ? "

" They did promise and vow three things in my name," answered Jack ; " first, that I should renounce the devil and all his works — "

" Yes, yes," cried my father rather hastily, for Postle was grinning. " We know all that. But would you take care of the basket, Jack, and leave the medicine for the neighbors at the right houses, and attend to your duty ? "

" My duty towards my neighbor," answered Jack, " is to love him as myself ; and to do to all men as I would they should do unto me. — Give us the lozenge."

My father gave him the lozenge, which the lad eagerly popped into his mouth, occasionally taking it out again, to look edgeways at its thinness, till all was gone ; and then deliberately licked his sweetened hand, beginning at the thumb, and ending with the little finger. My father, who had watched

every motion with intense interest, mechanically turned round
to the drawer for another "Tolu;" but falling into a fit of
musing at the same time, forgot the destination of the lozenge,
and eventually clapped it into his own mouth, to the infinite
discomfiture of Jack, who by a sudden depression of his features, while his head dropped on his bosom, and his arms fell
straight by his sides, typified very vividly the common catastrophe of the Hope going down with all hands.

"Yes, my mind is made up," said my father, awakening
from his reverie. "At any rate the unfortunate creature shall
have a chance. With a little looking after at first, he will do
very well."

Mr. Postle looked earnestly at my father, with an expression which might be translated "What next?"—then up at
the ceiling with a shrug which signified "Lord, help us!"—
and then performed "Confound it!" by a frantic worrying of
his hair, as if it had been wool or flock that required teazing.
To remonstrate, he knew was in vain. My father, in ordinary
cases, was not what is called pig-headed; but in matters of
feeling, his heart, as Postle said, was "as obstinate as the in-
fluenza, which will run its own course." In fact, from that
hour "the Idiot" was virtually engaged *vice* Job, — for the
parish of course made no objection to the arrangement; and
as to the old dame, his guardian, my father found means,
never exactly known, to reconcile her to the loss of her charge
and the stipend. So the thing being settled, Mr. Postle made
the best of it, and endeavored to initiate his subordinate in his
duties: but it was hard work, and accordingly Kezia volunteered her help to convert Jack into our Doctor's Boy.

"To be sure," she said, "his faculties were not over bright,
and he would protrude his catechiz at unseasoned times; but
he was very willing, and well-disposed, and an orphan besides,
and, as such, every woman ought to be his mother." And
truly, however she found time for the labor, she turned him
out daily so trim and clean, that could she have scoured up
his dull mind to the same polish, Jack would have been one
of the smartest boys in the parish.

CHAPTER XII.

OUR GODFATHER.

A MONTH and two days of our little lives had passed away, and another evening was in the wane, without any appearance of our worthy Uncle and Godfather elect, the rich and respectable Mr. Jinkins Rumbold.

He had written, briefly indeed, to accept the sponsorship, and to beg that the spare bed might be regularly slept in, seeing that he was subject to the rheumatism : but, although the morrow was appointed for the Christening, still he came not. No — although his mattress, thanks to the indefatigable Kezia, was well shaken, his blankets thoroughly aired, his sheets sweetly lavendered — a fire laid ready for lighting in the grate — a bowpot, daily renewed, on the mantel-shelf — and the Book of Common Prayer, with the leaf turned down at the Public Baptism of Infants, deposited on the walnut-wood table.

My mother was in despair; for she was a devotee of a very ancient and numerous sect, renowned for self-torture and voluntary martyrdom. Not that she ever scourged or flagellated her own body with cords or rods, or gashed her flesh with knives, or scored it with uncut talons, or wore sackcloth next her skin, or emaciated her frame by long fast or frequent vigils ; but for such painful exercises as lying on metaphorical thorns, sitting on figurative pins and needles, or hanging on colloquial tenter-hooks, she was a first-class saint of the self-tormenting order of the Fidgets.

" It don't signify ! " she said, in a crying tone, and flouncing down in the great white dimity-covered chair in the bed-room, as if her legs had suddenly struck work. " I 'm quite worn out ! If my brother means to stand for his nephews, he ought to be here by this time. Here we are, as I may say, on the very brink of the font, and no godfather ! — at least not certain. It is running it cruelly fine ; it is, indeed ! "

As my mother during these observations had first looked down at the floor, as if addressing the spirits under the earth, and then up at the ceiling, as though appealing to all the angels in heaven, Mrs. Prideaux, in her intermediate sphere, did not feel called upon to reply, but continued quietly to rock the cradle.

"A stranger," continued my mother, "might be excused for indifference; but when a brother and an uncle exhibits such apathy, what *is* one to think?"

Still the nurse remained silent; for the speaker, during her apostrophe, had fixed her eyes on the neglected twins. But my mother was yearning for sympathy, and, therefore, aimed her next appeal point blank at the mark.

"I confess it does fret and worry me; but it is too bad, Mrs. P.; is it not?"

"Not having the pleasure to know the gentleman," replied Mrs. P., "I must beg to decline hazarding an opinion. The delay may have proceeded from procrastination, or it may have arisen from some accident."

"Gracious Heaven!" exclaimed my mother, clasping her hands, as if wrung by some positive calamity. "Yes, you are right! There must have been an accident! You only echo my own misgivings. There have been heavy rains lately, and the waters are out of course. O my poor, dear, drowned brother! To think that, perhaps, whilst I am blaming and reproaching you —"

She stopped, for at that very instant the door opened; and, ushered in by my father, and closely followed by Kezia, the dear undrowned brother walked into the chamber, perfectly safe and dry, and not a little astonished at the hysterical scream and vehement caress with which he was welcomed.

At last my mother untwined her arms from his neck, and sank again into the easy-chair.

"Thank God!" she exclaimed, "you are safe! But oh! how changed!" an observation she prudently whispered to herself; but which, nevertheless, was plainly telegraphed by the workings of her features. And truly the alteration she beheld would have justified a louder exclamation. From top to toe, the former Jenkins Rumbold had undergone a complete metamorphosis. Instead of his old-fashioned wig — formal, as if cut in yew, by some Dutch topiarian — he wore his own hair, or rather a fringe of it, to his bald head; — the quaint pigtail, which used to dangle at his nape, was also retrenched; but his chin, by way of compensation, displayed a beard like

a French sapper's. And where was his precise white cravat,
with its huge bow? Discarded for a black silk kerchief,
carelessly tied round his neck in the sailor style, with a lax
double-knot. His silver knee and foot-buckles were likewise
gone; for his square-toed shoes were replaced by a kind of
easy buskins, and his kerseymere shorts had become longs, as
wide and loose as the trousers of a marine. His waistcoat
was unique; and his coat — cut after some original pattern of
his own — was remarkable for the number and amplitude of
its pockets: fit, there was none. He seemed to have won a
suit of clothes in a raffle, and to have adopted them for his
own wear from the sole merit of being so easy and roomy that
he could roll about in them — like a great oracle of those
days, Dr. Johnson.

What an Uncle! — what a Godfather!

Well might Kezia gape and gasp like a hooked gudgeon at
such a phenomenon! Nay, the genteel nurse herself opened
her eyes to a most vulgar width, and stared at the strange
gentleman with a pertinacity quite inconsistent with her usual
good manners.

My father alone was unmoved. Accustomed to the extraordinary whims and crotchets of sick and insane humanity,
he was not surprised by the oddities of his kinsman, which he
ascribed to their true source. The truth is, whilst the worthy
drysalter remained in trade the monotonous routine of business
induced and required a corresponding precision and formality
of conduct and character. He had neither leisure nor leave to
be eccentric. To caper and curvet on the commercial railroad
is as dangerous as inconvenient and inconsistent. But once
released from business, and its habits, like the retired tradesman who sets up his fancy carriage, or builds his " Folly,"
he started his hobby. Its nature chance helped to determine,
by throwing into his way a certain treatise, by some cosmogony
man of the Monboddo school, if not actually an unacknowl-
edged work from the pen of the speculative philosopher,
who maintained that Man, at the creation, had a tail like the
Monkey. However, the original uncle Rumbold had so
translated himself as to be hardly recognizable by his next
of kin.

" Ah! I see how it is," he said. " You miss my wig
and tail, and are boggling at my beard. A manly ornament,

is n't it — as intended by the Creator?　For eighteen months, sister — for a year and a half, brother-in-law — no razor has touched my chin, and please God, never shall again — never ! — at least while I preserve my reason.　As for shaving, it 's a piece of effeminacy, the invention of modern foppery ; to say nothing of the degradation of having your nose, that very sensitive feature, and one of the seats of honor, pulled here and there, right and left, up and down, at the will of a contemptible penny barber."

"Very degrading, indeed," said my father, stroking his own chin with his hand, as if coaxing a beard to grow from it.

"If there 's a ridiculous spectacle in the world," continued Uncle Rumbold, "it 's a full-grown man, a son of Adam the Great, with his human face divine lathered like a dead wall at its whitewashing — now crying with the suds in his eye, and then spitting with the soap in his mouth — and undergoing all this painful, and absurd, and disgusting penance for what? Why, to get rid of the very token that gives the world assurance of a man."

"Ridiculous enough !" said my father.

"My wig, on the contrary, was an artificial appendage, and accordingly I have abandoned it.　If, as a sign of mature age, nature ordains me to be as bald as a coot, so be it — I will go to my grave with an unsophisticated bare sconce. The same with my queue.　If she had intended me to wear a pig's tail bound in black ribbon, at my nape, she would have furnished me with one, or at least the germ of one, at my birth — but she did not, and therefore I have docked off the substitute."

"So I perceive," said my father.

"Yes, sir, as a foreign anomaly.　But a beard," resumed Uncle Rumbold, "is quite another thing — a hair-loom, as I may say, from our first ancestor.　Its roots were implanted in Paradise — and its shoots grew and flourished on the chins of the patriarchs.　And what can we conceive more awful and majestic than the beards, white as the driven snow, and reaching down to the girdle of Abraham, Isaac, or Jacob, in their old age?　But would they have been looked up to and implicitly obeyed by the people, as God's own vicegerents if they had shaved?　Not they !— And what I should like to know, intimidated the barbarian Gauls when they invaded the Roman Capitol ? "

"A flock of cackling geese," replied my mother, who had some random recollections of ancient history.

"A flock of cackling fiddlesticks!" cried Uncle Rumbold. "It was the beards, the venerable beards, of the Roman Senators. And I cannot help thinking that if our Members of Parliament adopted that classic fashion, and no men appeal oftener to the classics, they would not only deliberate with far more gravity and decorum, but frame laws much more wise, and profound, and just, than they do at present. In fact, all the great lawgivers wore beards. Look at Moses! — look at Solon! — look at Lycurgus! — look at our Alfred."

"If you please, sir," said Kezia — her patience worn out to the last thread — "won't you look at our twins?"

"Eh? what?" snapped Uncle Rumbold, annoyed in his turn, and waving off the maid of all work with an impatient sweep of his oratorical right arm. "By and by, my good woman, by and by. The twins, I suppose, are pretty much the same as other infants — little fat human squabs."

"As you please, sir," replied Kezia, with a courtesy, but heightening in color and expression towards a Red Lioness. "All I know is, they are such a pair of twin nevies as any uncle might be proud of — if he was the Grand Turk himself!"

"Well, well," said Uncle Rumbold, rather pleased than piqued by the allusion to his Oriental appendage. "Where are they? O, yonder! — Poor little wretches!"

"Poor little wretches!" exclaimed an echo, very like the voice of Kezia; but attributed by Uncle Rumbold to Mrs. Prideaux.

"Yes, poor little wretches!" he repeated, addressing himself to the nurse. "I do pity them — for of course they are to be bound up and bandaged like young mummies of the Nile."

"I presume you mean swaddled, sir," replied Mrs. Prideaux.

"I do, ma'am," said Uncle Rumbold, "that is to say, imprisoning their young, tender, free-born limbs with linen rollers, and flannel fetters, and other diabolical contrivances for cramping the liberty of nature. But perhaps, ma'am, you wear garters?"

The genteel nurse assented, with a slight bend of acquiescence.

"Because I never do," said Uncle Rumbold. "I detest all ligatures; they check the circulation of the blood, and consequently the flow of ideas. I once got upon my legs, with garters on, to speak in public, and I broke down at the very first sentence — I did, indeed! No, no — no ligatures for me! Look here, ma'am — and he threw open the bosom of his waistcoat — "no braces, you see! — but one garment buttoned on the other, like a schoolboy's."

"I am no judge, sir, of masculine habiliments," replied the genteel nurse; "but of the infantine costume I can speak, which is the same as custom prescribes in the highest families."

"Custom!" exclaimed Uncle Rumbold. "Confound custom! Why not be guided by the light of nature?" And he gave such a rhetorical blow on the head of the cradle, that the twins started broad awake in a fright, and began to pipe in concert like a double flageolet. In another moment they were sending their smothered cries through stuff and linen, into the bosom and very heart of the maid of all work, who, with an infant on each arm, hurried to the door, which she nevertheless contrived to unfasten, and then pushed wide open, with one leg and foot.

But Uncle Rumbold either overlooked or withstood the hints, and continued his harangue to the nurse.

"In the savage state, ma'am, the human animal has no swaddling. Look at the wild American pappoose."

"But ours an't pappooses," cried Kezia, — "they're babbies."

"Pshaw! — nonsense, woman!" said Uncle Rumbold. "Go to your kitchen. I say, ma'am, the human animal, in a state of nature, is never swaddled! — never! For example, the American Indians. Let us suppose that those two infants there, in the housemaid's arms, were young Crows, or Dog-Ribs — "

"I won't suppose any such falsities!" cried the indignant housemaid.

"Hush! hush, pray hush!" whined my mother. "Kezia, do hold your tongue, or I shall go distracted!" As in fact she was, poor woman, between her dread of offending our wealthy Godfather, and her horror of his doctrines. But my father enjoyed the discussion, and was sawing away with his forefinger across the bridge of his nose, as if it had been that of a fiddle.

In the mean time my mother's interruption had drawn Uncle Rumbold's discourse upon herself. "I don't know, sister," he said, "if my spiritual capacity of Godfather invests me with any control over their physical education; but if those two boys were mine, every blessed day of their lives, wet or dry, shade or shine, hot or cold, they should enjoy for an hour or two the native liberty of their limbs, and sprawl and crawl as naked as they were born, on the grass-plot."

"Gracious goodness! — On the damp lawn!"

"Ay, or soaking wet, if it so happened; and what's more, the youngsters should have to climb some tree or other for their suspended victuals."

"Why, the poor things would starve!" exclaimed my mother.

"Not they," said Uncle Rumbold. "Trust to the light of nature! Hunger and instinct would soon teach them to scramble up the stem, like young monkeys — ay, as nimble as marmosets!"

My mother shook her head. "But they would sprawl and crawl into the fish-pond."

"So much the better," said Uncle Rumbold, "for then they might have a swim."

"But does that come by nature, too?" inquired my mother.

"Of course," answered Uncle Rumbold, "as it does to a fish. Look at the savage islanders — I forget what author relates it — but when one of the native canoes or proas was upset, a little Carib, of a week old, who had never been in the water before, kept swimming about in the sea, till the vessel was righted, as spontaneously as a dog."

My mother again shook her head.

"Fact, and in print," said Uncle Rumbold; "he was paddling about like a water-spaniel; and why not? The art of swimming is innate. Take your own twins, there, and chuck them into the river opposite — "

"The Lord forbid!" ejaculated my mother, to which Kezia responded with as fervent an "Amen."

"I say, chuck them into the river," repeated Uncle Rumbold, "and you will see them strike out with their arms and legs as naturally as frogs. In fact, it is my decided opinion that man in his pristine state was intended by the Creator to be amphibious."

"Did you ever make, personally, any experiments in natation?" inquired my father, in his most serious voice.

"Why, I can't say that I ever did, exactly," replied Uncle Rumbold. "But what does that signify, when I 'm convinced of my theory? However, as I said before to my sister, if I am to have any share in the physical education of my godsons, those are the principles upon which, guided by the light of nature, I mean to act."

. My father made a low bow, so low, that it would have seemed farcical, but for the air of profound gratitude which he contrived to throw into his countenance; but my mother irvoluntarily uplifted her hands and eyes, while Kezia, forbidden to speak, gave a low groan or rather grunt.

"In the mean time," resumed Uncle Rumbold, "I have not forgotten a sponsorial offering," and diving his hand into one of the many huge cloth closets or pockets in his coat, he extricated with some difficulty a brown paper parcel, which he presented rather ostentatiously to my mother.

"No trumpery spoons, sister, or jingling corals," he said, as her fingers nervously fumbled at the string — "but something that, rightly employed, will increase in interest and be a benefit to the boys through life."

My mother's fingers trembled more than ever at these words, and twitched convulsively at the double-knot, whilst a score of vague images, including a pile of bank-notes, to be invested in twin annuities, passed through her agitated mind. Kezia, with held breath, and broad, undisguised anxiety in her party-colored face, intently watched the unfolding of the successive coverings; and even in the well-bred Mrs. Prideaux curiosity triumphed so completely over courtesy, that she jostled and incommoded our Godfather in her eagerness to partake of the revelation. At last the inmost veil of lawnpaper was removed.

"A book!" murmured my mother.

Kezia fetching her breath again with a deep-drawn sigh, deposited the dear twins in the cradle and hastily left the room; while the genteel nurse, giving her head the slightest toss in the world, resumed her seat and her needlework.

"A book!" repeated my mother.

"Ay, the Book of books, as I call it," said Uncle Rumbold, —"the Bible, of course excepted."

"And a presentation copy," remarked my father, adroitly catching the volume as it slid off my mother's knees, "with the writer's autograph on the fly-leaf!"

"Yes — and a tall copy and unique, and privately printed," said Uncle Rumbold. "A work as original as scarce — as logical as learned — as correct as copious — as sensible as sublime — as captivating as convincing — as playful as powerful — as elegant as elevating — the life-long study of a profound philosopher — in short, a work worthy of its title — 'The Light of Nature!'"

"It is all very fine, no doubt," said my mother.

"A perfect treasury — a mine of riches!" exclaimed Uncle Rumbold. "The Holy Testament excepted, the world has never received such a legacy. And this, as I believe, the only copy extant! A gift, let me tell you, sister, that nothing but our near relationship, and my anxiety for the future welfare of two — I say *two* nephews — could have extorted from me."

"A mine — a treasury — and a legacy," repeated my mother, with a tear, that might or might not be a pledge of sincerity, gushing from either eye. "You are very kind, I'm sure — very kind and considerate, indeed. — Who's there?"

It was Catechism Jack, come to announce that supper was on the table, in the parlor. So the conference in the bed-chamber broke up. Uncle Rumbold offered his arm to my mother to lead her down stairs; and my father, whistling a march, in a whisper, brought up the rear. Nothing worthy of record passed during the meal, except that the guest received and relished the mixture which had been promised to him by letter at the suggestion of Mr. Postle, namely, "a draught of something comforting to be taken the last thing at night — say, diluted alcohol sweetened with sugar." The dose was even repeated — and then the parties separated, and retired to their respective chambers.

"Well, my dear," asked my father, as he stepped into bed, "how do you like the 'Light of Nature'?"

"I wish," said my mother — but stopping short in the middle of her wish to give a vehement puff at the candle — "I wish I could blow it out!"

CHAPTER XIII.

OUR OTHER GODFATHER, AND THE GODMOTHER.

" George !"

" Well ? "

" How is the morning?" asked my mother, entering full-dressed, and accosting my father, as he looked over the Venetian half-blind of the parlor-window.

" Why, I think," replied my father, considering those low dirty-looking clouds, with tattered dripping skirts, lounging about the horizon, like ragged reprobates who have slept all night in the open air and the gutter, that we shall have a general sprinkling to-day, as well as the particular one in the church."

" I am always unlucky in my weather," grumbled my mother, " especially when it is wanted to be fine.　We shall be nicely soaked and draggled, of course ; for the glass-coach must draw up at the turnstile-gate ; and we shall have to paddle up the wet, sloppy churchyard, and the path has been new-gravelled, and the dripping yew-trees will green-spot all our things."

" You must take umbrellas and clogs," said my father.

" To go clattering up the avenue, and cluttering with into the porch !　And the poor children will catch colds, and have the snuffles," added my mother, taking a desponding look at the dull sky over my father's shoulder.　" Yes, it will rain cats and dogs, sure enough ! "

" There will be the less mobbing," suggested my father.

" That's no comfort ! " retorted my mother.　" I don't mind a crowd, or being a spectacle, or I should certainly object to walk in public with my brother ; for, unless I 'm mistaken, we shall have all the tag-rag and bobtail boys in the parish running after him like a Guy Fox.　And Kezia too — as if it was necessary at a christening to dress up like a she-Harlequin, with cherry ribbons on a Mazarine blue bonnet, and a scarlet shawl over a bright green gown ! "

" And our twins ? "

" O, Mrs. Prideaux has kept *them* genteel — though it was

a struggle too — what with the rosettes and lace quiltings that Kezia wanted to stitch on their caps and robes. And then Jack —"

"What of him?" asked my father, with some alarm.

"I have only had one glimpse of him," replied my mother, "in his new livery; and clean washed and combed, and smartened up respectable enough, if he had n't ornamented his jacket with a parcel of strips of French gray cloth, as well as a great bow stuck in his hat, with a white-headed nail. But Mr. Postle has stripped off his finery, and sent him out with the basket."

"Very good," said my father; "and my bearded brother-in-law, has he been called? He ought to be dressed and down by this time, for he has n't to shave."

"O, pray don't joke about him," exclaimed my mother; "as it is, I 'm sadly afraid he 'll be affronted before he goes. Do all I can, I can hardly keep myself from flying out at his daring doctrines about the poor children — and, as to Kizzy, I verily believe she suspects he is an ogre in disguise. She can't bear him even to come near the infants, though he has only kissed them once since he came, and then she wiped their dear little faces directly, as if she thought they would catch his beard."

"And if they had," roared the gruff voice of Uncle Rumbold, as he pushed open the parlor-door which had been ajar; "if they had caught my beard, it 's better than catching the chin cough. But come, come, no apologies; I 'm not easily offended, or I should have been huffy just now with your housemaid, who told me to the hairy thing itself, that it ought to have been blue."

"Poor Kizzy," said my father, "she is plain and plain-spoken, but as honest and faithful as unrefined."

"Ah! a child of Nature," said Uncle Rumbold; "well, I like her all the better; and, if she has a sister disengaged in the same capacity, I 'll hire her on the spot. The true old breed of domestic servants is almost worn out, nearly extinct in England, like the bustard and the cock-of-the-wood — partly their fault and partly our own, by always setting them too high or too low — over our heads or under our heels — either pampered like pet monkeys, or snubbed like born slaves — never treated according to the light of nature. For instance, there 's the tender passion. It 's notorious that nine tenths of the poor girls in Bedlam went crazy from suppressed sweethearts, and yet, forsooth, no followers are to be allowed; so that unless Molly falls in love with my lord, and John nourishes a flame for my lady, as he often does, by the way, they might as well have no human hearts in their bosoms. Whereas, servants have passions and feelings as well as ourselves — the same natural capacities for liking and loving — ay, and perhaps stronger at it too, as they are at scouring floors and scrubbing tables!"

How long this harangue might have proceeded is uncertain, probably till church time, but for a new arrival, our second godfather, the proctor from Doctors' Commons. In all outward and visible signs he was the direct antagonist of his co-sponsor. His beard and whiskers were cleanly shaved off; and although he was not bald, his hair was cropped as close as a pugilist's. Then his cravat was starched so stiffly, and tied so tightly, that he seemed in constant peril of strangulation: his coat fitted him like a skin, exhibiting a wasp-like figure suspiciously suggestive of stays; and his tight pantaloons were as tight as those famous ones, into which the then Prince of Wales could not get, it was said, without supernatural assistance. In his manners besides, he was as prim and reserved as our uncle was free and easy. — so that while introducing Mr. Titus Lacy to Mr. Jenkins Rumbold, my father could not help adding to himself, "*alias* Lord Chesterfield and Lord Rokeby."

Another tap at the parlor-door, and in stalked our godmother, Miss, or, as she was generally called, Mrs. Pritchard, a spinster as virtuous in reputation as Cato's daughter, and as towering above her sex, for she stood nearly six feet high without her cap. In features she rather countenanced the Rumbold practice, for though her upper lip was decidedly hairy she never shaved; but in her figure she inclined to the Titus Lacy persuasion, her waist was so very slender — whilst in her notions of the powers and duties of a sponsor, she differed from both; mysteriously hinting that by some mystical spiritual connection with the twins, she became more their mother than their mother, who was simply their parent in the flesh, and as such only entitled to wash, feed, and clothe their bodies, or to whip them if naughtiness required. My mother, it may be supposed, did not greatly relish or approve of this doctrine : but the truth is, the unexpected refusal of a female friend, at the eleventh hour, had compelled her to accept the proffered sponsorship of Mrs. Pritchard, in spite of that lady's former declaration, that if she did become a religious surety, she would not be a nominal one, but fulfil her vows and act up to the character : the nature of which character she painted during breakfast in such colors, that, as Uncle Rumbold whispered to my father, "she promised to make a devil of a god-mother !"

CHAPTER XIV.

THE CHRISTENING.

My mother was out in her forebodings. By the time that breakfast was over, the ragged, dirty-looking clouds had skulked off, and the tall poplar over the way shot up into a clear blue sky. The narrow strip of river that was visible above the grassy bank glittered like a stream of molten gold ; and the miller's pigeons, a sure sign of settled weather, were flying in lofty circles in the sunny air, casting happy glances, no doubt, at the earth beneath and the heaven above, instead of a steak under and a crust over them.

Even the little shabby boys who kept jumping over the post on the near side of the road, evidently reckoned on " Set Fair," for while many of them were without hat or cap, and some had no coat, great or small, none had brought umbrellas, — few had even water-proof shoes on their feet, much less clogs. A great comfort and relief it was, the said solitary post, to the young expectants, most of whom had to wait a couple of hours, more or less, before the glass-coach, driven by one man and a nosegay, and drawn by a pair of horses and two peonies, pulled up at the Doctor's door.

The mob in the mean time greatly increased, for a rumor of the bearded godfather, exaggerated, as the tale travelled, into the Grand Turk and the Great Mogul, had flown throughout the parish, so that when the gentlemen — who preferred to walk to the church — issued from the house, it was through an avenue planted with men, women, and children, six deep, and amidst a cheer which only the united Charity Schools, of both sexes, could have composed.

"Huzza!" they shouted,—"Moses forever!—Huzza! for the Great Mogul!" with other cries which our eccentric uncle would fain have loitered to enjoy and retort, but for the hauling at one arm of Mr. Titus Lacy, who was disgusted with the familiarity of the lower orders, and the dragging on the other side of my father, anxious to be in good time. But the mob was not to be shaken off or left behind any more than the swarming flies that encircle a horse's head. Even so, a buzzing cluster of satellites, male and female, old, middle-aged, and young, kept running, shuffling, trotting, behind, beside, and before the persecuted trio, whom, with a suffocating cloud of dust, they accompanied along the road, through the churchyard, and up the yew-tree avenue to the ancient porch, where an offcast of the curious but less active inhabitants, the lame, the infirm, and the indolent, awaited their arrival.

Thanks to this diversion, the glass-coach followed with a smaller escort, yet not so few but that there was constantly at each window the bobbing head of some long-legged lad or lass snatching peeps, by running jumps, at my mother and god-mother, in full dress, sitting bolt upright on the back-seat, and on the front one Mrs. Prideaux and Kezia, both in their best, and each holding a remarkably fine twin in her arms or on her lap. But it was otherwise when the females alighted at the churchyard-gate and walked up the avenue, where the minority joined the majority of the mob. Then all the clamor was renewed. "Huzza! Old Close! Longbeard forever! Huzza for the Great Mogul! Who's lost his Billy Goat?" with other cries more or less jocose, and some hostile ones, indicative, alas! of my poor father's declining popularity.

"Who frightened Sally Warner into fits?" screamed a gawky girl, pointing with her coarse red finger at Kezia.

"And who wanted to 'natomize her?" bawled an old lame woman, shaking her crutch at the Doctor.

"And won't sell opie!" grumbled a surly-looking laborer.

"And prescribed a child to sleep with a sick monkey," cried a woman with a green shade over her eyes.

"And a parish-burying for our poor Sukey," muttered a tall man with a black hatband on his brown hat.

"And begrudged us our Godsend!" murmured a woman in rusty mourning.

"That is untrue at any rate," said my father to himself; and with the serenity of a good man conscious of the rectitude of his intentions, he stepped smilingly into the church, where the curate was waiting, and the whole party being assembled the baptismal ceremony immediately began. And for a time the service proceeded with due decorum, till about the middle of it, when the clergyman had to demand, "Dost thou in the name of this child renounce the Devil and all his works?"

"I do," shouted a voice from one of the pews, "and all the sinful lusts of the flesh."

Every eye instantly turned in the direction of the sound, and at once recognized a well-known face, with its mouth sucking at a forefinger just clapped into it.

It was Catechism Jack, — who had been betrayed, by a familiar phrase in the service, into one of his old responses.

The curate paused, and made a signal to the beadle, who proceeded to eject the unlucky respondent from the church, — not without an altercation and a struggle, for Jack pleaded piteously to be allowed to see the christening, and even clung to the pew-door, from which at length he was wrenched, with a crash and a jingle of broken glass, whilst a powerful and disagreeable odor quickly diffused itself throughout the building. ·

"There goes a whole basketful of physic," said my father *sotto voce* to himself.

"So much the better," said Uncle Rumbold, in the same suppressed tone. "Trust to nature."

"O, I shall die! I shall swoon away!" murmured my mother, showing a strong inclination to go into a fit on the spot, but the hysterical passion was scared away by a stern, emphatic whisper from Mrs. Pritchard.

"Don't faint HERE!" and then turning to the curate and pointing with her long bony forefinger to the font, she added aloud: "I object, sir, to that consecrated element being used for reviving!"

The protest, however, was unnecessary, for my mother recovered without any relief from water, save what stood in her own eyes; and order being restored, the ceremony proceeded to the end without interruption, or anything extraordinary —

except that at the final exhortation, when every one else was standing up according to the printed direction, Kezia was observed on her knees, evidently offering up a private extempore prayer, — a departure from the orthodox rite, which incurred a severe rebuke from Mrs. Pritchard the moment the curate had pronounced the last syllable of the service.

" Well," said Kezia, mistaking the drift of a lecture that insisted on a strict observance of the ceremonials, " and if I did kneel down without a cassock — " she meant a hassock.

" But you were putting up a heterodox petition of your own framing," interrupted the angry spinster.

" Well, I own I was," answered Kezia ; " for the two dear little lively members just admitted into the church. And where 's the harm if it did proceed from my own heart and soul, instead of the Common Prayer Book ? — It was religiously composed, and I do hope," she added, unconsciously adopting the language of her bakery, " I do hope and trust it won't rise the worse for being home-made."

Here the controversy dropped ; and the usual entries and signatures having been made in the vestry, the family party reissued from the porch, saluted by the same cries as before, along the yew-tree avenue, and through the churchyard-gate, where the majority of the mob dispersed in different directions, so that the Great Mogul and the glass-coach were followed by only the idlest of the boys and girls, and of those one or two dropped off in every dozen yards.

The moment my father reached home he hurried into the surgery, and related to Mr. Postle what had occurred in the church with the medicine and Catechism Jack.

" I knew it ! Say I told you so !" exclaimed Mr. Postle. " What else could come of intrusting the basket practice to an idiot ! But of course, sir, you will discharge him directly."

" Certainly," replied my father, his good sense immediately recognizing the policy of the measure, but his humanity as promptly suggesting a loophole for evasion. " Yes, he shall be discharged on the spot, — that is to say, should the beadle be dismissed, for from what I saw of the scuffle, he had quite as much to do with the downfall of the basket as poor Jack."

By a curious coincidence, whilst Mr. Postle in the surgery was thus advising my father to send away the footboy, Mrs.

Pritchard, in the parlor, was recommending to my mother a month's warning for Kezia, and with a similar result.

"Why, she does forget her own sphere, dreadfully," said my mother; "and puts herself very forward in the parlor, and in the nursery, and even in the surgery, besides behaving very improperly and independently, as you say, ma'am, in the church. — Yes, I must and will part with her — at least as soon as I can find another like her, to do the work of three servants — and which I never shall."

CHAPTER XV.

THE SUPPER.

THE clock struck nine.

As settled in domestic conclave, the dinner had been only a plain early meal, at which the two godfathers and the godmother were treated as three of the family, the grand festival in honor of the christening being reserved for the evening; and my mother, attended by Mrs. Pritchard, had just slipped from the drawing-room to inspect the preparations.

"Beautiful, is n't it?" she said, looking along the supper-table, gay with flowers and lights, and brilliant with plate, of which there was an imposing display.

"Very genteel, indeed I might say elegant," replied Mrs. Pritchard, fixing her gaze especially on her own epergne. "And those silver branches, too, they are almost as handsome and massive as the Cobleys', and of the same pattern."

"Between you and me," said my mother, "they *are* the Cobleys'; and the tankard, you know, is Mr. Ruffy's, a present from one of his rich clients."

"And those silver-gilt salts are the curate's, I believe," said Mrs. Pritchard, "a parting gift from his late flock?"

"I believe it was," said my mother.

"And the dessert-spoons," inquired the tall spinster who had made the tour of the table; "all with different crests and initials — pray is that a new fashion?"

"They are the school spoons from Mrs. Trent's," said my mother, reddening. "But the knife-rests are our own."

"And if I may ask," said Mrs. Pritchard, "how many friends do you expect?"

"Why, all those who have lent plate, of course," replied my mother — namely, "the curate, the Cobleys, the Ruffys, Mrs. Trent, and Mrs. Spinks."

"Who!" exclaimed Mrs. Pritchard, in a tone like the pitch-note of an Indian war-whoop.

"Why, she is rather unpleasant, to be sure," said my mother; "but that is her salver on the sideboard. Then there's Colonel Cropper of the Yeomanry, who is to come in his uniform, and the Squire has half promised to drop in — and if it had n't been for that nasty little Brazilian Marmot — I ought to have said Marmoset — we might have hoped for the lady at the great house. Then there's Doctor Shackle, and the Biddles — and the Farrows — and young Fitch, altogether about fourteen or fifteen, besides ourselves."

"Just a nice number for a party," said Mrs. Pritchard, "if they all come."

"They are late, certainly, very late," replied my mother, her heart sinking like the barometer before a storm, at the mere suggestion of disappointments. "But hark! there is an arrival!" and with the tall spinster, she hurried into the drawing-room to receive her guest. It was the unpleasant Mrs. Spinks. Next came Doctor Shackle; and then, after a long interval, the wit of the neighborhood, young Mr. Fitch, a personage against whom Uncle Rumbold instantly felt that violent antipathy which he invariably entertained towards a dandy, or, in the language of those days, a buck.

"I 'm early, I 'm afraid," said the wit, looking round at the circle of unoccupied chairs.

"Or like myself, a little behind the mode," said Doctor Shackle. "I forgot that nine o'clock with fashionable people means ten."

"Then we are to have a fashionable squeeze, I suppose," said young Fitch, "a rout as they call it — a regular cram?"

"O no!" cried my mother, eagerly, "only a few, a very few friends, quite in a quiet way."

"About twenty," said Mrs. Pritchard.

"And there are only six come!" observed the unpleasant Mrs. Spinks, deliberately counting heads.

"Are you sure, my dear," inquired Mrs. Pritchard, "that your invitations were correctly dated?"

"O, quite!" replied my mother, "for I wrote all the notes myself, and to make sure had them delivered —"

"By Catechism Jack," said Doctor Shackle.

"No, indeed!" cried my mother, "but by a special messenger."

"Yes, a charity boy," said Mrs. Spinks. "And I know personally that Mrs. Trent had her note; and so had the curate, and the Biddles."

"It's very odd," muttered my mother; "the Biddles were always early, and I made sure of Mrs. Trent. She ought indeed to have come to tea. It is very strange — very strange, indeed!"

"Pooh! pooh!" said my father. "By and by they will all come in a lump; and if they don't we shall only be the snugger."

"And in the mean time," said young Fitch, "the great Bashaw there with the black beard will perhaps amuse us with one of his three *tails!*"

"I am sorry, young man," said Uncle Rumbold, in his gruffest voice, "that I am not a naval Bashaw, or I would amuse you with nine."

At this retort, delivered with the look and growl of an enraged lion, the abashed wit hastily retreated to a chair; and the little buzz of conversation which had sprung up, was hushed as by a clap of thunder. There was a pause — a long, dead pause — and to make it more dreary, the family clock — an old-fashioned machine with stout works and a strong pulse — stood in the hall, so near the drawing-room door, that its tick! tack! was distinctly audible, like the distant hammering of endless nails into an eternal coffin. Tick! tack! — tick! tack! O, that monotonous beat, — only broken by a sudden "click!" like the cocking of a gigantic pistol, and which made every one start, as if Death had actually given warning instead of Time! And then, tick! tack! again, — till with an alarming preliminary buzz the clock struck ten. The odious Mrs. Spinks was the first to speak.

"Quite a quakers' meeting!"

But nobody replied to the remark. The wit continued mute — the tall spinster merely looked wonderingly at my mother, who looked inquiringly at my father, who slightly shrugged his shoulders, and looked up at the ceiling. Mr. Titus Lacy was habitually taciturn, and Doctor Shackle only opened his lips in a sardonic smile.

At last, at a private signal from my mother, my father came and placed his ear to her mouth.

"For heaven's sake, George, do talk! — and get young Fitch to rattle — why don't he rattle?"

"The Bashaw killed him," whispered my father. "But I will do what I can." And by a desperate rally, he contrived to get up a brief conversation; but the fates were against him. Doctor Shackle seemed determined to answer in monosyllables; and Uncle Rumbold's hobby, in spite of a dozen allusions to the light of nature, refused to be trotted out. At last my father's own spirit began to share in the general depression — the discourse, such as it was, again dropped, and then — tick! tack! tick! tack! — Oh! it was horrible! — the only sound, it seemed, in the wide world. Not a knock — not a ring! No one came — nobody sent an apology. — What on earth could be the matter! The clock struck eleven!

"I believe," said my mother in a faint voice, "we need not wait any longer."

"We have waited too long already," said Uncle Rumbold; "at least I have — and long to satisfy the cravings of nature."

"Give your arm, then, to Mrs. Pritchard," said my father. "Mr. Lacy will escort Mrs. Spinks; the Doctor will convey my wife, and I will take care of Fitch;" and in this order the company, if company it might be called, marched, melancholy as a walking funeral, into the supper-room — joined, in their progress through the hall, by Mr. Postle.

My poor mother! A demon might have pitied her, as she took her place, and cast a rueful look at my father at the bottom of the table, flanked on each side by six empty chairs. A fiend would have felt for Kezia, as she stood, death-pale, behind the back of Doctor Shackle, not from any partiality to that sneering personage, but that she might exchange looks and signs of wonder and grief with Mr. Postle, who sat opposite.

"A pity, is n't it?" said Mrs. Spinks across the table to Mrs. Pritchard; "such a beautiful supper!—enough for thirty—and only nine to sit down to it!"

"We must make up in mirth," said my father, "for our lack of numbers," and again he made a gallant but vain attempt to revive the spirits of his guests. Besides the common gloom, he had to contend with the animosity of Mr. Postle against Doctor Shackle, and the antipathy of Uncle Rumbold to Mr. Fitch. An unlucky joke hastened the catastrophe. The wit, emboldened by wine, had the temerity again to attack the Bashaw.

"Allow me," he said, "to recommend a little of this," at the same time thrusting a frothy spoonful of trifle as near as he dared to the redoubtable beard.

"Sir," said Uncle Rumbold, snatching up a full glass of ale, "if I consulted the law of retaliation—which is one of the laws of nature—in return for your lather, I should present you with this wash for the face. I say, I should be justified in so doing; but from respect to the present company I shall only drink to your better manners."

A momentary silence followed this rebuke; and then came a sound which startled all the company, but one, to their feet. As in pile-driving, there is a point beyond which the weight, called the monkey, cannot be screwed up; so there is a certain pitch at which human fortitude gives way,—and my mother's had reached that limit. The agitation, the mortification, the mental agony she had so long suppressed, had at last overstrained her nerves, and with an involuntary scream, such as is said to come from persons who have swallowed prussic acid, she went into strong hysterics. My father and Kezia instantly hastened to her assistance, but to little effect; either the fit was so obstinate, or the patient.

"Nothing serious," said Dr. Shackle, "she will soon recover, and in the mean time her best place is bed."

The hint was taken; the company immediately broke up; and whilst my mother was carried up stairs to her chamber, her grand christening party—of two gentlemen and two ladies—unceremoniously departed.

"Only four out of twenty!" gasped Kezia to Mrs. Prideaux, whom she had dragged apart into a corner of the bedroom; "only four out of twenty!—What, in mercy's name, can it all mean!"

"The meaning is plain enough," answered the genteel nurse, in her calm, sweet voice,—"your master is a ruined man."

CHAPTER XVI.

A MYSTERY.

OUR family was in bed. My mother had sobbed herself to sleep; my father lay dreaming by her side; the twin infants were in their cradle; the whole house was quiet, except only the ticking of the old clock in the hall, the chirping of the cricket in the kitchen, and a dull, intermitting sound from one of the upper bedrooms, as if from somebody imitating through his nose the croaking of a frog in the fens.

The clock had struck one, and was about to strike again, when the door of the back attic opened, and Kezia, stepping forth in her night-clothes, and without any candle, walked deliberately down the stairs to the door of the room in the first floor appropriated to the nursery. Here for a moment she paused, the attraction within having overcome or diverted her original impulse; but her true errand speedily recurred to her, and descending the other flight, she crossed the hall, and entered the surgery, to the extreme alarm and astonishment of the two persons who were conversing therein.

The one was a female in a flannel wrapper, tied with green ribbon, and occupying the wooden arm-chair devoted to the accommodation of patients or impatients awaiting the making up of their prescriptions; the other, a strange man, with his hat on, was seated on the counter, whence, with his elbows resting on his knees, he stooped down towards his companion, his face close to hers, in earnest communion. At a glance, he was what was called in the slang of those days a Blood or Buck; in the cant of our own times, a Swell. Cigars were not yet in vogue; or, to a certainty, he would have had one between his lips: but he wore his beaver with the rakish, jaunty air still affected by gentlemen and journeymen who conceive themselves superior in acuteness, spirit, and an extensive knowledge of life, to the rest of the world. His clothes were expensive and fashionable. Round his throat he wore a very fine white cravat, so ample that his neck seemed poulticed, the ends being tied in a large ostentatious bow. His coat was blue, with fancy gilt buttons, a deep turned-down collar, and lappels, that for size might have served for ears to a Newfoundland dog. His waistcoat, of buff or primrose color, was double-breasted, long in the waist, and flapped, with a black ribbon crossing it from the left shoulder to the gold-mounted quizzing-glass in the left-hand pocket. His lower limbs were clad in gray stocking-pantaloons, tight as skin, and cased up to the well-made calf in Hessian boots, but somewhat deficient in polish, and minus one tassel. His coat, too, had the fluffy tumbled appearance of having occasionally taken its own nap with its master's on a feather-bed, or one of flock; his waistcoat was ill-washed; his pantaloons were soiled in sundry parts, and especially at the knees; and his cravat, besides its dingy hue, was wrinkled and flaccid. Altogether, there was as much of the sloven as of the beau in his costume — in his physiognomy, a corresponding mixture of the gentleman and the reprobate. His face was handsome; but had the faded, jaded look consequent on habitual debauchery. His large dark eyes were dry and bloodshot, with crowfoot wrinkles at the corners; and under each organ a flabby bag, as if for secreting the tears to be shed in the maudlin stage of intoxication. His cheeks were of a dull white, blotched with yellow and red, that deepened in his prominent nose to a crimson. His lips were parched and cracked; his chin was neutral-tinted by a bluish beard of two days' growth; and his long black hair and whiskers were foul and matted. Smart and slovenly; well featured, but with a sinister expression; dashing, but dirty; unbrushed, unwashed, uncombed, unshorn, he looked the rake, with a strong spice of the ruffian, whose attribute, a thick knotted bludgeon, lay handy beside him on the counter. On the other side, stood something of indefinite shape tied up in a cotton shawl; and near the bundle, the nursery rushlight, and an empty rummer, with a silver spoon in it. There could hardly be a greater contrast than between the female in the arm-chair and her nocturnal visitor; and yet the time, the scene, and the manner of their *tête-à-tête*, inferred the most confidential and familiar intercourse. Was it possible that the repulsive, dissolute, villanous-looking man on the counter was anything near or dear to the genteel, sweet-spoken, well-bred, lady-like Mrs. Prideaux?

To confirm and justify an affirmative answer, certain chronological characteristics must be taken into consideration. In these, our own times, so remarkable for a refined taste in art and literature, in manners and morals, the Court Callendar possesses more attractions for females than the Newgate one. There is no longer a rage for genteel highwaymen or eminent housebreakers. As pets, Brazilian monkeys are preferred to malefactors, and parrots to jail birds. Our mothers, wives, sisters, and daughters no longer admire the chivalrous courage of a horse-pad, whose utmost deed of daring — the presentment of a loaded pistol at an unarmed man — has been outdone by every light or heavy dragoon who has seen service. They no longer fall in love with a Knight of Roads for robbing them like a gentleman, and paying compliments to their beauty, and calming their feminine fears, at the cost of their purses, watches, brooches, bracelets, and finger-rings and earrings. A vulgar burglar, renowned for breaking into houses and out of prisons, is hardly reckoned on a par with the hero of successful sieges and sorties; or an obdurate ruffian who goes to the gallows with a bold face as a rival of the gallant veteran who leads a forlorn hope. A common murderer is no longer a lady-killer to boot; nor does a dashing pickpocket triumph in female preference over a plain honest man "innocent of stealing silver spoons." But it was otherwise formerly; when, in the current phrase, a daring felon became a darling fellow, and a precious rascal a charming rogue. It was then quite usual for ladies of rank and breeding, of family and fortune, to visit condemned criminals in Newgate — entwining with fair and noble arms the neck destined to an ignominious rope, — beseeching keepsake locks from the head soon to be shrouded in an infamous nightcap; and hanging with aristocratical fondness on a plebeian body about to swing shamefully from Tyburn Tree.

Thus, as worn-out fashions descend, like cast-off clothes, from mistress to maid, the example set by a lady of quality in the time of the First George, might very well be followed by a nurse in the reign of George the Third. However, robber or rake, there was the strange man, admitted, in the middle of the night, to a mysterious interview in the surgery, the door of which opened, round the corner of the house, into a lane.

At the entrance of Kezia the parties both started, and the man would have sprung up and spoken but for the warning of the nurse, who raised one hand with its forefinger on her lips, whilst she held him down with the other. In truth, the figure of the housemaid in its white garments, obscurely seen by the dim gleam of the rushlight, was quite spectral enough to shake the courage of a dissolute man, with nerves unsettled by drink. His frame trembled, his face turned ashen pale, and his teeth chattered as he exclaimed in a hoarse whisper —

" A stiff-un walking — by G—d ! "

The nurse, with a dissenting shake of the head and her lips indicating a silent " No ! " repeated her warning gesture to her companion, who, open-mouthed but breathless, watched with straining eyes every movement of the apparition. In the mean time Kezia, walking behind the counter, took her usual station beside the desk, but in silence, as if awaiting the leisure of her confidential adviser in all difficulties, Mr. Postle.

" All safe ! " said the nurse in a very low but distinct whisper : " she 's sleep-walking ! "

The man, as if suddenly relieved of a pectoral spasm, immediately drew his breath in a long deep sigh, and set himself intensely to watch and listen to the sayings and doings of the somnambulist, who at length spoke.

" This is a dreadful mysterious business, Mr. Postle. Twenty invited, and only four to come ! What can it all mean ? " and she paused for a reply, which having dreamed, she resumed : —

" No, the night was not bad enough for that. Besides, the Cobleys have their own carriage, and so has the Colonel and the Squire, who would have brought the Curate along with him. Then the Biddles have the mule cart, and the Ruffys always hire a po-shay. As for Mrs. Trent and the rest, they don't mind wind and rain, but lap up and visit in all weathers. No, — it couldn't be that ! And such a beautiful supper, too ! And such a splendid turkey — with a giver under one wing

and a lizard under the other — I should say quite the reverse. And then the sweets! I could have cried into hysterics myself, to see all the nice jellies, and creams, and custards,
and nobody to eat them, for they *was* nice — if they did taste
a little of the shop, as that odious Doctor Shackle said, meaning, I suppose, the almond flavor you was so kind as to oblige
me with out of the surgery."

The imaginary Mr. Postle here probably vented an oath,
for which she checked him.

"Yes, he certainly is malicious — but don't imprecate. It's
profane, and forbid in Scripture. Swear not at all — no, not
even at an enemy or a buzzum friend. To be sure, the
Doctor was very sneering and provoking, and especially
about the wine being good enough to need no bush except out
of our own garden. I could have found in my heart to drop
a blank mange on his medical head! And that foolish young
Fitch, to affront Mr. Uncle Rumbold to his very beard, instead
of having a perfect haw of it, as any one would in their senses,
it makes him look so like a conjurer. And then that abominable Mrs. Spinks as' would n't let the thing drop, but kept
counting the empty chairs, and saying that every one had a
banker's ghost in it — Banko's I should say — I declare she
made the hair stand upright on my very head. Though for
that matter, I would almost as soon have seen a ghost in
every seat, and Scratching Fanny among them. rather than
nobody at all! I never knew such a case afore — never, except once, — and that was at my first place."

The ideal assistant asked, of course, for the story.

"Why, the way was this. Master had come home with a
prodigious wealth of money from foreign parts, and on setting
up his establishment in London, determined to give a very
grand party, by way of housewarming, to his neighbors. Well,
the night came, with the rooms chalked for dancing, and all
lighted up with wax-candles and cut-glass chandeliers, and the
most elegant supper set out, only for seventy people instead
of twenty, — but nobody came. Nine o'clock, ten, eleven, —
the same as at our own unfortunate regalia, but not a soul —
not a knock or a ring, except the cook's cousin, the footman's
sister, and the housemaid's brother and uncle — at least not
till about twelve, when a single gentleman asked to speak with
master in private, and then out it all came, for we listened at

the study-door. Some spiteful person, in revenge for not being invited, had ferreted out master's secret history, and had whispered about in unanimous letters that he were a returned convert — I should have said a convict — from Botany Bay. He had been sent there for some errors in youth, but had reformed himself, and got rich by opulence, like Dick Whittington, and so got leave to come home again. But of course that don't apply to us, whom have never been arranged in court or transported, though fought as shy of by society as if we had. What is your own notion of it, Mr. Postle ? "

A long silence ensued, of which the nurse took advantage to whisper to her companion, whom she beckoned with her finger, and then pointed to the door. " She must not wake and see you. Come; but move cautiously — as quiet as death."

" Is this all ? " asked the man in a low grumble, and with a motion of his head towards the bundle.

" It must serve for this turn," whispered the nurse. " Quick ! and away ! "

The fellow instantly slid gently down from the counter and clutched the bundle, whilst the nurse turned down the rush-light in the socket. Then there was a slight rustle, with the sound of two or three hasty kisses. The next moment the outer door was partially opened — a cool gust of air came inwards, as the dark figure of the man passed outwards — the door slowly closed again, and the fastenings were replaced with less noise than is made by a mouse. The nurse then groped to the counter, where she found her candlestick and the empty rummer, but not the spoon, a loss she instantly comprehended — the bundle had not quite served for the turn — but her equanimity was undisturbed; and cautiously feeling her way out of the surgery, she crept, silent as a spirit, up the stairs to the nursery, leaving Kezia to her dreaming conference with Mr. Postle.

" Yes," she said, " there is some dreadful misfortune hanging over us, no doubt. My poor dear master ! Mrs. Prideaux foretells he is a ruinated man. But oh ! Mr. Postle ! — and the tears oozed from her eyelids while she clasped her hands in earnest appeal to him — " whatever comes of it, don't let nothing tempt us two to leave and better ourselves, and forsake them, whose bread we eat, in their adversity. For my part, I 'm ready and willing to take a solemn religious oath on my bended knees " — and she suited the action to the word — " and trust you will do the same ; never, never, never to give warning, nor take it neither, but to stand by the family and do for it to my last grasp, — namely, my poor dear master and missis, and them two lovely, helpless, innocent twin babes ! "

What promise the imaginary Mr. Postle made, and whether with the prescribed ceremony, is unknown ; but it gave the liveliest satisfaction to the devoted maid of all work. The expression of her features was indeed invisible in the dark to human ken ; but heaven, with its starry eyes, beheld her face shining with joy and gratitude.

" The Lord bless you, dear, dear Mr. Postle, for that comfort," she said, rising from her knees, and wiping her eyes with the sleeve of her only garment. " It 's exactly my own feeling and sentiments. Yes, if I was courted at this very moment by twenty prostrated lovers at my feet, with bags of gould in one hand, and wows of constancy in the other, I would n't change my state, but refuse them all, and live single for the sake of the family — and which reminds me it 's eight o'clock, and the breakfast to make."

So saying, led by that mysterious guidance which directs the somnambulist — whether some supernatural *clairvoyance*, or more probably an internal geographical scheme, corresponding with the external locality, and producing an exquisite consciousness by touch, independent of sight, of long familiar distances and habitual turns and windings — however, without blunder or collision, the sleeping Kezia passed hastily from the surgery, through the hall, into her kitchen, to prepare the morning meal to which she had referred. But here the guiding faculty was at fault. Besides the old furniture and utensils, on every article of which she could, blindfolded, have laid her hand, the floor was occupied by sundry novel and strange contrivances for holding the superabundant relics of the festival overnight. Against one of these extempore dressers she walked, with a force and a clatter that startled her wide awake, with one hand in a jelly, and her nose seemingly testing the sweetness of a boiled ham. The darkness, the cold, her undress, and the remembrance of former nocturnal excursions, instantly suggested the truth; her mind however retaining no trace of her recent dream; so, after a single exclamation of surprise, she quietly groped for the tinder-box, lighted a spare candle, and yawning and shivering, crept up stairs to the back garret, to get a brief rest, before the very early hour at which she regularly resumed the multifarious labors of her industrious days.

CHAPTER XVII.

A CLEW.

In the surgery — so lately the scene o. a double mystery, of a clandestine midnight meeting and unconscious somnambulism — of treacherous, heartless vigilance and honest devotion faithful even in sleep — at his old desk stood Mr. Postle, apparently studying some medical work, but in reality thinking over the supper of the night before and puzzling himself to account for the absence of the guests. But his meditations were in vain: to use one of his own favorite illustrations, he might as well have tried to make a nosegay with Flowers of Sulphur.

Meanwhile, in looking at his old prompters, along the wall from shelf to shelf, with all the parade of nice-looking nastiness arranged thereon in rows of glass bottles and white jars, marked with cabalistical signs, — his eye detected one receptacle breaking the uniformity of the series by being turned with its label to the wall. But he did not need to see the gilt scroll to know its inscription — " Tinct. Opii."

" Confound that idiot!" he muttered. " He will poison himself yet with his sweet tooth and his tastings. I can trace the mark of his wet finger on the bottles and drawers like the track of a snail. Only yesterday I had to teach him that Ferrum Tart. does not stand for pastry, nor Cerat. Plumb. for almonds and raisins, — and now he has been at the laudanum ?"

For once, however, Catechism Jack was mistakenly accused. No finger of his, wet or dry, had approached the dangerous narcotic. Another meddler, rather sharp than dull of intellect, had removed the stopper for a less innocent purpose than to test the flavor of the tincture. The dear Twins owed their very sound sleep in the night to a minute dose from that displaced bottle.

The assistant carefully rectified its position, and returning to his desk began, with pen and ink, to sketch — another of his habits — on the quire of blotting-paper before him, his designs being generally of the anatomical class, outlines of bones, muscles, and organs, rarely deviating into landscape, or rather scraps of foliage, and even then what was meant for a tree resembled rather a drawing of the Vena Porta or Vena Cava, with its branching veins. This time, however, his subject was the human face, not dissected, but in its natural state ; and as very commonly happens to artists, fine or unfine, the features took the form and expression of a countenance remotely present to his thoughts, so that without any premeditated portraiture, he had just achieved a rather striking but ugly likeness of Doctor Shackle, when a shadow fell across the paper, and looking up, he beheld the original of the picture standing right before him.

The Doctor was accompanied by a Mr. Hix, a parish official, and a very active one — but especially notable for a double propensity to turn private business into public, and public business into private — at once an indefatigable meddler in, and advertiser of, the personal concerns of his neighbors, and the uniform advocate of select vestries, secret committees, private reports, sealed books, suppressed accounts, the exclusion of reporters, and closed doors. Indeed, so far did he carry this love of mystery that, when certain parochial notices were to be posted, according to law, for the benefit of the community at large, he was said to have seriously recommended their being pasted up with their printed sides to the wall.

The ostensible errand of Doctor Shackle was merely to ask, in a friendly way, after the heads of the family, and how they had passed the night after the trying disappointments they had endured ; an inquiry urged with such seeming interest, that in the absence of any authentic bulletin, Mr. Postle deemed it expedient to fetch my father himself to reply personally to the application.

His back was no sooner turned, than Shackle, reaching his long arm over the low rail in front of the desk, snatched up something which he exhibited to his companion — namely, a fragment of French gray cloth in one hand, and in the open palm of the other two silver-washed nails. The pantomime that followed was silent, but expressive.

"*Do you see these, and understand what they mean?*" asked the fixed, significant look of the Doctor, as plainly as in words.

"*I do,*" replied the intelligent nod of Mr. Hix.

The Doctor raised his eyebrows and shrugged his shoulders. "*Could there be a clearer case?*"

The Churchwarden shook his head, and made a grimace. —"*Nor a more ugly business.*"

"I'm sorry for it — very!" said Shackle, hastily replacing the cloth and nails on the desk, and then suddenly turning his back on them, and fixing his eyes on a large glass jar full of snow-white magnesian bricks, as if projecting how to build with them some castle in the air. So intensely, indeed, was he occupied with this ideal fabric, as not to be aware of the entrance of my father, till the latter came close up to him, and shook him cordially by the hand. Then he awoke, and how delighted he was, or said he was, to find my father not merely as well, but better than could have been expected, after the late untoward events — a series of disappointments borne, he must say, with an equanimity worthy of the palmy days of the Stoic Philosophy.

"Had it been my own case," said Shackle, "to say nothing of the dead convivial failure, yet to meet with such a slight from the whole neighborhood, as it were — the cut wholesale as well as direct — I really think, with my own more sensitive, irritable temperament, I should either have gone there," — and he pointed to the laudanum bottle — "for oblivion, or there" — and he indicated another drug — "for annihilation."

"No, no," said my father, "you know better. And besides, there was no great stoicism needed in the matter. A medical man, and a Christian, who had walked the hospitals and the poor-house, and seen human misery and anguish in all their complicated shapes, and who could not bear such a petty mishap — provoking as I confess it was — would be a disgrace to his profession and his religion. As to the absence of our friends, no doubt it will be accounted for."

"No doubt," said Dr. Shackle.

"For the rest," continued my father, " the worst we are threatened with is to be cloyed with sweets for a few days to come, or surfeited with cold victuals ; evils for which between young folks and poor ones, we may easily find a remedy."

"I am glad to find you so well armed against trouble," said Dr. Shackle ; "and wish I had a little of your philosophy. I have equal need of it — for we are likely to be mutually involved in a very disagreeable business."

"A parochial, and perhaps a public business," said Mr. Hix. My father looked inquiringly from one speaker to another.

"The short of the matter is this," said Dr. Shackle. "You have heard, of course, of the pauper family, who gave their dead child that ridiculous funeral ? — "

"The Hobbeses," said Mr. Hix. "Indulged themselves with a genteel burial — and on our books for three shillings a week ! "

"Yes, inconsistent enough," said my father. "I was accidentally an eyewitness of the procession."

"Well," said Shackle, "the grave was robbed the other night, and the child's body stolen. The whole village is in a ferment about it — the poor especially — the paupers outrageous, and the Hobbeses rampant."

"Poor things," said my father.

"Yes, poor enough," said Shackle ; wilfully wresting my father's phrase of commiseration into another sense.

"And idle enough, and troublesome enough, and more than enough," added Mr. Hix.

"And scandalous enough," said Shackle. "to say that their beggarly corpses are less cared for than the carcasses of brute beasts."

"The coarse expression," said my father, "of a strong but natural prejudice."

" O. quite natural," sneered Dr. Shackle ; "and quite harmless, if their prejudices went no further. But, as human corpses are not eaten, except by ghouls, hyænas, and beasts of prey, of which there are none in this blessed Lincolnshire, the natural inference is that graves are robbed, and bodies snatched for other than pantry purposes. In short, in their own low language, that the poor are only poked into pit-holes, to be hoked up agin, and cut and hacked about like dog's meat, by raw 'prentices and Sawboneses,— and heaven knows what vulgar libels besides."

" Well, and what then ? " asked my father. " As a surgeon, *you* are not going, I presume, to deny the practices of the resurrectionists, or the uses to which the articles they deal in are applied ? "

" Not I," said Shackle. " The thing is too notorious ; and, as you say, too surgical ; though I never had, directly, a finger in any cold meat-pie of the kind. Probably, you have. However, the popular suspicion necessarily falls on the medical men of the place ; under which category we share the odium between us : at least, *pro tempore ;* for, as regards myself, as we doctors say, I shall very soon remove all that ; and hope you are in as good case."

" Most decidedly," said my father.

" So much the better," said Shackle. " Your official connection with the poor, as parish doctor, makes your exculpation of even more importance than my own."

" There must be a parochial inquiry ! " exclaimed Mr. Hix.

" Of course, with closed doors," said Shackle ; unable to resist a sarcasm, even on a friend and ally — a propensity that explained his otherwise unaccountable influence in a place where so few persons liked, but so many feared him.

" In fact," he continued, " the wretches do not scruple to say that the anatomizing of their remains is winked at by the workhouse authorities."

" And if we did," cried Mr. Hix, " every ounce of flesh on their bones was composed of parish victuals. There is n't a pauper dies, man, woman, or child, but in equity we have a mortgage, as I may say, on their bodies."

" That 's undeniable," said Shackle. " However, the paupers are all up in arms, and declare openly that they won't work ; and even that they won't die, unless assured of decent and safe interment."

" Won't die ! " exclaimed Mr. Hix.

" So they say," answered Shackle.

" Won't die ! " repeated the churchwarden. " That must be looked to."

My father, who had been lost in thought, here awoke from his reverie and addressed himself to Shackle.

7

"Yes, Doctor, you are right. This is a very disagreeable business, and a very serious one, at least for me."

"And for the parish too," said Mr. Hix, "to have such a slur on it."

"Especially," said Shackle, "as it is not a matter that can be shelved, or cushioned, or hushed up."

"And ought not to be," said my father, "must not! Last night's mystery is now solved. I am socially excommunicated. How or why, I know not,—but a suspicion has fallen upon me, which I must remove, or give up my practice, and quit the neighborhood. A public inquiry will be necessary, for my own sake."

"And for mine too," said Shackle.

"For all our sakes!" cried Mr. Hix. "The excitement of the lower orders will be sure to fall first on the authorities — the churchwardens and overseers. The least I expect is, to be hung or burnt in effigy, or to have my windows smashed!"

My father mechanically looked up over the surgery-door at the yellow glass globe, so often broken; and true to his misgivings, if not actually smashed, it was starred in all directions by some missile that had struck it in the centre. He pointed it out to his visitors.

"There is a token of the popular feeling — the local current that has set in against me. For some time past I have fancied myself treated with coldness and aversion by the humbler class of the inhabitants; but a clear conscience and my good-will towards them repelled the supposition. Now, however, there is a direct imputation on me which I must at once rebut, or be a ruined man."

"The Board sits this morning," suggested Mr. Hix.

"In that case," said my father, "I will at once go before it, and clear my character. I need not say, I hope, that I am altogether innocent in the matter — as innocent as those leeches" — and he pointed to the bottle — "of the blood of Julius Cæsar."

"I am truly happy to hear you say so," cried Shackle, seizing and squeezing my father's hand; "and shall be still more happy to hear you prove it."

The churchwarden expressed a similar wish, but instead of shaking hands, contented himself with a stiff bow, externally taking a simple leave of my father, but internally bidding good by to him, though somewhat precociously, as the parish doctor. The real functionary, in his eyes, was the medical gentleman with whom he walked off arm in arm.

"A clew at last!" cried my father to Mr. Postle, whose entrance into the surgery was synchronous with the exit of Dr. Shackle — a hint that Animal Magnetism ought properly to have two poles, — of repulsive Antipathy as well as of sympathetic Attraction. "A clew at last! We have found out the disease!" And my father imparted to his assistant the substance of the information he had just obtained.

"Say I told you so!" cried the assistant; an exclamation he would have made, however, if just informed of a shower of addled brains from the moon. "And that, then, is why we were sent last night to Coventry — to sup by ourselves! Not that they would have touched the supper if they had come — they would have fancied human brains in the blanc-mange, and coagulated blood in the currant jelly. Yes — for the future we are ghouls, vampires, carrion vultures — and nobody will come near us. There is nothing that unscientific people are so squeamish about as violating graves and desecrating their remains — though why the suspicion should fall on us, more than on Doctor Shackle, he knows best. If any one wants a refresher in anatomy, he does. And what, sir, do you mean to do?"

"Confront the report," said my father. "Go before the Board and demand an inquiry. Is not that always the best course — to take the bull by the horns?"

"Perhaps so — except you're run at by a polled cow," answered Mr. Postle. "For my part I'd as soon go at once at Farmer Nokes's bull with a board over his eyes, with 'beware' upon it. It's the Board, or a parcel of it, that wants to get you out, and have Shackle in your place."

"I don't — I can't — I won't believe it!" cried my father.

"As you please," said Mr. Postle. "If *they* don't, the paupers will, which comes to the same thing. I know them well: when the poor once catch a prejudice in their heads, it's as obstinate as ringworm. I lost my own practice by it when I was a doctor on my own account. My patients were mostly provincials of the lower and middle class, but all brutally ignorant, and of course superstitious, and devout believers in witchcraft. And how do you think I lost them?

By a joke, — sir, a mere joke — through telling a credulous old woman, — ass as I was ! — that I could show her Mindererus's Spirit, dancing with Saint Vitus, round Saint Anthony's Fire ! ”

“ But surely a jest,” said my father, “ might have been explained.”

“ Not it,” said Mr. Postle. “ To the vulgar, a doctor with his hieroglyphics on his bottles, and his Latin, is already half a conjurer. and I had made myself a necromancer outright. There was no revoking it. You may make an ignorant stomach give up its poison, but an ignorant faith never gives up a legend it has once swallowed.”

“ I should like to hear your definition of an ignorant stomach,” said my father, straying, as he was too apt, from serious matters after a whim.

“ We are likely to know practically,” answered the assistant, in a gloomy tone, “ if ignorance and emptiness be synonymous, as they are in the head ; for I don't suppose, as the practice goes, that the Board will board us.”

“ That 's true,” said my father. “ I must go to the workhouse.” And with a smile at the unintentional equivoque, he put on his hat, and set out for the parochial meeting.

Had he delayed a minute longer, he would have been startled and stopped by a sound ringing in his own house from hall to attic, — that sudden, shrill cry which only comes from a female in distress, anguish, or alarm, — and electrifies the hearer like a flash of lightning turned from visible into audible. As it flew first from the kitchen to the surgery close at hand, Mr. Postle was soonest at the spot, where, close to the ironing-board, the movable supports of which she had knocked away in her fall, lay Kezia in a strong hysterical fit, in the middle of a chaos of crockery, glasses, decanters. knives, forks, tongue, cold fowls, tarts, salad, cakes, and jellies, — amidst which she kicked and struggled like a passenger desperately swimming. or trying to swim, from the wreck of some well-provisioned steamer.

Having dashed into her face the first water at hand, the assistant stepped back into the surgery for the Sal. Vol. or Liq. Vol. C. C.. but with so much professional deliberation — knowing such fits may be safely left to run their course — that when he returned to the kitchen, he found the patient propped up against the wall, in a sitting posture, between Mrs. Prideaux and Uncle Rumbold, the first loosening the sufferer's dress, and the last, having lent a hand in her removal, gazing calmly on, very like a bearded Turk confiding in Predestination, and still more like himself "trusting to Nature." Mr. Postle nevertheless plied the stimulants.

"One more application of the restoratives," said Mrs. Prideaux, "and she will revive. There!—she is resuming her senses."

As she spoke, the color began to return to the claret-bald cheeks of Kezia, who, after a gasp or two, opened her eyes—sneezed—stared at each person in turn,—then suddenly turned pale again—closed her eyes—clasped her hands wildly together—and shrieking "the plate! the plate!" relapsed into insensibility.

The restorative process was again applied, and with success. The maid-of-all-work, after a short struggle, sprang up, as if galvanized, on her feet; and amidst gulps, sobs, broken ejaculations, and distracted gestures, informed her audience by bits and snatches that " there had been thieves in the house,—and Mr. Ruffy's silver tankard — and the Reverend Curate's silver-gilt salts — and all Mrs. Trent's school spoons — were missing!"

Poor faithful, devoted Kezia! No hand had she in that felonious abstraction; and yet, for all her innocence, how fearfully within the range of suspicion, whilst Guilt stood by in comparative safety, without a tremor in her silvery voice, or a faltering in her correct carriage! Had some wakeful ear, startled by the unseasonable issuing of the housemaid from her bedroom, heard her descending the stairs, marked her passage from hall to surgery, from surgery to kitchen, and recognized, by listening, her voice in conversation though but with a shadow, and then her stealthy retreat before dawn to her own attic, she was in all human probability a lost, undone, ruined creature. Like other Somnambulists, who, in their nocturnal, unconscious wanderings, step, dream-led, on the narrow window-sill or perilous parapet, she had walked to the very verge of a moral precipice — would she keep her footing or fall?

CHAPTER XVIII.

THE PARISH BOARD.

It was a sad journey, though a short one, for my father, from his home to the Workhouse. At every step he was painfully reminded of his position. In return for the ready smile and friendly greeting for everybody he met, he received only cold looks, and sullen or fierce replies. The very children, with whom he had been so popular, shrank from him inspired by the common prejudice: little heads, that used to nod to him, were immovable on their shoulders; little faces, that used to brighten at his approach, were frowning their aversion; not a few of the youngsters ran indoors as from the minister of a new Herod. And yet so innocent was he of the revolting act attributed to him, that he had yet to learn particulars which were known to almost every man, woman, and child in the place — that the grave of the little Hobbes had been reopened; the removed earth being placed, as the practice was in such operations, in a sheet, so that the mould might all be returned to its place without leaving a vestige to tell the tale of disturbance; but the resurrectionists had been alarmed at their work, and had decamped with the corpse, leaving the clay in the sheet, at one side of the yawning void, and the shattered coffin on the other.

To add to his discomfort, when my father arrived at the Workhouse, a number of applicants for out-door relief were in waiting at the gate; a squalid group, including the ungrateful Mrs. Hopkins, the bitter Mrs. Pegge, with her green shade, and the old deaf cripple, with her crutch and her ear-trumpet. As several of these persons were his patients, he inquired as usual after their complaints; but his questions were met by a dogged silence, or rude answers; whilst the three shrews were loud in their revilings, the deaf woman screaming high above the rest.

"Yes, ax 'em, do, poor things! when they mean to go to the pit-hole. And much rest they'll get in it, — just earthed over at night, and dug out again afore morning; that's all we enjoy of our narrow homes! Well, you've snatched one at any rate — poor Sukey Hobbes! Ay, you may shake your head — you did n't do it, — not you, — nor she is n't you know where, with her bones surgically picked into a skeleton, to stand behind a green curtain in a glass case. But, mark my words, — she 'll harnt ye some day! She 'll harn't ye in her little shrowd!"

My father rang the bell: the sliding panel in the gate moved aside; and a hard red face looked through the grating; but the porter still delayed to withdraw the bolt. He was an officer whose duty it was to admit rags and tatters, and as a character was being torn to shreds outside, he resolved to afford time for the operation. So the vituperation went on.

" Yes, go in to the Board, and hush and huddle it up among ye! It was not body-snatching — O no — poor paupers have not bodies, but only carcasses like brute beasts, so it was n't body-snatching at all! And if it was, who cares for the remains of the like of us? If we make away with ourselves, we 're mangled and mammoked with stakes through our corpses; and if we die nateral, we 're cut up like Haggerty and Holloway! Who did poor Sukey kill that she 's to be made a 'natomy? — But murderers is dissected, and so is paupers!"

The gate here opened; and my father entered, bestowing on the porter a gentle rebuke, that was received with a sneer, and revenged by leaving the panel open, so that as the Doctor crossed the yard he received through the grating a parting salute.

"Take care of John Hobbes, that 's all. If *he* comes nigh your body, he 'll snatch it alive!"

With these sounds ringing in his ears, my father entered the Workhouse; not unmarked by sundry dingy paupers, who were in waiting as messengers, and nodded and winked to each other, but omitted the customary tokens of respect as he passed them in the passage. Not a creature seemed to recognize him but the master's dog.

My father, for all his virtues, was not a favorite with the Board. In those days of general prosperity, and under the Old Poor Law, the expenditure for the maintenance of paupers was in many parishes very liberal, in some lavish; yet there were examples even then of a harsher spirit and sterner system; and in certain localities, the sole aim of the parochial authorities was to reduce the poor and their rates to the lowest possible pitch. In our own district especially, the management of the Workhouse had gradually fallen into the hands of rigid utilitarians and strict economists, who were continually seeking to discover that minimum of support on which human life can subsist; and their rules, by augmenting labor and diminishing food, had already brought their Work Tables and Dining Tables to proportions that would have astonished an upholsterer.

My father, from natural disposition, was ill-adapted to second such views; and was, in the opinion of the authorities, an expensive doctor: he was too apt to prescribe wine and a generous diet for very reduced patients; and to recommend extra comforts in clothing, and improvements in lodging the poor. Moreover, his evidence at inquests on defunct paupers was not always exactly what could have been wished; and in one case had tended directly to induce a verdict of " Died from Neglect." He was therefore no favorite with the Board, who, as Postle suspected, had secretly encouraged the establishment of a rival doctor, in whose private opinion the milk of human kindness, to say nothing of the cream of it, was a luxury to be reserved for the wealthy classes. With the poor, on the other hand, my father ought to have been popular: but his good intentions towards them were nullified by orders that were disobeyed, and recommendations that were disregarded; he was supposed, by some, to drink the wine that did not follow his prescription, and when it did, that *he* changed the Port into Elder, and the Sherry into Raisin. Thus he was associated with all sins of omission and commission; and as one of the Parochial Body, shared in the general odium that attached to it. His kind manners indeed, his prompt attendance, tender treatment, and private charity, as far as his very limited means allowed, might have procured an exemption in his favor; but his decided opposition to the local and growing habit of opium taking, by the lower classes, had excited a discontent, sedulously fostered by the opposite practice and secret machinations of Shackle, into a dislike, which the imputed outrage in the churchyard had aggravated to abhorrence. And so — a Martyr Elect — my father entered the Boardroom, and placed himself in one of the vacant seats at its long table.

The senior churchwarden, Mr. Peckover, was in the chair;

supported on his right by Mr. Hix, who had lost no time in circulating the story of his visit to the Doctor's surgery, with the discovery of the scraps of French-gray cloth and the silver-washed nails — but ending with a recommendation to bury the matter in their own bosoms. There were present, besides, Mr. Bearcroft the overseer, Mr. Poplitt the assistant-overseer, Mr. Tally the vestry clerk, and a few more official gentlemen. The greater part of the business of the meeting had been already disposed of: several tenders had been accepted; a complaint against the Master and Matron, and another against the Porter, had been heard and dismissed; a retrenchment in the Dietary had been agreed to; and the last question, the better punishment of the refractory paupers, was under discussion. Bread-and-water and solitary confinement were soon decided on; and then came a pause. The Boardmen looked at each other, and at the Doctor, and then with one accord at the chairman; who rose, coughed, stammered, and proceeded to lay before them a very disagreeable business — the desecration of the churchyard, the violation of a grave, and the abstraction of a corpse — according to popular rumor — by their own medical officer. The gentlemen would no doubt recollect the remarkable funeral bestowed by one John Hobbes, a pauper on the parish books, on his deceased child, who was interred in an elegant coffin, covered with French-gray cloth, and richly ornamented with silvered nails? It was her grave that had been disturbed; and her body which had been stolen for anatomical purposes. He thought, with his friend on his right, such a slur ought not to rest on the parish and its officers. The Doctor himself, he understood, wished for an immediate inquiry. It would have been more regular, no doubt, to have given notice, but as he was present for the purpose, the Board would perhaps dispense with the form, and hear what he had to say on the subject."

This course being assented to, my father rose, promptly yet embarrassed, for the old difficulty of proving a negative reduced his eloquence to little more than an assertion.

"All I can say is, gentlemen, that I am an innocent man. As for any guilty knowledge of this matter, it was only this very morning — within an hour ago — that I knew of any grave being robbed, or any body stolen · my informants being Mr. Hix, there, and Doctor Shackle."

"Yet it was pretty widely known last night, before your christening supper," observed Mr. Poplitt, who had been one of the uninvited.

"The surer proof of my having nothing to do with it," replied my father, "that I was behind the whole parish in the information. That I was suspected, nay, condemned, was indeed signified to me, at the family festival just alluded to, in a very marked and painful matter — but it is only recently that I have become aware of the cause of that general desertion. On what grounds the charge is grounded it is impossible to divine; my long practical acquaintance with anatomy, in the schools and hospitals, and my professional knowledge, vouched for by the most eminent surgeons of the day, place me beyond the need of such studies of the human subject; and if I did require any aid from dissection, my principles publicly avowed, deprecate the exclusive application of the remains of the poor to purposes equally beneficial to the rich."

"That is true," said the Vestry Clerk. "I have heard the Doctor express that sentiment on various occasions."

"No doubt of it," said Mr. Poplitt; "but people's practice don't always square with their professions."

"Well, let me be judged by my practice then," said my father. "What have I ever done, as a medical man, that such a suspicion should fall on me rather than on any one else?"

"If you mean to glance at Doctor Shackle," said the Chairman, "I myself can speak to his alibi; for he was in close attendance on my wife, who was confined on the night in question."

"I glanced at nobody, Mr. Chairman," replied my father, "nor have an aim beyond my own exculpation. I repeat, that I knew nothing of the affair till this morning; and if you will send for my assistant, Mr. Postle, he will confirm my statement."

"Mr. Postle!" exclaimed half a dozen voices.

"Phoo! phoo! Doctor," said the Chairman, "you know better than that! In a little quiet bit of body-snatching for the surgery, assistant and accomplice are synonymous."

"So be it," said my father. "Postle had certainly quite as much to do with the matter as myself; and I was sound asleep in my own bed. But that rests, too, on domestic, and therefore, I presume, on questionable evidence."

"I think," said Mr. Poplitt, appealing to Mr. Hix, "you told us something about some French-gray cloth and silver-headed nails that were seen in the Doctor's surgery?"

"I did," replied Mr. Hix, looking rather confused; "but on the understanding that the communication was to be suppressed as strictly confidential."

"There is no need of suppression," cried my father; "the articles were taken from my basket-boy, Catechism Jack, who is weak of intellect, and had childishly adorned himself with them on the morning of the christening."

"A likely story!" mumbled Mr. Hix, in a tone between publishing and smothering the remark.

"And pray, Doctor, how did *your* boy become possessed of the cloth and nails?" inquired Mr. Poplitt.

My father was silent: he could not form the remotest guess; for he was still ignorant that the coffin had been left above ground by the maranders.

"Why, of course," suggested the Vestry Clerk, "the boy picked up the things in the churchyard —"

"Yes, when he were there delivering their sleeping draughts to the dead folks," said Mr. Bearcroft, the Overseer, with a grim smile. Mr. Hix bestowed an approving nod on the Overseer, and Mr. Poplitt cast a sneer at the Vestry Clerk.

"Perhaps," said a little withered man with a pigtail, an Auditor and Trustee, "we had better send for the lad and examine him?"

"It would be to no purpose!" exclaimed my father. "The poor creature is so timorous, that, if seriously interrogated, he would recur to his old laps, and nothing would be got out of him, except that he would be a good boy, and say his Catechism, and not tumble down stairs. However, gentlemen, the suspicion attached to that cloth and those nails extorts from me a confession which nothing else should have induced me to make"—and my father blushed, as if about to plead guilty to the charge against him.

Now, then, it was coming! Mr. Hix nudged his neighbor, and the Overseer winked across the table at Mr. Poplitt.

"It was I, gentlemen, resumed my father, in a faltering tone, "who supplied the Hobbeses with the means for that preposterous funeral." The Boardmen looked at each other, and interchanged signals of various import: brow-raisings of wonder, head-shakings of disbelief, and shrugs of doubt.

"If you mean the money chucked in at the Hobbes's door, or window," said Mr. Poplitt, "that gift has generally been attributed to Dr. Shackle."

"Universally so," said Mr. Hix.

"And might be still," replied my father, "if nothing but common humanity were in question. I trust the Doctor is as capable as I am of feeling for a bereaved father and mother. The deed is only claimed because it tends directly to contradict the charge that has fallen upon me. Were I capable," and the speaker's eyes filled with tears as he recalled the poor dead child, with her flowers and toys about her, as he had seen through the cottage-window — " were I capable of robbing a churchyard, *that* little grave would have been the very last on earth I should have dreamed of violating!"

This speech, emphatically delivered, with the air and tone of the deepest feeling, caused a visible sensation amongst the auditors: several seemed affected, and one or two looked foolish, the only softness of which they were capable; but the impression was transient.

"Why, as to that," said the burly overseer, "if the trick had been clearly done, the father and mother would have been never the wiser, while the purse may be, you considered in the light of purchase-money, like, for the body."

My father's face flushed, his eyes glistened, his lips quivered, and he was about to start up for some angry explosion, when the vestry clerk laid his hand on his arm, held him down, and rose in his stead.

"Mr. Chairman, allow me to propose that this business be dropped. There is much more mystery about it than we can hope to unravel except by course of time. As yet, we are all in the dark, and where there is a doubt we are bound to give the benefit of it to the accused, and to suppose him innocent, as in this case I honestly believe he is."

Mr. Hix, Mr. Poplitt, and Mr. Bearcroft, rose together; but the loud voice of the big overseer soon found itself in possession of the air.

"The benefit of the doubt! Ay, that's very well for a legal friction, I should say fiction — but what's to benefit us, the parochial authorities, if we connive at such doings to dead paupers, surrounded as we are by such a vast proportion of live ones, and uncommon audacious and refractory? Their excitement is awful."

" They will easily be pacified," said the vestry clerk. " Post a few handbills with a reward for the discovery of the offender — "

" When we have discovered him gratis!" growled Mr. Bearcroft. " Not a shilling, sir, not a shilling! The parish funds are not to be rewarded away in any such manner. The offender is before us, and his guilt or innocence ought to be established at once."

" By all means!" exclaimed my father; "it is for that purpose that I am here, — that every equivocal circumstance may be explained away or contradicted, before I visit another parish patient, or set my foot again in the Infirmary."

" I believe that is the general feeling of the Board," said the Chairman, stooping sideways to receive the communication which Mr. Hix was whispering into his ear. " We will come, therefore, to the point. Perhaps, Doctor, you can tell us the mark or marks on your family linen ? "

My father started, and stared at what seemed so strangely irrelevant a question ; but to a repetition of it, replied that he presumed the marks would be the initials of himself and wife, or G. E. B. with the number.

" And in what color ? "

" Either red or blue — red to the best of my recollection."

The Chairman made a signal to a subordinate official who was in attendance, and delivered his order.

" Budge, produce the sheet to the Board."

Budge immediately proceeded to a cupboard in one corner of the room, and unlocking it, drew forth a large, strong sheet, soiled with clay, which he laid on the table, when it was eagerly inspected by the Boardmen, — and alas ! there were the fatal signs, G. E. B., No. 4, worked with red marking-cotton in one corner !

The Vestry Clerk having satisfied himself of the fact by occular inspection, sank back into his chair, violently striking the Minute Book before him with his open hand.

My father was petrified !

" In that cloth, gentlemen," said the Chairman, " the earth was deposited, which had been taken out of the grave, with a view to its being all returned to its place. The discovery of the robbery was made by the sexton, who reported it to me, and by my orders brought away the sheet, which has remained in the possession of Budge, under lock and key, ever since."

"A clear case! palpable! undeniable! a clencher! a settler!" resounded from different quarters of the room.

"Doctor," asked the Vestry Clerk, in an aside tone, "do you employ a laundress?"

"No," replied my father, with a sorrowful shake of the head, for he understood the drift of the question. "The washing is all done at home."

The Chairman, Mr. Hix, Mr. Bearcroft, and Mr. Poplitt were busily writing on strips of paper, which they passed across the table to each other. To judge by their looks and signals, the communications were generally approved; and some secret resolution having been passed by a succession of affirmative nods, they bent their eyes on the Doctor. He was gazing on vacancy, as a man gazes who seeks at once to comprehend the past, the present, and the future.

"Yes," he said, speaking half aloud to himself, "that sheet is certainly mine, though how it was obtained for such a purpose is an impenetrable mystery. I cannot pretend to fathom it. Time and Providence some day may clear it up — but now, and from me, an explanation is impossible. Gentlemen!" here he raised his voice; "you MUST think me guilty. The presumption is too strong against me, — the current of circumstances too violent to be stemmed by a simple though solemn denial. Hereafter the dark cloud that is hanging over me may disperse; and its shadow that now blackens me so deeply may pass away. In the mean time there is but one course for me to pursue. I cannot — I feel that I cannot — remain your medical officer any longer. The place is vacant. I will send my formal resignation as soon as I get home."

There was a dead silence of assent: nobody said, "Stop! — consider — take time!"

My father rose, and bowed to the Chairman, and the Board, and made a movement to shake hands with the Vestry Clerk, but observing no sign of encouragement, bowed to him too, and hurried out of the room.

The pauper messengers, who had learned the whole business by relays of listeners, made jeering comments as he passed through their lounging place — the Matron, whom he encountered in the passage, read in his face ere she arose from her courtesy, that he was disgraced, skipped aside into her parlor, and shut the door. Only the Master's dog still recognized him with his old salutes, and trotting across the forecourt with him, licked his hand for the last time. The hard red-faced porter, the moment the Doctor emerged from the Workhouse, had set the gate as wide open as it would swing; my father passed through it, and it closed with a loud slam.

Perhaps in the whole course of his days his heart had never felt so heavy as it weighed on his way home. In his progress to the Workhouse, he had been shocked and grieved by the frequent manifestations of dislike, and the sad change he had suffered in the golden opinions of all sorts of people; but on his return, the same tokens were embittered by tormenting reflections of more domestic interest. His prospect in life, within the last hour, had altered materially for the worse; and particularly resembled a natural one that was often before him — the Fens on a bad day. The situation of Parish Doctor was attended, indeed, with little direct emolument. The fees were calculated on a scale that only allowed for moderate mor- buses, reasonable rheumatisms, cheap agues, and very low fevers; and afforded little profit to a conscientious practitioner, who was not content, in treating a sick pauper, to do it very well for the price. But the parochial connection was valuable: and by his secession from the Board, he would lose as patients the churchwardens and overseers, their spouses and children. In short, he saw before him, very distinctly, a Wife, two dear Twins, and a household to support, but no clear prospect of that indispensable requisite,

A LIVELY-HOOD.

CHAPTER XIX.

AMONGST the minor difficulties of our perplexing family affairs, none was more puzzling than the communication of the robbery, or breaking the plate as Kezia called it, to my mother. She had slept all through the alarm of the discovery, and had risen, and was about to come down, quite unconscious that Fate, which had mixed up such a black dose for her over night, had prepared another bitter draught for her in the morning. That the revelation would kill her poor mistress stone-dead on the spot like a thunderbolt was broadly predicted by the weeping maid-of-all-work. Mrs. Prideaux anticipated that a very hysterical tendency might bring on a succession of fainting fits, and Mr. Postle compared the disclosure to imparting a blow to a packet of fulminating mercury.

At last Uncle Rumbold, in virtue perhaps of his likeness to a philosopher, undertook to deliver the evil tidings, and after some reflection determined to do it at the late breakfast which in my father's absence he was to enjoy *tête-à-tête* with my mother.

The task, nevertheless, was a nervous one for an inexperienced bachelor. A dozen times he stopped short in his meal, and clutching his beard in his hand — a trick he had in any case of perplexity — fixed his large speculative eyes on the face before him, asking himself will she scream? or go off in a fit? will her tea go the wrong way? will she choke with her muffin? or jump up and knock over the tea-urn? If she did not wear ligatures, thought he, I would not mind; but a woman wears so many bands and ties and laces, that when nature attempts a gallop in her veins she bursts a blood-vessel.

All this while he was eating an egg, out of which, all at once plucking the spoon he held it up, in a line with my mother's nose, and very solemnly exclaimed:

" Egad! my little fellow, it is well you did not go too! "

This opening, however, was a failure; my mother thought that the spoon had merely escaped being swallowed with one of those very large mouthfuls of food which her brother was in the habit of bolting. He therefore tried another tack; and began, in his oratorical tone, as follows : —

" In former times, sister, there was a certain sect of philosophers who professed to endure the severest pain with the most perfect indifference."

" Yes," said my mother, " they swallowed melted lead, and washed their hands in boiling oil, and carried about red-hot pokers by the red ends, and allowed any of the company to satisfy themselves that the things were actually burning and scalding hot."

" I alluded to the Stoics," said Uncle Rumbold.

" And so did I," said my mother.

" Humph !" said Uncle Rumbold. " However, that was the Stoic doctrine ; and the young Spartans were brought up in its principles. You remember the story of the Spartan boy who had a stolen fox under his cloak, and allowed the animal to gnaw away his bowels, rather than betray himself by crying out ? "

" Ah ! I see," said my mother, closing her eyes, and shuddering. " You want your two nevies to be brought up like young Stoics and Spartans — but what I call hardened little wretches."

" I was not thinking of my nephews at all," replied Uncle Rumbold. " In referring to the Stoic philosophy, what I wanted, sister, was to incite you to summon up your own fortitude."

" Then why did you not say so at once ? " said my mother. " Is there anything the matter ? "

" Of course there is," replied Uncle Rumbold, " or what occasion would there be for the Spartan virtue ? But before you hear it, let me recommend to you to finish your breakfast."

" Good gracious !" exclaimed my mother, pushing away the tea, and toast, and egg, to which she had helped herself, " as if I could eat, with my heart in my mouth ! I do wish you had kept it till George's return. He has ten times more fortitude than I have, — indeed it sometimes amounts to apathy. With his example before me, I might bear up against what might tempt me to stick myself with a breakfast-knife, or to run out and fling myself in the river."

" Well, I will wait," said Uncle Rumbold, " for my brother-in-law's return."

"O no, no, no," cried my mother; "I must hear it now. If there is one thing I cannot bear, it is suspense. Dear me! What can it be? Is it anything more about my poor supper party?"

"No," said Uncle Rumbold. "Though the origin of that cut by the neighborhood, as I have just learned from Mr. Pestle — or Postle — is an awkward affair too. In short, sister — but you must first solemnly promise me not to shriek, or faint away, or do yourself any mischief, or tip over the urn —"

"I won't! I won't!" reiterated my mother.

"Well, then, the silver plate —"

"The plate! I knew it was the plate!" exclaimed my mother, with difficulty suppressing the forbidden scream. But she had not promised anything about the bell, so she jumped up, and tugged at it till one bell-rope gave way with its blue and yellow rosette, and then she began jerking at the other.

Kezia answered the summons, — pale as a ghost.

"The plate — where's the plate?"

The maid-of-all-work wrung her hands, and looked piteously at Uncle Rumbold.

"Where's the plate, I say!"

Poor Kezia dropped on her knees with a *plump* that would have split any pans but those common brown ones, so hardened by frequent scrubbing, and with uncouth gesticulations referred her mistress to the gentleman with the beard.

"The truth is, sister," said Uncle Rumbold, "the plate — which was all borrowed I believe — has been fetched away in the night; but whether by the right parties is very doubtful."

"Thieves! — robbers!" gasped Kezia, in a hoarse whisper.

My mother had heard enough. Without speaking, she went and threw herself at full length on the horsehair sofa; whither Kezia, by a mode of progression familiar to housemaids that scour, shuffled after her on her knees. Uncle Rumbold, in the mean time, deliberately drew out his gold watch and gravely laid it on the breakfast cloth before him, determined to allow sorrow exactly five minutes of uninterrupted indulgence before he and comfort interposed.

Such was precisely the position of the parties in the parlor — the door of which Kezia had left open — when my father quietly entered!

If a domestic man is especially to be pitied, it is when after
the rebuffs, conflicts, defeats, disappointments, affronts, losses,
and crosses he has encountered abroad, in his business, he returns baffled, tired, disgusted, dejected, to be indemnified by
the comforts of home — and finds it desolate — that whilst
the reptiles of that foul hag Adversity had been stinging, biting, hissing, and spitting at him in his path out of doors, others
of the same malignant brood had been spawning and hatching
on the household hearth. That was precisely my father's
case. He stood wonder and thunderstruck — looking from
Uncle Rumbold to Kezia, and from her to my mother, on the
sofa, trying vainly to catch the purport of her broken ex-
clamations.

"Brother-in-law — Kezia — Wife — what is the meaning
of this?"

At the sound of his voice, my mother exchanged her
recumbent for a sitting position, and began incoherently to
inform him of the catastrophe.

"O George, George — we are ruined at last! We can
never hold up our heads again in the place — never, never,
never! What the curate will say — and what Mr. Ruffy
may do, for he's a lawyer — and then that horrid Mrs.
Spinks —"

"She had hern, ma'am! — she had hern!" cried Kezia —
"for she carried it away under her shawl!"

"Thank Heaven for that!" exclaimed my mother, with
extraordinary fervor. "*She* can't ride, then, on our necks!"

"In the name of common sense," said my father, appealing to his brother-in-law, "what is all this about?"

"Why, the house has been robbed," answered Uncle Rumbold, "and the plate carried off."

In making this abrupt communication, the Philosopher had
reckoned on the cheerful, manly, and generally sanguine disposition of my father, whom he was surprised therefore to
see turn pale and stagger into a seat. But the Doctor's spirits
were unusually jaded and depressed by the trial they had so
recently undergone, and made him keenly sensible of a loss,
which he felt bound to make good; but yet knew to be an
impracticable obligation, in the present hopeless posture of
his affairs.

"Yes, it really is a heavy trouble, is n't it, George?" said my mother. "No wonder I felt it deeply, when you take it to heart so seriously. But what is to be done?"

"Ought n't we to raise the hue and cry, and print handbills, and offer a reward for the stolen plate?"

"Turned into white soup by this time!" said Uncle Rumbold. "Melted down almost into a state of nature. All we can do is to report the robbery to the next magistrate, and leave him and his myrmidons to find the thieves, if they can. As the Doctor is tired, and may be wanted, I will step down myself to his Worship: but before I go, I should like to know, brother-in-law, the upshot of the body-snatching story of which Mr. Pestle or Postle has given me the heads — and the result of your visit to the Board."

"The result is simply," said my father, "that I am no longer the Parish Doctor."

At this announcement there was a general expression of surprise, the exclamatory "We an't!" of Kezia ringing high above all.

"But how, George?"

"On what grounds, brother-in-law!"

"To be candid," said my father, "though some of the members of the Board were less friendly than I expected, they had sufficient grounds, founded on circumstantial evidence, to go upon — that the mould cast out of the poor child's grave was deposited in one of my own sheets."

"One of our own sheets!" screamed my mother.

"Our sheets!" echoed Kezia.

"Yes; I saw it produced," said my father. "It was marked G. E. B. No. 4, with red cotton."

The description was no sooner complete, than, after a collision that made our bearded uncle reel like a classic Bacchanalian, Kezia dashed out of the parlor, and was heard racing up the stairs at a horse-gallop.

"We shall soon know if any of the linen is deficient," said my mother. "For Kizzy is very careful of it, and that it is worn fairly, turn and turn about."

"I wish she had been more careful of the plate," growled Uncle Rumbold, "instead of trusting to country fastenings — a thin deal shutter, and a strong oaken bar.

"Did the thieves break in, then, at the kitchen window?" asked my father.

"If they broke in anywhere," muttered Uncle Rumbold, "which his Worship's two-legged ferrets must determine;" and our godfather was setting out on that errand, when he was delayed by the return of Kezia, with the result of her search on her lips and in her face. The household linen was all correct, with the exception of the identical sheet in question, which was missing, though she remembered marking it, as described, with her own hands. Our godfather immediately left the room, and the next minute his bearded profile, surmounted by a very broad-brimmed hat, was seen to pass above the blind of the parlor-window.

My father and mother, released from the restraint which all persons felt more or less in the presence of our strange uncle, immediately became confidential; the first relating what had taken place at the Workhouse, and the last commenting bitterly on a mass of trouble, not spreading itself fairly like a flood on the Flats, but discharging itself, like a terrific waterspout she had lately read of in the county paper, on one devoted house and family.

Kezia, meanwhile, repaired to her old post beside the desk in the surgery, to derive comfort and counsel from Mr. Postle; and was about to reveal to him the mysterious disappearance of the fatal sheet, when she perceived that a very little woman, with a straw-colored face, was shivering in the patient's chair. The influence of old habits instantly took possession of her.

"Ah! a case for chinchony. My good woman, you've got the ha-gue, and I should say the stertian. You must take bark; and the best form is in canine pills."

"No, no," said the woman; "I'm weary of that old dose. I've took bark enough to turn me into a holler tree. But I'm not come about myself, but my sister, who is troubled about her legs — she has such very coarse veins."

"Has she any occasion to be showing her legs?" inquired Kezia, not a little puzzled by the novelty of the complaint.

"Pshaw! she means varicose veins," said Mr. Postle.

"Yes, so I suppose," said Kezia. "It's very kind of her, I'm sure, to come to us, instead of Doctor Shackle, after all the falsities that has been spread about us, and has gone thro' the parish like an infection of a malignant nature —"

"She was interrupted by the entrance of Uncle Rumbold,

who swept through the surgery like a bearded meteor, with
the parish constable in his vortex, in which, by an imperative
beckon, he involved the maid-of-all-work, who was hurried
along with them into the parlor.

"Dear me!" exclaimed my mother, "what is all this,
brother? Who is that strange gentleman with the paper?"

"I am the Constable, ma'am, at your service," said the
stranger, referring to the document in his hand; "and this
here is a sarch warrant, for sarching the box or boxes of one
Kezia Jenks."

"Mine!" faltered Kezia, — who, like many very innocent
persons, had nevertheless a most intense dread and awe of the
law, and all that belonged to it. "Mine!"

"I do wish, brother-in-law," said my father, in a tone of the
deepest vexation, "I do wish you had been less precipitate!
What has this faithful, devoted, hardworking, and affectionate
creature done, that she should be affronted by suspicion, and
have her character tarnished by such a proceeding? I would
pledge my life for her honesty."

"I know you would!" replied Uncle Rumbold, "and therefore acted without consulting you, on my own judgment and re-
sponsibility. But I do nothing without grave deliberation; no
man does, who wears this — and he touched his beard. "Listen. In the dead of the night, with my own ears I heard your
paragon of fidelity open her chamber-door, and proceed stealthily down stairs, where, by listening over the banisters, I heard
her voice, which I can swear to, in conversation with some
person or persons unknown. The words I could not distinguish. — Silence, woman, and let me proceed —"

But Kezia was not to be silenced; but dropping on her
knees, appealed to Heaven, and her master and mistress, to
testify to her innocence.

"I was only sleep-walking, —which I have done afore, in
this house, and other places besides, — being my misfortune,
and such as will kill me, some day, off a parapet, or out of a
window — as there is a judge in Heaven, it was only sleep-
walking! And I waked up in the kitchen, by stumbling over
the cold supper things, with my face on an 'am."

"A pretty story!" said Uncle Rumbold — echoed by his
satellite, the constable.

"But a true one," said my father. "The poor girl is, to
my knowledge, a somnambulist."

"A bamboozleist!" exclaimed Uncle Rumbold. "If you believe in such fables, brother-in-law, I do not — and never will. They're contrary to nature. And the spoons walked off too in their sleep! Bah! Then you will not allow her box to be searched?"

"I will NOT," said my father.

"In that case," said Uncle Rumbold, "I shall remove my own person and property from the premises."

My mother looked horror-struck; yet not more so than her housemaid, as deeply interested in the hopes, for the dear twins, that hung on the smiles and frowns of Godfather Rumbold.

"O pray, pray," she sobbed, "don't quarrel and differ about me. I'm not worth it, whatever becomes of me. O Master — consider those dear, precious, innocent twins. Let my box be searched — I want to have it searched — it will do the things good to give them a fresh airing!"

"You had better, George," whispered my mother, with a twitch at my father's sleeve, — "there will be nothing found in it."

"Well — I wash my hands of it!" cried my father, — and the company in a body proceeded up stairs to the attic landing, whither Kezia's box, that she kept in her bedroom, was lugged and ransacked. And never did searcher, legal or fiscal, expose such a heterogeneous medley of articles, of so little intrinsic value! A few clothes — scraps of ribbon, and fragments of patchwork — bits of dried orange and lemon-peel, various ha'penny ballads, and last dying speeches, with one solitary play-bill — a Moore's Almanack, and a Dream-Book — keepsakes innumerable — locks of hair, of all colors, folded up in papers inscribed with female names, and one long silver tress, labelled "My deer Muther's," — with a date, — a red leather heart pin-cushion — several double nuts — a reel-in-a-bottle — and a little bone needle-case, in the shape of a closed umbrella, with a paper tied to the handle, "*Presented me by Mister Postle,*" — an old-fashioned wooden spice-box, and last, not least, a yellow canvas sampler, with its worked alphabets and numerals, and Adam and Eve and the Apple Tree, and Kezia's own name, and the date at the bottom. On the whole, the impression produced by the exhibition was decidedly in favor of the honesty of the proprietor — that she was disinterested, and affectionate, somewhat superstitious, and had one more grain of romance than was suspected in her homely composition.

"Well, I 've sarched many a sarvant's box in my time," said the constable, "and I never come across a more innocenter one than that!"

As the party returned down stairs, they were met at the door of the nursery by Mrs. Prideaux, who, dropping a very lady-like courtesy to Uncle Rumbold, tendered a bunch of keys on a steel ring. She was in that house, she said, a hired nurse, and so far in the capacity of a servant, and therefore begged to submit her boxes to inspection. But Uncle Rumbold as politely declined the offer: he had had quite enough of searching, and had become irksomely indebted in an apology to the maid-of-all-work; for he was a proud man in his way, and of all the things that disagreed with his stomach, none was more indigestible than the proverbial Pasty of Humility,

HUMBLE PIE.

CHAPTER XX.

OUR LUCK.

Our Uncle Rumbold, though fierce of aspect and manner, was not absolutely hard-hearted; and his pride relented considerably when he saw the maid-of-all-work come down stairs, with her eyes red and swollen with weeping. But his apologies were disclaimed. "It wasn't the searching her box," she said, "she didn't mind that, nor the being suspected, that made her cry, but the sight of her dear mother's hair, who died, poor soul! of a bilious calculation."

"Calculus," said my father, "calculus. But come, brother-in-law, let us inspect the premises, and have the constable's opinion of the burglary."

The trio accordingly repaired to the kitchen, where they minutely inspected the window and its fastenings, from which it appeared that a piece had been cut out of the shutter, so as to allow of the removal of the bolt, the sill was scratched and soiled with clay, and the ground, on the outside, bore in several places the imprint of a man's shoe or boot, thickly studded with hobnails. There was no doubt of the manner in which the entrance had been effected; and the parties having come to an unanimous conclusion on the subject, the constable was despatched to take the necessary steps for the discovery and apprehension of the offender or offenders. Uncle Rumbold undertook to order the printing and issue of the handbills, whilst my father, with a heavy heart, proceeded to his escritoire in the parlor, with a task before him which, to a man who disliked letter-writing in general, was a heavy infliction — seeing that he had to indite three several epistles, all on subjects of the most painful and disagreeable nature, namely, to the Board, with his resignation of office; to Mr. Ruffy, communicating the fate of his presentation tankard; and to the curate, conveying the loss of the silver-gilt salts. It would have moved a heart of nether millstone to have seen how he spoiled pen after pen, and sheet after sheet of paper, vainly turning his eyes for inspiration from the mirror, with its bird and ball, to the ceiling or the floor, the wall or the window, the poplar-tree, and the blue sky.　O, if my father ever envied a rich or great man, it was then, just then, for the sake of his private secretary !

To add to his distress, his usual resource in such emergencies was unavailable.　In reply to his application for help, Mr. Postle had excused himself, under the pretence of urgent business in the surgery ; but, in reality, the assistant was indisposed with a fit of spleen.　He had heard of the affair of the search-warrant ; and after indignantly asking of the jar of conserve of roses why Mrs. Prideaux had not been suspected instead of Kezia, had solemnly promised the pestle and mortar to pluck old Rumbold, at the very first opportunity, by the beard — a threat he would probably have put into execution but for a positive injunction from the injured maid, who overheard him pledging himself to the same effect to the bottle of leeches.

"No, Mr. Postle," she said, "you will do no such thing. It's a heathen fashion, to be sure, and makes him look more like a satire of the woods than a Christian : but when you consider what hangs on it, namely, the future prospects in life of our poor, helpless, innocent twins, you'll respect his beard as if it belonged to Moses or Aaron. As for my being suspected, it comes natural to a servant, and, like a part of her work, to clear up her character sometimes, as well as her kitchen : and as regards the searching of my box, it's nothing to the rummaging of one's thoughts and feelings, which I have had to undergo in other places.　But so long as master, and missis, and you don't suspect me, I can bear it from any one else. So, for the sake of the dear twins, you must let the matter drop, and not offend Mr. Rumbold by look, or word, or deed, and especially by touching his beard, which would be cutting off young heirs with a shilling."

Having extorted a promise to this pacific effect, Kezia repaired to the nursery, where she relieved her full heart and excited feelings by a good cry and a hearty fondling of the precious babes.　But, beyond this solace, she had a secret project of her own, in accordance with which she addressed herself to the genteel nurse.

"O, Mrs. Prideaux, is n't it a shocking thing to see a family like ours, for no fault of their own, coming step by step, deeper and deeper into misfortune and misery !　First, that dreadful supper, and then the robbery, and then the loss of the parish — it reminds me of one of my own runs of bad luck, when first I was knocked down by a runaway horse, and then picked up by a pickpocket, and then sent home in a hackney-coach that had just carried a patient to the hospital with a putrid fever."

"The planets," said the nurse, "are decidedly sinister."

"Then you think," said Kezia, delighted with the astrological turn of the conversation, "that it is our ill stars are in fault?"

"Of course," said the nurse. "The aspects of the planets, at this juncture, and as affects this house, are particularly malignant."

"They must be, indeed!" said Kezia, with a melancholy shake of her head. "According to the Almanac, their bad influences affect sometimes one part and sometimes another, and at different times; but here they are, as I may say, smiting us back and belly, hip and thigh, all at once!"

"The natural effect," said the nurse, "of the planetary configurations, and especially of the position of Saturn."

"Ah! with his ring!" exclaimed Kezia. "Mr. Postle once showed him to me through his refractory telescope."

"A refracting one, I presume," said the nurse.

"I believe it was," said Kezia; "and it brought down the moon till it looked as big as a silver waiter. Talking of which reminds me of the stolen plate; and which it is my private notion that you know as much or more about than any one else."

"That *I* do!" exclaimed the nurse, with a slight start, and fixing her keen eyes on the face of the maid-of-all-work as if she would read her very soul. "That I know who stole the plate!"

"Yes," said Kezia, "by means of the heavenly bodies. I have heard of many persons recovering their lost things through star-gazers and fortune-tellers; and of course, as you can cast nativities, *you can do the other*."

This was the very point at which she had been aiming; but the answer of the nurse put an extinguisher on her hopes.

"Between ourselves," she said, "I have cast some figures on purpose; but there is a mystery in the matter that defies my art."

"The more's the pity," said Kezia; "for I made sure that you could discover the thief.   And then that lost sheet, as was found in the churchyard, — how it was abstracted from a press to which nobody but ourselves had access: I own to thoughts, and suspicions, and misgivings about it, that make me shudder!"

"Then do you really suppose," asked the nurse, "that your master was guilty of stealing the dead child?"

"The Lord forbid!" exclaimed Kezia.   "I would as soon suspect him of kidnapping live ones for the Plantations! No, I was not thinking of him, but of a treacherous, deceitful being, whom to think of under the same roof, and in the same room with one, makes my very blood in a curdle."

The nurse again fixed one of her scrutinizing looks on Kezia; but the latter was thinking of quite another personage, as implied by her next question.

"What is your real opinion, Mrs. Prideaux, of supernatural agency?"

"The same as your own," was the prompt answer of the nurse.

"In that case," said Kezia, "I don't mind saying it's my belief that our sheet was purloined away by Satan himself, whose delight is in casting down the good and the godly, and for the express purpose of ruining my poor master."

"It is quite possible," said the nurse, who seemed to take delight in pampering the credulity of her simple-minded and single-hearted companion. "Such an act would be perfectly in unison with the diabolical character. My belief coincides with your own.   But remember, Kezia, the age is a sceptical age, and its infidels especially repudiate astrology and demonology; so that the less we say of our own convictions the better.   Indeed, it would cost me my bread were it known that I had cast the nativity of these dear twins."

"But it never shall be," cried Kezia, — "never! Do you think I would break the solemn oath you made me take on the Testament?"

"No — I know that you would not," said the nurse, in her sweetest tone; "for if you did, there are lightnings to burn your body, and other fires to scorch your soul for the perjury." And so the conference ended.

My father, meanwhile, had toiled on at his irksome task in

the parlor — blotting, blundering, erasing, correcting, tearing up, and beginning *de novo*, in a way that a corresponding clerk would have gone crazy to witness; for if my parent's sustenance had depended on the exercise of his pen, he must have died of starvation.   At last, after infinite trouble, he had completed the whole of the missives, and was just in the act of drawing that long sigh of satisfaction with which a weary man is apt to hail the accomplishment of his labor, when my mother entered the room, drew a chair beside him, seated herself, and laid her hand on his arm.   There was nothing in her face to indicate any interruption of the mental repose and relief which my father had promised himself; her looks were as cheerful as the tone with which she uttered her preluding monosyllable.

" George ! "

" My dear ! "

" Can you forgive me for keeping from you a little secret ? "

"Of course I can," replied my father, with his old smile. " But will your own sex for being so unwomanly ? "

" No matter for them," said my mother.   " I meant to have hoarded it up for an agreeable surprise ; but with such troubles as have come upon us, it seems only fair that you should share in any comfort which I am enjoying myself.   You remember the 20 *l.* note that you gave me last week ? "

" Yes — for Mr. Lobb."

" Ah, Mr. Lobb must wait a bit," said my mother.   " That note went quite a different way, and for another purpose.   Up to London, George, and for a purchase.   " Can you guess ? "

" For winter clothing, perhaps," said my father, " or a fresh stock of household linen."

" For winter wealth, George," said my mother, " and a stock of good luck.   What do you think of a lottery ticket ? "

My father made no reply — he was confounded by this new blow.

" Do you hear, George ? " cried my mother, — " a lottery ticket ! "

" Yes, twenty pounds gone," murmured my father.

" But they are not gone ! " said my mother.

" As completely," said my father, " as if the note had lighted a candle.   The last money in the house, too, and which ought to have paid the butcher.   That accounts, then, for Lobb's insolence about the tainted mutton."

"Well, well," said my mother, "we shall soon get rid of Lobb after the drawing. The ticket is sure to come up a prize."

"I wish it may!" said my father.

"It is sure to come up a prize," repeated my mother, "for I dreamt three times running of the number."

My father jumped up from his seat, and after pacing a few turns up and down the room, suddenly stopped short and addressed himself to himself in the mirror.

"If ever there was a minister deserved impeachment — if ever a chancellor of the exchequer who ought to have lost his head on the block — it was the man who first invented a mode of raising money by the encouragement of public gambling!" He then turned abruptly to my mother, and inquired whether the ticket was registered.

"Yes, and the lottery was to be drawn on the 16th."

"And this is the 18th," said my father.

My mother instantly started from her seat, and rang the bell, to know if the post had come in, and whether there were any letters.

"Yes, one," which Kezia had laid on the kitchen shelf, where, in the unusual bustle of the morning, it had been forgotten. It was addressed to my mother, who seized the letter, broke the seal, glanced over the contents, and dropping the paper from her hand, sank, gasping, on the sofa — the blankness of her face sufficiently indicating the nature of the intelligence.

"Then the money is gone!" exclaimed my father.

My mother sobbed, and covered her face with her hands; Kezia wrung her's in mute despair. Our evil stars were verily shooting ones, and were practising on our devoted family as at a target!

"Well, what is this new disaster?" inquired the voice of Uncle Rumbold, who had just entered the parlor, but stopped short at two paces from the door, clutching his beard in his right hand.

"Nothing, nothing," replied my father, forgetting his own vexation in the affliction of my mother — "only a lost banknote."

"What, another robbery?"

"No," replied my father, "thrown into the fire — blown out of window — washed down the sink — a mere trifle."

"A trifle!" exclaimed my mother, unwilling to forego any benefit to be derived from her brother's sympathy — "our last twenty pounds in the world — intended to pay the butcher."

But her indirect appeal had no effect. Liberal of advice and personal exertion, Uncle Rumbold, from habit and inclination, was slow in drawing his purse-strings. The amount, he admitted, was no trifle; but sometimes a loss became a gain in the end, by teaching those who had neglected their twenties to take care of their fifties. This new misfortune, however, seemed gradually to touch him, for shortly afterwards, having deliberately seated himself, he addressed his unlucky relatives as follows : "Sister, I have been thinking over your various troubles, and have come to the conclusion, brother-in-law, that, what with your loss of the parish appointment and other drawbacks, your affairs are, or soon will be, in anything but a prosperous condition. Such being the case, I feel called upon, as a near relative, to step a little beyond my original intentions for the family benefit, and especially as regards my twin nephews, though I trust I have sufficiently testified my regard for them already by that invaluable present, the Light of Nature. However, as I said before, I have determined to stretch a point, but on the condition that what I do shall be done in my own way."

"I am sure," said my mother, "we shall be truly grateful for your kindness in any way."

"I am not so certain of that," replied Uncle Rumbold: "however, what I propose is this, — to relieve you altogether of the care and maintenance of one of those two boys. As soon, therefore, as my godson can run alone, I am ready to adopt him ; to board, lodge, and educate — in short, to provide for him through life at my own cost and charge, and of course according to my own system and views."

Here he paused, expecting an answer, whereas his proposition was met by a dead silence. My father, taken by surprise, was at a loss what to say, and my mother looked absolutely aghast. She had not forgotten certain features of the system alluded to, and in her mind's-eye saw her poor offspring, now climbing a tree for his food, at the risk of his neck, and now thrown dog-like into a river, to sink or swim as might happen — in short, undergoing all the hard discipline associated with a young Indian savage, or child of nature.

"Humph! I see how it is," said Uncle Rumbold; "but I do not press an immediate answer. Perhaps you will make up your minds before my departure. I have ordered a chaise at five o'clock, which will carry me to Wisbeach, where I shall meet the coach;—no words; my arrangements once made are never altered, and, let me add, my offers once refused are never repeated."

So saying, he rose and walked off to make his preparations for his departure; whilst my mother took the opportunity of expressing her sentiments to her helpmate on the godfatherly offer.

"No, I never will consent to it," she said,—"never, never! To have a child of mine climbing trees, and swimming ponds, and sleeping in the open air, like a gypsy, or Peter the Wild Boy! And taught bird's-nesting and tomahawking and all sorts of savage tricks, instead of the accomplishments of a young gentleman—and, at any rate, dressed up more like a Guy Fawkes than a Christian—and with a beard, when he's old enough, like a Jewish rabbi,—O, it would break my heart, it would indeed, George! to have a boy of mine begin the world with such a prospect before him!"

"Well, well," said my father, "so be it. I am as loath as you are to have a son of mine bred up into a bearded oddity, like his uncle, or old Martin Van Butchell. So go and see to the dinner, and in the interim I will invent the best excuse I can to offer to my redoubtable kinsman."

Thus comforted, my mother applied herself to the arrangement of the dinner, which, thanks to what Kezia called the "supperfluities" of the night before, presented an unusual variety and profusion of the delicacies of the season. The meal, nevertheless, passed off very drearily. The spirits of the presiding pair were weighed down by the communication they had to make, and the certain resentment that awaited their decision; whilst the temper of Uncle Rumbold himself was still ruffled by a short but sharp argument on somnambulism with Mr. Postle in the surgery. The conversation, such as it was, had flagged into silence, when the post-chaise drew up at the door.

"Now then, sister," cried Uncle Rumbold, rising from his seat, "now then, brother-in-law, for your ultimatum. Am I to have the boy or not?"

"Why then, brother," began my mother, but her voice failed and died away in an articulate croak.

"The truth is," said my father, "we are deeply sensible of your kindness, and sorry to decline it. If the children had not been twins, we might have felt and decided otherwise; but we really cannot find in our hearts to separate, so early in life, a pair of brothers, that nature herself has so closely united."

"That's enough!" said Uncle Rumbold. "A plain offer has met a plain refusal — no offence on either side; but, by my beard, if ever I offer to adopt a child again — " What followed was inaudible or suppressed: he hastily shook hands with his relatives, and hurried into the gaping vehicle, wherein he threw himself back, as if determined on sulks and silence. In another moment, however, his face and beard appeared at the open window.

"God bless you, sister," he said; "brother-in-law, God bless you, — though how you are to be blessed, is more than I know, for you will never be guided by the light of nature!"

Every word of this leave-taking was overheard by Kezia, who with outstretched neck and straining ears listened eagerly for his least syllable. But those words were his last, — not a breath about the dear twins, his own nephews. The whip cracked, the horse-shoes clattered, the wheels rattled, and the few boys who had assembled set up a cheer for the Grand Mogul. The last chance was gone. In another minute, the black and yellow body, which contained Uncle Rumbold, was out of sight; and with it vanished, alas! all the hopes that he had engendered!

CHAPTER XXI.

A DEMONSTRATION.

"So much for relatives!" said my mother, as she poured out the tea, and handed a cup of the beverage to my father. "My precious brother, who would not shave off a hair of his beard for love or money, will now cut off his own nephews without a scruple!"

"Nothing more likely," said my father.

"Do you really think then," inquired my mother, "that he will leave them quite out of his will?"

She waited in vain for an answer; and at last obtained, in lieu of it, another query, far wide of her mark. Throughout his troubles and vexations, my father's mind had been haunted by a vague sense of a something amiss; but his thoughts had always been diverted elsewhere before his fears could assume a definite shape; now, however, his misgivings, after many gleamings and vanishings, suddenly recurred to him, and taking a distinct character prompted the abrupt question— "Where is Catechism Jack?"

Nobody knew. In the crowding events of the day he had not been missed; there had been no medicine to deliver, so that his services were not in requisition, and even Mr. Postle could not tell what had become of him. On comparing notes, he had not been seen by any one since an early hour in the morning, when he had slipped out at the surgery door.

Here was a new cause of anxiety for my father; if any mischance happened to the idiot, the blame in the present temper of the parish was certain to be visited on the master, who had taken the half-witted boy from the care of the old dame, and become responsible for his safety and welfare. Many were the conjectures that were hazarded on the cause of his absence. In my father's opinion, Jack had gone on a visit to his former guardian, and was spending the day with her: my mother, prone to dream of disasters, at once pronounced him drowned in the river; Kezia's fancy sent him tramping after a recruiting party which had passed through the village; and the assistant supposed that he was playing truant and chuck-farthing with other young dogs as idle as himself. The last guess was most probably the true one; however, in the midst of their speculations, his voice was clearly recognized, and in another moment Jack, in an unusual state of excitement, burst into the parlor, round which he pranced with a sort of chimney-sweep's caper, exclaiming with ecstasy, "The tongs and bones! The tongs and bones!"

"Why, Jack," asked my father, "what is the matter with you?"

"The tongs and bones," said Jack, standing still for a moment and then resuming his dance and his song.

"Speak, idiot!" cried Mr. Postle, seizing the boy by the shoulder and shaking him. "What is the meaning of this mummery?"

"O don't, pray don't beat me," whined Jack. "I will say my catechism."

"Poor fellow!" said my father. "Be gentle with him."

"Huzza! The tongs and bones!" shouted Jack, extricating himself by a sudden twist from the grasp of the assistant; and darting through the parlor-door, and across the hall, into the kitchen, to the infinite horror of Kezia, who really believed, as she declared afterwards, that the boy had been bitten by "a rapid dog." Here he continued his capering and his cry; till observing the table with food on it, by one of those abrupt transitions common to weak intellects, his thoughts fastened on a new object; and at once subsiding into his usual demeanor, and seating himself at the board, he asked Kezia to give him his supper. The maid-of-all-work immediately complied; and as after some minutes he continued to eat and drink very quietly, Mr. Postle returned to the surgery and my parents to the parlor.

"The tongs and bones," muttered my mother as she resumed her seat at the tea-table, "what on earth can it mean?"

"Why, I suspect it means," said my father, "that the tag-rag and bobtail of the village have been treating some quarrelsome couple with what is called rough music; and Jack has been present, and perhaps performing at the concert."

This explanation was so satisfactory to both parties, that Jack and his chorus were speedily forgotten; and the pair had resumed their quiet, confidential intercourse, when Mr. Postle entered, with an ominous face, and placed in my father's hands something which he said he had just found upon the counter. It was a scrap of dirty, coarse paper, folded note-fashion, and containing only the following words: "Let the Dockter and Fammily keep in Dores to nite And look to yure Fastnings. A Frend."

"Well, and what do you make of this document?" asked my father.

"That it is what it professes to be," answered the assistant, looking uneasily at my mother, as if embarrassed by her presence. — "I will put the thing technically. There is, you know, sir, a certain local epidemic in the parish, of a very malignant type, and attended with extensive irritation. Now this party intends to say that probably there will be an eruption."

"I understand," said my father, with a nod of intelligence — "but doubt very much if the disease will take that active turn."

"There is no doubt at all," said Mr. Postle. "I know a party who has been round amongst the infected, on purpose to feel their pulse; and the symptoms are of a most unfavorable character. For instance, tongue hot — breath acrimonious and offensive — voice loud and harsh — with the use of expressions bordering on furious mania."

"A mere temporary fever," said my father, "that will pass off without any dangerous paroxysm."

"I wish it may," said Mr. Postle, "and without a nocturnal crisis."

My mother's head during this mysterious discussion had turned mechanically from speaker to speaker, as if moved by internal clock-work; but she could gather no more information from their faces than from their words; and as the consultation might be a long one, and she hated medical matters, she briefly intimated to my father that she should go up-stairs to the children, and left the room.

"And do you really suppose," asked my father, "that there is going to be any disturbance or outrage? Phoo, phoo — I can't and won't believe it."

"So you said of the hostility of the parish Board," retorted the assistant.

"Well, well, do as you please," said my father. "I leave the matter entirely in your own hands."

"In that case," said Mr. Postle, "I shall at once lock all the doors, and secure the lower windows, and this one to begin with;" — and accordingly he pulled up the sliding parlor-shutter, and inserted the screws. "Now then for the others."

"Very good," said my father, "and then come to supper with us in the parlor. Poor Postle," he continued, as the assistant departed to look to the household defences, "he was always an alarmist, and I'll be bound expects the premises to be stormed and sacked, on the strength of an anonymous letter, intended, most probably, to play upon his fears."

True to his plan, the alarmist, meanwhile, proceeded from window to window, and from door to door, locking, bolting, barring, screwing; the surgery door alone, for convenience, being left but partially fastened by a single latch, which, however, could only be raised on the inside. The fanlight above he barricaded with a stout board; and ascertained, shutter by shutter, that the defences of the window were all sound and secure. He then took a final peep at Jack, who was still quietly making an interminable meal in the kitchen; and finding all safe, repaired to the parlor, and took his usual place at the supper-table; not without some bantering from my father as to the preparations in a certain fortress for a state of siege, and the strength of its garrison. But the joke was mistimed.

The meal was about half finished, when, attracted by the attitude of my mother, whose sense of hearing was remarkably acute, my father laid down his knife and fork, and began listening; in which he was soon imitated by Mr. Postle; and for a while the three, silent and motionless, seemed stiffened into as many statues. There was certainly some unusual humming in the air.

"It sounds," said my father, "like the distant murmer of the sea."

"More like the getting up of a gale," said Mr. Postle.

"It 's the noise of a mob!" exclaimed my mother; "I hear voices and the tramping of feet!"

"Say I told you so!" cried Mr. Postle, jumping up from his chair, and resuming the knife with which he had been cutting his cold meat.

"And if it be a mob," said my father, "it may not be coming to us."

"Hark! it comes nearer and nearer," said my mother, turning pale. "In the name of wonder, George ——" she stopped, startled by a loud noise and a sudden outcry close at hand.

The distant sounds, which excited so intense an interest in the parlor, had reached the kitchen; where they no sooner struck on the tympanum of Jack, than, like a young savage who recognizes the warwhoop of his tribe, he started up, overturning his heavy wooden chair, and shouting his old cry, the

"Tongs and bones — tlie tongs and bones!" rushed through the hall, and the surgery, and out of the door, which he left wide open. Kezia, in hot pursuit, with my father and Mr. Postle, were soon on the spot; but only just in time to distinguish the flying figure of the idiot, before he disappeared in the gloom of the lane; his cry being still audible, but getting fainter and fainter till it was lost in the general murmur of the mob.

" 'They are coming up the lane — there is no time to be lost," said Mr. Postle, pushing Kezia, and then drawing my father by the arm into the surgery; the door of which he bolted and locked. They then hurried to the parlor; but my mother, with hen-like instinct, had flown up to her young ones, and was sitting in the nursery to meet whatever might happen, with her twin babes at her bosom. Kezia, by a kindred impulse, was soon in the same chamber; while my father and his assistant posted themselves at a staircase-window which overlooked the lane. It was quite dusk; but at the turn of the road the crowd was just visible, a darker mass amid the gloom, and a moving one, which, as it approached, occasionally threw out a detatched figure or two in front, barely distinguishable as of human shape. Now and then there was a shout; and more rarely a peal of hoarse laughter. As the mob neared the house, its pace quickened.

" There's Jack!" exclaimed Mr. Postle, whose eyesight was much keener than my father's; " he's winding in and out among them like an eel!"

" And, if I mistake not," said my father, " they have something like a black flag."

" Yes, — borne by a tall, big fellow," answered the assistant. " As I live, it's John Hobbes!"

" Poor man," sighed my father.

" As yet I can make out no firearms," said Mr. Postle; " but they have pitchforks and sticks. And yonder's a stuffed figure like a Guy — they are going to burn us in effigy. Yes, they've got fagots and a truss of straw. Here they come at a run! But ah, ah! my fine fellows, you are too late. Look! — they are trying the surgery door!"

The foremost of the mob, in fact, were endeavoring to effect an entrance as described; but, being foiled, commenced a smart rattling with their sticks on the doors and shutters, accompanied by frequent and urgent invitations to the doctor and his assistant to come out and receive their fees. Tired at last of this pastime, they set up a cry "to the front! — to the front!"

Anticipating this movement, my father and his companion hurried into the nursery, the abode of Terror and Despair. My mother, with an infant in each arm, was seated in the easy-chair, her eyes closed, and her face of a ghastly white; so that she might have been taken for dead, or in a fit, but for occasional ejaculations. Kezia, with her apron thrown over her head, knelt beside her mistress; whilst the nurse, with folded arms, leaned her back against the wall between the windows — a position secure from any missile from without. The two babes alone were unconscious of danger — the one smiling and crowing; the other fast asleep.

Taking the hint from Mrs. Prideaux, my father removed his partner and her progeny into a safe nook beyond the angle of projectiles, and only in good time; for the arrangement was hardly completed when a large stone came crashing through the window, and rebounded on the floor.

"Put out the lights!" cried Mr. Postle; "they only serve for marks to aim at," — and, in spite of the remonstrances of the females, the candles were extinguished.

The whole mob by this time had weathered the corner of the house; and having vainly tried the front-door, and thoroughly battered it, as well as the parlor-shutter with their bludgeons, proceeded to organize that frightful concert of rough music with which the lower orders in the provinces were accustomed to serenade an obnoxious character — a hideous medley of noises extracted from cow-horns, cat-calls, whistles, old kettles, metal pans, rattles, and other discordant instruments, described by Jack as the tongs and bones. The din was dreadful; and yet far less so than the profane imprecations and savage threats that were shouted out at every pause of the wild band. There were women too in the crowd; and the cry of "Where's Sukey Hobbes? — Come out, you body-snatcher!" were frequently repeated by voices much shriller than the rest.

"I must — I will speak to them," said my father; and before Mr. Postle could remonstrate or interpose, he had thrown up the sash, and uttered the first three words of his address.

But he was heard no further. His appearance was the signal for one of those yells of execration so awful to hear from a multitude of human throats: a ferocious howl fit only to salute an incarnate fiend, and from which my father recoiled in soul, more than he shrank in body from the ensuing volley of stones. His place, however, was immediately occupied by another orator, in the person of Kezia, who, regardless of the pelting, presented herself to the assembly, screaming at the highest pitch of her voice : —

"You sanguine monsters! do you want to kill us with fright, and our poor innocent babbies?"

"Yes — and to make skeletons of you," replied a hoarse voice from the crowd; a retort applauded by so vociferous a cheer, and such atrocious expressions, that Kezia, with an exclamation of horror, precipitately withdrew to her old position.

Her retreat was hailed with a loud huzza, mingled with derisive laughter, and as it ceased ringing, the dark room was suddenly illuminated by a red glare that projected the shadow of the window-frames, inwards, upon the ceiling. The mob had ignited a quantity of straw and wood, forming an enormous bonfire, by the light of which the persons and features of the ringleaders were easily recognized.

"There is Jack again!" said Mr. Postle, "flitting amidst the smoke like an imp of mischief. And John Hobbes is waving his black flag about like a madman — and yonder is Roger Heap, with a child's bonnet on a pitchfork!"

"And there am I, burning by proxy," said my father, pointing to the dark stuffed figure that was dangling from a triangle of poles in the midst of the blaze. "I shall soon be done to a cinder, and then the cooks will disperse."

"I wish they may," said Mr. Postle, "but the faces they turn up to us are desperately fierce and vicious, as well as their words. I hardly think that their excitement will be satisfied without an attack on the premises, and perhaps taking a few ounces of blood. But what is the matter now?"

As he spoke there was an uncertain stir and movement among the crowd, with a confused outcry, amidst which the words "justice" and "constables" were prominently audible. But it was a false alarm : his worship and his myrmidons either did not or would not know of the tumult, and were snugly and safely housed at home, or in their usual haunts. The report, however, served the same purpose that their presence would have done; for after some hesitation and wavering of the mass to and fro, Roger Heap thrusting his pitchfork into the burning effigy, ran with it up the river bank, and pitched the half-consumed figure, still blazing, into the stream. The mob then dispersed in different directions, the last of them being Catechism Jack, who, after tossing about the glowing sparkling embers, squib-fashion, for a minute or two, ran after the main body.

The smouldering figure meanwhile slowly floated along on the surface of the sluggish river, silently watched by my father and his assistant; till after a few turns and windings, it vanished like the last twinkle of a burnt paper, in the black, blank, distance.

"So ends the *auto-da-fé*," exclaimed Mr. Postle. "Now, then, for candles to inspect and repair our damage."

It was less than might have been expected. Thanks to the precaution of extinguishing the lights, the majority of the stones had missed the windows: only a few panes were broken; and the holes were soon stopped with paper and rags.

"Are the wretches all gone, George?" asked my mother, before she ventured to unclose her eyes.

"All," answered my father—"man, woman, and boy!"

Thus reassured, my mother, with many broken phrases of thanksgiving, came out of her corner, and willingly resigned the dear twins to Kezia, who covered them with her kisses. The nurse also quitted her position, and in her usual calm, sweet voice suggested that her mistress, after her fright and exhaustion, would be the better for some restorative; to which the assistant added that nobody, the infants excepted, would be the worse for some sort of stimulant.

Accordingly the brandy, the kettle, the sugar, tumblers, and spoons, were fetched from below; and cheered by a cordial mixture, the nerves of the company, manly and womanly, soon recovered their tone, and enabled the parties to discuss the circumstances of the recent riot. It was generally agreed that, for that night at least, there would be no futher disturbance; they, nevertheless, continued to sit up, keeping a vigilant watch, back and front, till two hours having elapsed without any fresh alarm, they retired to their respective chambers.

"And how is all this dreadful work to end, George?" inquired my mother, as soon as she found herself, with her husband, in their bedroom.

"Heaven knows!" replied my father. "Only one thing is certain — that the practice must be given up, and we must quit the neighborhood."

"What, sell the business!" exclaimed my mother.

"Yes, if anybody will buy it," said my father. "He must be a liberal man, indeed, who, after this night's demonstration, will bid me anything for the good-will."

"Why then we are ruined!" cried my mother.

"Or something very like it," responded my father — as indeed appeared but too probable when my unlucky parents came to talk over their future prospects; the only comfort before them being that very forlorn hope held out by the old proverb —

WHEN THINGS ARE AT THE WORST, THEY WILL MEND.

CHAPTER XXII.

AN INVALID.

THE moment my father opened his eyes in the morning, they rested on the shattered window-panes, with their holes patched with paper or stuffed with rags, the transparent and the opake, as they admitted or excluded the early sunshine, forming strong diversities of light and shadow. Still, the events of the overnight seemed so dream-like, that he mechanically stepped out of bed, and went to look abroad for confirmation. And, alas! there it was, in the road; that great dark mark, indicating the site of the opprobrious bonfire — a round black spot, a blot as it were, on the parish. The leaves on one side of the poplar-tree were visibly scorched; and he could even trace where Roger Heap had run up the bank to heave the burning effigy in the river. On these tokens he looked, however, with more pain than resentment. Accustomed, as a medical man, to witness the infirmities, frailties, frenzies, and morbid irritability of human nature, he made large allowance for its violence and its weakness; and felt little more anger at the outrage of the mob, than if he had been struck by a crazy patient, or abused by a delirious one.

My mother, on the contrary, was no sooner awake to the dilapidations in the casement, with all their suggestions of glaziers, and new panes, and putty, than she burst out into the most bitter reproaches on the whole parish; and especially the authorities, who ought to have preserved the peace, from the justice down to the beadle. They were a set, she said, of hapless, cowardly sots, and deserved to be locked in their own cage and set in their own stocks for neglecting their duties.

" Well, well," said my father, " thank Heaven, we are all safe and unhurt; for nobody has even received a scratch; which, considering such missiles as those " — and he pointed to a large stone on the floor — " must be regarded as providential."

" It's that," replied my mother, " that makes me so mad! One had better be murdered at once, than subjected to such dreadful alarms, and scared out of one's senses;" and again she launched out in vituperation of the village wretches. The truth is, there is nothing that people resent more strongly, or forgive less easily, than a thorough frightening; the absence of personal injury serving to aggravate the offence. Thus my mother, finding herself safe and sound, as well as all who belonged to her, begrudged, miser-like, the needless expenditure of terror, or so little real damage; just as a certain traveller reproached the highwayman, who pleaded in extenuation of having shot at him, that there was no bullet in the pistol. "So much the worse," exclaimed the indignant old gentleman; "so much the worse, you villain; for then you frightened me for nothing!"

My mother's denunciations, however, did not confine themselves to the inhabitants of the neighborhood; but gradually took a wider range; and finally involved so large a portion of mankind in general, as to compel my father to remind her, that, with such sentiments, one ought to renounce society, and retire into solitude.

"And why should n't we renounce society?" cried my mother. "Did n't society renounce us on the night of the christening? For my part, I could begin to-morrow — and go into a desert!"

"No doubt of it," replied my father, very gravely. "The only difficulty is to dwell there. It may do very well for a lone man or woman, disgusted with society, to become a recluse, and live in a cave, a cell, or a grotto; but I fear it would be extremely inconvenient, if not impraticable, for married people, with a young family, to turn hermits."

"No matter," said my mother. "I know what I mean. I hate the world, and I wish I could fly from it."

"Phoo, phoo!" said my father.

"And what am I to do then," whined my mother, "if I am not to complain?"

"Why, come here," said my father, "and look at the flight of the miller's pigeons; how pretty and playful and harmless they look, after the burning flakes that were fluttering in the air last night."

My mother immediately slid out of bed, and slipped on her dressing-gown; but, instead of looking at the miller's pigeons, went off to her own dove-cote, the nursery, to assure herself of the welfare of her twin-babes. They were fast asleep; and their calm, chubby, innocent faces soon put to flight whatever remained of her misanthropy. An effect they had previously produced on Kezia, who, like her mistress, had waked up in such a virulent humor against the whole county, that, as she delared, " Provided the family had an Ark, she should n't care if all Lincolnshire was under water."

My father, meanwhile, dressed himself with professional celerity, and went down to the surgery; which he no sooner entered, than to his astonishment he found himself in utter darkness. The shutters had not been taken down; and the fanlight over the door was still blocked up by its temporary barricade. It was the first time that the assistant had failed to begin business at the usual hour, and my father hastened into the kitchen, and anxiously inquired if anything was the matter with Mr. Postle.

" I am afraid there is, sir," said Kezia, " for I overheard him very restless in the night. He got up several times, and walked about his room, a talking to himself. Afterwards, towards morning, he was quiet; so thinking he was asleep, instead of calling him, I thought best to let him indulge a little."

" Quite right, Kizzy," replied my father. " The poor fellow's zeal and excitement last night have been too much for him."

" I believe they have, indeed," said Kezia, with great animation; " for to be sure Mr. Postle takes as much excitement and interest in us as if he had been born and bred in the family; and its good or bad luck comes home to him like a blood relation."

" Yes," said my father, " and more than to some blood relations with long beards:" an allusion that Kezia understood and intensely relished. " But I must go and open shop;" and, rejecting the housemaid's assistance, he took down the surgery shutters, and locking the outer door, repaired to the breakfast-parlor, where he found my mother and two unopened letters awaiting his presence. The first, from the curate, was kind and considerate. He did not deny some temporary vexation at the loss of the plate, as the gift of his late congregation; but fortunately their regard and good-will were not removable with the salt-cellars; the intrinsic value of which was so immaterial to him, that he begged my father would think no more of the matter. The lawyer's letter from Mr. Ruffey was more rigid: clients, he said, were not so grateful a class in general, as to make presentation tankards to attorneys of common occurrence. He did therefore set a very high value on the testimonial to his professional zeal and ability, independent of its worth as solid silver. The exact value he could not state; but it was considerable. To bring home such a robbery to the perpetrators was a duty to society He relied accordingly that for the public interest my father would leave no stone unturned, and spare no expense, to trace the stolen property, and thereby bring the offender, or offenders, to justice. In this hope he would say nothing about compensation, or an equivalent — at least for the present.

"Humph!" said my father, "the lawyer, at any rate, must be indemnified."

"And here," said my mother, holding out a three-cornered epistle, "is the answer to a note which I wrote to Mrs. Trent." My father took the billet and read as follows: —

"Madam, —

"In answer to your distressing communication, what can I say, or, indeed, what can be said, where necessity extorts submission? My plate is gone — and by this time melted down — and consequently irretrievable.

"My poor silver souvenirs! Every spoon represented a young lady! I have others left; but those were my favorites. All massy and solid, and stamped with the Goldsmiths' mark, and each recalling some interesting young female, now a highly polished and well-educated woman. One of the spoons, with a ducal crest, was left me by a charming, accomplished creature, just finished, and now moving in the first circles of rank and fashion. Another, with a plain cipher, belonged to the present Lady Mawbey, and retained the marks of her little aristocratic teeth. To a preceptress, such memorials of the juvenile objects of her affectionate solicitude have a preciousness beyond Potosi and Peru. Of course, as regards mere metallic value, they may be replaced by an equal number of spoons of equal weight, or coalesced into a silver teapot; but, alas! all the endearing associations are obliterated forever!

"I am, Madam,
"Your very obedient, humble servant,
"Amelia Trench."

"She must have a silver teapot!" exclaimed my father. "Though where it is to come from, in the present state of our finances, is beyond my guess. And talking of teapots, Postle is poorly this morning, my dear, and must have his breakfast in bed — Kezia will take it up to him." Had my father looked at the maid-of-all-work as he spoke, he would have perceived a sign of prudency that would have greatly diverted him, for both her cheeks seemed flushed with a claret-mark ; but his attention was attracted towards his own meal, and the blush evaporated without a comment. Kezia quietly placed a great cup of tea and a small plate of toast on her waiter, and proceeded up stairs, to introduce his breakfast, with all proper discretion, into the bedchamber of Mr. Postle.

"Well I must and will say," cried my mother, "we are a persecuted family. Our misfortunes never come single — they never rain but they pour. After all our other troubles, here is Mr. Postle taken ill — breeding an infectious fever perhaps — and with those dear children in the house — I declare I shall go distracted !"

"Make yourself easy," replied my father ; "Postle is only a little out of sorts, and rest and quiet will soon set him to rights. And in the mean time the burden of his illness will fall chiefly on myself; for I shall not only have to make up the prescriptions, but, as that Catechism Jack has absconded, I must carry out my own physic."

"I wish it may be so," said my mother, shaking her head. "But I am far from satisfied in my mind. Mr. Postle is a very feverish subject, and when he shakes hands with one his palm is always burning hot. If he breaks out with anything catching, I shall go wild ! "

"At any rate, ma'am," said Kezia, who had returned in time to hear the latter part of the discussion, "fever or no fever, we'll use all the preventives. The dear infants shall have camphor bags directly, and Mr. Postle's landing shall be well fumigated with hot vinegar, and we'll burn bastilles all over the house."

" Pastils," said my father, " pastils."

" Well, pastils. And, perhaps, if somebody was to smoke about the house," added Kezia, with a look that applied the " somebody " to her master, " for they do say that in the Great Plague, the tobacconists were the only unaffected people in London."

"You are quite correct," said my father; "and if needful, the house shall stink like a tap-room. Only in that case, as I never could stomach even a cigar, and your mistress does not smoke, and I will venture to answer for Mrs. Prideaux, you must take to the pipe yourself, Kezia, and do the fumigations."

"And I would, too!" cried Kezia, with energy, "if it made me as sick as a dog!"

"Ah, you don't know what you undertake," said my mother. "The truth is, I did once try to smoke my favorite geraniums, to destroy the insects."

"And didn't it kill 'em, ma'am?" asked Kezia.

"By no means," replied my mother. "Quite the contrary; for your master found me insensible in the greenhouse, and the vermin as lively as ever."

My mother's anecdote put an end to the discussion; and my father having finished his breakfast, repaired to the surgery, and posted himself at the desk usually occupied by Mr. Postle. A glance at the blotting-book showed how the assistant's thoughts had been lately occupied, for the paper was covered with rough pen and ink illuminations, in the style called the Grotesque. Amongst the figures, two were particularly prominent, and plainly recognizable by their features, however otherwise transformed. Thus the bearded profile of a certain goat was obviously that of Uncle Rumbold—he was, of course, the rampant Bear with the turbaned head of the Great Mogul; and as unmistakably he was the hideous Ogre, elsewhere striding along, and clutching a fat naked child in each hand by the hair of its head. The Demon with horns and a tail was a strong likeness of Doctor Shackle; and the bottle-bellied Spider, with a human face, was evidently the same obnoxious personage. In a third design, he was dangling from a gibbet; and in a fourth, he lent his marked physiognomy to a huge Serpent, which, after a natural coil or two, twisted off into a corkscrew that went wandering half over the paper, as if in search of something to draw. Other emblems were equally significant of the assistant's despondency and the decay of the practice. The mortar, turned into a garden-pot, had a rose growing in it; and from the physic-basket, converted to domestic uses, protruded a bunch of carrots.

And, in truth, the gloomy prospect entertained by the artist seemed likely to be realized : hour after hour passed away, and still the doctor found himself in the surgery without a patient or a prescription. At last the confinement became so irksome, that he ran up-stairs to the assistant's bedroom, to ascertain the true state of his case. The invalid was still asleep, but restless, grinding his teeth, turning from side to side, muttering, and occasionally tossing his arms and clenched hands, as if laboring under the influence of some horrible dream. Nevertheless he did not awake, when the doctor felt his forehead and examined his pulse ; for, conscious of an impending illness, and to counteract his nervous excitement, he had taken a narcotic.

"This is more serious than I thought," muttered my father. "He is really ill, and must be looked to when he wakes." And with a heavy heart and step the doctor slowly descended the stairs ; at the foot of which he was intercepted by Kezia, with an inquiry after poor Mr. Postle.

"Worse than I could wish," replied my father ; and, with a deep sigh, he passed into the surgery, paralyzed, so to speak, in his professional right arm.

Still there came no customer ; a dearth of business less annoying, however, to the proprietor than to another party who looked on. Led by the impulse of old habit, Kezia every now and then made a move towards the surgery, but on looking through the glass door, and seeing my father at the desk instead of Mr. Postle, immediately retreated. Yet these brief glimpses sufficed to fret her with the fact that, come when she would, there never was a living creature with the doctor, except the leeches. "It's well," she said, "that our cordials and compounds are so nasty ; for many a publican in such a case would take to drinking and swallow up his own stock in trade."

At last, on one of her visits to the surgery, there was actually a strange man in it ; no patient, however, but the carrier, who, having delivered a small parcel, and received the carriage money, immediately departed. My father opened the packet, briefly inspected the contents, and then with an audible remark deposited it in a drawer. The remark was meant for himself ; but the glass door being ajar, the observation reached another, and not indifferent ear.

All this time my mother was in the nursery discussing with Mrs. Prideaux the topics appropriate to the locality, and, in particular, the merits of various kinds of food for babes ; not forgetting her favorite story of the man-servant who was sent to the biscuit-baker's for the infant victual, and forgetting the name of tops and bottoms, clapped his shilling on the counter, and said, " Head or tail." This anecdote she had told, and was just beginning another, when Kezia entered the room, with a melancholy face, of faded red and white, like an ill-dyed handkerchief with the color partly washed out. She was evidently the bearer of evil tidings, which my mother immediately guessed referred to Mr. Postle.

" Yes, poor Mr. Postle is very poorly," replied Kezia. "The doctor does not say so, implicitly, but he shakes his head, which stands, medically, for the same thing."

" Why, then, we may have a fever in the house after all !" exclaimed my mother.

" And I have bad news besides," said Kezia, her looks becoming still more gloomy, and her voice more dismal. " Master has got his nymph down from London."

" His what !" cried my mother.

" His nymph," repeated Kezia.

" I conceive she means lymph," suggested Mrs. Prideaux.

" Yes, lymph, or nymph," said Kezia, " it's a pleasanter word than vaccinating matter. However, it's come down from town, — and I wish Doctor Jenner had been hung, I do, before he invented it."

" But are you certain or it ? " inquired my mother.

" Quite," answered Kezia ; " I saw the parcel. And as soon as Mr. Postle goes down, you will have master up here, at those dear babes to scarify their poor arms, and introduce the beastly virus into their little systems."

Her prophecy was correct. In about half an hour my father made his appearance in the nursery, packet in hand, and proceeded to impart to my mother a piece of intelligence, of which to his surprise he found her already in possession.

CHAPTER XXIII.

OUR VACCINATION.

THE practice of Vaccination, which has since proved such a blessing to mankind, was received at its first introduction into England with anything but a gracious welcome. Like other great public benefits, it had of course to encounter the opposition of that large class of persons who set their stereotype faces against all innovations ; but besides this resistance, active or passive, it involved, in its most material feature, a peculiarity adverse to its popularity. The mere notion of deriving a disease from a brute beast was sufficient to excite a prejudice against it in the minds of the million ; and the most absurd stories of the deplorable effects of the cow-pock were currently circulated and believed by the ignorant and the credulous, especially in the provinces. Narratives were gravely repeated, and swallowed, of horns that sprouted from human heads ; — of human feet that hardened into parted hoofs ; — of human bodies that became pied or brindled with dappled hair ; — in short, the ancient metamorphosis of Iö seemed to have been only an extreme case of Vaccination.

My mother, prone to misgiving, and easily *cowed*, readily entertained the common fears and doubts on the subject ; an impression in which she was strongly backed by Kezia, who adopted the vulgar opinions to their utmost extent, and devoutly put faith in all the extravagant tales that were told of the victims of the operation. It may be supposed, therefore, that the two females looked with no favorable eye on my father's preparations ; indeed, as far as wishing could effect it, the " nymph " and the lancet were more than once thrown out of the window.

" And are you really going, George, to vaccinate the children ? " asked my mother, with a faltering voice.

" I really am," replied my father, and then resumed his quiet whistle, whilst he carefully charged a sharp lancet with the vaccine matter.

" Well, if you must you must," said my mother. " But for my part I cannot reconcile my mind to it ; and I'm afraid I never shall. There seems something so unnatural and revolting in transferring the humor of a diseased brute beast into the human frame!"

"Ah! the old story," said my father. "That we may expect to see the bovine humor break out again in horns and a tail. And do you really believe, my dear, that there is any foundation for such popular romances?"

"Heaven knows!" said my mother. "But very strange things are said to have happened from it. Ask Kezia."

"And pray what is your legend?" said my father, turning towards the maid-of-all-work.

"It's about a little girl, sir," replied Kezia, "as was vaccinated down in our part of the country, namely, Suffolk."

"And was turned into a heifer, eh?" said my father.

"Why no, at least not in corporal shape," said Kezia. "And I won't speak positive, though some do, to a pair of little knobs of horns, that one could just feel under the skin on her forehead. But this I know, it was moral impossible to keep her out of the fields, and from running about the common, and wading up to her knees in pools of water."

"Pshaw! a mere country hoyden," said my father.

"Perhaps she were," said Kezia, reddening. "Only in that case she need n't have moo'd whenever a cow did; and what's more, in summer-time she always had a swarm of flies about her nose and ears."

"I think I could account for that," said my father.

"Well, then," cried Kezia, "there was one thing that was cow-like at any rate. She could n't abide scarlet; and when they wanted to put her into a red frock, she tore, and butted so with her head, that they were forced to give it up."

"Very good," said my father, again turning towards my mother. "Well, my dear, I have heard Kezia's story, and in spite of it, I think we may safely vaccinate the children, and run the risk of being tossed by them afterwards."

"It's no joke," said my mother, in a crying tone, "though you make one of it. It's introducing an animal change into the constitution, and who knows, if such a thing as a murrain was to break out among the cattle, but the children might have it too?"

"Why, it would only be according to the old doctrine of sympathy," said my father.

"And why not?" said my mother.   "It is well known that if a man is bit by a dog, and the dog afterwards runs mad, the man will go crazy too!"

"A vulgar error, my dear," said my father.   "An exploded fallacy.   But come; make your mind easy. There is no more danger of the children's having the murrain than of their bursting themselves, as a cow sometimes does, in a clover-field. As to the operation itself, it is a mere flea-bite, and I will be responsible for the consequences. — Mrs. Prideaux, may I trouble you to hold this little one on your lap," — and the wilful doctor took one of the twins from the cradle and placed it in the arms of the genteel nurse.

"I can't — I won't see it done!" screamed Kezia, turning her face to the wall, and throwing her apron over her head.

"Nor I neither," exclaimed my mother, covering her face with her hands.   And they were sincere in their horror. We, of this year of grace, 1845, convinced by experience of the beneficial effects of the discovery of Jenner, and consequently wiser in our *Jenneration*, cannot sympathize with the ludicrous terrors that prevailed when Vaccination was a new thing. They were nevertheless both strong and general, and hundreds and thousands of females would have had the same dread of the operation as my mother and her maid.

My father, meanwhile, grasping a little plump arm so firmly as to tighten the skin, thrice plunged his lancet obliquely into the flesh; the infant expressing its sense of the proceeding by as many squalls.   Had it *bellowed*, there were two persons in the room who would not have been surprised in the least. My father then charged his lancet with fresh lymph, which he introduced into the wounds; and then, having repeated the whole process on the other little fat arm, the babe was exchanged for his twin-brother, who underwent *seriatim* the same operations.

"There!" said my father, as he finished the work, — " there, they are insured for life against the small-pox and its disfigurations." ·

"I wish they may be, and from all disfigurations besides," said my mother, taking her hands from her eyes; while Kezia removed her apron, and turning round from the wall, gazed mournfully on each little arm, scarred with what she called mentally, " the mark of the beast."

*   *   *   *   *

ROMANCES AND EXTRAVAGANZAS.

MR. WITHERING'S CONSUMPTION AND ITS CURE.

A DOMESTIC EXTRAVAGANZA.

> " Come away, come away, death,
>   And in sad cypress let me be laid;
> Fly away, fly away, breath;
>   I am slain by a fair cruel maid.
> My shroud of white, all stuck with yew,
>   O, prepare it! "
>
> TWELFTH NIGHT.

CHAPTER I.

" AND who was Mr. Withering ? "

Mr. Withering, Gentle Reader, was a drysalter of Dowgate-hill. Not that he had dealt in salt, dry or wet — or, as you might dream, in dry salt stockfish, ling, and Findon haddies, like the salesmen in Thames Street. The commodities in which he trafficked, wholesale, were chiefly drugs, and dye-woods, a business whereby he had managed to accumulate a moderate fortune. His character was unblemished, — his habits regular and domestic, — but although advanced in years beyond the middle age, he was still a bachelor.

" And consumptive? Why then according to Dr. Imray's book, he had hair of a light color, large blue eyes, long eye-lashes, white and regular teeth, long fingers, with the nails contracted or curved, a slender figure, and a fair and bloom-ing countenance."

Not exactly, miss. Mr. Withering was rather dark —

" O yes — as the doctor says, the tuberculous constitution is not confined to persons of sanguineous temperaments and fair complexion. It also belongs to those of a very dif-ferent appearance. The subjects of this affection are often of a swarthy and dark complexion, with coarse skin, dark hair, long, dark eyelashes, black eyes, thick upper lip, short fingers, broad nails, and a more robust habit of body, with duller intellect, and a careless or less active disposition."

Nay, that is still not Mr. Withering. To tell the truth, he was not at all like a consumptive subject : — not pigeon-breasted, but broad-chested — not emaciated, but plump as a partridge — not hectic in color, but as healthily ruddy as a redstreak apple — not languid, but as brisk as a bee, — in short, a comfortable little gentleman, of the Pickwick class, with something, perhaps, quizzical, but nothing phthisical in his appearance.

"Why, then, what was the matter with the man?"

A decline, madam. Not the rapid decay of nature, so called, but one of those declines which an unfortunate lover has sometimes to endure from the lips of a cruel beauty; for Mr. Withering, though a steady, plodding man of business, in his warehouse or counting-house, was, in his parlor or study, a rather romantic and sensitive creature, with a strong turn for the sentimental, which had been nourished by his course of reading — chiefly in the poets, and especially such as dealt in Love Elegies, like his favorite Hammond. Not to forget Shenstone, whom, in common with many readers of his standing, he regarded as a very nightingale of sweetness and pathos in expressing the tender passion. Nay, he even ventured occasionally to clothe his own amatory sentiments in verse, and in sundry poems painted his torments by flames and darts, and other instruments of cruelty, so shockingly, that, but for certain allegorical touches, he might have been thought to be describing the ingenious torture of some poor white captive by a red Indian squaw.

But, alas! his poetry, original or borrowed, was of no more avail than his plain prose against that petrifaction which he addressed as a heart, in the bosom of Miss Puckle. He might as well have tried to move all Flintshire by a geological essay; or to have picked his way with a toothpick into a Fossil Saurian. The obdurate lady had a soul above trade, and the offer of the drysalter and lover, with his dying materials in either line, was met by what is called a *flat* refusal, though it sounded, rather, as if set in a *sharp*.

Now in such cases it is usual for the Rejected One to go

into something or other, the nature of which depends on the temperament and circumstances of the individual, and I will give you six guesses, Gentle Reader, as to what it was that Mr. Withering went into when he was refused by Miss Puckle.

" Into mourning?"

No.

"Into a tantrum?"

No.

"Into the Serpentine?"

No — nor into the Thames, to sleep in peace in Bugsby's Hole.

"Into the Army or Navy?"

No.

"Into a madhouse?"

No.

"Into a Hermitage?"

No — nor into a Monastery.

The truth is, he opportunely remembered that his father's great aunt, Dinah, after a disappointment in love, was carried off by Phthisis Pulmonalis; and as the disease is hereditary, he felt, morally as well as physically and grammatically, that he must, would, could, should, and ought to go like a true Withering into a Consumption.

"And did he, sir?"

He did, miss; — and so resolutely, that he sold off his business at a sacrifice, and retired, in order to devote the rest of his life to dying for Amanda — *alias* Miss Susan Puckle. And a long job it promised to be, for he gloried in dying very hard, and in pining for her, which of course is not to be done in a day. And truly, instead of a lover's going off, at a pop, like Werter, it must be much more satisfactory to a cruel Beauty, to see her victim deliberately expiring by inches, like a Dolphin, and dying of as many hues, — now crimson with indignation, then looking blue with despondence, anon yellow with jaundice, or green with jealousy — at last fading into a melancholy mud-color, and thence darkening into the black tinge of despair, and death. It is said, indeed, that when the cruel Miss Puckle was informed of his dying for her, she exclaimed, " O, I hope he will let me *crimp* him first, — like a skate!"

CHAPTER II.

"But did Mr. Withering actually go into a consumption?"

As certainly, miss, as a passenger steps of his own accord into an omnibus that is going to Gravesend. He had been refused, and had a strong sentimental impression that all the Rejected and Forsaken Martyrs of true love were carried off, sooner or later, by the same insidious disease. Accordingly his first step was to remove from the too keen air of Pentonville, to the milder climate of Brompton, where he took a small detached house, adapted to the state of single unblessedness, to which he was condemned. For with all his conviction of the propriety, or necessity of the catastrophe, his dying for love did not involve a love for dying; he might soon have to breathe his last, but it should be of a fine air.

His establishment consisted but of two female servants; namely, a housemaid, and a middle-aged woman, at once cook, housekeeper, and nurse, who professedly belonged to a consumptive family, and therefore knew what was good or bad, or neither, for all pulmonary complaints. Her name was Button.

She was tall, large-boned, and hard-featured; with a loud voice, a stern eye, and the decided manner of a military sergeant — a personage adapted, and in fact accustomed, to rule much more refractory patients than her master. It did not indeed require much persuasion to induce him to take to wear " flannin next his skin," or woollen comforters round his throat and wrists, or even a hareskin on his chest in an east wind. He was easily led to adopt cork soles and clogs against wet, and a great-coat in cold weather — nay, he was even outtalked into putting his jaw into one of those hideous contrivances called Respirators. But this was nothing. He was absolutely compelled to give up all animal food and fermented liquors — to renounce successively his joint, his steak, his chop, his chicken, his calves' feet, his drop of brandy, his gin-and-water, his glass of wine, his bottled porter, his draught ditto, and his ale, down to that bitter pale sort, that he used to call his *Bass* relief. No, he was not even allowed to taste the table-beer. He had promised to be consumptive, and Mrs. Button took him at his word. As much light pudding, sago arrow-root, tapioca — or gruel — with toast-

and-water, barley-water, whey, or apple-tea, as often as he pleased — but as to meat or " stimuluses," she would as soon give him " Alick's Acid, or Corrosive Supplement."

To this dietary dictation the patient first demurred, but soon submitted. Nothing is more fascinating or dangerous to a man just rejected by a female than the show of kindness by another of the sex. It restores him to his self-love — nay, to his very self, — reverses the sentence of social ex-communication just pronounced against him, and contradicts the moral annihilation implied in the phrase of being " nothing to nobody." A secret well-known to the sex, and which explains how so many unfortunate gentlemen, crossed in love, happen to marry the housemaid, the cook, or any kind creature in petticoats — the first Sister of Charity, black, brown, or carroty, who cares a cus —

" Oh ! — "

—a custard for their appetite, or a comforter for their health. Even so with Mr. Withering. He had offered himself from the top of his Brutus to the sole of his shoe to Miss Puckle, who had plumply told him that he was not worth having as a gift. And yet, here — in the very depth of his humiliation, when he would hardly have ventured to bequeath his rejected body to an anatomical lecturer — here was a female, not merely caring for his person in general, but for parts of it in particular — his poor throat and his precious chest, his delicate trachea, his irritable bronchial tubes, and his tender lungs. Nevertheless, no onerous tax was imposed on his gratitude; the only return required — and how could he refuse it ! — was his taking a Temperance, or rather Total Abstinence Pledge for his own benefit. So he supped his semi-solids and swallowed his slops ; merely remarking on one occasion, after a rather rigorous course of barley-water, that if his consumption increased he thought he should " try *Madeira*," but whether the island, or the wine, he left in doubt.

CHAPTER III.

In the mean time Mr. Withering continued as plump as a partridge, and as rosy as a redstreak apple. No symptoms of the imputed disease made their appearance. He slept well, ate well of sago, &c., drank well of barley-water and the like, and shook hands with a palm not quite so hard and dry as a dead Palm of the Desert. He had neither hectic flushes nor shortness of breath — nor yet pain in the chest, to which three several physicians in consultation applied their stethoscopes.

Doctor A. — hearing nothing at all.

Doctor B. — Nothing particular.

Dr. C. — Nothing wrong.

And Doctor E. distinctly hearing a cad-like voice, proclaiming "all right."

Mr. Withering, nevertheless, was dying — if not of consumption, of *ennui* — the mental weariness of which he mistook for the physical lassitude so characteristic of the other disease. In spite, therefore, of the faculty, he clung to the poetical theory that he was a blighted drysalter, withering prematurely on his stem; another victim of unrequited love, whom the utmost care could retain but a few short months from his cold grave. A conviction he expressed to posterity in a series of Petrarchian sonnets, and in plain prose to his housekeeper, who only insisted the more rigidly on what she called her "regimental rules" for his regimen, with the appropriate addition of Iceland Moss. A recipe to which he quietly submitted, though obstinately rejecting another prescription of provincial origin — namely, snails beaten up with milk. In vain she told him from her own experience in Flanders, that they were reckoned, not only nourishing, but relishing by the Belgians, who after chopping them up with bread-crumbs and sweet herbs, broiled them in the shells, in each of which a small hole was made, to enable the Flemish epicure to blow out the contents.* Her master decisively set his face against the experiment, alleging, plausibly enough, that the operation of snails must be too slow for any galloping complaint.

There was, however, one experiment, of which on his own recommendation Mr. Withering resolved to make a trial — change of air, of course, involving change of scene. Accordingly, packing his best suit and a few changes of linen in his carpet-bag, he took an inside place in the Hastings coach, and was whirled down ere night to that favorite Cinque Port.

---

* The origin perhaps of the vulgar phrase, "a good blow out."

And for the first fortnight, thanks to the bracing yet mild air of the place, which gave tone to his nerves, without injury to his chest, the result exceeded his most sanguine expectations. But alas! he was doomed to a relapse, a revulsion so severe, that, in a more advanced stage of his complaint he ought to have "gone out like a snuff."

" What, from wet feet, or a damp bed?"

No, madam — but from a promenade, with dry soles, on a bright day in June, and in a balmy air that would not have injured a lung of lawn-paper.

CHAPTER IV.

Poor Mr. Withering !

Happy for him had he but walked in any other direction — up to the Castle, or down to the beach — had he only bent his steps westward to Harlington, or Bexhill, or eastward to Fairlight, — or to the Fish-ponds — but his sentimental bias would carry him towards Lover's Seat, — and there — on the seat itself — he beheld his lost Amanda, or rather Miss Puckle, or still more properly, Mrs. Scrimgeour, who, with her bridegroom, had come to spend the honeymoon at green Hastings. The astounded Drysalter stood aghast and agape at the unexpected encounter; but the lady, cold and cutting as the East wind, vouchsafed no sign of recognition.

The effect of this meeting was a new shock to his system. He felt, at the very moment, that he had a hectic flush, hot and cold fits, with palpitation of the heart, — and his disease set in again with increased severity. Yes, he was a doomed man, and might at once betake himself to the last resource of the consumptive.

" Not," he said, "not that all the ass's milk in England would ever lengthen his years."

Impressed with this conviction, and heartily disgusted with Hastings, he repacked his carpet-bag, and returned by the first coach to London, fully convinced, whatever the pace of the Rocket, or the nature of the road, that he was going very fast, and all down hill.

CHAPTER V.

It was about ten o'clock at night when Mr. Withering arrived at his own residence in Brompton; but although there was a light in the parlor, a considerable time elapsed before he could obtain admittance.

At last, after repeated knockings and ringings, the street-door opened, and disclosed Mrs. Button, who welcomed her master with an agitation which he attributed at once to his unexpected return, and the marked change for the worse, which of course was visible in his face.

" Yes, you may well be shocked — but here, pay the coach-man and shut the door, for I'm in a draught. You may well be shocked and alarmed, for I'm looking, I know, like death, — but bless me, Mrs. Button, the house smells very savory!"

" It's the drains as you sniff, sir," said the Housekeeper; " they always do smell strongish afore rain."

" Yes, we shall have wet weather, I believe — and it may be the drains — though I never smelt anything in my life so like fried beefsteaks and onions!"

" Why, then, to tell the truth," said Mrs. Button, " it *is* beef and inguns; it's a favorite dish of mine, and as you're forbid animal food, I thought I'd jest treat myself, in your absence, so as not to tantalize you with the smell."

" Very good, Mrs. Button, and very considerate. Though with your lungs, I hardly approve of hot suppers. But there seems to me another smell about the house, — yes — most decidedly — the smell of tobacco."

" O, that's the plants!" exclaimed the Housekeeper — " the geraniums that I've been smoking, — they were eaten up alive with green animalculuses."

" Humph!" said Mr. Withering, who, snuffling about like a spaniel, at last made a point at the Housekeeper herself.

" It's very odd — very odd, indeed — but there is a sort of perfume about *you*, Mrs. Button — not exactly lavender or Eau de Cologne — but more like the smell of liquor."

" Law, sir!" exclaimed the Housekeeper, with a rather hysterical chuckle, " the sharp nose that you have sure*ly!* Well, sure enough, the tobacco-smoke did make me squeamish, and I sent out for a small quantity of arduous spirits just to settle my stomach. But never mind the luggage, sir, I'll see to that. while you go up to the drawing-room and the sofy, for you do look like death, and that's the truth."

And suiting her actions to her words, she tried to hustle her master towards the staircase; but his suspicions were now excited. and making a pig-like dodge round his driver, he bolted into the parlor, where he beheld a spectacle that fully justified his misgivings.

"Lord! what did he see, sir?"

Nothing horrible. madam; only a cloth laid for supper, with plates, knives. and forks, and tumblers for two. At one end of the table stood a foaming quart-pot of porter; at the other a black bottle, labelled "Cream of the Valley," while in the middle was a large dish of smoking hot beefsteaks and onions. For a minute he wondered who was to be the second party at the feast, till, guided by a reflection in the looking-glass, he turned towards the parlor-door. behind which, bolt upright and motionless as wax-work, he saw a man, as the old song says,—

"Where nae man should be."

"Heydey! Mrs. Button. whom have we here?"

"If you please, sir," replied the abashed Housekeeper, "it's only a consumptious brother of mine, as is come up to London for physical advice."

"Humph!" said Mr. Withering, with a significant glance towards the table, "and I trust that in the mean time you have advised him to abstain, like your master, from animal food and stimulants."

"Why you see, sir, begging your pardon," stammered Mrs. Button, "there's differences in constitutions. Some people requires more nourishing than others. Besides, there's two sorts of consumption."

"Yes, so I see," retorted Mr. Withering; "the one preys on your vitals and the other on your victuals."

Just at this moment a scrap of paper on the carpet attracted his eye, and at the same time catching that of Mrs. Button, and both parties making an attempt together to pick it up, their heads came into violent collision.

"It's only the last week's butcher's bill," said the Housekeeper, rubbing her forehead.

"I see it is," said the master, rubbing the top of his head

with one hand, whilst with the bill in the other, he ran through the items, from beef to veal, and from veal to mutton, boggling especially at the joints.

"Why, zounds! ma'am, your legs run very large!"

"My legs, sir?"

"Well, then, *mine*, as I pay for them. Here's one I see of eleven pounds, and another of ten and a half. I really think my two legs, cold one day and hashed the next, might have dined you through the week, without four pounds of my chops!"

"Your chops, sir?"

"Yes, my chops, woman,—and if I had not dropped in, you and your consumptive brother there would be supping on my steaks. You would eat me up alive?"

"You forget, sir," muttered the Housekeeper, "there's a nousemaid."

"Forget the devil!" bellowed Mr. Withering, fairly driven beyond his patience, and out of his temper, by different provocatives; for all this time the fried beef and onions, — one of the most savory of dishes, — had been steaming under his nose, suggesting rather annoying comparisons between the fare before him and his own diet.

"Yes, here have I been starving these two months on spoon-victuals and slops, while my servants, my precious servants, — confound them! were feasting on the fat of the land! Yes, you, woman! you — with your favorite dishes, — my fried steaks, and my boiled legs, and my broiled chops, but forbidding *me* — *me* your master, — to dine even on my own kidneys, or my own sweetbread! But if I'll be consumptive any longer I'll be —"

The last word of the sentence, innocent or profane, was lost in the loud slam of the street-door — for Mrs. Button's consumptive brother, disliking the turn of affairs, had quietly stolen out of the parlor, and made his escape from the house.

"And did Mr. Withering observe his vow?"

Most religiously, madam. Indeed, after dismissing Mrs. Button with her "regimental rules," he went rather to the opposite extreme, and dined and supped so heartily on his legs and shoulders, his breast and ribs, his loins, his heart, and liver, and his calf's-head, and moreover washed them down so freely with wine, beer, and strong waters, that there was far more danger of his going out with an Apoplexy than of his going into a Consumption.

THE CAMBERWELL BEAUTY.

A CITY ROMANCE.

"She entered his shop, which was very neat and spacious, and he received her with all the marks of the most profound respect, entreating her to sit down, and showing her with his hand the most honorable place."

ARABIAN NIGHTS.

CHAPTER I.

Mr. BOOBY was in his shop, his back to the fire and his face to the *Times*, when happening to look above the upper edge of the newspaper, towards the street, he caught sight of an equipage that seemed familiar to him.

Could it be!

Yes, it was the same dark-brown chariot, with the drab liveries, — the same gray horses, with the same crest on the harness, and above all the same lady-face was looking through the carriage-window.

In a moment Mr. Booby was at his glass-door, obsequiously ushering the fair customer into his shop, where with his profoundest bow and his sunniest smile he invited her to a seat at the counter. Her commands were eagerly solicited and promptly executed. The two small volumes she asked for were speedily produced, neatly packed up, and delivered to the footman in drab, to be deposited in the dark-brown chariot. But the lady still lingered. Thrice within a fortnight she had occupied the same seat, on each occasion making a longer visit than the last, and becoming more and more friendly and familiar. Perhaps, being past the prime of life, she was flattered by the extremely deferential attentions of the young tradesman ; perhaps she was pleased with the knowledge he possessed, or seemed to possess, of a particular subject, and was gratified by the interest which he took, or appeared to take, in her favorite science. However, she still lingered, smiling very pleasantly, and chatting very agreeably in her low, sweet voice, whilst she turned over the pretty illustrated volumes that were successively offered to her notice.

In the mean time the delighted Booby did his utmost in the conversational way to maintain his ground, which was no easy task, seeing that he was not well read in her favorite science, nor indeed in any other. In fact he did not read at all; and although a butcher gets beefish, a bookseller does not become bookish, from the mere smell of his commodity. Nevertheless he managed to get on, in his own mind, very tolerably, adding a few words about Egypt and the Pyramids to the lady's mention of the Sphinx, and at the name of Memnon edging in a sentence or two about the British Museum. Sometimes, indeed, she alluded to classical proper names altogether beyond his acquaintance; but in such cases he escaped by flying off at a tangent to the new ballet, or the last new novel, of which he had derived an opinion from the advertisements — nay, even digressing at need, like Sir Peter Laurie, on the Omnibus nuisance, and the Wooden Pavements. To tell the truth, the lady, as sometimes happens, was so intent on her own share of the discourse, that she paid little attention to his topics or their treatment, and so far from noticing any incongruity would have allowed him to talk unheeded of the dulness of the publishing trade, and the tightness of money in the City. Thanks to this circumstance, he lost nothing in her opinion, whilst his silent homage and assiduities recommended him so much to her good graces, that at parting he received an especial token of her favor.

"Mr. Booby," said the lady, and she drew an embossed card from an elegant silver case, and presented it to the young publisher, "you must come and see me."

Mr. Booby was of course highly delighted and deeply honored; not merely verbally, but actually and physically; for as he took the embossed card, his blood thrilled with delight to the very tips of his fingers. Not that he was in love with the donor; though still handsome, she was past the middle-age, and, indeed, old enough, according to the popular phrase, to have been his mother. But then she was so ladylike and well-bred, and had such a carriage — the dark-brown one — and so affable — with a footman and a gold-headed cane — quite a first-rate connection — with a silver crest on the harness — and oh! such a capital pair of well-matched grays! These considerations were all very gratifying to his ambition; but above all, his vanity was flattered by a condescension which confirmed him in an opinion he had long indulged in secret — namely, that in personal appearance, manners, and fashion, he was a compound of the Apollo Belvidere and Lord Chesterfield, with a touch of Count D'Orsay. But the lady speaks.

"Any morning, Mr. Booby, except Wednesday and Friday. I shall be at home all the rest of the week, and shall leave orders for your admittance."

Mr. Booby bowed, as far as he could, after the fashion of George IV., — escorted the lady into the street, as nearly as possible in the style of the Master of the Ceremonies at Brighton, and then handed her into her carriage with the air, as well as he could imitate it, of a French Marquis of the *ancien régime*.

"I shall expect you, Mr. Booby," said the lady, through the carriage-window. "And as an inducement" — here she smiled mysteriously, and nodded significantly — "you shall have a peep at my Camberwell Beauty."

CHAPTER II.

"AND did he go?"

Why, as to his figure, it had been three times cut out, at full-length, in black paper — once on the Chain Pier at Brighton — once in Regent Street, and once —

"But did he go?"

Then, for his face, he had twice had it done in oil, thrice in crayons, and once in pencil by Wageman. Moreover, he had had it miniatured by Lover — and he had been in treaty with Behnes for his bust, but the marbling came so expensive —

"But did he go, I say?"

— so expensive that he gave up the design, and contented himself with a mask in plaster of Paris.

"But did he go?"

Yes — to both. To Collen for a half-length, and to Beard for a whole one. I think that was all — but no — he went to

What's-his-name, the modeller, and had a cast taken of his
leg.

"Hang his leg!   Did he go or not?"

To be sure he was a tradesman; but his line was a genteel
one; and his shop was double-fronted, in a first-rate thoroughfare, and lighted with gas.   Then as to his business, with
strict assiduity and attention, and a little more punctuality
and despatch—

"Confound his business!— Did— he— go?"

To the Opera?   Yes, often.   And had his clothes made at
the West End— and gave champagne— and backed a horse
or two for the Darby— and smoked cigars— and was altogether, for a tradesman, very much of a gentleman.

"But, for the last time, did he go?"

Where?

"Why, to see the Beauty!"

He did.

"What, to Camberwell?"

No; but to the looking-glass, over the mantel-shelf in his
own dining-room, and where, Narcissus-like, he gazed at his
reflected image till he actually persuaded himself that he was
as unique as the Valdarfer Boccaccio, and as elegantly got up
as Lockhart's Spanish Ballads.

CHAPTER III.

THE dark-brown chariot was gone.

As it rattled away, and just as the drab back of the footman disappeared, Mr. Booby turned his attention to the
embossed card, and deliberately read the address thrice
over.

"Mrs. E. G. Heathcote, Grove Terrace, Camberwell."

To what wild dreams, to what extravagant speculations did
it give birth!   He had evidently made a favorable impression on the mature lady, and might not his merits do him as
good service with her daughter, or niece, or ward, or whatever
she was, the young lovely creature to whom she had alluded
by so charming a title.   The Camberwell Beauty!   The
acknowledged Venus of that large and populous parish!

The Beauty of all the Grove, and Grove Lane — of the Old road and the New — of all the Green — of Church-row and the Terrace, of all Champion and Denmark Hills — of all Cold Harbor Lane! The loveliest of the lovely, from the Red Cap on the north to the Greyhound on the south — from the Holland Arms in the east to the Blue Anchor in the west!

"Here, Perry, reach me the Book of Beauty."

The shopman handed the volume to his master, who began earnestly to look through the illustrations, wondering which of those bewitching countesses, or mistresses, or misses, the fair *incognita* might resemble. But such speculations were futile, so the book was closed and thrown aside; and then his thoughts reverting to his own personal pretensions, he passed his fingers through his hair, adjusted his collar, and drawing himself up to his full height, took a long look at his legs. But this survey was partial and unsatisfactory, and accordingly striding up the stairs, three at once, he appealed to the looking-glass in the dining-room, as stated in the preceding chapter.

The verdict of the mirror has been told, and the result was a conviction in the mind of Mr. Booby, that some time, and somewhere, the Beauty must have been smitten with his elegant appearance — perhaps in an open carriage at Epsom — perhaps in the street — but most probably as he was standing up, the observed of all observers, in the pit of Her Majesty's Theatre.

For the rest of the day Mr. Booby retired from business; indeed, he was in a state of exaltation that unfitted him for mercantile affairs, or any of the commonplace operations of life. The cloth was laid, and the dinner was served up, but he could not eat; and as usual in such cases, he laid the blame on the cook and the butcher. The soles were smoked, the melted butter was oiled, the potatoes were over-boiled, the steak was fresh killed, the tart was execrable, and the cheese had been kept too dry. In short, he relished nothing except the bumper of sherry, which he filled and drank off, dedicating it mentally to the Camberwell Beauty.

The second glass was poured out and quaffed to his own honor, and the third was allotted to an extempore sentiment, which rolled the two former toast into one. These ceremonies performed, he again consulted the mirror over the mantel-shelf, carefully pocket-combing his hair, and plucking up his collar as before. But these were mere commonplace manœuvres compared with those in which he afterwards indulged.

Now of all absurd animals, a man in love is the most ridiculous, and of course doubly so if he should be in love with two at once, himself and a lady. This being precisely the case with Mr. Booby, he gave a loose to his twofold passion, and committed follies enough for a brace of love-lunatics. It would have cured a quinsey to have seen and heard how he strutted, and chuckled, and smiled, and talked to himself — how he practised bowing, and sliding, and kneeling, and sighing — how he threw himself into attitudes and ecstasies, and then how he twisted and wriggled to look at his calves, and as far as he could all round his waist, and up his back ! Never, never was there a man in such a fever of vanity and love-delirium, since the conceited Steward, who walked in yellow stockings, and cross-gartered, and dreamt that he was a fitting mate for the Beauty of Illyria !

CHAPTER IV.

ALL lovers are dreamers —
"In real earnest !"
Perfectly, miss. They are notorious visionaries, whether asleep or awake.
"Why, then, of all things, let us have the dream of Mr. Booby about the Camberwell Beauty. It must have been such a very curious one, considering that he had never seen the lady !"
It was, and, remembering his business, rather characteristic to boot. I have hinted before, how vainly he had tried, during the day, to paint an ideal portrait of the Fair Unknown, and no sooner were his eyes closed at night, than a similar series of vague figures and faces began to tantalize him in his sleep. Dim feminine shapes, of every style of beauty, flitted before him, and vanished like Daguerreotype images, which there was not light enough to fix. Before he could examine, or choose, and say "this must be the Idol," the transitory phantom was gone, or transfigured. The blonde

ripened into a brunette, the brunette bleached into a blonde before he could decide on either complexion. Flaxen tresses darkened into jet — raven locks brightened into golden ringlets, and yellow curls into auburn, before he could prefer one color to another. Black eyes changed at a wink into gray; blue in a twinkling to hazel, — but no, they were green! The commanding figure dwindled into a sylph, the fairy swelled into the fine woman, the majestic Juno melted into a Venus, the rosy Hebe became a pale Minerva — who in turn looked for a moment like the lady in the frontispiece to the " Book of Beauty ; " and then, one after another, like all the Beauties at Hampton Court!

Alas ! amid such a bewildering galaxy, how could he fix on the Beauty of Camberwell !

One angelic figure, which retained its shape and features somewhat longer than the rest, informed him, by the mysterious correspondence of dreams, that she was the Beauty of Buttermere. Another lovely phantom, who presented herself rather vividly, by signs understood only in visions, let him know that she was the beauty who had espoused the gentle Beast. And, finally, a whole bevy of Nymphs and Graces suddenly appeared at once, but as suddenly changed —

" Into what — pray what ? "

Why, into a row of books, and which signified to him by their lettered backs that they were " the Beauties of England and Wales ! "

CHAPTER V.

Thursday morning ! —

It was the first day on which Mrs. E. G. Heathcote, of Grove Terrace, Camberwell, was to be " at home ; " and the eager Mr. Booby had resolved to avail himself of the very earliest opportunity for a visit. A determination not formed so much on his own account, as for the sake of the enamored love-sick creature, whom his vanity painted as sitting on pins, needles, thorns, tenter-hooks, and all the other picked pointed articles which are popularly supposed to stuff the seats, cushions, pillows, and bolsters of the chairs, beds, sofas, and settees, of anxious and impatient people.

Accordingly, no sooner was breakfast over, than snatching up his hat, he set out —

"Ah, to Gracious Street for the homnibus!"

No ma'am — to the Poultry for a pair of exquisitely-made French gloves, that fitted better than his skin, and were of the most delicate lemon-color that you ever, or never, saw. Thence he went to Cheapside, where he treated himself to a superfine thirty-shilling beaver, of a fashionable shape, that admirably suited the character of his physiognomy; after which he bought, I forget where, a bottle of genuine Eau de Cologne — the sort that is manufactured by Jean Marie Farina, and by nobody else — and finally, looking in at a certain noted shop near the Mansion-house, he purchased a bouquet of the choicest and rarest flowers of the season.

"Well, and then he went to the bus."

No — he returned home to dress — namely, in his best blue coat with the brass buttons, a fancy waistcoat, black trousers, and patent-leather boots. His shirt was frilled — with an ample allowance of white cuff — and his silken cravat was of a pale sky-blue. Of course, he did not fail to consult the looking-glass in the dining-room, which assured him that his costume was complete. The shopmen, however, to whom he afterwards submitted the question, were more inclined to demur. The clerk thought that an Union pin would have been an improvement to the cravat, and the porter would have preferred a few Mosaic studs in the shirt-front. In answer to which, the master, who had consulted them, declared that they knew nothing about the matter.

In the mean time the hour struck which he had appointed in his own mind for the start, so hastily striding up Cornhill and turning into Grace-church Street, he luckily obtained the last vacant place in an omnibus, which was already on the move. As usual, the number of the passengers was considerably reduced ere the vehicle reached the Red Cap, at the Green — in fact, there remained but three gentlemen besides Mr. Booby, who after some preliminary conversation, contrived to turn the discourse on the subject that lay nearest his heart. But he took nothing by his motion. A little cross-looking old fellow, in the corner-seat, looked knowing, but said nothing: the other two passengers declared that they had never heard of the Camberwell Beauty.

"I am going to see her, however," said Mr. Booby.

"Are you, sir?" retorted the little crabbed-looking old gentleman in the corner-seat. "Well, I hope you may get her!"

"I hope, in fact I have reason to believe that I shall," replied the self-confident Mr. Booby, and twitching the Mackintosh of the conductor, he desired to be set down at the bottom of the Grove.

"It is rather strange," he thought, as he walked slowly up the hill, "that they have not heard of her. The little old chap in the corner though, seemed to know her, and to be rather jealous of me. But, no — it's impossible that he can be a rival;" and as he said this, there occurred a corresponding alteration in his gait — "perhaps he's her father or her uncle."

CHAPTER VI.

Bravo, Vanity!

Of all friends in need, seconds, backers, confidents, helpers, and comforters, there is none like Self-Conceit! Of all the Life Assurances in England, from the Mutual to the Equitable, there is none like Self-Assurance! It defies the cold water of timidity and the wet blankets of diffidence — and against the aguish, chilly, and hot fits of modesty it is as sovereign as Quinine!

How many men, for instance, on a similar errand to that of the young bookseller, would have felt nerve-quakes and *tremor cordis*, and have scarcely mustered courage enough to pull the bell at the gate! How many would have remained in the front garden shilly-shallying like Master Slender, till the Camberwell Beauty herself came forth, as sweet Anne Page did, to entreat her bashful wooer to enter the premises!

Not so with Mr. Booby; as soon as he had ascertained the right house, he walked resolutely up to the door, and played on the knocker something very analogous to a flourish of trumpets. The well-known footman in the drab livery appeared to the summons and admitted the visitor, who contrived during his progress through the hall to smooth his coat-tails, pluck up his collar, pull down his white cuffs, and pass his pocket-comb through his hair. He was going, moreover, to hang up his hat; but luckily remembered the present mode, and that the beaver was bran-new, wherefore he carried it with him into the drawing-room — a very indifferent fashion, be it said, and particularly in the case of an invitation to dinner, for what can be more ridiculous than to see a guest sitting hat in hand, as if he had dropped in unasked, and was far from certain of a welcome.

" And did he see the Beauty ? "

No, madam. Mrs. Heathcote was alone : but obviously prepared for the visit. A number of handsomely bound books almost covered the round table, some of them open, and exhibiting colored plates illustrative of Conchology, Geology, and Botany ; others were devoted to Ornithology and Entomolgy — hinting, by the way, that the lady was rather multifarious in her studies.

In manner she was as condescending, affable, and agreeable as ever, and as chatty as usual, in her low, sweet voice. Nevertheless, her visitor did not feel quite so much at his ease as he had anticipated. After the first compliments, and commonplace remarks on the weather, the lady's conversation became perplexingly scientific, her allusions distressingly obscure, while technical terms, and classical proper names, fell in quick succession from her lips. Some of the names seemed familiar to the ear of the listener, but before he could determine whether he had heard them at school, or in his business, or at the opera, he was obliged to " give them up," and direct his guesses to a fresh set of riddles. Every moment he was getting more mystified ; — he knew no more than a dog whether she was talking mythology, or metaphysics, or natural history, or algebra, or alchemy, or astrology, or all six of them at once.

This ignorance was sufficiently irksome ; but it soon became alarming, for she began to make more direct appeals to him, and occasionally seemed surprised and dissatisfied with his answers. His old shifts, besides, were no longer of any avail — she turned a deaf ear to his quotations from the *Times* and *Herald* — the theatrical movements, the odds at Tattersall's, and the progress of the New Royal Exchange. Above all, he trembled to find that the extraordinary mental efforts he was compelled to make in order to keep pace with her,

were fast driving out of his head all the pretty speeches which
he had prepared for a more interesting conference. In a word,
he was thoroughly flabbergasted — as completely topsyturvied
in his ideas as the fly that walks on the ceiling, with its head
downwards. What course to take he knew no more than that
vainly enlightened man, the man in the moon. He fidgeted in
his seat, coughed, sighed, blew his nose, sniffed at the bouquet,
looked " all round his hat," then into it, and then on the crown
of it, but without making any discovery. The lady meanwhile
talking on, in a full stream, for all he knew, like Coleridge on
the Samo-Thracian Mysteries!

" Well, well, never mind her nonsense."

Poor Booby! His conceit was fast being taken out of him.
His vanity was oozing out at every pore of his body — his
assurance seemed peeling off his face, like the skin after a
fever. He was dying to see the Beauty — but alas! there
was that eternal tongue, inexhaustible as an Artesian spring,
still pouring, pouring, — by the way, ma'am, did you ever read
the " Arabian Nights "?

" Of course, sir."

Well, then, you will remember the story of the tailor who,
burning, broiling, and frying to see his beauty of Bagdad by
appointment, was detained, half-shaved, hour after hour, by
Es-Sámit, the garrulous barber. Now, call the tailor Mr.
Booby, and put the babbling tonsor into petticoats, and you
will have an exact notion of the case — how the lady gossiped, and how the perplexed lover fretted and fumed, till,
like the Oriental, he felt " as if his gall-bladder had burst," and
was ready to cry out with him, " For the sake of heaven, be
silent, for thou hast crumbled my liver!"

" Dear me, how shocking!"

Very! In spite of the rudeness of the act, he could not
refrain from looking at his watch — an hour had passed, and
yet there had been no more mention of the Beauty than if she
had been doomed, like the Sleeping one, to lie dormant for a
hundred years. The most distressing doubts and misgivings
began to creep over him. For example, that the talkative
lady was not precisely of sound mind — she was certainly
rather flighty and rambling in her discourse — and consequently that the lovely being she had promised to introduce to
him might be altogether a fiction! His spirits sank at the

idea, like the quicksilver before a hurricane, and he heartily wished himself back in his own shop, or his warehouse, — anywhere but alone in the same room with a crazy woman, who talked Encyclopædias, till he was as heavy at heart, as confused in his head, and as uneasy all over, as if he had just feasted with a geologist on pudding-stone and conglomerate.

Never had he been so mystified and confounded in all his life! Accustomed to revolve in the circle of his own perfections, his thoughts were utterly at fault when called to the consideration of circumstances and combinations at all complex or extraordinary; whilst his superficial knowledge, limited to the covers of books, failed to furnish him with any hint towards the unravelment of a mystery quite equal, in his estimation, to the intricacies of romance. What would he not have given for a few minutes' private consultation with his Co., with his Clerk, or even with his Porter!

A dozen of times he was on the point of rising, determined to plead a sudden headache, a bleeding at the nose, or a forgotten engagement; and certainly erelong he would have said or done something desperate if the eccentric lady had not, of her own accord, put a period to his suspense by saying abruptly, —

"But we have gossiped enough, Mr. Booby, and I must now introduce you to my Camberwell Beauty."

The crisis was come! The important interview was at hand! Mr. Booby sprang to his feet, twitched his collar, plucked his cuffs, set up his hair, clapped his bran-new hat under his left arm, and smelling and smiling at his bouquet walked jauntily on his tiptoes, at the invitation of the lady, into a sort of boudoir.

*　　*　　*　　*　　*　　*

*　　*　　*　　*　　*　　*

CHAPTER VII.

"And was the Beauty in the little room?"

Yes. There was also a couch in it, and a most luxurious library-chair. One side of the wall was covered with cases of stuffed birds of the smaller species, the opposite side was occupied by cases of shells, and specimens of minerals, and metallic ores, and the third side was taken up with cases of beetles, moths, and butterflies.

" But the Beauty ? "

On the sofa-table lay a Hortus Siccus for botanical specimens, and a Scrap-book, — both open.

" But the Beauty ? "

In one corner of the room, on a kind of a pedestal, was a bust of Cuvier ; in the opposite corner, on a similar stand, a head of Werner ; in the third nook was that of Rossini ; and in the fourth stood a handsome perch for a parrot, but the bird was dead or absent.   Over the door —

" No, no — the Beauty ? "

Over the door was a half-length of the lady herself, in a fancy dress ; and from the centre of the ceiling hung a small Chinese lantern.

" The Beauty ? "

In the recess of the solitary window, on a stand, stood a compound birdcage, à la Bechstein, enclosing a globe of gold-fish, and surmounted by a basket of flowers.   The floor, — which was Turkey carpeted —

" The Beauty? the Beauty ? "

The floor was littered with various articles, including a guitar, — a large porcelain jar, — and a little wicker-work kennel for a lapdog, — but the dog, like the parrot, was deficient.

" The Beauty ? the Beauty ? the Beauty ? "

My dear madam, pray have a little patience, and read " Blue Beard ; " how nearly his last wife was destroyed by her curiosity.   My mystery is not yet ripe, and you have even less right to the key of my Romance than Fatima had to the key of the Bloody Chamber.

CHAPTER VIII.

Every person of common observation must have remarked the vast contrast between the carriage of a man going *up*, and the bearing of the same going *down* in the world !

In the first case how he trips, how he brightens, how he jokes, how he laughs, how he dances, how he sings, how he

whistles, how he admires, how he loves; in the second predicament — how he stumps, how he glumps, how he sneers,
how he satirizes, how he grumbles, how he frowns, how he
vilifies, how he hates — in short, how he behaves, with a
difference, like Mr. Booby.

As he ascended Grove-Hill his step was brisk and elastic;
he simpered complacently, held his bouquet mincingly in his
lemon-colored glove, and had his new hat stuck jauntily a little
on one side of his head.

As he descended the steep, his tread was heavy, sometimes
amounting to a stamp, the flowers had been thrashed into a
bundle of stalks, the delicate kid-glove was being gnawed into
a mitten, and the bran-new beaver was sullenly thrust down
over his eyebrows.

As he mounted, his eyes were cast upward towards the
elm-tree tops, as if looking for birds'-nests.

As he descended, his eyes were turned to the gravel-path,
as if in search of Brazilian pebbles.

As he went up, he hummed " La çi darem."

As he went down, he muttered curses between his teeth.

In going up, he had carefully picked his way, avoiding
every dirty spot.

In going down, he tramped recklessly through the mud, and
stepped into the very middle of the puddles.

" And had the Beauty slighted him ? "

Why, those persons who saw him come out of the house-
door, remarked as he stumbled down the steps, that his face
was as red and hot as a fiery furnace : others who did
not notice him till he had cleared the front garden-gate, observed that his complexion was as pale as ashes. And both
reports were true, for like the Factions of the Red and White
Roses, did Anger and Vexation alternately domineer and
hoist their colors by turns in his countenance.

" But had the Beauty really behaved ill to him ? "

Why, in going to the house he had conducted himself
towards men, women, and children with a studied and almost
affected courtesy; whereas in going from the premises he
jostled the gentlemen, took the wall of ladies, punched each
little boy who came within reach of his arm, and kicked every
dog that ran within range of his foot.

" Then she *had* been scornful to him ! "

Everybody in the street looked after him. Some thought that he was mad; some, that he was in liquor — others, that he was walking for a wager, and from his ill-temper, that he was losing it.

"Poor man!"

However, on he went, striding, frowning, muttering, and swearing, gnawing one kid-glove, and shaking the other like a muffin-bell. On he went — like an overdriven beast — on through Church Street, and away across the Green, kicking hoops, tops, and marbles; thumping little boys, and poking little girls, snubbing nursemaids, making faces at their babies, and grinning viciously at everything in nature that came within his scope. He was out of humor with heaven and earth. It pleased him to know, by a sudden yell in the road, that a cur was run over; and he was rather glad than otherwise to see a horse in the pound.

"Poor fellow! how cruelly he must have been treated!"

Well, on he went to the Red Cap, where an omnibus was just on the point of starting.

It was invitingly empty, so without asking whether it went to the East or West End, in jumped Mr. Booby, and threw himself on the centre seat at the further end of the vehicle. And now, for the first time, he had leisure to feel that he had been worked and walked, morally as well as physically into a violent heat. He let down all the windows that would go down, tugged out his handkerchief, wiped the dew from his face, and then fanned himself with his hat. The process somewhat cooled the outer man, but his temper remained as warm as ever, and at last found vent.

"Confound the old fool!" he exclaimed, with an angry stamp on the floor of the omnibus, — "Confound the old fool with her Camberwell Beauty! Why did n't she tell me it was a Butterfly!"

12

THE CONFESSIONS OF A PHŒNIX.

"How! dead!
How dead? Why, very dead indeed!"

KILLING NO MURDER.

CHAPTER I.

I WAS once dead.

"Eh! how! what!" interrupts the Courteous Reader, naturally startled by such a posthumous announcement.

"What! dead, dead, dead!" inquires a Criminal Judge, unconsciously using the legal formula.

"What! food for worms?" exclaims a great Tragedian.

"What! gone to another and a better world?" says a sentimental spinster.

"Or to a wus," snuffles a sanctified shoemaker.

"What, to that bourne," says a Bagman, "to which no traveller makes more than one journey?"

"What,—unriddled that great enigma!" cries a metaphysician, "of which we obtain no solution but by dissolution?"

"Or, in plain English, *Hic Jacet?*" puts in an Undertaker.

"What, hopped the twig?—kicked the bucket?—bowled out?—gone to pot?—mizzled?—ticked off?—struck off the roster?—slipped your cable?—lost the number of your mess?" ask as many professional querists.

"Oh! a case of suspended animation—hung and cut down!"

"Or a cut throat and sewed up?"

"Poisoned and pumped out?" hints a Medical Student.

"Drowned, and 'unsuffocated gratis'?" quotes a reader of "Don Juan."

"Or buried in a trance?" guesses a Transcendental Speculator.

"Poo, poo! he means dead-beat," cries a Sportsman.

"Or dead lame," prompts a Veterinarian.

"Or dead asleep," proposes a Mesmerizer

"Or dead drunk," mutters a Tea-totaller.

"Or only metaphorically," suggests a Poet.

But begging the pardon of the Poet, the Tea-totaller, the Mesmerizer, the Horse-Doctor, and the Student, I had no such meaning: but that I was departed, deceased, demised, defunct, or whatever term may denote the grand Terminus.

"What! as dead as a house — as a herring — as a door-nail — as dumps — as ditch-water — as mutton — "

Yes — or as Cheops, or Julius Cæsar, or Giles Scroggins, or Miss Bailey. In short, as declared before, I was once dead — a regular subject for the Necrologist — an entry for the Registrar — an item for the Obituary as thus : —

On the 3d instant, suddenly, Peregrine Phœnix, Esq., of Clapham Rise.

CHAPTER II.

"To be sure," murmurs Memory, applying her right forefinger to her forehead, and pressing on her own organ. "to be sure there have been many persons who, though seemingly dead, and even interred, have afterwards returned to life. For example: the wife of Reichmuth Adolch, the Councillor of Cologne, who died of the plague, and was buried with a diamond ring on her finger, and was revived by the violence of the thievish sexton in wrenching off the ornament. Then there was Monsieur François de Civille, thrice coffined and thrice restored; not to forget the romantic tale of the lady of Nicholas Chassenemi, who was rescued from the grave by her old lover Cariscendi. Also, the Honorable Mrs. Godfrey, Mistress of the Robes to Queen Anne, and sister of the great Duke of Marlborough, who lay in a trance for a week. Then there was Isabella Wilson, who, after eleven days of rigid insensibility, would have been entombed but for the interference of the Doctor, who felt some warmth about the heart; and Mr. Cowherd of Cartmell, Lancashire, who revived after being laid out; and Isaac Rooke, who revived after a coroner had been summoned; and Walter Wynkbourne, executed on the gallows at Leicester in 1350 — but jolted to life in a cart. Above all, there was Anne Green, who, after being hung and pulled by the legs, and struck on the chest by the but-end of a musket, yet recovered, and married and bore three children."

"Hout aye," chimes in a Scottish Mnemosyne. "And there was yon Ill-hangit Maggie, as they ca'd her."

"Yaw, yaw," adds a Teutonic Remembrancer. "Also dere vas de Yarman, Martin Grab, who comed to himself quite lively, after he was a copse."

And so he did. And thereby hangs a tale of the DEAD-ALIVE, which will serve for a fresh chapter.

CHAPTER III.

IN the Free City of Frankfort-on-the-Maine, the bodies of the dead are not kept for several days, as with us, in the house of mourning, but are promptly removed to a public cemetery. In order to guard, however, against premature interment, the remains are always retained above ground till certain signs of decomposition are apparent; and besides this precaution, in case of suspended animation, the fingers of the corpse are fastened to a bell-rope, communicating with an alarum, so that on the slightest movement the body rings for the help which it requires for its resuscitation — a watcher and a medical attendant being constantly at hand.

Now the duty of answering the Life-bell had devolved on one Peter Klopp — no very onerous service, considering that for thirty years since he had been the official " Death Watch," the metallic tongue of the alarum had never sounded a single note. The defunct Frankforters committed to his charge had remained, one and all, man, woman, and child, as stiff, as still, and as silent, as so many stocks and stones. Not that in every case the vital principle was necessarily extinct: in some bodies out of so many thousands it doubtless lingered, like a spark amongst the ashes — but disinclined by the national phlegm to any active assertion of its existence.

For a German, indeed, there is a charm in a certain vaporous dreamy state, between life and death, between sleeping and waking, which a Transcendental Spirit would not willingly dissolve. Be that as it might, the deceased Frankforters all lay in their turns in the Corpse-Chamber, as passive as statues in marble. Not a limb stirred — not a muscle twitched — not a finger contracted, and consequently not a note sounded to startle the ear or try the nerves of Peter Klopp.

In fine, he became a confirmed sceptic as to such resuscitations. The bell had never rung, and he felt certain that it never would ring — unless from the vibrations of an earthquake. No, no — Death and the Doctors did their work too surely for their patients to relapse into life in any such manner. And truly, it is curious to observe that in proportion to the multiplication of Physicians, and the progress of Medical science, the number of Revivals has decreased. The Exanimate no longer rally as they used to do some centuries since — when Aloys Schneider was restored by the jolting of his own coffin, and Margaret Schöning, leaving her death-bed, walked down to supper in her last linen.

So reasoned Peter Klopp, who, long past the first tremors and fancies of his novitiate, had come, by dint of custom, to look at the bodies in his care but as so many logs or bales of goods committed to the temporary custody of a Plutonian warehouseman, or Lethean wharfinger. But he was doomed to be signally undeceived.

In the month of September, just after the autumnal Frankfort Fair, Martin Grab, a middle-aged man, of plethoric habit, after dining heartily on soup, sour-krout, veal-cutlets with bullace sauce, carp in wine-jelly, blood sausage, wild boar brawn, herring salad, sweet pudding, Leipsic larks, sour cream with cinnamon, and a bowlful of plums, by way of dessert — suddenly dropped down insensible. As he was pronounced to be dead by the Doctor, the body was conveyed, as usual, within twelve hours, to the public cemetery, where being deposited in the Corpse-Chamber, the rest was left to the care and vigilance of the Death-Watch, Peter Klopp.

Accordingly, having taken a last look at his old acquaintance, he carefully twisted the rope of the Life-Bell round the dead man's fingers, and then retiring into his own sanctorum, lighted his pipe, and was soon in that foggy Paradise, which a true German would not exchange for all the odor of Araby the Blessed, and the society of the Houris.

"And did the fat man come to life again?"

Patience, my dear madam, patience, and you shall hear.

It was past midnight, and in the Corpse-Chamber, hung with dismal black, the lifeless body of Martin Grab was lying in its shroud as still as a marble statue. At his head, the solitary funeral lamp burned without a flicker — there was no breath of air to disturb the flame, or to curve the long spider-lines that hung perpendicularly from the ceiling. The silence was intense. You might have heard the ghost of a whisper or the whisper of a ghost, if there had been one present to utter it — but the very air seemed dead and stagnant — not elastic enough for a sigh even from a spirit.

In the adjoining room reposed the Death-Watch, Peter Klopp. He had thrown himself, in his clothes, on his little bed, with his pipe still between his lips. Here, too, all was silent and still. Not a cricket chirped — nor a mouse stirred — nor a draught of air. The light smoke of the pipe mounted directly upward, and mingled with its cloud-like shadows on the ceiling. The eye would have detected the flitting of a mote, the ear would have caught the rustling of a straw, but all was quiet as the grave, still as its steadfast tombs — when suddenly the shrill hurried peal of the alarm-bell — the very same sound which for fifteen long years he had nightly listened for — the very same sound that for as many long years he had utterly ceased to expect — abruptly startled the slumbering senses of Peter Klopp!

In an instant he was out of bed and on his feet, but without the power of further progress. His terror was extreme. To be waked suddenly in a fright is sufficiently dreadful; but to be roused in the dead of the night by so awful a summons — by a call, as it were, from beyond the grave, to help the invisible spirit — perhaps a Demon's — to reanimate a cold, clammy Corpse, — what wonder that the poor wretch stood shuddering, choking, gasping for breath, with his hair standing upright on his head, his eyes starting out of their orbits, his teeth chattering, his hands clutched, his limbs paralyzed, and a cold sweat oozing out from every pore of his body! In the first spasm of horror his jaws had collapsed with such force, that he had bitten through the stem of his pipe, the bowl and stalk falling to the floor, whilst the mouth-piece passed into his throat, and agitated him with new convulsions. In the very crisis of this struggle, a loud crash resounded from the Corpse-Chamber—then came a rattling noise, as of loose boards, followed by a stifled cry—then a strange, unearthly shout, which the Death-Watch answered with as unnatural a shriek, and instantly fell headlong, on his face, to the stone-floor!

"Poor fellow!　Why, it was enough to kill him!"

It did, madam.　The noise alarmed the resident doctor and the military patrole, who rushed into the building, and lo! a strange and horrid sight!　There lay on the ground the unfortunate Death-Watch, stiff and insensible; whilst the late Corpse, in its grave-clothes, bent over him, eagerly administering the stimulants, and applying the restoratives that had been prepared against its own revival.　But all human help was in vain.　Peter Klopp was no more—whereas Martin Grab was alive, and actually stepping into the dead man's shoes, became, and is at this day, the official Death-Watch at Frankfort-on-the-Maine.

CHAPTER IV.

"AND do you really mean to say, sir," exclaims a vulgar-looking personage, in a black rusty suit, with black-silk gloves, black-cotton stockings, and a hat of two colors, black and sleek at bottom, and brown and shabby at top; a figure, a good deal like a decayed apothecary of the old school,—"do you really mean to say, sir, that you hactually obiited and re-surgam'd like the apoplectic German gemman as ate such a wery hearty last meal?"

Well, and what then?

"Why, then, sir, it's the beer, that's all."

The bier?

"Yes, the double X.　You see, sir, the truth is, I've laid myself three quarterns of rum to a pot of ale, as how it was not a regular requiescat, not a boney fide Celo quies, but only a weekly dispatch."

A *Weekly Dispatch?*

"Yes, or a Morning Post Mortum.　Not a natural hexit, you know.　Not a true Bill of Mortality,—but that you was only killed by the perodical press, like Lord Brougham!"

Humph!　That such a rusty raven should pluck out the

heart of my mystery! That such a walking shadow should throw a light on my enigma! But the fellow's guess is correct. I died only in print. The great Composer had no hand in it: my everlasting rest was set up by a compositor of the *Morning Herald!*

"*On the 3d instant, suddenly, Peregrine Phœnix, Esq., of Clapham Rise.*"

CHAPTER V.

WHAT a strange sensation it caused, the reading of that mortal paragraph! A feeling only to be understood by those who have been put out of the world by the Globe, had their days ended by the Sun, been posted to eternity by the Post. or sent on their last journey by the Evening Mail!

The newspaper that morning came late; and when the fatal sentence met my glance, I was, like Hamlet's father, "full of bread." I had already finished my morning's repast, but by an instinctive impulse, I took another egg, and began breakfasting over again. A sort of practical assertion of the animal functions — and I never enjoyed a meal so much in my life. What a zest it had! Each separate morsel by its peculiar substance, flavor, or aroma, giving the lie, backed by the three senses of Touch, Taste, and Smell, to that abominable announcement! The noble Athelstane, when he escaped in his grave-clothes from the funeral-vault of St. Edmond's Abbey, did not attack the venison-pasty and the wine-bottle with more relish! There was a certain pleasure even in a crumb's going the wrong way!

"What!" exclaims Civic Apoplexy, his face as crimson as the wattles of an enraged turkey-cock, his tongue struggling for utterance, and his eyes protruding, like pupils about to be expelled by the head-master, "a comfort in choking!"

Yes, my dear Alderman, as an evidence of active existence. Unlike the race-horse, every cough is in your favor.

For my own part, O how vividly I delighted in the grating in the throat, the soreness of the lungs, the watering of the eyes, which told, how instead of being dead, I had merely lost my breath! How deliciously I enjoyed every symptom, otherwise disagreeable, of vitality! The imputed absence of my

life made me intensely sensible of its presence. I felt, methought, the warm blood coursing through my veins and
arteries, and tingling in the very nails of my fingers and toes.
Every movement of the machine, beforetime withdrawn from
notice, had become decidedly perceptible. I had a distinct
notion of the peristaltic motion, and seemed absolutely conscious of the growth of my hair!

"What, without Macassar! Impossible!"

Perhaps so, Mr. Rowland, but it seemed probable. And
then how delightedly I strutted about, and boxed with Nobody,
and fenced with my own shadow, and spouted like a 'Bartlemy
Tragedian. No, no — I was not dead. A gentleman who
eats two breakfasts

> "And lightly draws his breath,
> And feels his life in every limb,
> What should he know of Death?"

My next act was to ring for my servant, who entered, and
found me grimacing before the looking-glass — dead men don't
make faces.

"John, where was I, and what did I do on Friday last, the
3d instant?"

"Let me see — you rowed on the river, sir, in the wherry."

"What, with Charon?"

"No, sir, with Mr. Emery."

"Very good, that will do, John."

And joyous as a blackbird in Spring, I began to whistle
Dibdin's air of "Jack's Alive." By an association of ideas,
Dibdin's verses put me in mind of Sterne, and darting off at
a tangent to my library I pulled down the first volume of
Tristram Shandy, and began to read aloud the extempore lecture of Corporal Trim on the text of " Are we not here now,
and are we not gone in a moment?" with his cocked hat illus-
tration of sudden death. "But I am alive," said the foolish,
fat scullion.

O, how I admired that fat scullion! I could have hugged
her in spite of her grease — our feelings, our sympathies
were in such perfect unison! Trim's Funeral Sermon had
been to her the same in effect as my obituary paragraph in
the *Herald.*

In the mean time, the ten o'clock Clapham omnibus called

for me as usual ; I put on my hat and gloves, took my walking-stick (the dead don't walk with sticks), got into the vehicle, seated myself, and remarked with a smile all round, —

"Well, this is better than a hearse."

A speech natural and significant enough under my peculiar circumstances, but to the rest of the company, who wanted the key, a mere impertinent truism.

One gentleman in particular seemed personally disgusted and offended by the observation, and on glancing at his beaver, I perceived he wore a hat-band. Somebody dead of course —but it was not Peregrine Phœnix, Esquire, of Clapham Rise, a reflection which made that vivacious personage as merry as the music after a soldier's funeral.

The confinement of the omnibus, and the reserve of its passengers, erelong became intolerable ; the first cramped the physical activity, and the last checked the flow of animal spirits of a man more alive than common. So taking a hearty tug at the conductor's dreadnought, I was set down, and walked off at the rate of four miles an hour and humming,

" Life let us cherish."

along the London road. But I was soon arrested by a spectacle of uncommon interest — an undertaker's shop, with all the grim and glittering emblems of the craft in the window. I had passed them a hundred times before without notice, but now the establishment had for me all the interest of an exhibition.

I examined every painted scutcheon, as if for an æsthetic critique — scrutinized the mottoes and inscriptions as for an archæological essay — examined each crest and blazonry with heraldic relish, and inspected the shining coffin-plates and handles with the zest of an antiquary poring over rusty pieces of antique armor. A device of a flying cherub was gazed at like a design of Raffaele's, and the notification of " Funerals Performed " was read over and over again like a love posy. But above all, I was smitten with an emblem which had formerly seemed rather a repulsive one — a Death's head and cross-bones — especially the dreary skull with its vacant eyelet holes, and that sardonic grin — whereas now, a laughing eye within the dark cavity seemed to tip me a knowing wink, and the ghastly grin was become a smile so contagious, that I felt myself smiling from ear to ear.

All this time the hammer had sounded merrily — yes, *merrily* from the interior of the shop, and looking in at the door, I saw the master, with his journeyman, busied in the last decoration of a handsome black coffin, lined with white satin — to some, perhaps, a dismal object, but to me a poetical one, like

> "A sable cloud
> That turns its silver lining on the night."

I read the name engraved on the silver plate thrice over, and with a novel but pleasant curiosity, informed myself minutely of all the particulars of the age, business, and circumstances of the deceased.

"And when, pray, did the poor gentleman die ?"

"On the 3d instant, sir, rather suddenly."

The very day that *I* did not ! — O, the electric thrill of life that ran through every fibre of my frame at that coincidence of dates ! The vivid revelation of a stirring, vital principle, that glowed from head to heel ! I am convinced that for a man to know, to feel, to enjoy his existence, to be properly conscious of his being, he must be put into the Obituary ! Till then, he is like the flounders that did n't flounder.

"But the fish are dead," objected the Cook.

"Not them," said the Fishwoman, tossing the last flounder into the blue and white dish. "Just see how they 'll kick when they comes to the hot lard. Why, bless ye, they 're as alive as you are, only they don't know it till they are put in the pan."

CHAPTER VI.

"THEN after all," says Mrs. Grundy, a lively, loquacious old lady, familiarly known to a very wide circle of friends and acquaintance, "it is not so very disagreeable to be killed by the press ?"

By no means, madam — rather reviving than otherwise — as good as a sniff of hartshorn, sal volatile, or aromatic vinegar, and much more agreeable than burnt-feathers — a bunch of black ostrich-plumes always excepted.

"Well, I should have thought that such a broad hint in

black and white would be a memento mori, — a sort of
'Philip, remember thou art mortal.' "

Quite the reverse, ma'am. A memento vitæ — a fillip to
the animal spirits — a "remember thou art alive." Dead
men, you know, don't read their own obituaries.

"True. Nevertheless, the sudden shock of such a frigid
announcement — "

Like the shock of a shower-bath, ma'am. Cold, but bracing;
and for a phlegmatic temperament, the finest and safest stimu-
lus in the world! Gives a glow to the skin — a healthy tone
to the nerves — improves the appetite, corrects the spleen, and
tickles the cockles of the heart and the risible muscles. You
have heard, ma'am, of a lightening before death?

"Yes — Romeo alludes to it."

Well, it's nothing to the lightening after it! I mean in
print. Talk of Parr's Life Pills, or the Elixir Vitæ! — a kill
by the press is the Grand Catholicon — a specific for ennui or
tedium vitæ, a sovereign remedy for Hypochondriasis, and in-
fallible for Suicidal Monomania! Only let a newspaper hint
that you are a corpse, and it makes you *quite another thing* —
a Harlequin, a Rope-dancer, a Tumbler, a Dancing Fakir, a
Springheeled Jack. But not to advertise a remedy without a
case, — there was Lord Cowdenknows, who was killed by the
Times.

"Ah, by an upset of his carriage."

Yes — with one horse's hoof on his sternum, another on his
os-frontis, a wheel on his epagastrium, and the broken axletree
through his abdomen. No mortal was ever *pressed* to death
more completely — and what is the result? Why, an intense consciousness of his existence, and the continual assertion of his vitality by a vivacious volubility and volatility
amounting almost to a nuisance. He reminds us that Lord
Cowdenknows is alive with a vengeance! — his enemies by
astounding pats on the head and confounding slaps on the
back; and his friends by disconcerting digs in the ribs, or
staggering punches in the stomach. No practical joker in the
exuberance of his animal spirits ever played more pranks.
On one head he pours melted butter, on a second cold water,
on a third vinegar, smears a fourth with honey, a fifth with
cantharides, a sixth with treacle, a seventh with tar, an eighth
with bear's-grease, a ninth with mustard, a tenth with cold

cream, an eleventh with paste, a twelfth with cowage, and then daubs an unlucky Quaker with ink. One he trips up, and astonishes another with a *coup de pied.* In short, he is all alive and kicking — 'all manner of ways.'"

CHAPTER VII.

"Now I think of it," says Mnemosyne, again pressing the organ of memory with her right forefinger, and gently smiling as if some pleasant image rose up before the mental eye, "there was Squire Foxall, a martyr to that melancholy humor called Hypochondriasis, and who was cured by the Press. Many a serio-comic scene there was between the master and his man Roger, a confidential servant of the old school, shrewd, trusty, and as blunt as a spade."

"Well, Roger," the master would say, after a very long and solemn shaking of his head, "I am going at last."

"Glad on it — to Swaffham, in course?"

"No, Roger, no — to another world."

"What, to Amerikey?"

"No, to another and a better one, Roger — to the world of spirits."

"Ah, that's along o' missing your brandy — you be low, you be."

"Not so low as I shall be, Roger. I'm at death's door — I have double knocked, and am scraping my shoes, and it will soon be, walk in. Now, Roger, remember when I'm gone that Mr. Bewlay —"

"Yes, yes — I know. He have got the last o' your last wills. Your nevy will come into the land, and your niece is to have your personal bulk."

"No, Roger — that was the will before. I've made another since then — but no matter. I've done with money and land. All I require now is a little turf."

"Well — there's a whole stack on it i' the rickyard, and when you've burnt out that —"

"Never, Roger, never! I'm burnt out myself — quite down in the socket, and shall go off like a snuff. I am ready, Roger, for the garner."

"Yes, yes, and corn for the sickle, and grass for the scythe, and a ripe plum for the basket, and a brown leaf for hopping the twig.   I know all that by heart."

"I 'm a dying man, Roger, and you know it.   I have n't twelve hours to live — no, not six, before I pay the debt of nature."

" Dang the debt o' nature !   I wish you had none to settle but hern.   But it arn't do yet it arn't."

" Due, and overdue, Roger.   The receipt 's made out, and before to-morrow you will have another master."

" No, I shan't.   I harn't had no warnin."

" But *I* have, Roger.   Here, feel my pulse.   It stopped just now for two minutes and a half.   The circulation is at a stand-still — the heart cannot perform its functions."

" All moonshine, master.   It 's performing its funkings at this minit.   It 's going as regular as the eight-day clock — I can a' most hear un tick."

" No, no, Roger — that 's impossible."

" Is it ?   Then why do Dr. Darby try to hear it with his telescope ?"

" Stethoscope, Roger — ste-thos-cope.   There may be hyper-trophy for all that.   But you know I can't argue with you.   My lungs are quite gone — quite ! "

" No wonder — you 've been blowin 'em up this ten year."

" They 're destroyed, Roger.   Pulmonary consumption has set in —"

" Yes, yes, I know — and they 're full of tuber-roses."

" Tubercles, man — and my liver is in no better state."

" No — they 're schismatic.   And you 've got an absence in your inside — "

" An abscess."

" Well, an abscess in your stomach, and can't digest prop-erly for want of gas-water."

" A deficiency of the gastric juice.   It is all too true, Roger.   Every organ I have is out of order."

" Then I would n't play on 'em.   Well, what next ?   Why, you 've got a gatherin in your lumbering progresses."

" Lumbar processes —"

" Which in course affects the head, and so you 've got a confusion of water on the brain.   Then you 've had an eclec-tic fit, and three parallel strokes — and there 's your stertian ague, and the intermediate fever—"

" Intermitting."

" Then, there's the inflammation of your mucus members —"

" Membrane, membrane."

" Well, membrane. Next there's your vertical headach —"

" Vertigo."

" And lord knows what in your intestates and viceruses. Then there's your legs with their various veins —"

" Varicose."

" And as to your feet, what with hoppin gout in them — and flying gout in your stomach — and swimming gout in your head — you're gout all over."

" Yes, Roger, yes — it has got hold of my whole system, sure enough. But it's apoplexy I'm afraid of — apoplexy, Roger. I have giddiness, tinnitus, congestion, lethargy — every symptom in the book ! "

" Dang the books — it's them has done it ! There's Doctor Imray's Family Physicker, you've giv yourself over ever since you brought it home. And then there's Doctor Winslow's book, and Doctor Frankum's, as made you believe between 'em, that you'd got a turned head and a pendulum belly — "

" Pendulous, Roger, pendulous."

" Well, it's all one. And then their plaguy formulus for making up your own prescriptions. You'll proscribe yourself into heaven, you will some day, with your blue pills and hydrangea powders — "

" Hydrarge powders."

" It can't be good for nobody to swallow so much calumny. And then your dabblin with them deadly pisons, though you know as well as I do, that three Prussian Acidulated Drops would kill a horse."

" You mean Prussic acid. But in some affections, Roger, it is of great service."

" Yes, like Oxonian acid, for boot-tops. Then, there's the newspapers. I do believe there an't a quack medicine advertised, but you've tried 'em all, from Cockle's Antibiling pills, and the Febrifudges, to Sarcy Barilla. Lord ! lord ! the heaps of nasty messes you have swallowed sure-ly ! Not to forget the Horse Physic you took arter readin in Doctor Elliotson that the human two-legged specious could ketch the glanders!"

"And was the poor man cured of his Hypochondriasis?"

Yes, by the *County Chronicle*, into which some wag introduced an announcement of his sudden demise, "*after a complication of disorders borne for a long series of years with unexampled cheerfulness and resignation.*" The effect on the patient was miraculous! Instead of damping his spirits or shocking his nerves, it set up his lumbagoed back, roused his sluggish spleen, stimulated his torpid liver, stirred his lethargic lights, warmed his congested blood till it boiled a-gallop, and turned his flagging heart to a *cœur de lion.* He declared loudly that the paragraph originated in a political spite — swore that it was intended as a hint for his assassination, and vowed that he would horsewhip the Editor of the diabolical newspaper in his own infernal office.

And he was as good as his word — for which practical sincerity he had to pay a hundred pounds for damages, and as much more in costs. The cure, however, was complete. His old affections vanished as if by magic : and now his only complaints in the world are of the impudence of counsel, the partiality of judges, the stupidity of juries, the uncertainty of the law, the murderous propensities of the Whigs, the rascality of venal Editors, and the intolerable licentiousness of the Press.

CHAPTER VIII.

"AND don't you think, sir," asked Self-Preservation, in a close ball-proof silk corslet, under his figured waistcoat, — "don't you think that the fellow who takes another man's life, though only in a newspaper, ought to be shut up forever, if not hung — as a Homicidal Monomaniac?"

By no means — nor will you either, my dear Number One, when your feelings, which temporary excitement has raised from Blood Heat to the Fever Pitch, have subsided to their natural temperature. For my own part, I blush for my countrymen. There is something of cowardice as well as cruelty in the present irrational outcry for chains, cells, straight-jackets, and — fie on it! — even halters for the lunatic. A return to the barbarous system of our ancestors, when insanity was treated as a crime, and punished with a severity beyond the severest prison discipline of the present day.

"No matter," says Number One, "I stick by the first law of Nature — so Protection! Protection! Protection!"

"Protection! Protection!" shrieks Fear, with her hand before her eyes.

"Protection, Pro—tection," shouts Folly, out of wantonness, — and the Spirit of Imitation, like Echo, repeats the cry.

Protection! Protection!" bawl a million of voices, while with better reason, Conscious Guilt — the poor man's Oppressor — the Robber of the Widow and the Orphan — the Heart-Breaker, and the Brain-Breaker, vociferously swells the clamor, aware in his felon soul how richly he has earned the stab or the shot from the weapon of frenzy!

For my own part, my fears look the other way, and my cry would be for better defence against the Sane. Not the half-witted, but the sharp-witted — not the crazy, but the clear-headed — not the noncompos, but the homicidal lucid fellows who do not babble of Covenants, or Chambers's Journal, or the Customs, who neither brandish knives, nor draw triggers, nor even " throw about fire " — and yet deliberately take our lives, for they do " take the means by which we live." Against such, O Law and Justice! defend *me*. Only protect me from the sane Foxes, and I will take my chance about the March Hares!

Still Society, with her numberless throats, roars " Protection! "

Heavens! what are a few bewildered creatures roaming the earth, though furnished with sticks, staves, swords, and guns, to the legion of sound Destructives who go at large, armed with "a little brief authority," and a billy-roller or a forge-hammer! When did Homicidal Monomania, with all her mischievous malignity, and all her weapons, when did she cripple a child per day, or poke out thirty pairs of eyes during one short court mourning?

But still the Hydra shouts, with all its mouths in chorus, for " Protection! "

Such popular outcries against a class are always perilous, and apt to lead to cruelty and injustice. So, perhaps, some centuries ago originated a prejudice and persecution against a description of human beings quite as forlorn and desolate, only the Homicidal Monomaniacs of those times were called Wizards and Witches.

It is fit and proper, no doubt, for the security of society, that dangerous Lunatics should be so confined as to prevent their carrying any murderous design into effect — but to judge by the popular ferment, and the vehemence of the outcry for more Protection, I fear Society would hardly be satisfied with anything short of the incarceration of every individual who happened to go ungartered, or to button his doublet awry ; and above all, the establishment of a Cordon Sanitaire between South and North Britain, with positive orders to shoot every Scotchman who crossed the Tweed with a bee in his bonnet. For, be it noted, that Scotland comparatively swarms with what she calls, in her own dialect, " daft, or dementit bodies " — every city, every town, nay, every pelting petty village has its crazy or imbecile Goose Gibbie, or Davie Gellatly. Nevertheless, even the Provosts and the Bailies sleep in whole skins, and would be intensely surprised if they could not get their lives insured at as low rates as their neighbors.

The truth is, the English public was always haunted — as Goldsmith points out in his Essays — by some popular Bugbear; and he instances an epidemic terror of Mad Dogs. There is something of this national characteristic in the present panic, which really amounts to a general monomania about monomaniacs. Every day some person or other denounces his or her homicidal lunatic ; and as human heads cannot be rung like bells or glasses, or sounded like sovereigns on wooden-counters or stone-steps, to ascertain if they are cracked, the magistrates are sorely puzzled, and half-crazed themselves by a question on which Lawyers with Physicians, and even Doctors with Doctors, are at issue. The dispute between the two learned Professions promises, indeed, to become "a very pretty quarrel."

"And pray, sir, how do you think it will end ? "

Heaven only knows, madam. But, between ourselves, I do not despair of a very Rabelaisian termination — namely, the Big Wigs proving that the Gold-Headed Canes know nothing about Mental Disease ; and the Gold-Headed Canes proving that the Big Wigs know nothing about Jurisprudence.

CHAPTER IX.

"HARK!" cries Alarm, holding up a warning finger, listening and looking as if she saw something.

"Eh!—what!—where?" inquires bewildered Surdity, dancing with excitement, and looking hastily North—Nor-Nor-East,—Nor-East,—East-Nor-East—East, and so all round the compass.

"A Comet of the first magnitude," says Rumor, bedecked in her old robe, all over tongues, and breathless with running down "all sorts of streets."

"A what?" asks Surdity, eagerly poking his acoustical mainpipe into his best ear, and trying to lay on the report. "A new Comedian?"

"No—a great new Comic that has appeared in the Hare," bawls officious Ignorance into the bell of the flexible Voice-Conductor. "A voluminous body, with an inflammatory tail, as reaches, they say, from Sir William Herschel in England, to Mr. Cooper in Italy."

"Three hundred and sixty degrees in length," puts in Popular Exaggeration.

"Why then we shall have a fiery belt all round us," exclaims a female voice from Prospect House—"like the Planet Satan."

"An awful Phenomenon!" says Mrs. Aspenall, trembling like a leaf.

"A Fiery Dragon!" mutters Superstition: "with a *sulfurious* tail of burning brimstone, from the bottomless pit."

"We shall all be burnt alive!" roars Vulgar Error, running into the back-yard, and plumping up to his chin in the water-butt.

"There will be another Deluge!" cries a Whistonian Theorist, determined at any price to purchase a life-boat and a cork-jacket; having proved in print, that Noah's Flood was certainly caused by a Comet.

"It will approximate into physical collision with our terrestrial globe," says the Schoolmaster, abroad, "and obliterate our sublunary planet into infinitesimal fractions!"

"We shall have changes and revolutions," murmurs a Continental Monarch with pale lips.

"War! Pestilence! and Famine!" bellows a Modern Astrologer!

"And Earthquakes," croaks an unshaken believer in the shocking predictions of the old Monk of Dree and Doctor Dee.

"It will blow up our Powder-Works," groans a resident near Waltham Abbey.*

"And dry up our Water-Works," moans a Chelsea Director, turning to all the colors of a *Dolphin* out of its element.

"It's played the dickens already with the Consternations," says Ignorance. "They do say as how it's singed the Ram, set fire to the Wirgin, roasted the Bull whole, scorched up the Man with the Watering-pot, and fried all the heavenly Fishes!"

"So much the better!" ejaculates the Lord Mayor.

"So much the better!" exclaims his Worship of Bow Street.

"So much the better!" cries his Worship of Marlborough Street.

"So much the better!" observes his Worship of Hatton Garden.

"So much the better!" remarks his Worship of Marylebone.

"So much the better!" echoes his Worship of Queen Square.

"So much the better!" says his Worship of Worship Street, briskly rubbing his hands together, and drawing a long, deep sigh of satisfaction from somewhere about the solar plexus, — "so much the better! The public panic will now perhaps take another direction, and instead of the daily monomaniac, and the everlasting question, "*How's his head?*" it will be, "*Where's its tail?*"

* As good a prophecy as any of Zadkiel's: for the Waltham Powder-Works actually blew up, about a fortnight after the hint in print.

CHAPTER X.

But Mr. Hatband —

The Undertaker was so delighted with the interest I had taken in his work, and the decoration of the coffin, that on parting, he presented to me his card, which he gave me with a pleasure only inferior to mine on receiving it, but derived from a very different source — he supposing that I had some funeral order in store for him, and I exulting that there had been no occasion, on my own behalf for his services — in reality, feeling very much like a man who has just escaped, untouched, from meeting with a dead shot.

The sun was shining brilliantly, and the morning was delicious; one of those Spring mornings when we seem to walk on spring-boards; but never on elastic wood, or turf, did man tread so lightly as Peregrine Phœnix, Esq., on the broad, flat flag-stones, pleasantly contemplating, now and then, the active shadow, which proved that he was not a shade. It was the most agreeable promenade I ever enjoyed — that solitary walk to the West End — making a dozen satisfactory purchases by the way; for example, a stick of red sealing-wax, simply because it was not black — a piece of Holland linen for shirting, which "was warranted to wear well," and two pair of trousers that were ticketed "Everlastings." The next shop but one to the draper's was a Circulating Library, a rather petty repository; but there was a placard of the terms in the window, and although the act cost me a guinea, I could not resist going in and subscribing *for a year.*

A Statuary's, a few yards further on, supplied me, like the Undertaker's, with some very comfortable cogitation. For the first time since my birth, I found a charm in potbellied monumental Urns — in stone-blind Cherubs with wigs *à la mode* and alabaster — and in petrified Angels, with wings of good solid masonry, blowing dumb coach-horns. They were finer to me, in my peculiar frame of mind, than Phidian sculptures. And then those polished snow-like marble slabs and tablets, how cheerfully they shone in the bright sunshine! It was indeed my lucky day, *marked with white stones!* Yes, lucky, although in turning away from the statuary's, I was run against, full butt, by a workman with a package of laths under his arm, that came in uncomfortable contact with my body, a little below the chest. But the poor fellow begged my pardon so humbly, that it was impossible for a Christian, and especially under my circumstances, to refuse it.

"Well, well, pick up my hat. That poke in the stomach has given me a strong conviction, at any rate, of my corporeal vitality."

"I'm sorry to hear it, sir," replied the workman, "I am indeed, and I hope it's a feeling as will soon wear off."

But my greatest triumphs awaited me at my Club. O, the indescribable look of the porter, when he saw my Ghost thrust open the glazed door!—the unutterable astonishment of the waiter when my Apparition orderd a biscuit and a glass of sherry—the profound mystification of my friend B. when my Spirit carelessly asked him the current price of Long Annuities. The other members present were equally amazed. Some started up—most of them ejaculated—all stared—one choked—and a tumbler of Bass's Pale Ale dropped with a crash on the floor. Had I walked into the room *à la* Phœnix, in a pair of incombustible asbestos trousers, blazing with burning spirits of wine, there could not have been a greater sensation. However, the excitement subsided at last, and gave place to boisterous congratulations. The news of my sudden demise had circulated amongst my club intimates and acquaintance, and to do them justice they hailed my resurrection from my ashes as cordially as if they had conjointly underwritten my life.

A House Dinner was proposed to celebrate my revival; and fixed for seven precisely. The interval I employed chiefly in the pleasant task of composing a public contradiction of the paragraph in the *Herald*, and writing bulletins of my perfect health to all my friends and acquaintances, and some few others, including a tradesman or two, and the actuary of the Eagle Assurance. And when the missives were done and delivered to the house-steward for the post, with what gusto I added, "Mind, not the Dead Letter Office!"—while the steward stared by turns at the enormous *red* seal, and the staring P. PHŒNIX, in the corner of each envelope, intended to *break my life* to my correspondents.

"And did the dinner go off well, Mr. Phœnix?"

Excellently, madam. The best I ever ate. Every delicacy

of the season — the most delicious fruits I ever tasted — the most exquisite wines I ever drank. Then everybody was in capital spirits, and myself above all (good reason why) — joking, punning, telling my best stories (dead men tell no tales), and laughing, like one of the Immortals. Then after the cloth was drawn, the toasts that were drunk — not in solemn silence — but vociferously, with all the honors, " The Arabian Bird," — " Never say Die," — " Many Happy Returns of the Day," and the songs that were sung, and the speeches that were made, including my own, in which I assured the company, with unusual sincerity, that upon my life (a phrase since become habitual with me) it was the happiest day of my life — one to be remembered to my last hour — but which, in spite of somebody putting on my clock, like the grim Covenanter in " Old Mortality," had not yet arrived.

" Hear, hear, hear ! " shouted my auditors, and to tell the truth, I joined lustily in their cheering, out of sheer self-congratulation. If ever a human biped enjoyed the nine-fold vitality of the feline quadruped, it was mine at that moment. I was full, brimming, overflowing with life ; there was enough in me, had I been chopped up like a polypus, to animate a dozen Phœnixes !

It was nearly dawn ere we broke up, when between two companions, who — these are Confessions — looked sometimes like four, I set out to walk home, not walking as a mechanic plods to his work, or as an invalid ambulates for exercise, but with occasional skips and curvetings, or a little run, in one of which courses my head came in collision with a lamp-post, and gratified me with occular demonstration of my existence in a shower of vital sparks. Nor yet did we proceed quite so mum-chance as quakers, or boarding-school misses, but whistling, warbling trios, and occasionally shouting in chorus, when just at the bottom of Waterloo Place, or it might be the top of the Haymarket — by some mystery not to be explained — through some *Casus Belli* never clearly defined — for it was in the days of Tom and Jerryism, when war was seldom formally declared — all at once I found myself engaged in battle royal, or rather republican — it was so free and independent — with an unknown number of opponents. My new life, probably, was in danger, for I fought

for it like a tiger, wrestling, hugging, tugging, kicking, pushing, striking right and left, and being kicked, pushed, and
belabored in return.   One unlucky punch, I suspect, punched
out my centre of gravity, from my difficulty afterwards in
keeping my legs.   Sometimes I was on my feet, sometimes on
my head, now on my back, then on my front, then on my side,
and then on my seat — bounding, scrambling, rolling, up again,
posturing, squaring, warding, and down again — at first dry,
next wet, then tattered and torn, but still fighting, encouraged
by shouts of "Go it, Lively!" though purblind, giddy, bleeding, and almost out of that precious article, my breath.   Still
the battle raged with various success; my spirit, or spirits, for
I seemed to have several within me, yet unsubdued, when
just in the middle of a furious rally, in the very crisis of vic-
tory, I was caught up horizontally, and before tongue could
cry rescue, Peregrine Phœnix, Esq., the Dead Man of the
Morning Herald, was borne off kicking and shouting at the
top of his voice "Hurrah for Life — Hurrah for Life — Hurrah for Life — Life — Life in London!"

DOGBERRY.

MRS. BURRAGE.

A TEMPERANCE ROMANCE.

"Water, water everywhere." — COLERIDGE.

"There 's nothing like grog." — DIBDIN.

"For the water swells a man." — FALSTAFF.

"Come, come, wine is a good familiar creature if it be well used — exclaim no man against it." — IAGO.

"Give it me without water; so, my friend, so." — RABELAIS.

"'I believe, an' please your Honor,' quoth the Corporal, 'that if it had not been for the quantity of brandy we set fire to every night, and the claret and cinnamon with which I plied your Honor off—'

"'And the Geneva, Trim,' added my Uncle Toby, 'which did us more good than all.'" — TRISTRAM SHANDY.

CHAPTER I.

TEMPERANCE is a Virtue.

"No doubt of it," cries a little fat, plethoric gentleman, with a sanguine complexion, and a very short neck — too short to be long in this world.

"It 's the summit of human Virtue," exclaims a tall, long, vinegar-faced female, holding up a Teatotal Tract.

"A Virtue that will preserve itself in any climate," shouts an advertiser of quack nostrums.

"And a Virtue that costs nothing," adds a Templar of Pump Court.

"It is virtuous for de outside of a man, and for de inside of a man," says a foreign water-curate.

"It 's a Cardinal Virtue," cries a Romish Priest, not hopeless, perhaps, of arriving by water at a Red Hat.

"And a primitive Virtue," puts in a friend in drab. "It was practised by our first parents."

"A Virtue that is its own reward," exclaims a scholastic copyholder.

Then what need, say I, of a Temperance Medal.

CHAPTER II.

HEAVENS! what a hubbub!

What an uproar from Teatotal Presidents, Vice-Presidents, Grand Masters, and Grand Mistresses! What an awful flourishing of white staves, and red hands, and brown cudgels! I shall have my eye punched out by a total abstinence fist, or my nose broken by Sobriety's flagstaff, or my skull fractured by a temperate shillelagh! Yes; I shall be brained by yonder red-headed hod-carrier, with the muddy knees, — who, for all his uproarious support of the element, would as soon be choked as drink Boyne Water! No matter: I must speak my mind.

"You shall do no such thing," screams a she-Rechabite, "unless you speak your mind on our side."

"Tell the brass band to play up, and drown his voice!" roars a brother-bite.

"He's a publican and sinner," squeaks a little old woman, the very model for a Water Witch. "Pump on him! Duck him! Drown him!" cries an admirer of aquatic sports.

"Make him take the pledge!" bellows Waterman No. 1.

"And kneel to the 'Postle!" bawls Waterman No. 2.

"And force him to be blest!" bellows Waterman No. 3.

"And to buy a medal!" suggests a Hebrew member of the Numismatic Society. Which brings us round again to the old question, as to the need of a temperance medal at all.

There are no such honorary badges for the other virtues — for example, Honesty, Charity, Veracity — then why a medal for Temperance?

"Vy!" exclaims the Wandering Jew. "Vy, becos if ve melts up all the metal for medals, there von't be no pewter left to make quart and pint pots."

Bravo, Moses! Thou hast extemporized the most reasonable reason yet advanced in favor of the ridiculous decoration! A sort of *Water*-loo medal, precociously worn before the moral battle is even fought — much less won!

CHAPTER III.

"AND do you really think, sir," asks a little woman, in an Eau du Nil colored bonnet, with watered ribbons, — "do you really think that there is any harm in wearing such an ornament?"

"No wickedness, ma'am, but great weakness. Something of that contemptible vanity which induces certain people to decorate themselves with the ribbon or insignia of foreign orders, conferred on themselves by themselves."

"Ah — you're agin the cause!"

"Far from it, madam. On the contrary, I was for many months a strict teatotaller. Nay, I not only abstained from wine, beer, and spirits, for my own good; but, from the same exalted motive, drank daily, almost hourly, the most nasty, filthy, nauseous, abominable, disgusting draughts, to smell and taste, that my doctor and apothecary could invent. But did I, therefore, bedeck myself with rewards of merit, or was I treated with any public honors? Who gave me a medal for swallowing, for my health's sake, vile tincture of bark? Who invested me with a Blue Ribbon, for improving my appetite by chamomile tea? Who waved a green banner over me, for drinking infusion of senna? Or ground even a hurdy-gurdy before me, for taking castor-oil? Faugh! my gorge rises at the remembrance! And your teatotaller, forsooth, is to be decorated, like a Knight of the Bath, for only quaffing, for soul and body's sake, nice, pure, sweet, delicious water! the Nectar of the Naiads!"

"Then of course, sir, with such sentiments, you would not kneel down, and be blessed by the Apostle of Temperance?"

"Certainly not, madam. When I kneel to mortal, it will be to my lady-love, or her Majesty the Queen; but to man, never!"

"Ah! because the father is a popish priest."

"Not at all. But because the posture, however common amongst the Neales and O'Neils, is not an English one. In the time of the 'Spectator,' indeed, it was usual for a dutiful son to kneel down to his parents for a blessing. But Father Mathew is not my father, nor, although an Irishman, is he my mother, to entitle him to such a filial genuflection. I can respect the man and honor the cause; but, as to dropping on my knees, like some of his proselytes, whenever I found myself in Theobald's Road——"

"Well, for my part, sir, I don't mind saying, I did kneel to him at the great Marrowbone meeting—I should say Maryle-bone."

"As you please, madam; but the hinges of my legs are not so pliant. Besides, consider the monstrous inconvenience that would result; for, after kneeling to Father Mathew, I should feel bound, on temperance principles, to drop on my pans to some thousand or so of other meritorious individuals —beginning with my friend Martin the Painter."

"A painter?"

"Yes—for his Plan for Supplying the Metropolis with Spring Water."

"Are you serious, sir?"

"Quite, madam. I decidedly think that every Protestant man, woman, or child, who has knelt to Father Mathew, is bound, in common consistency, to fall on his or her knees, shine or shade, wet or dry, dust or mud, rough or smooth, easy or greasy, not only to Mr. Martin, but to Mr. Pedley, Mr. Robins, Mr. Schweppe, Captain Pidding, and the Directors of the Chelsea Water-Works, the East London Water-Works, the New River Company, the East India Company, the Master Wardens and Members of the Grocers' Company, Captain Claridge, Mr. Braidwood, the Parish Turncocks; in short, every notable patron of tea and water in the kingdom."

"Mercy on us!"

"Nay, more, ma'am; I venture to say, that if any person ever kissed Father Mathew, he or she is bound by the movement to kiss every one of the personages I have just enumerated,—and Mr. Mackay into the bargain,—for so strongly recommending the Thames and its Tributaries."

CHAPTER IV.

"Now really, really," says the fat, red-faced gentleman with the short neck,—"really now, you are really—too bad! To turn such a cause into ridicule!"

"Who, I, my dear sir? Heaven forbid! It is its own

watery-headed pumpkins of followers — temperate perhaps in body, but certainly not sober-minded — who render it ridiculous. A great authority has compared public meetings to farces; but what with its processions and its brass bands, its banners and crosses, its green scarfs and blue sashes, — its foppery and its poppery — its stepfathers, Roman monks, and bearded pilgrims — its terrific combats between the Wapping bullies and the pot-valiants — and its teatotal chorusses, from its six foolish virgins in white, — a Mathewite meeting bade fair to become —"

"What, sir — what?"

"A GRAND MELODRAMATIC PANTOMIME WITH REAL WATER!!!"

"Very well, sir — very well, indeed! I see you are not for the promotion of temperance amongst the lower classes!"

"On the contrary. But, my dear Moses, just cease for a moment the jingling of your medals — my dear female Rechabite, have the goodness to take your wet tract out of my eye, — and my dear little printseller, be off with your portraits of the apostle. If the poor man must lay out his pence or shilling in a picture, let him have a cheap print, at cost price, of Hogarth's Gin Lane."

"Humph! Why then, sir, you do approve of temperance in the lower orders?"

"Yes; certainly. But I have some misgivings, when I see a flock of bleating human animals plunging, helter-skelter, follow-my-leader, into the fresh water — as Dingdong's sheep rushed into the herring-pond — not from principle, but gregarious impulse. I should like to know how many of the converted have already broken their rash pledges — how many are at this hour writhing, like poor Mr. Brunel, with their temperance medals sticking in their throats."

"Why, then, you are against the Movement after all?"

"Nay. I would move still further — for I would water not only the bodies of the poor and ignorant, but their minds — open to them not merely the parish pump, but the springs of knowledge. In plain words, I would educate them, — furnish schools for them, and, as in the schools abroad, ' la morale ' should form a distinct and prominent item in the prospectus. They should be taught that temperance involves something more than a mere abstinence from strong drinks — that it forbids man to be 'drunk with pride'—to be 'intoxicated with vanity'—to be overcome with anger—to be far gone in hatred; and, above all, that he must renounce bloodthirstiness, as well as his thirst for mountain-dew or Cream of the Valley.

"Then we shall see the humble bricklayer and his laborer become such builders as Young describes,— men who

> ' On reason build resolve,
> That column of true majesty in man!'

Then will the artisan kneel down to God—his true father—and regard as his best temperance pledges those little living ones that prattle around him. Then he will walk steadily and soberly, without a white wand,—eschew blue-ruin without a blue scarf,—drink his glass of water without a medal for it, —and sip his cup of Bohea without a teatotal hullabaloo from six young women in white."

"Well, for all your skits, sir," says the florid, bull-necked gentleman, "I must and will say I admire a Mathewite meeting."

"And so do I," cries the little woman, in the Eau du Nil colored bonnet, with the watered ribbons. "It's such a beautiful sight!"

"It's such a powerful moral engine," says the stout florid gentleman.

"Then I wish," mutters a simple Fire-Brigade man, "we had had it at the fire at Topping's wharf."

CHAPTER V.

"But Mrs. Burrage!"

Patience, dear Reader, patience. She was not quite in a fit state to be introduced to you: I was obliged to enter into that little preliminary discussion on temperance to allow her time to get tipsy.

But now—lo! there she sits, that little plump woman, with her moist blue eye, with a drop in it, like a violet wet with dew—her nose nubbly and red as a rose-bud—her cheeks blushing like the full-blown damask flower—and her mouth half open, like a street-door left ajar—according to the Arabian superstition—for the Evil Spirits to drop in. The

forefinger of her right hand is crooked round the stem of an
empty wine-glass, and with her other hand she gives a twitch
at her cap and the row of brown curls under it, which having
gone a little a-jee on one side, she tugs as far awry on the
other.

Yes, there she sits—in melancholy contrast to the scene
around her; for Mr. Burrage, a strict teatotaller, has fitted
up his parlor to match his principles. Nothing, you see, but
the most chaste and cool colors;—none but the most temperate images. The curtains are of a pale sky-blue,—the
carpet is of sober drab and browns—the paper of a cream-
color ground, with a meandering pattern of aquatic weeds, and
white water-lilies, interwoven with that vegetable emblem of
sobriety, the Pitcher Plant—and in each curve of the pattern
a little fish. On the mantle-shelf—in the middle—stands
one of those Fountain Clocks, that eternally pour forth a
limpid stream, clear as glass, and spirally twisted like a stick
of barley-sugar. On each side of the clock is a large marine
shell, and at either end of the shelf, a biscuit-ware River God,
with his urn under his arm. Over the fireplace hangs a
large framed print of Rebecca at the well, and on the opposite wall, an engraving of Moses smiting the Rock. On the
right of the door is an original drawing in water-colors of the
New River Head,—and on the left, on a bracket, and under
a bell-glass, a cork model of Aldgate Pump. From the
centre of the ceiling, in lieu of chandelier, hangs a huge pumpkin,—and on the little table near the window, is an alabaster
vase, with a cluster of little doves on the brim, sipping the
imaginary pool, with one bird, which should be looking heaven-
ward, as if in gratitude for the draught, but that Female Intemperance, in too rudely washing it, had wrung off its little
head. .What else? Why, if you could look into that corner
cupboard, you would see a splendid Silver Tea Pot, presented
by Mr. B. to his helpmate, in the vain hope of attaching her
to the Chinese beverage.

"No, no," mutters Mrs. Burrage with a nod and a wink
and a smile at nobody, "He won't get *me* to be a te—a to—,
a to-tittler!"

CHAPTER VI.

Now, exactly as Mrs. Burrage mispronounced the last word of her soliloquy, the Teatotaller entered the room, and catching the jumbled syllables, guessed immediately at the cause.

"Ellen! — you have been drinking again!"

"Only the least drop, John — only the least modicus — nothing but a drain of rum."

"*Nothing* but ardent spirits! — *Only* fermented liquor; only liquid fire! — *You* had better drink poison at once!"

"Perhaps — I had!"

"I say, woman, you might as well swallow arsenic or oxalic acid!"

"Yes, or corrosive sub—sublimity," stammered the Bacchanal, for she had got into her old cups, the hiccups. "Well, perhaps I shall!"

"Ellen, Ellen, you will break my heart! You will drive me mad!" —and the afflicted man, throwing himself into a chair, leaned his arms and head on the round table. His face was hidden; but his wife could hear his sobs, and see the heaving of his shoulders, — and a change came over her countenance. The vacant stare, and the idiotic simper, gave place to a sober gravity; and, hastily rising from her seat, she staggered towards her husband and threw her arms round his neck.

"John — dear John — I will take tea — or water — whatever you like."

"O that you would only drink water!" groaned John, getting up on his legs, and mechanically stretching forth his right arm like an orator; for, on temperance themes, that greatest of all water-drinkers, the whale, was not more of a spouter, — "O that you would but drink water! The beverage of our first parents before they knew sin! The pure fluid of the founting! The dimond of the dessert! (he meant desert.) O that you would take to water, hard or soft, river or pump, plain or mineral, callybeat, or sulfurious."

"Or fly-water — or lau—lau—laurel water," muttered his perverse helpmate.

The Teatotaller dropped into his chair again as if he had been shot.

"I will, I WILL poison myself!" screamed the repentant woman, running and throwing herself at full length on the sofa, in a passion of grief, which at last subsided into a heavy sleep. But even in her slumbers, she continued to murmur of poison, arsenic, laudanum, oxalic acid, and "corrosive sublimity."

"And she will, too!" exclaimed the disconsolate husband, with a violent gesture of his right arm, as if he were dashing to the ground some bottle of deadly fluid, — "she will, too, in some of her low fits!"

For, as happens to all persons with the same unhappy failing, the physical excitement was succeeded by exhaustion and depression, — a "flow of spirits" by a flood of tears. Her most volatile flights always ended in a plunge in the Slough of Despond. What more likely than that, under the weight of bodily discomfort and mental anguish, from dejection and remorse, she would fulfil the dreadful threat?

"And she will, too!" repeated the poor Teatotaller, as he carefully searched the table-drawer and the cupboard, anxiously sniffing at every vial, and tasting every powder. But he only found a little Sal Volatile, some pounded rotten-stone, and a paper of common salt.

And nothing else?

Yes — a black bottle half full of some liquid which by the smell and taste he ascertained, at some risk to his pledge, to be very fine Pine-apple Rum.

"The horrid creature!" exclaims our She Rechabite, — whose nose, by the way, is of a deeper crimson than becomes her sober professions, though she may be an aquatic bird notwithstanding, as even the Water Hen has sometimes a very red beak, — "the horrid creature! such Silenuses are a disgrace to our sex!"

CHAPTER VII.

POOR Mr. Burrage! what a night he passed, — or rather what a night passed him, — for, could he have given it the goby, most assuredly it would have been at a quicker pace.

The moment he closed his eyes in sleep, the image of his wife stood before him, with a large packet marked "Poison"

in one hand, and a great bottle labelled " Laudanum " in the
other. He tried to snatch them from her; but from a stroke
of that universal paralysis, so common in dreams, he was utterly powerless — helpless — speechless. A passive spectator,
he could only look on at the dreadful tragedy enacted before
him, in a succession of rash acts. For slowly, slowly, the
wretched woman unfolded the packet and uncorked the vial,
— then, deliberately, so deliberately that the operation seemed
to occupy an age, she licked up the fatal powder, and next
drank the deadly dose, taking after it an enormous white lump
of what he understood by intuition to be sugar of lead. A
strange imitation of the ordinary process of taking medicine
— but dreams are often mere *parodies* of the realities of life.

All this while the Teatotaller made frantic efforts to arrest
the suicidal deed — and if desperate *willing it* could have sufficed, according to the theory of the Magnetizers, he would
certainly have mesmerized the visionary arms and hands of
his partner into some stiff and safe attitude — but alas! the
most intense volition would not even lift his own finger. No
man ever intended more energetically to bawl out, but he
could not even accomplish the squeak of a mouse; never was
the Spirit of Determination so swaddled up in the Mummy of
Imbecility!

In the mean time the features of the poisoned woman exhibited the most awful changes. Her face — at first of a cadav-
erous white, except the mouth, which was of an unnatural
red — a face of dough with lips of sealing-wax — suddenly
became flushed with crimson, that deepened into purple, and
thence almost to black. Her eyes, one moment closed as if
under the influence of the narcotic, at the next started wide
open, and began protruding from her head like those of a snail
— anon turning inwards, they disclosed nothing but the whites
— and finally, mocking a catastrophe not uncommon to wax-
dolls, dropped bodily into her head. As for her cheeks, they
had attained to a frightful puffiness; but, instead of being
white or crimson, they were now discolored with dreadful
blotches, blue, yellow, or green, and at last turning to large
spots of a livid color with red edges, — like rounds of ship-
beef.

It was a dismal sight! but how more so, when, suddenly
falling on the floor, she became spasmodically convulsed, and

threw herself into more postures and contortions than any tumbler on the stage. But at last these ceased; and her body swelled prodigiously, — her head thrice the natural size. The death-rattle was heard in her throat — but with supernatural loudness — a white foam, afterwards bloody, oozed from her black lips; the eyes, returning to their sockets, rolled horribly — most horribly! and, after a long, deep-drawn sigh, she puffed into his face, as he bent over her, the last parting breath — smelling powerfully of pine-apple rum!

She was gone! — but no — she was not — for the shock to his nerves awoke the Teatotaller, — and turning on his pillow he saw his wife by his side — she was alive and breathing, and her face was of its natural complexion, — but her lips were moving, and, approaching his ear, he distinctly heard her murmur — " Yes — I will — I will take it."

" And did she, sir ? "

My dear, curious Reader, — *she did.*

CHAPTER VIII.

The next morning the Teatotaller arose, and went to his occupation abroad, as usual, for he was the Co. of a small linen-drapery establishment in the City; but he was sadly unfit for business; as who could be otherwise, with his heart as heavy as a slack-baked loaf, his head as confused as mixed pins, his nerves as unstrung as the harp of Tara's halls, and altogether as unhinged as the Gates of Somnauth. In fact, he entered the shop with such a melancholy face, — as if he had forsworn even animal spirits, — that his partner inquired anxiously after his health.

" Why, middling, had a bad night ; " but he did not add that he was having almost as bad a day from his waking dreams; nor that, from the perturbation of the optic nerves, the pink sprigs on the printed cotton before him seemed to be wriggling about like clusters of worms. There was a half-mourning chintz, too, with round black spots on it that rolled about, distressingly like *her* eyeballs.

" And how was Mrs. B. ? " inquired the partner.

" Why, pretty well, thankee," as indeed she might be for all he knew; but alas! for all he knew, she might be, at that very moment, as he had seen her in his vision, namely, with her whole frame drawn into an arch, only resting on the heels and the back of the head. She was, perhaps, even then swelling to that portentous bulk, with a head huge as three, and a face changing from pink to purple, like the shot silk in the window. He even seemed to smell — it might be the odor of the dye, from the stuffs and bombazines: but in his nostrils it was the smell of a narcotic associated with sleep everlasting.

In vain he tried to get rid of the gloomy impression; it clung to him like a wet garment, chilling him to his very soul. At sight you would have set him down, not a Teatotaller, but a confirmed drunkard; his hand shook so, he never snipped the linen with the scissors at the right nick; his eyes dazzled so, he offered puce-ribbons to match with snuff-color, and declared blue satin to be the best raven black. As for the bills, he could neither make them out nor sum them up correctly; he was too busy with the Bills of Mortality; and he invariably gave the wrong change. In short, to use a common phrase, his mind was poisoned, and, as a natural consequence, his thoughts were corroded, his fancies discolored and distorted, and Reason in a high delirium. As usual in such cases, his brain swarmed with horrible images; whilst the most trifling realities assumed a prophetic significance.

"What a frightful pattern!" exclaimed a maid-servant, as she turned over some remarkably cheap ginghams.

The Teatotaller glanced at the piece she pointed at, and thought so too, for it was sprinkled over with spots of *a livid color with red edges.*

"And that is not much better," said the girl, tossing aside a remnant of a *flesh-colored* ground, *blotched with yellow, green, and purple.*

"And that's wus," said the female, rejecting a third sample. "I don't see nothing I like;" and she proceeded to deposit her small purchases of pins and tape, and half a yard of flannel, in her basket, out of which she first took an article that either occupied too much room or would have endangered the rest — a bottle of some deleterious mixture for the flies, and marked "Poison," in large letters. The linen-draper shuddered at the sight, but attempted a grim pleasantry.

"Are you going to drink that, my dear?"

"No; it's for Missus."

"Good God!" ejaculated the Teatotaller, out under his breath, and hastily pushing three shillings and two penny pieces towards his customer, as the change out of her half crown, for he was almost crazy at the ominous coincidence: "It's meant, yes, it's meant for a warning." And snatching up his hat, without more notice or ceremony than if he had absconded with the till or the cash-box, he bolted out of the Emporium, and ran home, if it was a home, and to his wife, if he had a wife. Of which he had quite as many doubts as one could tie up in a yard of black crape.

CHAPTER IX.

Rap — rap — rap! — No one came to the door.

Ring — ding — ding! — Nobody answered the bell.

"My worst fears then are realized!"— but the conclusion was premature, for the door suddenly opened, whilst his hand again convulsively grasped the knocker, and pulled him into the passage. With trembling nerves, and a palpitating heart, he instantly rushed into the parlor; she was not there! Nor yet in the drawing-room! But her bonnet and shawl lay on the round table. His wife had been out! Perhaps to lay in a fresh stock of pine-apple rum, for he had made way with the bottle in the cupboard. Perhaps, dreadful thought! to purchase some or all of the deadly drugs she had threatened to swallow. With renewed alarm he hurried up stairs to the bedchamber, and threw open the door. Yes, thank Heaven! there she was, and alive, and without a blotch on her face. But he had yet his minor misgiving.

"Ellen, you have been out."

"Well, I know I have."

"To the King's Head."

"No, John, no; but no matter. You'll be troubled no more with my drinking."

"What do you mean?"

"I mean what I say, John," replied the wife, looking very serious, and speaking very solemnly and deliberately, with a strong emphasis on every word. "You — will — be — troubled — no — more — with — my — drinking — I HAVE TOOK IT AT LAST."

"I knew it!" exclaimed the wretched husband, desperately tossing his arms aloft, as when all is lost. "I knew it!"— and, leaving one coat flap in the hands of his wife, who vainly attempted to detain him, he rushed from the room,—sprang down the stairs, both flights, by two and three stairs at a time —ran along the passage, and without his hat or gloves, or stick, dashed out at the street-door, sweeping from the step two ragged little girls, a quartern loaf, a bason of treacle, and a baby. But he never stopped to ask if the children were hurt, or even to see whether the infant dripped with gore or molasses. Away he ran, like a rabid dog, straight forward, down the Borough, heedless alike of porter's load, baker's basket, and butcher's tray.

"I say," muttered the errand-boy as he staggered from the collision.

"Do that agin," growled the placard man, as he recovered the pole and board which had been knocked from his shoulder.

"Mind where you're goin'," bawled a hawker, as he picked up his scattered wares; whilst a dandy, suddenly thrust into the kennel, launched after the runner one of those verbal missiles which are said to return, like the boomerang, to those who launch them.

But on, on, on scampered the Teatotaller, heedless of all impediments — on he scoured, like a he Camilla, to the shop, number 240, with the red, blue, and green bottles in the window, — the Chemist and Druggist's, into which he darted, and up to the little bald man at the desk, with barely breath enough left to gasp out "My wife!" "Poison!" and "Pump!"

"Vegetable or mineral?" inquired the Surgeon-Apothecary, with professional coolness.

"Both — all sorts — ladnum — assnick — oxalic acid — corrosive sublimity," — and the Teatotaller was about to add pine-apple rum, amongst the poisons, when the Doctor stopped him.

"Is she sick?"

"No," but remembering the symptoms overnight, the Teatotaller ventured to say, on the strength of his dream, that she was turning all manner of colors, like a rainbow, and swelling as big as a house.

"Then there is not a moment to lose," said the Esculapius,

and accordingly clapping on his hat, and arming himself with
the necessary apparatus — a sort of elephantine syringe with
a very long trunk — he set off at a trot, guided by the Teatotaller, to unpoison the rash and ill-fated bacchanalian, Mrs.
Burrage.

"And did he save her?"

"My dear madam, be content to let that issue remain a
little, and accumulate interest, like a sum in the Saving
Bank.

CHAPTER X.

Now, when the Teatotaller, with the medical man at his
heels, arrived at his own house, Mrs. Burrage was still in
her bedroom; which was a great convenience, for before
she could account for the intrusion of the stranger, nay, even
without exactly knowing how it was done, she suddenly found
herself seated — more zealously than tenderly or ceremoniously — in the easy-chair; and when she attempted to
expostulate, she felt herself choking with a tube of something, which was certainly neither macaroni, nor stick-licorice,
nor yet pipe-peppermint.

To account for this precipitancy, the exaggerated repre-
sentations of her husband must be borne in mind; and if his
wife did not exhibit all the dying dolphin-like colors that he
had described, — if she was not yet quite so blue, green,
yellow, or black as he had painted her, the apothecary made
sure that she soon would be, and consequently went to work
without delay, where delays were so dangerous.

Mrs. Burrage, however, was not a woman to submit quietly
to a disagreeable operation, against her own consent; so with
a vigorous kick and a push, at the same time, she contrived to
rid herself at once of the doctor and his instrument, and indignantly demanded to know the meaning of the assault upon
her.

"It's to save your life — your precious life, Ellen," said
the Teatotaller, very solemnly.

"It's to empty the stomach, ma'am," said the doctor.

"Empty a fiddle," retorted Mrs. B., who would have added
"stick," but the doctor, watching his opportunity, had dexter-

ously popped the tube again into her open mouth : not without a fresh scuffle from the patient.

"For the Lord's sake, Ellen," entreated the Teatotaller, confining her hand, "do, do, pray do sit quiet."

"Pob—wob—wobble," said Ellen. "Hub—bub—bub—bubble," attempting to speak with another pipe in her throat besides the windpipe.

"Have the goodness, ma'am, to be composed," implored the doctor.

"I won't," shouted Mrs. Burrage, having again released herself from the instrument by a desperate struggle. "What am I to be pumped out for ? "

"O Ellen, Ellen," said the Teatotaller, "you know what you have taken."

"Corrosive salts and narcotics," put in the doctor.

"Assnic and corrosive sublimity," said the Teatotaller.

"Oxalic acid and tincture of opium," added the doctor.

"Fly-water and laurel-water," said Mr. Burrage.

"Vitriol, prussic acid, and aqua fortis," continued the druggist.

"I 've took no such thing," said the refractory patient.

"O Ellen, you know what you said."

"Well, what ? "

"Why, that your drinking should never trouble me any more."

"And no more it shall ! " screamed the wilful woman, falling, as she spoke, into convulsive paroxysms of the wildest laughter. "No more it shall, for I 've took — "

"What, ma'am ; pray what ? "

"In the name of Heaven ! What ? "

"Why then — I 've took the PLEDGE ! "

MRS. PECK'S PUDDING.

A CHRISTMAS ROMANCE.

"The disappointment will be dreadful," said Mrs. Peck, speaking to herself, and looking from the dingy floor, up the bare wall, at the blank ceiling. "But how to get one, Heaven only knows!"

It was the afternoon of the 24th of December. Christmas Day was at hand, and for the first time in her existence Mrs. Peck was without a plum-pudding. For years past she had been reduced in life; but never so reduced as that! She was in despair. Not that she particularly doted on the composition; but it was a sort of superstition with her that, if she failed to taste the dish in question on that festival, she should never again enjoy luck in this world, or perhaps in the next. It was a foolish notion: but many enlightened Christians cling religiously to similar opinions; for example, as to pancakes on Shrove Tuesday, or hot cross buns on a Good Friday. So with Mrs. Peck a plum-pudding on Christmas Day was an article of her faith.

Yes — she must have one, though it should prove but a dumpling of larger growth. But how? Buying was out of the question: she had not half a farthing in the house — a widow without a mite! — and stealing was not to be thought of — she must borrow or beg. Once arrived at this conclusion, she acted on it without delay. There were plenty of little emissaries at hand, in the shape of her own children, for the necessary errands — namely, Careful Susan, Dirty Polly, Greedy Charley, Whistling Dick, Little Jack, and Ragged Peter, so called from a fragment of linen that usually dangled behind him, like a ship's ensign from its stern.

"Children!" said Mrs. Peck, "I am going to have a Christmas plum-pudding."

At such an unexpected announcement, the children shouted, jumped about and clapped their skinny hands. But their mirth was of brief duration. Second thoughts, for once none of the best, soon reminded them that the cupboard was as bare as Mother Hubbard's; while the maternal pocket was equally empty. How the thing was to happen, therefore, they knew not — unless by some such fairy feat as sent black puddings tumbling down the chimney; or some such scriptural miracle as showered quails and manna in the Wilderness; or that one, which Greedy Charley remembered to have seen depicted in blue and white on a Dutch tile, of horned cattle and sheep coming down from heaven to St. Peter, in a monster bundle. But having vainly watched the hearths, the walls, and the ceiling, for a minute or so, they gave up all such extravagant expectations. The hopes of Ragged Peter were, like his nether garments, in tatters; and the dingy face of Dirty Polly looked darker than ever. There was a dead silence, at last broken by Little Jack.

"But, mammy, you have got no plums."

"And no flour," said Careful Susan.

"And no suet," said Dirty Polly.

"Nor no sugar," said Ragged Peter.

"And no almonds and orange-peel," said Greedy Charley.

"No eggs," said Careful Susan.

"And never a saucepan," said Whistling Dick.

"As to almonds and orange-peel," said Mrs. Peck, "we must do without. Our pudding will be a very plain one. That is to say, if we get it at all, for there is not one ingredient in the house. We must borrow and beg; so get ready, all of you, to run on my errands."

"Let me go for the plums, mother," said Greedy Charley; but knowing his failing, she assigned to him to plead to Mr. Crop, the butcher, for a morsel of suet. Dirty Polly was to extract a few currants and raisins and some sugar, if she could, out of Mr. Perry, the grocer; Little Jack was to wheedle a trifle of flour from Mr. Stone, the baker; and Careful Susan was to get three eggs of Mrs. Sankins, who did mangling in her parlor and kept fowls in her cellar. Whistling Dick undertook to borrow a saucepan; and as Ragged

Peter insisted also on a commission, he was sent to hunt about the streets, and pick up a little orange-peel — candied, if possible.

As the children had no promenade dresses to put on, they were soon ready. Susan merely reduced the angles of her bonnet front to something of a semicircle; and Dirty Polly, with a single tug, made her short, scanty garment look a little more like a frock, and less like a kilt. She might, indeed, have washed her face, as Ragged Peter might have tucked in some dingy linen, with personal advantage; but as they were not going to a juvenile party, they waived the ceremony. Little Jack clapped on his crownless hat; Greedy Charley took his jew's-harp, the gift of a generous charity-boy; Whistling Dick set up his natural pipe; and away they went, in search of a pudding by instalments.

As soon as they were gone, Mrs. Peck, having made up the fire, washed her hands and arms very clean, and then seating herself at the round deal-table, with her elbows on the board, and her chin between her palms, began to calculate her chances of success. The flour, provided Mr. Stone, and not his wife, was in the shop, she made sure of. The fruit was certain — the suet was very possible — the eggs probable — the saucepan as good as in her own hand — in short, being of a sanguine temperament, she dreamed till she saw before her a smoking hot plum-pudding, of respectable size, and dappled with dark spots, big and little, like a Dalmatian dog.

In the mean time, Charley, twanging all the way on his jew's-harp, arrived at the butcher's, who was standing before the shop with his back to the road, admiring, as only butchers can admire, the rows of fat carcasses and prime joints on the tenter-hooks before him. Could that meat have known his sentiments concerning it, what proud flesh it would have been! Hearing a step behind him, and anticipating a customer, he turned round with the usual " What d' ye buy ? "

" I have n't got no money to buy with," said Charley, " or else " — and looking round for the desired object, he pointed to it with his finger — " I 'd buy that ere lump of suet."

" And what do you want with suet ? " asked the butcher.

" If you please, sir," replied Charley, " it 's for our pudding. But mother is out of money; so if you don't let her have that bit of suet, either on credit or for charity — "

" Well, what then ? " said the butcher.

" Why then," said Charley, " it will be the first time in our lives that we 've gone without plum-pudding on this blessed festival."

The butcher was a big florid man, bloated and reddened, as persons of his trade are said to be, by constantly imbibing invisible beef-tea and mutton-broth, or as it is called, the smell of the meat. But, although thus appropriating by minute particles the flesh and fat of sheep, oxen, and pigs, he was far from becoming a brute. He cast a kindly glance at the poor boy, who looked sickly and ill-fed, and then a triumphant one at his halves and quarters, glorious with nature's red and white, and gay with sprigs of holly, suggesting the opportune reflection that Christmas comes but once a year.

" There — take it, boy — you 're welcome to it, gratis, by way of a Christmas-box — and my compliments of the season to your mother."

" So saying, he tossed the suet to Charley, who, forgetting in his joy to thank his benefactor, ran straight home with the treasure, as delighted as if he had just won the Prize Ox in a Beef-Union Lottery.

The success of Dirty Polly was less decisive. Before entering the grocer's shop, she took a long, longing look through the window, unconsciously nibbling at her own fingers, instead of those delicious Jordan almonds, and that crisp candied citron and orange-peel — and sucking in imagination at those beautiful Smyrna figs, and Damascus dates, and French plums, so temptingly displayed in round drums and fancy boxes, with frills of tinted paper round each compartment. And there, too, were the very articles she wanted — new currants from Zante — rich Malaga raisins, or of the sun, or sultanas — with samples of sugar of every shade and quality, from a fine light sand to a coarse dark gravel; but alas! all ticketed at impracticable rates, in obtrusive figures! The owner had marked a price on everything except the long twisted sticks of sugar-candy and the canes of cinnamon that leaned against the China figure. " Will he give anything away for nothing," she asked herself, " if I beg ever so ? " The China mandarin nodded his head, and she stepped in.

The grocer himself was in the shop, in his snow-white apron, busily dusting, with a clean cloth, some imaginary impurities from the polished counter. He was not a harsh man, but a particular one, scrupulously neat in his apparel, and cleanly in his person. The slovenly frock and grubby flesh of dirty Polly did not therefore prepossess him in her favor. He hastily took down a pair of dazzling bright scales and asked her what she wanted. But Polly was silent. She was haunted by those large black numerals, no figures of fun, but formidable to penniless poverty as giants with clubs. The grocer again inquired what she wanted.

" Why then, if you please, sir," said Polly, " it 's raisins, and currants, and brown sugar."

" How much of each ? "

" As much, sir," replied Polly, dropping a low courtesy, " as you 'll please to give us."

" Pshaw ! " said the grocer.

" It 's for a Christmas pudding," said Polly, beginning to whimper ; " and if you don't take pity on us, we shall have none at all."

The grocer was silent, and turned away from her towards his shelves and canisters.

" Do, sir — pray do," said Polly, wringing her hands and beginning to cry, not much to the advantage of her looks, as the tears washed away the dirt in stripes ; and still less when she wiped her cheeks and eyes with the skirt of a frock that was draggled with mud. Luckily the grocer's back was still turned, so that he did not see the grimy drops which fell on his bright mahogany.

" Pray, pray, pray — only a few plums and currants, and a little, a very little sugar," said Polly, between her sobs.

" There," said the grocer, turning suddenly round, and thrusting a square paper of something into her hand. " Take that, and tell your mother to make a good use of it."

In the eagerness of her joy, for the thing felt like a money-box, Dirty Polly hurried out of the shop, and sure in the absence of sugar and plums of the means of buying them, she ran home to her mother with the speed of a young heifer.

The next subject for experiment was Mr. Stone, the baker ; but unfortunately Mr. Stone was from home, and his helpmate was at the desk in the shop, in charge of the pecks, quarterns, and half quarterns, the fancy twist, and the French rolls. She was a little pale woman, with quick gray eyes, and a sharp-pointed nose, so sharp and pointed that she might have drilled with it the holes in the butter-biscuits. A glance at little Jack and the receptacle he carried informed her at once of his errand.

"Flour, eh? And in that odd thing!"

"Yes, ma'am." said little Jack. "When poor daddy was alive it was one of his double nightcaps; but mammy has turned it into a flour-bag by cutting off one end."

"A quartern, I suppose," said Mrs. Stone, going towards the large tin scale.

"If you please. ma'am," said Jack, "and be as good as not to let it be seconds or middlins, but the best flour."

"There then, child," said Mrs. Stone, holding out one hand with the full bag, and the other for the money.

"There's no money, ma'am," said little Jack. "Mammy's not got any. The flour isn't to be paid for."

"No, no — that won't do," said Mrs. Stone; "I'm not going to book it."

"We don't want you to," said Little Jack.

"You don't?" exclaimed Mrs. Stone.

"No, ma'am," said little Jack. "I'm begging, ma'am,— it's for charity."

"In that case," said Mrs. Stone, deliberately returning the flour into the great tin scale, "charity begins at home." So saying. she tossed the empty nightcap into the blank face of the urchin, who, beginning to cry, and having nothing else to wipe his eyes with, made use of the flour-bag, which soon converted his woe into dough.

"It's for our Christmas pud—pud—pudding," he blubbered. "We only had a very tiddy one last year, and now there won't be none at all."

"A Christmas fiddlestick!" exclaimed Mrs. Stone. "Here, come hither, you little wretch, and I will give you something worth all the creature comforts in the world."

"Is it good to eat?" asked little Jack.

"To eat!" cried Mrs Stone, with upraised hands and eyes. "O, belly gods! belly gods! belly gods!"—a singular ex-clamation enough for a woman who sold fancy bread and took in bakings. "When will the poor leave off hankering after the flesh-pots of Egypt?"

"I don't know," said little Jack.

"No, but your mother might!" retorted Mrs. Stone. "A quartern of flour indeed! When will she ask for heavenly manna?"

"Perhaps she will," said Jack, "arter she's finished her pudding."

"There again!" exclaimed Mrs. Stone, "nothing but gluttony. But come this way;"—and she led little Jack into the parlor, behind the shop, where she first unlocked her bureau, and then opened a private drawer. "There!" she said, thrusting a paper parcel into his tiny hand—"there's spiritual food—go home, and tell your mother to feed you well with it."

Little Jack took the gift with the best bow he could make. To be sure it was not flour, but the packet might contain Embden grotts, which was better than nothing, and he was fond of gruel; so he made the best of his way home, not quite so well pleased as Greedy Charley, or Dirty Polly, but better satisfied than Careful Susan.

She had picked her way through the dirt to Mrs. Saukins's, before whose door a spangled bantam, with a magnificent red comb and wattles, was strutting about, cocksure of possessing the handsomest feather-trousers in the whole parish; and responding at intervals with a screeching chuckle to a more distant cackle in the cellar. Accepting the hint of this bird of good omen, Susan at once ascended the steps, and walking into the mangling parlor, explained her wants to the proprietor.

"By all means," said Mrs. Saukins. "Three eggs—yes, certainly—I'll fetch 'em directly—warranted new-laid—hark! there's Polly Phemus."

"Polly who?" said Susan.

"Polly Phemus. I give female names to all my hens; and know every one by her voice. Yes, that's her—black with a white tuft—a Polish everlasting layer—she's in her nest, in the old candle-box up in the dark corner. Well—three eggs—I think you said three?—Yes, certainly—you shall have them warm, as I may say, from the hen."

"Thankee, ma'am," said Susan. "Mother can't pay for them now, but she will out of her very first money."

"Dear me!" exclaimed Mrs. Saukins. "That alters the

ease. I'm very sorry to deny — but eggs is eggs now, and the new-laid uns fetches tuppence apiece. Besides, it's not the season, and my poultry don't lay."

"*Kuk-kuk-kuk-a-larcock!*" cried the hen in the cellar.

"*Larcock!*" echoed the spangled bantam.

"No, they don't lay!" said the unblushing Mrs. Saukins. "And if they did, my fowls pay ready money for their barley, and can't afford to give credit."

"Then you won't let us have them?" said Susan.

"It's impossible," said Mrs. Saukins. "My poultry has suffered such bad debts already. If they once knew I booked, they'd turn pale in the combs, and leave off laying directly. They've done it afore — yes — often and often. I'm very sorry, I'm sure — and if it was anything else — for example, a little mangling —"

"You're very kind," said Susan, "but we've got no linen. So you won't oblige us with the eggs?"

"Dear me, no — I said no," replied Mrs. Saukins. "My poultry is my partner, and would dissolve directly. Their terms for new-laid is tuppence apiece, cash down, or three for sixpence. That's the lowest; but to a friend I'd venture to go so far as to give one in — that one there, in the little moss basket in the window. To be sure the flies has spotted it a little, till it looks more like a thrush's, but it's a hen's — and as fresh a one as ever was broke in a basin."

"But I haven't got sixpence," said Susan.

"The more's the pity," said Mrs. Saukins, "for my hens is imperative. My mangle sometimes accommodates with credit, but my poultry won't. Birds is so cunning, and my fowls in particular. I do really believe they would know a bad shilling from a good one."

"But mother promises faithfully to pay," said Susan.

"No, no," said Mrs. Saukins. "My poultry won't take promises. They know pence from piecrust — you might offer them a bushel of promises, and promissory notes besides, without getting an egg out of them — but only show them the money, and they go off to their nests and lay like lambs."

"There goes our pudding, then!" said Susan, in a tone of deep dejection.

"Do you mean a Christmas pudding — a plum one?" inquired Mrs. Saukins.

"I do," replied Susan. "It will be the first time that we have missed having one, and mother will feel it dreadfully. It's quite a religious point with her."

"Well, that's lucky!" exclaimed Mrs. Saukins; "for if I can't oblige with the eggs for a pudding, I can favor with a receipt for making one — rich, yet economical."

"I would rather have the eggs," thought Susan; but as the pudding promised to be anything but a rich one, and the recipe professed to be a cheap one, she thought it prudent to take advantage of the offer. Accordingly, the document having been transcribed, she put the copy in her pocket, and returned home; the least satisfied of all the foraging party with the result of her expedition.

Ragged Peter, it is true, had failed equally in his search for orange-peel. Whether some elderly lady or gentleman had stepped on a piece, at the cost of a compound fracture, and so had sharpened *pro tempore* the vigilance of the police, or whether it had become the fashion to eat the rind with the fruit, there was not a morsel of it to be picked up, candied or uncandied. But to make amends for this disappointment, in passing along a street at the West End, the ragged boy had the good luck to be espied by a personage who had before time noticed him, on account of some fancied resemblance to a deceased nephew. Peter's eyes twinkled with joy as he recognized his old acquaintance in his splendid livery; and the more from remembering that at their last meeting he had been presented with some of the requisites for a plum-pudding. He crossed the road, therefore, with alacrity, in compliance with the friendly signal from the powdered gentleman at the open street door.

The porter was a very tall and very portly man, with a very convex chest, and a very stiff frill projecting from it, from top to bottom, like a palisade to keep off all intruders on his heart or bosom. Nor was there anything very promising to poor boys in general in his livery, blue turned up with red, and trimmed with gold lace, making him look merely a free translation of a parish beadle. Nevertheless the porter was a good-natured fellow; and his glance was genial, and his voice was kindly, as he accosted the ragged child.

"Well, young un! Where now? — Do you remember me?"

"Yes, sir," said Peter, with a cheerful smile. "You give me once a pocket full of almonds and reasons."

"Ah, that was after our dinner-party," said the porter. "I've none to-day."

Peter sighed, and was turning away from the steps,— a movement that exhibited the dilapidations in his rear,— when he was recalled by the same friendly voice. Peter stopped.

"Stay here till I come back." And the gentle giant went inwards, whence he presently returned with a bundle, which he placed in Peter's arms. "There, take that — it's good stuff — and tell your mother to do her best with it."

"We shall have a pudding, anyhow," thought Peter, not doubting that the bundle of good stuff had been made up by contributions from the cook and housekeeper; wherefore, spluttering some broken thanks to the porter, he ran home, with his rags fluttering in the wind, as fast as he could scamper.

The last of the adventurers was Whistling Dick. To the tune of "O where, and O where," he had successively visited the whole of his mother's friends and acquaintance — no great number in all, as often happens to a widow with a limited income — but from nobody could he obtain a loan of the indispensable culinary utensil. One had lent her saucepan already; another had burnt a hole in it ; a third had it on the fire with the family dinner ; a fourth had pawned it, but his mother was welcome to take it out ; and a fifth, an Irishwoman, had never had any saucepan at all except the frying-pan.

"I do believe," said Dick, "if there is such things as saucepans in kitchens, they have all asked for a holiday, like the servants, and gone out for a day's pleasure."

At last he gave up the search in despair, and was walking slowly homewards, when his attention was attracted by a tapping at a parlor-window. He looked up, and recognized over the Venetian blind the three faces of the young Masters Britton, who had once called him into the house to whistle to them.

"Who knows," thought Dick, "if I am invited in again, but I may make friends with the cook, and so get the lend of a saucepan ?"

But the hope was fallacious. He was indeed asked in ; but the moment he mentioned the object of his expedition, and confessed his design on the kitchen, the youngsters, one and all, declared that the thing was impossible. Their mamma was out, and the cook was such a termagant, and, that morning particularly, in so fierce a temper, that he might as well confront a fiery dragon. But what did he want with a saucepan?

"To bile our puddin in," said Dick. "It's Christmas time, you know; and we don't like to miss keepin it."

At the mention of Christmas and keeping it, the young Brittons withdrew into a corner, and held a whispered consultation, which seemed a long one, before they broke up, and clustered again round their *protégé*.

"Do you ever play at a round game?" inquired Master John.

"Sometimes," answered Dick. "Only I harn't got a hoop."

The young Brittons looked in some perplexity at each other.

"You know what counters are, don't you?" asked Master William.

"Yes," replied Dick; "they nail bad ha'pence to them."

The young Brittons were again disconcerted by this answer.

"He don't understand us," observed Master William.

"Give it him at once," said Master Benjamin.

Thus instructed, Master John advanced close up to Dick, and poked something into his hand, which the receiver thoroughly looked at, and then in turn at each of the young gentlemen.

"It's to play with," said Master John.

"You'll find it very amusing," said Master William.

"But you must whistle us a tune for it," said Master Benjamin.

Dick immediately complied, and struck up "Sich a gettin up Stairs," but rather dolefully: he would have preferred a good-sized, well-tinned saucepan to the thing in his hand, or all the toys in the world. However, a trifle is better than nothing; so, thrusting it into his pocket, he took leave of the young gentlemen, and returned home, whither we will follow him.

The Widow Peck has been described as a woman of sanguine disposition. We left her sitting with her elbows on the table, and her chin between her hands, with a dreamy steamy plum-pudding in all its glory before her — a vision not at all dispelled by the arrival of Greedy Charley with a real substantial lump of suet. He was closely followed by Dirty Polly, but, alas! without those conical paper bags associated with sugar and spice, and all that is nice, in grocery.

"What! no raisins — no currants — no sugar — no nothing!"

"Yes, — that!" said Dirty Polly, throwing her packet on the table ; "and you 're to make a good use of it."

The mother caught up the packet, and impatiently tearing off the envelope, in a faint voice proclaimed the contents.

"A square of yellow soap!"

"A square of yellow soap!" repeated both of the children.

"I should like to know of Heaven," said the widow, holding up the article towards the ceiling, "how I am to use *that* in a pudding!"   But Heaven made no answer.

"It 's for washing my face with!" cried Dirty Polly, very indignantly.   "I saw him stare at me!"

"Well, there can't be a plum-pudding without plums," said the widow, looking the very picture of despair. But her lamentations were cut short by the entrance of Little Jack : he had brought the flour, of course.

"No, mammy," said Jack, "I 've got no flour at all; but there 's grits.'

"Grits!" exclaimed the widow.   "Who wants grits?" But the case, when opened, appeared even worse.   "Grits indeed!   It 's a parcel of religious tracks!"

"It a'n't my fault," said little Jack, blubbering, and again having recourse to the old nightcap for want of a handkerchief. "It was Mrs. Stone's.   She said it was for spiritous food, and I thought she meant gruel, with rum in it."

"Well, well," said the widow, forgetting, mother-like, her own troubles in the grief of her little one.   "Don't cry. We shall, perhaps, have a pudding yet — who knows? Susan, maybe, will have better luck."

As she spoke, Susan stepped into the room, and walking gravely up to the table, began to search under her frock.

"Why, in Mercy's name!" exclaimed the alarmed widow,

"what is the girl fumbling at! You surely have not brought the eggs in your pocket?"

"I have n't brought the eggs in anything," said Susan, still groping among her petticoats.

"No! Then what *have* you brought?"

"A receipt for a plum-pudding."

"A receipt!" screamed the excited widow, — "a receipt! Why it 's the only thing I don't want! I can write a receipt myself. Take a pound of suet, a pound of currants, a pound of plums — but how am I to take 'em? Where 's my materials!"

"Here they are, mother," shouted the well-known voice of ragged Peter, as he bounded into the room and threw a good-looking bundle on the table. "There 's the materials!"

"Then we 're in luck after all!" said the widow, nervously tugging at the knots of the old handkerchief, which suddenly gave way and allowed the materials to unfold themselves.

"O Lord! O cri! O criminy!" ejaculated Peter and Charley and little Jack, the girls using similar interjections of their own.

"Hold me!" cried the widow, "lay hold of me or I shall run away. I 'm going off my head — I 'm half crazy — take 'em out of my sight! — A pair of old red plushes!"

"I thought," whined Peter, "they was things from the pantry. But that comes of turning my back to the porter and exposing my rags. I wish, I do, that I was all front!"

"There 's Dick," exclaimed Susan; "I hear his whistle in the distance. I wonder if he has got the saucepan!"

"O, of course we shall have that," said the widow with great bitterness: repeated disappointments had brought her to the mood for what she called arranging Providence. "Yes, we shall have the saucepan, no doubt, just because we 've nothing to put in it." She was wrong. In another minute Dick was standing amongst his brothers and sisters, but empty-handed.

"Why, bless the boy! He has n't brought the saucepan after all!"

"No," said Dick, — "nor even a tin-pot. But I 've brought this," and he chucked his present on the table.

"As I live!" cried the widow, — "it 's an ivory totum!"

"Yes," said Dick. "It was given me by the young Brittons. They seemed to think as we had no pudding, we should like to divert our hungers."

"Divert a fool's head!" cried the poor widow, throwing herself back in her chair, and laughing hysterically. "The world's gone mad! — the world's gone mad, and everybody is crazy! The more one wants anything, the more they give one something else — and the more one don't want anything, the more they force it upon you! Here am I, going to make a plum-pudding — or rather wanting to make one — and what have I got towards it?"

"A lump of suet!" muttered Charley.

"Yes, that's something," said the widow. "But what else — tell me, what else have I got towards my pudding? Why, a square of yellow soap — a bundle of tracks — a written receipt — a pair of red plushes, — and a tetotum!"

The circle of children, down-hearted as they were, could not forbear a titter at the idea of the comical pudding to be made of such ingredients; but their mirth was speedily damped by the tears of their mother.

"It's all over," she said, "and Christmas must go by without its pudding! What will come of it, Lord knows! Once break through a religious rule, and who knows the consequence? There was your poor father and me: every wedding-day in our lives, as sure as it came round, we made a point to have pickled streaky pork and pea-pudding, the same as at our nuptials; but one year somehow or another we missed — and in less than a week after he was called away."

"And why, mammy," asked little Jack, "why didn't you die too, then?"

The widow, doubtless, would have answered this artless question; but unfortunately she was seized with such a violent fit of coughing as almost took away her breath. At last she recovered, rather suddenly, and assumed the attitude of a listener.

"Hush! there's somebody tapping at the door."

The children immediately rushed to the latch, and let in a tall thin man, in black clothes and green spectacles, with an umbrella in one hand, and a red book in the other. A glance at the breast of his coat confirmed the widow's worst fears;

an inkhorn with a pen in it was dangling from one of the buttonholes.

"If it's rates or taxes," she said, "you must seize at once —for I have n't a farthing."

The man in black made no answer, but kept prying through his green glasses at the circle of young faces, and at length fixed upon Dick.

"Did n't I see you, my lad, looking in at the window of a cookshop?"

"Yes," answered Dick, "and you asked me about the family, and if we was n't in distress."

"Very good," said the man in black. "And you replied that you were in very deep distress indeed."

"Yes, for a sarcepan," said Dick.

"It was to boil our Christmas pudding," said the widow. "But we have n't got one, sir, nor no hopes of one."

"Very good," said the man in black. "I am a Perambulating Member of the District Benevolent Visitation Society, and am come to relieve your wants."

"You are very good, I'm sure," said the widow, quite flustered by such moral plunges from hot to cold, and then to hot again. "As you say, sir, I have seen better days," — though how or when the gentleman said so was known only to herself. "Yes, for twenty years I have been a householder, and up to this time have never missed celebrating my Christmas in a respectable way. And I do own it would go nigh to break my heart."

"Very good, very good," said the man in black, busily writing in the red book, from which he eventually tore out a leaf, that he folded up and presented to the widow.

"There's an order, ma'am, for what you want."

"The Lord in heaven bless you!" cried the widow, starting up from her chair, with a first impulse to throw herself on the good man's neck; and a second one, to go down on her knees to him; but which she checked just as the genuflection arrived at the proper point for a very profound courtsey.

"O, sir!—but I'm too full to speak. Yet, if the prayers of a widow and six fatherless children—"

"Very good, very good, very good," said the man in black, waving off the six ragged dirty, grateful fatherless children, who wanted to hug and kiss him — and shuffling as fast as he could to the door, through which he bolted more like a detected swindler than a professed Samaritan.

"Well, that comes of trusting to Providence," said the widow, quite forgetting a recent lapse, the least in the world, towards atheism. "Come, children, sing 'O be joyful,' for we have got our pudding at last."

The children needed no further hint; but at once joined hands, and began dancing round the table, as if the grand object of their hopes had been already smoking in the middle — Dick whistling "Merrily danced the Quaker's wife," as loud and fast as he could rattle it, whilst the mother ecstatically beat time with her head and foot. At last they were all out of breath.

"There, that will do," said the widow. "Now then, some of you put on your hats and bonnets to fetch the things; for, of course, it's an order on the baker and the grocer."

"It's an order," said Careful Susan, reading very deliberately the paper which she had taken from her mother's passive hand, — "an order for six yards of flannel."

"Flannin !"

"Yes, flannel."

The widow snatched the paper; glanced at it; threw it from her; and dropped into her chair; not as if for a temporary rest, but as though she would fain have sunk through the bottom of it, and right through the floor, and down through the foundation of the house, and six foot of earth beneath, for a quiet grave.

In a moment she had six comforters at her neck; not woollen ones, but quite as warm and more affectionate, though their loving assiduities were repelled.

"Don't hang on me — don't! And don't tell me to hope, for I won't! I can't be consoled! So don't come nigh me — no, not even if you see me fainting away — for I'm grown desperate, like an over driv beast, and don't know what I may commit !"

The panic-stricken children instinctively backed into a distant semicircle, and fixing their eyes on their parent, as if she had really been the enraged animal she had described, awaited in awful silence her next words. At last they came in a fierce, harsh voice.

"Wipe Jackey's nose."

A brother and sister on either hand of the little one immediately performed the desired office; and then trembling waited the next command.

"Tear up that devilish paper!"

Susan immediately picked up the unfortunate order, but as she hesitated, with her usual prudence, to destroy what was equivalent to six yards of flannel, Dirty Polly snatched the paper from her, and tore it up as small as she could mince it.

"I have hoped as long as I could," cried the widow, suddenly starting to her feet, "but now I give up! When bad luck sets in that way, blow upon blow, it's for good. We shall never prosper again — never, never, never! We're a ruined family, root and branch — and if it was not for the sin, I'd wish nothing better at this blessed moment than to have you all six tied round my waist, enjoying a Serpentine death!"

At this horrible picture, which the speaker dramatized by frantically throwing up her arms, as at the fatal plunge, and then letting herself sink gradually, by a sort of courtsey, as if subsiding into the mud, the poor devoted children set up a general howl; and then broke into a series of sobbings and ejaculations, only checked by the opening of the door and the entrance of another stranger.

If the former visitor resembled a tax-gatherer, his successor hardly made a more favorable impression on the widow, from whom, had he asked the same question as the Baronet in the Poor Gentleman, "Do I look like a bailiff?" he would probably have received the same answer — "I don't know but you do." He had no red book in his hand, and no inkhorn at his buttonhole; but he carried a very formidable bludgeon, and wore a very odd wig, and a very broad-brimmed hat, as much on one side as a yacht in a squall. Altogether there was such an air of disguise about him, that if not a bailiff, he was certainly, as the next best guess, a policeman in plain clothes.

"I believe, ma'am," said the stranger, "you have just had a visit from an agent of a Benevolent Society?"

"Yes, and be hanged to him!" thought the widow; "and perhaps you're another!" but she held her tongue. The

stranger, therefore, repeated his question to Susan, as the
eldest of the children, and was answered in the affirmative.

"I knew it," said the stranger. "And he asked if you were
not in distress; and you said that you were, and he told you
he was come to relieve it."

"Yes, with six yards —" burst from several voices.

"Hush — hold your little tongues! I know it all — with
an order for six yards of flannel — wasn't it so? Six yards
of flannel for a Christmas pudding — ha! ha! ha!"

The children would have laughed too, but they were afraid.
The stranger had suddenly turned into a conjurer, who knew
their thoughts and wishes.

"You are right indeed, sir," said the widow. "He called
himself by some hard name."

"Yes, an ambulating member," said the stranger, "of the
District Visitation. I know them well. Six yards of flannel
— just like them. That's their way. There was poor Biddy
Hourigan, an Irish Catholic, ma'am — they visited her, too,
and found her in deep distress, not about a pudding though,
but because she had not a farthing in the world to get her
husband out of purgatory. And how do you think, ma'am,
they relieved a poor soul in purgatory? Why, with a bushel
of coals!"

"Is it possible?" exclaimed the widow; adding, in the simplicity of her heart, "that perhaps it was in the winter?"

"No, ma'am, there's no winter *there*," said the stranger.
"But to business. You have seen better days."

The poor widow cast a piteous glance at the bare walls
and rickety furniture of her humble dwelling.

"You have been a housekeeper many years in this parish,"
continued the stranger, "and have been accustomed all your
days to a plum-pudding at Christmas; and you cannot bear to
go without it — hush! not a word! — I know it all by sympathy. I like myself to keep up old customs — better, most
of them, than the new ones."

"They are, indeed," said the widow, shaking her head.
"But if it is not a liberty, may I ask, sir, if you belong to any
Society yourself?"

"Why, yes, ma'am," said the stranger. "In one sense, I
do — namely, the Universal Society of Human Nature. But
if you mean such as the District Visitation, I do not. I tread

in their steps, it is true, but it is to do what they leave undone. Their ambulators serve me for pointers to find my birds."

"And a noble sort of sporting, if ever there was one!" exclaimed the widow, with enthusiasm. "It's a thousand pities more rich people don't take out licenses, and follow the same game."

"It is, indeed, a thousand pities, ma'am," said the stranger; "and a thousand shames to boot. In this motley world of ours, some people have their happiness cut thick, and buttered on both sides; and some have it thin, and no butter at all. As one of the former class, it's my duty to bestow some of my greasy superfluity on my poorer fellow-creatures. But what are all those heterogeneous articles on the table, neither eatables nor drinkables — have you been visited, ma'am, by half a dozen Societies?"

The widow, with the help of her family, related their adventures in search of a pudding, at the end of which the stranger laughed so long and immoderately, and choked, and got so black in the face, that the children shrieked in chorus for fear he should go to heaven before his time. But ready-made angel as he was, heaven spared him a little longer by letting him come to; at which, however, instead of seeming overjoyed, he looked very grave, and shook his head, till the widow feared he had "bust a vessel."

"Too bad," he said at last, "too bad of me to laugh at such distress. I must make amends on the spot — and the best way will be to make you all, if I can, as merry as myself. There, ma'am" — and he placed in the widow's hand a purse, through the green meshes of which she perceived the glitter of sovereigns, like gold-fish among weeds. "Properly laid out, that money will purchase all the requisites for a Christmas plum-pudding, and some odd comforts and clothing besides. Hush — no words, I guess them all by sympathy! Only a shake of the hand all round, and a kiss from the little one. There! Be good boys and girls! God bless you all! Good by!"

The children watched the exit of the generous stranger till the last bit of him had disappeared, and then, as if "drowned in a dream," still continued gazing on the door.

"He was a real gentleman!" cried Dick.

"A saint! a saint!" exclaimed Mrs. Peck, "a real saint

upon earth — and I took him for a bailiff! but no matter. He don't know it, that's one comfort; and if he did, such an angelical being would forgive it. But come, children, what are you all staring at? Why don't you huzza now, as you did afore, and whistle, and take hands, and dance round the table? Vent yourselves how you like — only don't quite pull the house down — for we've got a Christmas Pudding at last!"

THE SCHOOLMISTRESS ABROAD.

AN EXTRAVAGANZA.

CHAPTER I.

> " She tawght 'hem to sew and marke,
> All manner of sylkyn werke,
> Of her they were ful fayne."
>
> ROMANCE OF EMARE.

A SCHOOLMISTRESS ought not to travel—

No, sir!

No, madam—except on the map. There, indeed, she may skip from a blue continent to a green one—cross a pink isthmus—traverse a Red, Black, or Yellow Sea—land in a purple island, or roam in an orange desert, without danger or indecorum. There she may ascend dotted rivers, sojourn at capital cities, scale alps, and wade through bogs, without soiling her shoe, rumpling her satin, or showing her ankle. But as to practical travelling,—real journeying and voyaging,—O, never, never, never!

How, sir! Would you deny to a Preceptress all the excursive pleasures of locomotion?

By no means, miss. In the summer holidays, when the days are long, and the evenings are light, there is no objection to a little trip by the railway,—say to Weybridge or Slough,—provided always—

Well, sir?

That she goes by a special train, and in a first-class carriage.

Ridiculous!

Nay, madam,—consider her pretensions. She is little short of a divinity!—Diana, without the hunting!—a modernized Minerva!—the Representative of Womanhood

in all its purity!—Eve, in full dress, with a finished
education!—a Model of Morality!—a Pattern of Propriety!—the Fugle-woman of her Sex! As such she must
be perfect. No medium performance—no ordinary good-
going, like that of an eight-day clock or a Dutch dial—will
suffice for the character. She must be as correct as a prize
chronometer. She must be her own Prospectus personified.
Spotless in reputation, immaculate in her dress, regular in her
habits, refined in her manners, elegant in her carriage, nice
in her taste, faultless in her phraseology, and in her mind
like — like —

Pray what, sir?

Why, like your own chimney-ornament, madam,—a pure
crystal fountain, sipped by little doves of alabaster.

A sweet pretty comparison! Well, go on, sir!

Now, look at travelling. At the best, it is a rambling,
scrambling, shift-making, strange-bedding, irregular-mealing,
foreign-habiting, helter-skelter, higgledy-piggledy sort of process. At the very least, a female must expect to be rumpled
and dusted; perhaps draggled, drenched, torn, and rough-
casted,—and if not bodily capsized or thrown a summerset,
she is likely to have her straitest-laced prejudices upset, and
some of her most orthodox opinions turned topsyturvy. An
accident of little moment to other women, but to a schoolmistress productive of a professional lameness for life. Then
she is certain to be stared at, jabbered at, maybe jeered at,
and poked, pushed, and hauled at, by curious or officious foreigners,— to be accosted by perfect and imperfect strangers,
—in short, she is liable to be revolted in her taste, shocked
in her religious principles, disturbed in her temper, disordered
in her dress, and deranged in her decorum. But you shall
hear the sentiments of a Schoolmistress on the subject.

O, a made-up letter!

No, miss,—a genuine epistle, upon my literary honor.
Just look at the writing,—the real copy-book running-hand,
— not a *t* uncrossed,—not an *i* undotted,—not an illegitimate
flourish of a letter, but each *j* and *g* and *y* turning up its tail
like the pug dogs, after one regular established pattern. And
pray observe her capitals. No sprawling K with a kicking
leg,—no troublesome W making a long arm across its
neighbor, and especially no great vulgar D unnecessarily

sticking out its stomach. Her H, you see, seems to have stood in the stocks, her I to have worn a back-board, and even her S is hardly allowed to be crooked!

CHAPTER II.

"Phoo! phoo! it's all banter," exclaims the Courteous Reader.

Banter be hanged! replies the Courteous Writer. But possibly, my good sir, you have never seen that incomparable schoolmistress, Miss Crane, for a Miss she was, is, and would be, even if Campbell's Last Man were to offer to her for the preservation of the species. One sight of her were, indeed, as good as a thousand, seeing that nightly she retires into some kind of mould, like a jelly shape, and turns out again in the morning the same identical face and figure, the same correct, ceremonious creature, and in the same costume to a crinkle. But no, — you never can have seen that She-Mentor, stiff as starch, formal as a Dutch hedge, sensitive as a Daguerreotype, and so tall, thin, and upright, that, supposing the Tree of Knowledge to have been a poplar, she was the very Dryad to have fitted it! Otherwise, remembering that unique image, all fancy and frost-work, — so incrusted with crisp and brittle particularities, — so bedecked allegorically with the primrose of prudence, the daisy of decorum, the violet of modesty, and the lily of purity, you would confess at once that such a Schoolmistress was as unfit to travel — *unpacked* — as a Dresden China figure!

Excuse me, sir, but is there actually such a real personage?

Real! Are there real Natives — Real Blessings to Mothers — Real Del Monte shares, and Real Water at the Adelphi? Only call her * * * * * instead of Crane, and she is a living, breathing, flesh and blood, skin and bone individual! Why, there are dozens, scores, hundreds of her Ex-Pupils, now grown women, who will instantly recognize their old Governess in the form with which, mixing up Grace and Gracefulness, she daily prefaced their rice-milk, batter-puddings, or raspberry-bolsters. As thus : —

"For what we are going to receive — elbows, elbows! — the Lord make us — backs in and shoulders down — truly thankful — and no chattering — amen."

CHAPTER III.

"But the letter, sir, the letter —"

"O, I do so long," exclaims one who would be a stout young woman if she did not wear a pinafore, — "O, I do so long to hear how a governess writes home!"

"The professional epistle," adds a tall, thin Instructress, genteelly in at the elbows, but shabbily out at the fingers' ends; for she has only twenty pounds per annum, with five quarters in arrear.

"The schoolmistress's letter," cries a stumpy Teacher, — only a helper, but looking as important as if she were an educational coachwoman, with a team of her own, some five-and-twenty skittish young animals, without blinkers, to keep straight in the road of propriety.

"The letter, sir," chimes in a half-boarder, looking, indeed, as if she had only half-dined for the last half-year.

"Come, the letter you promised us from that paragon, Miss Crane."

That's true. Mother of the Muses, forgive me! I had forgotten my promise as utterly as if it had never been made. If any one had furnished the matter with a file and a rope-ladder, it could not have escaped more clearly from my remembrance. A loose tooth could not more completely have gone out of my head. A greased eel could not more thoroughly have slipped my memory. But here is the letter, sealed with pale blue wax, and a device of the Schoolmistress's own invention, — namely, a note of interrogation (?) with the appropriate motto of "An answer required." And in token of its authenticity, pray observe that the cover is duly stamped, except that of the foreign postmark only the three last letters are legible, and yet even from these one may *swear* that the missive has come from Holland; yes, as certainly as if it smelt of Dutch cheese, pickle-herrings, and Schie * * * ! But hark to Governess!

"My dear Miss Parfitt, —

"Under the protection of a superintending Providence we have arrived safely at this place, which as you know is a seaport in the Dutch dominions — chief city Amsterdam.

" For your amusement and improvement I did hope to compose a journal of our continental progress, with such references to Guthrie and the School Atlas as might enable you to trace our course on the map of Europe. But unexpected vicissitudes of mind and body have totally incapacitated me for the pleasing task. Some social evening hereafter I may entertain our little juvenile circle with my locomotive miseries and disagreeables ; but at present my nerves and feelings are too discomposed for the correct flow of an epistolary correspondence. Indeed, from the Tower-stair to Rotterdam I have been in one universal tremor and perpetual blush. Such shocking scenes and positions, that make one ask twenty times a day, is this decorum ? — can this be morals ? But I must not anticipate. Suffice it, that, as regards foreign, travelling it is my painful conviction, founded on personal experience, that a woman of delicacy or refinement cannot go out of England without going out of herself !

" The very first step from an open boat up a windy shipside is an alarm to modesty, exposed as one is to the officious but odious attentions of the Tritons of the Thames. Nor is the steamboat itself a sphere for the preservation of self-respect. If there is any feature on which a British female prides herself, it is a correct and lady-like carriage. In that particular I quite coincide with Mrs. Chapone, Mrs. Hannah More, and other writers on the subject. But how, let me ask, — how is a dignified deportment to be maintained when one has to skip and straddle over cables, ropes, and other nautical *hors d'œuvres*, — to scramble up and down impracticable stairs, and to clamber into inaccessible beds ? Not to name the sudden losing one's centre of gravity, and falling in all sorts of unstudied attitudes on a sloppy and slippery deck. An accident that I may say reduces the elegant and the awkward female to the same level. You will be concerned, therefore, to learn that poor Miss Ruth had a fall, and in an unbecoming posture particularly distressing, — namely, by losing her footing on the cabin flight, and coming down with a destructive launch into the steward's pantry.

" For my own part, it has never happened to me within my remembrance to make a false step, or to miss a stair : there is a certain guarded carriage that preserves one from such sprawling *dénouemens ;* but of course what the bard calls the ' poetry

16

of motion ' is not to be preserved amidst the extempore roll-ings of an ungovernable ship. Indeed, within the last twenty-four hours, I have had to perform feats of agility more fit for a monkey than one of my own sex and species. Par example : getting down from a bed as high as copybook-board, and, what really is awful, with the sensation of groping about with your feet and legs for a floor that seems to have no earthly exist-ence. I may add, the cabin-door left ajar, and exposing you to the gaze of an obtrusive cabin-boy, as he is called, but quite big enough for a man. O, *je ne jamais !*

" As to the Mer Maladie, delicacy forbids the details ; but as Miss Ruth says, it is the height of human degradation ; and to add to the climax of our letting down, we had to give way to the most humiliating impulses in the presence of several of the rising generation, — dreadfully rude little girls who had too evidently enjoyed a bad bringing up.

" To tell the truth, your poor Governess was shockingly in-disposed. Not that I had indulged my appetite at dinner, being too much disgusted with a public meal in promiscuous society, and, as might be expected, elbows on table, eating with knives, and even picking teeth with forks ! And then no grace, which assuredly ought to be said both before and after, whether we are to retain the blessings or not. But a dinner at sea and a school dinner, where we have even our regular beef and batter days, are two very different things. Then to allude to indiscriminate conversation, a great part of which is in a foreign language, and accordingly places one in the cruel position of hearing, without understanding a word of, the most libertine and atheistical sentiments. Indeed, I fear I have too often been smiling complacently, not to say engagingly, when I ought rather to have been flashing with virtuous indignation, or even administering the utmost severity of moral reproof. I did endeavor, in one instance, to rebuke indelicacy ; but un-fortunately from standing near the funnel, was smutty all the while I was talking, and, as school experience confirms, it is impossible to command respect with a black on one's nose.

" Another of our cardinal virtues, personal cleanliness, is totally impracticable on ship-board ; but without particulariz-ing, I will only name a general sense of grubbiness ; and as to dress, a rumpled and tumbled *tout ensemble,* strongly indi-cative of the low and vulgar pastime of rolling down Greenwich-hill! And then, in such a costume to land in Holland, where the natives get up linen with a perfection and purity, as Miss Ruth says, quite worthy of the primeval ages! *That* surely is bad enough, — but to have one's trunks rummaged like a suspected menial, — to see all the little secrets of the toilet, and all the mysteries of a female wardrobe, exposed to the searching gaze of a male official, — O shocking! shocking!

" In short, my dear, it is my candid impression, as regards foreign travelling, that, except for a masculine tallyhoying female, of the Di Vernon genus, it is hardly adapted to our sex. Of this at least I am certain, that none but a born romp and hoyden, or a girl accustomed to those new-fangled pulley-hauley exercises, the Calisthenics, is fitted for the boisterous evolutions of a sea-voyage. And yet there are creatures calling themselves women, not to say ladies, who will undertake such long marine passages as to Bombay in Asia, or New York in the New World! Consult Arrowsmith for the geographical degrees.

" Affection, however, demands the sacrifice of my own personal feelings, as my Reverend Parent and my Sister are still inclined to prosecute a Continental tour. I forgot to tell you, that during the voyage Miss Ruth endeavored to *parlez fran-çois* with some of the foreign ladies, but as they did not understand her, they must all have been Germans.

" My paper warns to conclude. I rely on your superintending vigilance for the preservation of domestic order in my absence. The horticultural department I need not recommend to your care, knowing your innate partiality for the offspring of Flora; and the dusting of the fragile ornaments in the drawing-room, you will assuredly not trust to any hands but your own. Blinds down of course — the front-gate locked regularly at 5 P. M., — and I must particularly beg of your musical *penchant*, a total abstinence on Sundays from the piano-forte. And now adieu. The Reverend T. C. desires his compliments to you, and Miss Ruth adds her kind regards, with which believe me,

" My dear Miss Parfitt,

" Your affectionate Friend and Preceptress,

" PRISCILLA CRANE.

"P. S. I have just overheard a lady describing, with strange levity, an adventure that befell her at Cologne. A foreign postman invading her sleeping-apartment, and not only delivering a letter to her on her pillow, but actually staying to receive his money, and to give her the change! And she laughed and called him her *Bed Post!* Fi donc! Fi donc!"

CHAPTER IV.

WELL, — there is the letter —

"And a very proper letter, too," remarks a retired Seminarian, Mrs. Grove House, a faded, demure-looking old lady, with a set face so like wax, that any strong emotion would have cracked it to pieces. And never, except on a doll, was there a face with such a miniature set of features, or so crowned with a chaplet of little string-colored curls.

"A proper letter! — what, with all that fuss about delicacy and decorum!"

Yes, miss. At least proper for the character. A schoolmistress is a prude by profession. She is bound on her reputation to detect improprieties, even as he is the best lawyer who discovers the most flaws. It is her cue, where she cannot find an indecorum, to imagine it; just as a paid spy is compelled, in a dearth of high treason, to invent a conspiracy. In fact, it was our very Miss Crane who poked out an objection, of which no other woman would have dreamt, to those little button-mushrooms called Pages. She would not keep one, she said, for his weight in gold.

"But they are all the rage," said Lady A.

"Everybody has one," said Mrs. B.

"They are so showy!" said Mrs. C.

"And so interesting!" lisped Miss D.

"And so useful," suggested Miss E.

"I would rather part with half my servants," declared Lady A., "than with my handsome Cherubino!"

"Not a doubt of it," replied Miss Crane, with a gesture of the most profound acquiescence. "But if *I* were a married woman, I would not have such a boy about me for the world, — no, not for the whole terrestrial globe. A page is unquestionably very *à la mode*, and very dashing, and very pretty, and may be very useful, — but to have a youth about one, so beautifully dressed, and so indulged, not to say pampered, and yet not exactly treated as one of the family, — I should certainly expect that everybody would take him —"

" For what, pray, what ? "

" Why, for *a natural son in disguise.*"

CHAPTER V.

But to return to the Tour.

It is a statistical fact, that since 1814 an unknown number of persons, bearing an indefinite proportion to the gross total of the population of the British empire, have been more or less " abroad." Not politically, or metaphysically, or figuratively, but literally out of the kingdom, or as it is called, in foreign parts.

In fact, no sooner was the continent *opened* to us by the Peace, than there was a general rush towards the mainland. An alarmist, like old Croaker, might have fancied that some of our disaffected Merthyr Tydvil miners or underminers were scuttling the island, so many of the natives scuttled out of it. The outlandish secretaries who sign passports, had hardly leisure to take snuff.

It was good, however, for trade. Carpet-bags and portmanteaus rose one hundred per cent. All sorts of guidebooks and journey works went off like wildfire, and even Sir Humphrey Davy's " Consolations in Travel " was in strange request. Servants, who had " no objection to go abroad " were snapped up like fortunes, — and as to hard-riding " curriers," there was nothing like leather.

It resembled a geographical panic, — and of all the country and branch banks in Christendom, never was there such a run as on the banks of the Rhine. You would have thought that they were going to break all to smash, — of course making away beforehand with their splendid furniture, unrivalled pictures, and capital cellar of wines ! However, off flew our countrymen and countrywomen, like migrating swallows, but at the wrong time of year ; or rather like shoals of salmon, striving up, up, up against the stream, except to spawn Tours and Reminiscences, hard and soft, instead of roe. And would that they were going up, up, up still, — for when they came down again, Ods, Jobs, and patient Grizels! how they did *bore* and *Germanize* us, like so many flutes.

It was impossible to go into society without meeting units, tens, hundreds, thousands, of Rhenish tourists, — travellers in Ditchland, and in Deutchland. People who had seen Nimagen and Nim-Again, — who had been at Cologne, and at Koöln, and at Colon, — at Cob-Longs and Coblence, — at Swang Gwar and at Saint Go-er, — at Bonn, at Bone, and at Bong!

Then the airs they gave themselves over the untravelled! How they bothered them with Bergs, puzzled them with Bads, deafened them with Dorfs, worried them with Heims, and pelted them with Steins! How they looked down upon them, as if from Ehrenbreitstein, because they had not eaten a German sausage in Germany, sour-krout in its own country, and drunk seltzer-water at the fountain-head! What a donkey they deemed him who had not been to Assmanshauser, — what a cockney who had not seen a Rat's Castle besides the one in St. Giles's! He was, as it were, in the kitchen of society, for to go " up the Rhine " was to go up stairs!

Now this very humiliation was felt by Miss Crane ; and the more that in her establishment for Young Ladies she was the Professor of Geography, and the Use of the Globes. Moreover, several of her pupils had made the trip with their parents, during the vacations, and treated the travelling part of the business so lightly, that in a rash hour the Schoolmistress determined to go abroad. Her junior sister, Miss Ruth, gladly acceded to the scheme, and so did their only remaining parent, a little, sickly, querulous man, always in black, being some sort of dissenting minister, as the " young ladies " knew to their cost, for they had always to mark his new shirts in cross-stitch, with the Reverend T. C. and the number — the " Reverend " at full length.

Accordingly, as soon as the Midsummer holidays set in, there was packed — in I don't know how many trunks, bags, and cap-boxes — I don't know what luggage, except that for each of the party there was a silver spoon, a knife and fork, and six towels.

" And pray, sir, how far did your Schoolmistress mean to go ?"

To Gotha, madam. Not because Bonaparte slept there on his flight from Leipsic, nor yet from any sentimental recollections of Goethe, — not to see the palace of Friedenstein and its museum, — nor to purchase an " Almanach de Gotha, — nor even because His Royal Highness Prince Albert, of Saxe Gotha, was the Husband Elect of our Gracious Queen.

"Then what for, in the name of patience?"

Why, because the Berlin wool was dyed there, and so she could get what color and shades she pleased.

CHAPTER VI.

"Now of all things," cries a Needlewoman, — one of those to whom Parry alludes in his comic song of " Berlin Wool," —" I should like to know what pattern the Schoolmistress meant to work !"

And so would say any one, — for no doubt it would have been a pattern for the whole sex. All I know is, that she once worked a hearth-rug, with a yellow animal, couchant, on a green ground, that was intended for a panther in a jungle: and, to do justice to the performance, it was really not so very unlike a carroty-cat in a bed of spinach. But the face was a dead failure. It was not in the gentlewomanly nature, nor indeed consistent with the professional principles of Miss Crane, to let a wild, rude, ungovernable creature go out of her hands; and accordingly the feline physiognomy came from her fingers as round, and mild, and innocent as that of a Baby. In vain she added whiskers to give ferocity, — 't was a Baby still; and though she put a circle of fiery red around each staring ball, still it was a mild, innocent Baby, — but with very sore eyes.

And besides the hearth-rug, she embroidered a chair-cushion, for a seat devoted to her respectable parent, — a pretty, ornithological design, — so that when the Reverend T. C. wanted to sit, there was ready for him a little bird's-nest, with a batch of speckled eggs.

And moreover, besides the chair-bottom — But, in short, between ourselves, there was so much *Fancy* work done at Lebanon House, that there was no time for any *real*.

CHAPTER VII.

THERE are two Newingtons, Butts, and Stoke: but the last has the advantage of a little village-green, on the north side of which stands a large brick-built, substantial mansion, in the comfortable old Elizabethan livery, maroon-color, picked out with white. It was anciently the residence of a noble family, whose crest, a deer's head, carved in stone, formerly ornamented each pillar of the front gate: but some later proprietor has removed the aristocratical emblems, and substituted two great white balls, that look like petrified Dutch cheeses, or the ghosts of the Celestial and Terrestrial Globes. The house, nevertheless, would still seem venerable enough, but that over the old panelled door, as if taking advantage of the fanlight, there sit, night and day, two very modern plaster of of Paris little boys, reading and writing with all their might. Girls, however, would be more appropriate ; for, just under the first-floor windows, a large board intimates, in tarnished gold letters, that the mansion is "Lebanon House, Establish-ment for Young Ladies. By the Misses Crane." Why it should be called Lebanon House appears a mystery, seeing that the building stands not on a mountain, but in a flat; but the truth is, that the name was bestowed in allusion to a remarkably fine Cedar, which traditionally stood in the fore court, though long since cut down as a tree, and cut up in lead pencils.

The front gate is carefully locked, the hour being later than 5 p. m., and the blinds are all down, — but if any one could peep through the short Venetians next the door, on the right hand, into the Music Parlor, he would see Miss Parfitt herself stealthily playing on the grand piano (for it is Sunday), but with no more sound than belongs to that tuneful whisper commonly called "the ghost of a whistle." But let us pull the bell.

"Sally, are the ladies at home ?"

"Lawk, sir ! — why, have n't you heard? Miss Crane and Miss Ruth are a-pleasuring on a Tower up the Rind, — and the Reverend Mr. C. is enjoying hisself in Germany along with them."

*   *   *   *   *

Alas, poor Sally! Alas for poor, short-sighted human nature!

"Why, in the name of all that 's anonymous, what is the matter?"

Lies! lies! lies! But it is impossible for Truth, the pure Truth, to exist, save with Omnipresence and Omniscience. As for mere mortals, they must daily vent falsehoods in spite of themselves. Thus, at the very moment while Sally was telling us — but let Truth herself correct the errata.

For "The Reverend Mr. C. enjoying himself in Germany —"

Read, "*Writhing with spasms in a miserable Prussian inn.*"

For, "Miss Crane and Miss Ruth a-pleasuring on a tour up the Rhine —"

Read, "*Wishing themselves home again with all their hearts and souls.*"

CHAPTER VIII.

IT was a grievous case!

After all the troubles of the Reverend T. C. by sea and land, — his perplexities with the foreign coins at Rotterdam, — with the passports at Nimeguen, — with the Douane at Arnheim, — and with the Speïse-Karte at Cologne —

To be taken ill, poor gentleman, with his old spasms, in such a place as the road between Todberg and Grabheim, six good miles at least from each, and not a decent inn at either! And in such weather, too, — unfit for anything with the semblance of humanity to be abroad, —a night in which a Christian farmer would hardly have left out his scarecrow!

The groans of the sufferer were pitiable, — but what could be done for his relief? on a blank, desolate common, without a house in sight, — no, not a hut! His afflicted daughters could only try to soothe him with words, vain words, —assuasive perhaps of mental pains, but as to any discourse arresting a physical ache, — you might as well take a pin to pin a bull with. Besides, the poor women wanted comforting themselves. Gracious heaven! Think of two single females, with a sick, perhaps an expiring parent, — shut up in a hired coach, on a stormy night, in a foreign land, — ay, in one of its dreariest places. The sympathy of a third party, even a stranger, would have been some support to them; but all they could get by their most earnest appeals to the driver was a couple of unintelligible syllables.

If they had only possessed a cordial, — a flask of *eau de vie!* Such a thing had indeed been proposed and prepared, but alas! Miss Crane had wilfully left it behind. To think of Propriety producing such a travelling accompaniment as a brandy-bottle was out of the question. You might as well have looked for claret from a pitcher-plant!

In the mean time the sick man continued to sigh and moan, — his two girls could feel him twisting about between them.

"O, my poor, dear papa!" murmured Miss Crane, for she did not "father" him even in that extremity. Then she groped again despairingly in her bag for the smelling-bottle, but only found instead of it an article she had brought along with her, heaven knows why, into Germany, — the French mark!

"O — ah — ugh! — hah!" grumbled the sufferer. "Am I — to — die — on — the road!"

"Is he to die on the road!" repeated Miss Crane through the front window to the coachman, but with the same result as before; namely, two words in the unknown tongue.

"Ruth, what is *yar vole?*"

Ruth shook her head in the dark.

"If he would only drive faster!" exclaimed Miss Crane, and again she talked through the front window. "My good man —" (*Gefalliy?*) "Ruth, what's gefallish?" But Miss Ruth was as much in the dark as ever. "Do, do, do make haste to somewhere —" (*Ja wohl!*) That phlegmatic driver would drive her crazy!

Poor Miss Crane! Poor Miss Ruth! Poor Reverend T. C.! My heart bleeds for them, — and yet they must remain perhaps for a full hour to come in that miserable condition. But no — hark! — that guttural sound which like a charm arrests every horse in Germany as soon as uttered, — "Burr-r-r-r-r!"

The coach stops; and looking out on her own side through the rain, Miss Crane perceives a low, dingy door, over which by help of a lamp she discovers a white board, with some great black fowl painted on it, and a word underneath that to her English eyes suggests a difficulty in procuring fresh eggs. Whereas the Adler, instead of addling, hatches brood after brood every year, till the number is quite wonderful, of little red and black eagles.

However, the royal bird receives the distressed travellers under its wing; but my pen, though a steel one, shrinks from the labor of scrambling and hoisting them from the Lohn Kutch into the Gast Haus. In plump, there they are, — in the best inn's best room, yet not a whit preferable to the last chamber that lodged the " great Villiers." But hark, they whisper, —

Gracious powers! Ruth!
Gracious powers! Priscilla! } What a wretched hole!

CHAPTER IX.

I TAKE it for granted that no English traveller would willingly lay up — unless particularly *inn-disposed* — at an inn. Still less at a German one; and least of all at a Prussian public-house, in a rather private Prussian village. To be far from well, and far from well lodged, — to be ill, and ill attended, — to be poorly, and poorly fed, — to be in a bad way, and a bad bed. But let us pull up, with ideal reins, an imaginary nag, at such an outlandish hostelrie, and take a peep at its " Entertainment for Man and Horse."

Bur-r-r-r-rrrr !

The nag stops as if charmed, — and as cool as a cucumber, — at least till it is peppered, — for your German is so tender of his beast that he would hardly allow his greyhound to *turn a hair* —

Now then, for a shout; and remember that in Kleinewinkel, it will serve just as well to cry " Boxkeeper!" as " Ostler!" but look, there is some one coming from the inn-door.

'T is Katchen herself — with her bare head, her bright blue gown, her scarlet apron — and a huge rye-loaf under her left arm. Her right hand grasps a knife. How plump and pleasant she looks! and how kindly she smiles at everybody, including the horse! But see — she stops, and shifts the position of the loaf. She presses it — as if to sweeten its sourness — against her soft, palpitating bosom, the very hemisphere that holds her maiden heart.   And now she begins to cut — or rather haggle — for the knife is blunt, and the bread is hard ; but she works with good-will, and still hugging the loaf closer and closer to her comely self, at last severs a liberal slice from the mass.   Nor is she content to merely give it to her client, but holds it out with her own hand to be eaten, till the last morsel is taken from among her ruddy fingers by the lips ;—— of a sweet little chubby urchin ? — no — of our big, bony, iron-gray post-horse !

Now, then, Courteous Reader, let us step into the Stube, or Traveller's Room ; and survey the fare and the accommodation prepared for us bipeds.   Look at that bare floor, — and that dreary stove, — and those smoky, dingy walls, — and for a night's lodging, yonder wooden trough, — far less desirable than a shake-down of clean straw.

Then for the victualling, pray taste that Pythagorean soup, —and that drowned beef, — and the rotten pickled-cabbage, —and those terrible hog-cartridges, — and that lump of white soap, flavored with caraways, *alias* ewe-milk cheese —

And now just sip that Essigberger, sharp and sour enough to provoke the " dura ilia Messorum " into an Iliac Passion — and the terebinthine Krug Bier !   Would you not rather dine at the cheapest ordinary at one, with all its niceties and nasties, plain cooked in a London cellar?   And for a night's rest would you not sooner seek a bed in the Bedford Nursery ? So much for the " Entertainment for Man and Horse," — a clear proof, ay, as clear as the author's own proof, with the date under his own hand —

Of what, sir ?

Why, that Dean Swift's visit to Germany — if ever he did visit Germany — must have been prior to his inditing the Fourth Voyage of Captain Lemuel Gulliver, — namely, to the Land of the Houyhnhnms and the Yahoos, where the horses were better boarded and lodged than mankind.

CHAPTER X.

To return to the afflicted trio — the horrified Miss Crane, the desolate Ruth, and the writhing Reverend T. C. — in the small, sordid, smoky, dark, dingy, dirty, musty, fusty, dusty best

room at the Adler. The most miserable "party in a parlor — "

" 'T was their own faults!" exclaims a shadowy personage, with peculiarly hard features, — and yet not harder than
they need to be, considering against how many things, and how
violently, she sets her face. But when did prejudice ever look
prepossessing? Never — since the French wore shoes *à la
Dryade!*

" 'T was their own faults," she cries, "for going abroad.
Why could n't they stay comfortably at home, at Laburnam
House ? "

" Lebanon, ma'am."

" Well, Lebanon. Or they might have gone up the Wye,
or up the Thames. I hate the Rhine. What business had
they in Prussia ? And of course they went through Holland.
I hate flats ! "

" Nevertheless, madam, I have visited each of those countries, and have found much to admire in both. For example — "

" O, pray don't ! I hate to hear you say so. I hate everybody who does n't hate everything foreign."

" Possibly, madam, you have never been abroad ? "

" O yes ! I once went over to Calais — and have hated
myself ever since. I hate the Continent ! "

" For what reason, madam ? "

" Pshaw ! I hate to give reasons. I hate the Continent —
because it 's so large."

" Then you would, perhaps, like one of the Hebrides ? "

" No — I hate the Scotch. But what has that to do with
your Schoolmistress abroad ? — I hate governesses — and her
Reverend sick father with his ridiculous spasms — I hate
Dissenters — They 're not High Church."

" Nay, my dear madam, you are getting a little unchar-
itable."

" Charity ! I hate its name. It 's a mere shield thrown
over hateful people. How are we to love those we like
properly, if we don't hate the others ? As the Corsair says,

> ' My very love to thee is hate to them.'

But I hate Byron."

" As a man, ma'am, or as an author ? "

"Both.   But I hate all authors — except Dr. Johnson."

"True — he liked 'a good hater.'"

"Well, sir, and if he did!   He was quite in the right, and I hate that Lord Chesterfield for quizzing him.   But he was only a Lord among wits.   O, how I hate the aristocracy!"

"You do, madam!"

"Yes — they have such prejudices.   And then they're so fond of going abroad.   Nothing but going to Paris, Rome, Naples, Old Jerusalem, and New York — I hate the Americans — don't you?"

"Why, really, madam, your superior discernment and nice taste may discover national bad qualities that escape less vigilant observers."

"Phoo, phoo — I hate flummery.   You know as well as I do what an American is called — and if there's one name I hate more than another, it's Jonathan.   But to go back to Germany, and those that go there.   Talk of Pilgrims of the Rhine! — I hate that Bulwer.   Yes, they set out, indeed, like Pilgrim's Progress, and see Lions and Beautiful Houses, and want Interpreters, and spy at Delectable Mountains — but there it ends; for what with queer caps and outlandish blowses — I hate smock-frocks — they come back hardly like Christians.   There's my own husband, Mr. P. — I quite hate to see him!"

"Indeed!"

"Yes — I hate to cast my eyes on him.   He has n't had his hair cut these twelve months — I hate long hair — and when he shaves he leaves two little black tails on his upper lip, and another on his chin, as if he was real ermine."

"A moustache, madam, is in fashion."

"Yes, and a beard, too, like a Rabbi — but I hate Jews. And then Mr. P. has learnt to smoke — I hate smoke — I hate tobacco — and I hate to be called a Frow — and to be spun round and round till I am sick as a dog — for I hate waltzing.   Then don't he stink the whole house with decayed cabbage for his sour crout — I hate German cookery — and will have oiled melted butter because they can't help it abroad? — and there's nothing so hateful as oiled butter. What next?   Why, he won't drink my home-made wine — at least if I don't call it Hock, or Rude-something, and give it him in a green glass.   I hate such nonsense.   As for con-

versing, whatever we begin upon, if it's Harfordshire, he's sure
to get at last to the tiptop of Herring-Brightshine — I hate such
rambling. But that's not half so hateful as his Monomanium."

"His what, madam?"

"Why his hankering so after suicide (I *do* hate Charlotte
and Werter), that one can't indulge in the least tiff but he
threatens to blow out his brains!"

"Seriously?"

"Seriously, sir. I hate joking. And then there are his
horrid noises; for since he was in Germany he fancies that
everybody must be musical — I hate such wholesale notions
— and so sings all day long, without a good note in his voice.
So much for Foreign Touring! But pray go on, sir, with the
story of your Schoolmistress Abroad. I hate suspense."

CHAPTER XI.

Now the exclamation of Miss Crane — "Gracious heavens,
Ruth, what a wretched hole!" — was not a single horse-
power too strong for the occasion. Her first glance round the
squalid room at the Adler convinced her that, whatever might
be the geographical distance on the map, she was morally two
hundred and thirty-seven thousand miles from Home. That
is to say, it was about as distant as the Earth from the Moon.
And truly had she been transferred, no matter how, to that
Planet, with its no-atmosphere, she could not have been more
out of her element. In fact, she felt for some moments as if
she must sink on the floor, — just as some delicate flower,
transplanted into a strange soil, gives way in every green fibre,
and droops to the mould in a vegetable fainting-fit, from which
only time and the watering-pot can recover it.

Her younger sister, Miss Ruth, was somewhat less disconcerted. She had by her position the greater share in the
active duties at Lebanon House : and, under ordinary circumstances, would not have been utterly at a loss what to do for
the comfort or relief of her parent. But in every direction
in which her instinct and habits would have prompted her to
look, the materials she sought for were deficient. There was no
easy-chair — no fire to wheel it to — no cushion to shake up
— no cupboard to go to — no female friend to consult — no

Miss Parfitt — no Cook — no John to send for the doctor. No English — no French — nothing but that dreadful "Gefallig" or "Ja Wohl" — and the equally incomprehensible "Gnädige Frau!"

As for the Reverend T. C., he sat twisting about on his hard wooden chair, groaning, and making ugly faces, as much from peevishness and impatience as from pain, and indeed sometimes plainly levelled his grimaces at the simple Germans, who stood round, staring at him, it must be confessed, as unceremoniously as if he had been only a great fish, gasping and wriggling on dry land.

In the mean time, his bewildered daughters held him one by the right hand, the other by the left, and earnestly watched his changing countenance, unconsciously imitating some of its most violent contortions. It did no good, of course: but what else was to be done? In fact, they were as much puzzled with their patient as a certain worthy tradesman, when a poor shattered creature on a shutter was carried into his Floorcloth Manufactory by mistake for the Hospital. The only thing that occurred to either of the females was to oppose every motion he made, — for fear it should be wrong, and accordingly whenever he attempted to lean towards the right side, they invariably bent him as much to the left.

"Der herr," said the German coachman, turning towards Miss Priscilla, with his pipe hanging from his teeth, and venting a puff of smoke that made her recoil three steps backward, — "Der herr ist sehr krank."

The last word had occurred so frequently, on the organ of the Schoolmistress, that it had acquired in her mind some important significance.

"Ruth, what is krank?"

"How should I know," retorted Ruth, with an asperity apt to accompany intense excitement and perplexity. "In English, it's a thing that helps to pull the bell. But look at papa — do help to support him — you're good for nothing."

"I am, indeed," murmured poor Miss Priscilla, with a gentle shake of her head, and a low, slow sigh of acquiescence. Alas! as she ran over the catalogue of her accomplishments, the more she remembered what she *could* do for her sick parent, the more helpless and useless she appeared. For instance, she could have embroidered him a nightcap —

> Or netted him a silk purse, —
> Or plaited him a guard-chain, —
> Or cut him out a watch-paper, —
> Or ornamented his braces with bead-work, —
> Or embroidered his waistcoat, —
> Or worked him a pair of slippers, —
> Or open-worked his pocket-handkerchief.

She could even — if such an operation would have been comforting or salutary — have rough-casted him with shell-work, —

> Or coated him with red or black seals, —
> Or incrusted him with blue alum, —
> Or stuck him all over with colored wafers, —
> Or festooned him —

But alas! alas! alas! what would it have availed her poor dear papa in the spasmodics, if she had even festooned him, from top to toe, with little rice-paper roses!

CHAPTER XII.

"Mercy on me!"

[N. B. Not on Me, the Author, but on a little, dwarfish "smooth-legged Bantam" of a woman, with a sharp nose, a shrewish mouth, and a pair of very active, black eyes, — and withal as brisk and bustling in her movements as any Partlet with ten chicks of her own, and six adopted ones from another hen.]

"Mercy on me! Why the poor gentleman would die while them lumpish foreigners and his two great, helpless daughters were looking on! As for that Miss Priscilla, — she's like a born idiot. Fancy-work him, indeed! I've no patience — as if with all her Berlin wools and patterns, she could fancy-work him into a picture of health. Why did n't she think of something comforting for his inside, instead of embellishing his out — something as would agree, in lieu of filagree, with his case? A little good hot brandy-and-water with a grate of ginger, or some nice red-wine negus with nutmeg and toast — and then get him to bed, and send off for the doctor. I'll warrant, if I'd been there, I'd have unspasmed him in no time. I'd have whipped off his shoes and stockings, and had his poor feet in hot water afore he knew where he was."

"There can be no doubt, ma'am, of the warmth of your humanity."

"Warmth! it's everything. I'd have just given him a touch of the warming-pan, and then smothered him in blankets. Stick him all over with little roses! stuff and nonsense — stick him into his grave at once! Miss Crane? Miss Goose, rather. A poor, helpless Sawney! I wonder what women come into the world for if it is n't to be good nusses. For my part, if he had been my sick father, I'd have had him on his legs again in a jiffy, — and then he might have got crusty with blue alum or whatever else he preferred."

"But, madam — "

"Such perfect apathy! Needlework and embroidery, forsooth!"

"But, madam — "

"To have a dying parent before her eyes, — and think of nothing but trimming his jacket!"

"But — "

"A pretty Schoolmistress, truly, to set such an example to the rising generation! As if she could n't have warmed him a soft flanning! or given him a few Lavender Drops, or even got down a little real Turkey or calcined Henry."

"Of course, madam, — or a little Moxon. And in regard to Conchology."

"Conk what?"

"Or as to Chronology. Could you have supplied the Patient with a few prominent dates?"

"Dates! what, those stony things — for a spasmodic stomach!"

"Are you really at home in Arrowsmith?"

"You mean Arrow-root."

"Are you an adept in Butler's Exercises?"

"What, drawing o' corks?"

"Could you critically examine him in his parts of speech — the rudiments of his native tongue?"

"To be sure I could. And if it was white and furry. there's fever."

"Are you acquainted, madam, with Lindley Murray?"

"Why no — I can't say I am. My own medical man is Mr. Prodgers."

"In short, could you prepare a mind for refined, intellectual intercourse in future life, with a strict attention to religious duties ? "

" Prepare his mind — religious duties? — Phoo, phoo ! he warn't come to that ! "

" Excuse me, I mean to ask, ma'am, whether you consider yourself competent to instruct Young Ladies in all those usual branches of knowledge and female accomplishments — "

" Me ! What me keep a 'Cademy ! Why, I've hardly had any edecation myself, but was accomplished in three quarters and a bit over. Lor' bless you, sir ! I should be as much at sea, as a finishing-off Governess, as a bear in a boat ! "

Exactly, madam. And just as helpless, useless, and powerless as you would be in a schoolroom, even so helpless, useless, and powerless was Miss Crane whenever she happened to be out of one. Yea, as utterly flabbergasted when out of her own element, as a Jelly Fish on Brighton beach !

CHAPTER XIII.

Relief at last !

It was honest Hans the hired Coachman, with a glass of something in his hand, which after a nod towards the Invalid, to signify the destination of the dose, he held out to Miss Priscilla, at the same time uttering certain gutturals, as if asking her approval of the prescription.

" Ruth — what is Snaps ? "

" Take it and smell it," replied Miss Ruth, still with some asperity, as if annoyed at the imbecility of her senior : but secretly worried by her own deficiency in the tongues. The truth is, that the native who taught French with the Parisian accent at Lebanon House, the Italian Mistress in the Prospectus, and Miss Ruth who professed English Grammar and Poetry, were all one and the same person : not to name a lady, not so distinctly put forward, who was supposed to know a little of the language which is spoken at Berlin. Hence her annoyance.

" I think," said Miss Priscilla, holding the wine-glass at a discreet distance from her nose, and rather prudishly sniffing the liquor, " it appears to me that it is some sort of foreign G."

So saying, she prepared to return the dram to the kindly

Kutscher, but her professional delicacy instinctively shrinking from too intimate contact with the hand of the strange man, she contrived to let go of the glass a second or two before he got hold of it, and the Schnapps fell, with a crash, to the ground.

The introduction of the cordial had, however, served to direct the mind of Miss Ruth to the propriety of procuring some refreshment for the sufferer. He certainly ought to have something, she said, for he was getting quite faint. What the something ought to be was a question of more difficulty, — but the scholastic memory of Miss Priscilla at last supplied a suggestion.

"What do you think, Ruth, of a little hoarhound tea?"

"Well, ask for it," replied Miss Ruth, not indeed from any faith in the efficacy of the article, but because it was as likely to be obtained for the asking for — in English — as anything else. And truly, when Miss Crane made the experiment, the Germans, one and all, man and woman, shook their heads at the remedy, but seemed unanimously to recommend a certain something else.

"Ruth — what is forstend nix?"

But Ruth was silent.

"They all appear to think very highly of it, however," continued Miss Priscilla, "and I should like to know where to find it."

"It will be in the kitchen, if anywhere," said Miss Ruth, while the invalid — whether from a fresh access of pain, or only at the tantalizing nature of the discussion — gave a low groan.

"My poor dear papa! He will sink — he will perish from exhaustion!" exclaimed the terrified Miss Priscilla; and with a desperate resolution, quite foreign to her nature, she volunteered on the forlorn hope, and snatching up a candle, made her way without thinking of the impropriety into the strange kitchen. The Housewife and her maid slowly followed the Schoolmistress, and whether from national phlegm or intense curiosity, or both together, offered neither help nor hinderance to the foreign lady, but stood by, and looked on at her operations.

And here be it noted, in order to properly estimate the difficulties which lay in her path, that the Governess had no distinct recollection of having ever been in a kitchen in the course of her life. It was a Terra Incognita — a place of which she literally knew less than of Japan. Indeed, the laws, customs, ceremonies, mysteries, and utensils of the kitchen were more strange to her than those of the Chinese. For aught she knew the Cook herself was the dresser; and a rolling-pin might have a head at one end and a sharp point at the other. The Jack, according to Natural History, was a fish. The flour-tub, as Botany suggested, might contain an Orange-tree, and the range might be that of the Barometer. As to the culinary works, in which almost every female dabbles, she had never dipped into one of them, and knew no more how to boil an egg than if she had been the Hen that laid it, or the Cock that cackled over it. Still a natural turn for the art, backed by a good bright fire, might have surmounted her rawness.

But Miss Crane was none of those natural geniuses in the art who can extemporize Flint Broth — and toss up something out of nothing at the shortest notice. It is doubtful if, with the whole Midsummer holidays before her, she could successfully have undertaken a pancake — or have got up even a hasty-pudding without a quarter's notice. For once, however, she was impelled by the painful exigency of the hour to test her ability, and finding certain ingredients to her hand, and subjecting them to the best or simplest process that occurred to her, in due time she returned, cup in hand, to the sick-room, and proffered to her poor dear papa the result of her first maiden effort in cookery.

"What is it?" asked Ruth, naturally curious, as well as anxious as to the nature of so novel an experiment.

"Pah! puh! poof — phew! chut!" spluttered the Reverend T. C., unceremoniously getting rid of the first spoonful of the mixture. It's paste — common paste!"

CHAPTER XIV.

Poor Miss Crane!

The failure of her first little culinary experiment reduced her again to despair. If there be not already a Statue of Disappointment, she would have served for its model. It

would have melted an Iron Master to have seen her with her
eyes fixed intently on the unfortunate cup of paste, as if asking herself, mentally, was it possible that what she had prepared with such pains for the refreshment of a sick parent,
was only fit for what?—Why, for the false tin stomach of a
healthy bill-sticker!

Dearly as she rated her professional accomplishments and
acquirements, I verily believe that at that cruel moment she
would have given up all her consummate skill in Fancy Work,
to have known how to make a basin of gruel! Proud as she
was of her embroidery, she would have exchanged her cunning in it for that of the plainest cook,—for oh! of what
avail her Tent Stitch, Chain Stitch, German Stitch, or Satin
Stitch, to relieve or soothe a suffering father, afflicted with
back-stitch, front-stitch, side-stitch, and cross-stitch into the
bargain?

Nay, of what use was her soldier knowledge?—for example, in History, Geography, Botany, Conchology, Geology,
and Astronomy? Of what effect was it that she knew the
scientific names for coal and slate,—or what comfort that she
could tell him how many stars there are in Cassiopeia's Chair
whilst he was twisting with agony on a hard wooden one?

"It's no use *talking!*" exclaimed Miss Ruth, *after a long
silence,* "we must have medical advice!"

But how to obtain it? To call in even an apothecary, one
must call in his own language, and the two sisters between
them did not possess German enough, High or Low, to call
for a Doctor's boy. The hint, however was not lost on the
Reverend T. C., who with a perversity not unusual, seemed
to think that he could diminish his own sufferings by inflicting
pain on those about him. Accordingly, he no sooner overheard the wish for a Doctor, than with renewed moanings and
contortions he muttered the name of a drug that he felt sure
would relieve him. But the physic was as difficult to procure
as the physician. In vain Miss Ruth turned in succession to
the Host, the Hostess, the Maid, the Waiter, and Hans the
Coachman, and to each, separately, repeated the word "Ru-
bub." The Host, the Hostess, the Maid, the Waiter, and
Hans the Coachman, only shook their heads in concert, and
uttered in chorus the old "forstend nicht."

"O, I *do* wish," exclaimed Miss Crane, with a tone and a

gesture of the keenest self-reproach,—"how I *do* wish that I had brought Buchan's Domestic Medicine abroad with me, instead of Thomson's Seasons!"

"And of what use would that have been without the medicine chest?" asked Miss Ruth; "for I don't pretend to write prescriptions in German."

"That's very true," said Miss Crane, with a long, deep sigh—whilst the sick man, from pain or wilfulness, Heaven alone knew which—gave a groan, so terrific that it startled even the phlegmatic Germans.

"My papa—my poor dear papa!" shrieked the agitated governess; and with some confused notions of a fainting-fit—for he had closed his eyes—and still conscious of a cup in her hand, though not of its contents, she chucked the paste—that twice unfortunate paste!—into the face of her beloved parent!

CHAPTER XV.

"And serve him right, too!" cries the little smart bantam-like woman, already introduced to the Courteous Reader. "An old good-for-nothing! to sham worse than he was, and play on the tender feelings of two affectionate daughters! I'd have pasted him myself if he had been fifty fathers! Not that I think a bit the better of that Miss Crane, who after all, did not do it on purpose. She's as great a gawky as ever. To think, with all her schooling, she couldn't get a doctor fetched for the old gentleman!"

"But, my dear madam, she was ignorant of the language."

"Ignorant of fiddlesticks! How do the deaf and dumb people do? If she couldn't talk to the Germans she might have made signs."

Impossible! Pray, remember that Miss Crane was a schoolmistress, and of the *ancien régime*, in whose code all face-making, posturing, and gesticulations were high crimes and misdemeanors. Many a little Miss Gubbins or Miss Wiggins she had punished with an extra task, if not with the rod itself, for nodding, winking, or talking with their fingers; and is it likely that she would personally have had recourse to signs and signals for which she had punished her pupils with such severity? Do you think that with *her* rigid notions of propriety, and *her* figure, she would ever have stooped to what she would called buffoonery?

"Why to be sure, if you have n't high-colored her picture she is starched and frumpish enough, and only fit for a place among the wax-work!"

And besides, supposing physiognomical expression as well as gesticulation to be included in sign-making, this Silent Art requires study and practice, and a peculiar talent! Pray, did you ever see Grimaldi?

"What, Joey? Did I ever see Lonnon! Did I ever go to the Wells!"

O rare Joe Grimaldi! Great as was my admiration of the genius of that inimitable clown, never, never did it rise to its true pitch till I had been cast all abroad in a foreign country without any knowledge of its language! To the richness of his fun — to his wonderful agility — to his unique singing and his grotesque dancing, I perhaps had done ample justice, — but never, till I had broken down in fifty pantomimical attempts of my own — nay, in twice fifty experiments in dumb show — did I properly appreciate his extraordinary power of making himself understood without being on speaking terms with his company. His performance was never, like mine, an Acted Riddle. A living Telegraph, he never failed in conveying his intelligence, but signalled it with such distinctness, that his meaning was visible to the dullest capacity.

"And your own attempts in the line, sir?"

Utter failures. Often and often have I gone through as many physical manœuvres as the Englishman in "Rabelais," who argued by signs; but constantly without explaining my meaning, and consequently without obtaining my object. From all which, my dear madam, I have derived this moral, that he who visits a foreign country, without knowing the language, ought to be prepared beforehand either to act like a Clown, or to look like a Fool.

CHAPTER XVI.

It was a good-natured act of honest Hans the coachman — and especially after the treatment of his Schnapps — but see-

ing the Englishers at a dead lock, and partly guessing at the
cause of their distress — he quietly went to the stable, saddled
one of his own horses, and rode off in quest of a medical man.
Luckily he soon met with the personage he wanted, whom
with great satisfaction he ushered into the little, dim, dirty
parlor at the Black Eagle, and introduced, as well as he could,
to the Foreigners in Distress.

Now the Physician who regularly visited at Lebanon
House, was, of course, one of the Old School ; and in correct-
ness of costume and professional formality was scarcely inferior
to the immaculate lady who presided over that establishment.
There was no mistaking him, like some modern practitioners,
for a merchant or a man about town.   He was as carefully
made up as a prescription — and between the customary
sables, and a Chesterfieldian courtesy, appeared as a Doctor
of the old school always used to do — like a piece of sticking-
plaster — black, polished, and healing.

Judge then of the horror and amazement of the Schoolmistress, when she saw before her a great clumsy-built M. D.
enveloped in a huge gray cloak, with a cape that fell below
his elbows, and his head covered with what she had always
understood was a jockey-cap !

" Gracious Heaven ! — why, he 's a horse-doctor ! "

" Doctor? — ja wohl," said Hans, with a score of affirmative little nods ; and then he added the professional grade of
the party, which happened to be one of a most uncouth sound
to an English ear.

" Ruth, what 's a medicine rat ! "

" Lord knows," answered Miss Ruth, " the language is as
barbarous as the people ! "

In the mean time the Medicin Rath threw off his huge cloak,
and displayed a costume equally at variance with Miss Crane's
notions of the proper uniform of his order.   No black coat,
no black smalls, no black silk stockings, — why, any undertaker in London would have looked more like a doctor !   His
coat was a bright brown frock, his waistcoat as gay and variegated as her own favorite parterre of larkspurs, and his trousers of plum color !   Of her own accord she would not have
called him in to a juvenile chicken-pock or a nettlerash — and
there he was to treat full grown spasms in an adult !

" Je suis medecin, monsieur, a votre service," said the

stranger, in French more guttural than nasal, and with a bow to the sick gentleman.

"Mais, docteur," hastily interposed Miss Ruth, "vous êtes un docteur à cheval."

This translation of "horse-doctor" being perfectly unintelligible to the German, he again addressed himself to his patient, and proceeded to feel his pulse.

"Papa is subject to spasms in his chest," explained Miss Crane.

"Pshaw — nonsense!" whined the Reverend T. C., "they 're in my stomach."

"They 're in his stomach," repeated Miss Crane, delicately laying her own hand, by way of explanation, on her sternum.

"Monsieur a mangé du diner?"

"Only a little beef," said Miss Crane, who "understood" French, but "did not speak it."

"Seulement un petit bœuf," translated Miss Ruth, who spoke French, but did not understand it.

"Oui — c'est une indigestion, sans doute," said the Doctor.

CHAPTER XVII.

Hark!—
"It 's shameful! abominable! atrocious! It 's a skit on all the schoolmistresses — a wicked libel on the whole profession!"

"But my dear Mrs. —— "

"Don't 'dear' me, sir! I consider myself personally insulted, "Manger un petty boof! As if a governess could n't speak better French than that! Why, it means eating a little bullock!"

"Precisely. *Bœuf*, singular, masculine, a bullock or ox."

"Ridiculous! And from one of the heads of a seminary! Why, sir, not to speak of myself or the teachers, I have a pupil at Prospect House, and only twelve years of age, who speaks French like a native."

"Of where, madam?"

"Of where, sir? — why of all France to be sure, and Paris in particular!"

"And with the true accent?"

" Yes, sir, with *all* the accents — sharp, grave, and circumbendibus — I should have said circumflex, but you have put me in a fluster. French! why it's the corner-stone of female education. It's universal, sir, from her ladyship down to her cook. We could neither dress ourselves nor our dinners without it! And that the Miss Cranes know French I am morally certain, for I have seen it in their Prospectus."

" No doubt of it, madam. But you are of course aware that there are two sorts — French French and English French — and which are as different in quality as the foreign cogniac and the British Brandy."

" I know nothing about ardent spirits, sir. And as to the French language, I am acquainted with only one sort, and that is what is taught at Prospect House — at three guineas a quarter."

" And do all your young ladies, ma'am, turn out such proficients in the language as the little prodigy you have just mentioned ? "

" Proficient, sir ? — they can't help it in my establishment. Let me see, — there's Chambaud on Mondays — Wanostrocht on Wednesdays — Telemaque on Fridays, and the French mark every day in the week."

" Madam, I have no doubt of the excellence of your system. Nevertheless it is quite true that the younger Miss Crane made use of the very phrase which I have quoted. And what is more, when the doctor called on his patient the next morning, he was treated with quite as bad language. For example, when he inquired after her papa —

" Il est très mauvais," replied Miss Ruth with a desponding shake of her head. " Il a avalé son médécin, — et il n'est pas mieux."

CHAPTER XVIII.

To return to the sick-chamber.

Imagine the Rev. T. C. still sitting and moaning in his uneasy chair, the disconsolate Miss Crane helplessly watching the parental grimaces, and the perplexed Miss Ruth standing in a brown study, with her eyes intently fixed on a sort of overgrown child's crib, which occupied one dark corner of the dingy apartment.

"It's very well," she muttered to herself, "for a foreign doctor to say '*laissez le coucher*,' but where is he to *coucher*?" Not surely in that little crib of a thing, which will only add the cramp in his poor legs to the spasms in his poor stomach! The Mother of Invention was however at her elbow, to suggest an expedient, and in a trice the bedding was dragged from the bedstead and spread upon the floor. During this manœuvre Miss Crane, of course, only looked on: she had never in her life made a bed, even in the regular way, and the touzling of a shake-down on the bare boards was far too Margery Dawish an operation for her precise nature to be concerned in. Moreover, her thoughts were fully occupied by a question infallibly associated with a strange bed, namely, whether it had been aired. A speculation which had already occurred to her sister, but whose more practical mind was busy in contriving how to get at the warming-pan. But in vain she asked for it by name of every German, male or female, in the room, and as vainly she sought for the utensil in the inn kitchen, and quite as vainly might she have hunted for it throughout the village, seeing that no such article had ever been met with by the oldest inhabitant. As a last resource she caught up a walking-stick, and thrusting one end under the blanket, endeavored pantomimically to imitate a chambermaid in the act of warming a bed. But alas! she "took nothing by her motion,"—the Germans only turned towards each other, and shrugging their shoulders and grinning, remarked in their own tongue, "What droll people they were, those Englishers!"

The sensitive imagination of Miss Crane had, in the interim, conjured up new and more delicate difficulties and necessities, amongst which the services of a chamberlain were not the least urgent. "Who was to put her papa to bed? Who was to undress him?" But from this perplexity she was unexpectedly delivered by that humble friend in need, honest Hans, who no sooner saw the bed free from the walking-stick, than without any bidding, and in spite of the resistance of the patient, he fairly stripped him to his shirt, and then taking him up in his arms, like a baby, deposited him, willy nilly, in the nest that had been prepared for him.

The females, during the first of these operations, retired to the kitchen,—but not without a certain order in their going.

Miss Crane went off simultaneously with the coat, — her sister with the waistcoat, and the hostess and her maid with the smallclothes and the shoes and stockings. And when, after a due and decent interval, the two governesses returned to the sick-chamber, — for both had resolved on sitting up with the invalid — lo! there lay the Reverend T. C., regularly littered down by the coachman with a truss of clean straw to eke out the bedding, — no longer writhing or moaning, — but between surprise and anger as still and silent as if his groans had been astonished away like the " hiccups ! "

You may take a horse to the water, however, but you cannot make him drink, — and even thus, the sick man, though bedded perforce, refused obstinately to go to sleep.

" Et monsieur a bien dormi ? " inquired the German doctor the next morning.

" Pas un — " began Miss Crane, but she ran aground for the next word, and was obliged to appeal to the linguist of Lebanon House.

" Ruth — what 's a wink ? "

" I don't know," replied Miss Ruth, who was absorbed in some active process. " Do it with your eye."

The idea of winking at a strange gentleman was, however, so obnoxious to all the schoolmistress's notions of propriety that she at once resigned the explanation to her sister, who accordingly informed the physician that her " pauvre père n'avoit pas dormi un morceau toute la nuit longue."

CHAPTER XIX.

" Stop, sir ! Pray change the subject. By your leave we have had quite enough of bad French."

As you please, madam, — and as the greatest change I can devise, you shall now have a little bad English. Please, then, to lend your attention to Monsieur De Bourg, — the subject of his discourse ought, indeed, to be of some interest to you, namely, the education of your own sex in your own country.

" Well, sir, and what does he say of it ? "

Listen, and you shall hear. Proceed, Monsieur.

" Sare, I shall tell you my impressions when I am come

first from Paris to London. De English Ladies, I say to myself, must be de most best educate women in de whole world. Dere is schools for dem every wheres, — in a hole and in a corner. Let me take some walks in de Fauxbourgs, and what do I see all round myself? When I look dis way I see on a white house's front a large bord wid some gilded letters, which say Seminary for Young Ladies. When I look dat way, at a big red house, I see anoder bord which say Establishment for Young Ladies by Miss Someones. And when I look up at a little house, at a little window, over a barber-shop, I read on a paper Ladies School. Den I see Prospect House, and Grove House, and de Manor House — so many I cannot call dem names, and also all schools for de young females. Day Schools besides. And in my walks, always I meet some Schools of Young Ladies, eight, nine, ten times in one day, making dere promenades, two and two and two. Den I come home to my lodging's door, and below the knocker I see one letter — I open it, and I find a Prospectus of a Lady School. By and bye I say to my landlady, where is your oldest of daughters, which used to bring to me my breakfast, and she tell me she is gone out a governess. Next she notice me I must quit my appartement. What for I say. What have I done? Do I not pay you all right like a weekly man of honour? O certainly, mounseer, she say, you are a gentleman quite, and no mistakes — but I wants my whole of my house to myself for to set it up for a Lady School. Noting but Lady Schools! — and de widow of de butcher have one more over de street. Bless my soul and my body, I say to myself, dere must be nobody born'd in London except leetle girls!"

CHAPTER XX.

THERE is a certain poor word in the English language which of late years has been exceedingly ill-used, — and it must be said, by those who ought to have known better.

To the disgrace of our colleges, the word in question was first perverted from its real significance at the very head-quarters of learning. The initiated, indeed, are aware of its local sense, — but who knows what cost and inconvenience the duplicity of the term may have caused to the more ignorant members of the community? Just imagine, for instance, a plain, downright Englishman who calls a spade a spade — induced perhaps by the facilities of the railroads — making a summer holiday, and repairing to Cambridge or Oxford, may be with his whole family, to see he does not exactly know what — whether a Collection of Pictures, Wax-Work, Wild Beasts, Wild Indians, a Fat Ox, or a Fat Child, — but at any rate an " *Exhibition!* "

More recently the members of the faculty have taken it into their heads to misuse the unfortunate word, and by help of its misapplication, are continually promising to the ear what the druggists really perform to the eye — namely to "exhibit" their medicines. If the Doctors talked of hiding them, the phrase would be more germane to the act : for it would be difficult to conceal a little Pulv. Rhei — Magnes. sulphat. — or tinct. jalapæ, more effectually than by throwing it into a man's or woman's stomach. And pity it is that the term has not amongst medical men a more literal significance ; for it is certain that in many diseases, and especially of the hypochondriac class — it is certain, I say, that if the practitioner actually made "a show" of his *materiel,* the patient would recover at the mere sight of the " Exhibition."

This was precisely the case with the Rev. T. C. Had he fallen into the hands of a Homœopathist with his infinitesimal doses, only fit to be exhibited like the infinitesimal insects through a solar microscope, his recovery would have been hopeless. But his better fortune provided otherwise. The German Medecin Rath. who prescribed for him, was in theory diametrically opposed to Hahnemann, and in his tactics he followed Napoleon, whose leading principle was to bring masses of all arms, horse, foot. and artillery, to bear on a given point. In accordance with this system, he therefore prescribed so liberally that the following articles were in a very short time comprised in his " Exhibition : " —

A series of powders, to be taken every two hours.

A set of draughts, to wash down the powders.

A box of pills.

A bag full of certain herbs for fomentations.

A large blister, to be put between the shoulders.

Twenty leeches, to be applied to the stomach.

As *Macheath* sings, "a terrible show!"—but the doctor, in common with his countrymen, entertained some rather exaggerated notions as to English habits, and our general addiction to high feeding and fast living,—an impression that materially aggravated the treatment.

"He *must* be a horse-doctor!" thought Miss Crane, as she looked over the above articles—at any rate she resolved—as if governed by the proportion of four legs to two—that her parent should only take one half of each dose that was ordered. But even these reduced quantities were too much for the Rev. T. C. The first instalment he swallowed, the second he smelt, and the third he merely looked at. To tell the truth, he was fast transforming from a Malade Imaginaire, into a Malade Malgré Lui. In short, the cure proceeded with the rapidity of a Hohenlohe miracle,—a result the doctor did not fail to attribute to the energy of his measures, at the same time resolving that the next English patient he might catch should be subjected to the same decisive treatment. Heaven keep the half, three quarters, and the whole lengths of my dear countrymen and countrywomen from his Exhibitions!

His third visit to the Englishers at the Adler was his last. He found the Convalescent in his travelling-dress,—Miss Ruth engaged in packing,—and the Schoolmistress writing the letter which was to prepare Miss Parfitt for the speedy return of the family party to Lebanon House. It was, of course, a busy time; and the Medecin Rath speedily took his fees and his leave.

There remained only the account to settle with the landlord of the Adler; and as English families rarely stopped at that wretched inn, the amount of the bill was quite as extraordinary. Never was there such a realization of the "large reckoning in a little room."

"Well, I must say," murmured the Schoolmistress, as the coach rumbled off towards home, "I do wish we had reached Gotha, that I might have got my shades of wool."

"Humph!" grunted the Rev. T. C., still sore from the recent disbursement. "They went out for wool, and they returned shorn."

"We went abroad for pleasure," grumbled Miss Ruth, "and have met with nothing but pain and trouble."

"And some instruction too," said Miss Crane, with even more than her usual gravity. "For my own part I have met with a lesson that has taught me my own unfitness for a Governess. For I cannot think that a style of education which has made me so helpless and useless as a daughter, can be the proper one for young females who are hereafter to become wives and mothers, a truth that every hour has impressed on me since I have been a Schoolmistress Abroad."

18

THE TOWER OF LAHNECK.

A ROMANCE.

AMONGST the many castled crags on the banks of the Rhine, one of the most picturesque is the ruin of Lahneck, perched on a conical rock, close to that beautiful little river the Lahn. The castle itself is a venerable fragment, with one lofty tower rising far above the rest of the building, — a characteristic feature of a feudal stronghold, — being in fact the observatory of the Robber-Baron, whence he watched, not the motions of the heavenly bodies, but the movements of such earthly ones as might afford him a booty, or threaten him with an assault. And truly, Lahneck is said to have been the residence of an order of Teutonic Knights exactly matching in number the famous band of thieves in the Arabian Tale.

However, when the sun sets in a broad blaze behind the heights of Capellen, and the fine ruin of Stolzenfels on the opposite banks of the Rhine, its last rays always linger on the lofty tower of Lahneck. Many a time, while standing rod in hand on one or other of the brown rocks which, narrowing the channel of the river, form a small rapid, very favorable to the fisherman, — many a time have I watched the rich warm light burning beacon-like on the very summit of that solitary tower, whilst all the river lay beneath in deepest shadow, save the golden circles that marked where a fish rose to the surface, or the bright corruscations made by the screaming swallow as it sportively dipped its wing in the dusky water, like a gay friend breaking in on the cloudy reveries of a moody mind. And as these natural lights faded away, the artificial ones of the village of Lahnstein began to twinkle, — the glowing windows of Duquet's hospitable pavilion, especially, throwing across the stream a series of dancing reflections that shone the brighter for the sombre shadows of a massy cluster of acacias in the tavern-garden. Then the myriads of chafers, taking to wing, filled the air with droning, — whilst the lovely fireflies with their fairy lamps began to flit across my homeward path, or hovered from osier to osier, along the calm waterside. But a truce to these personal reminiscences.

It was on a fine afternoon, towards the close of May, 1830, that two ladies began slowly to climb the winding path which leads through a wild shrubbery to the ruined Castle of Lahneck. They were unaccompanied by any person of the other sex; but such rambles are less perilous for unprotected females in that country than in our own, — and they had enjoyed several similar excursions without accident or offence. At any rate, to judge from their leisurely steps, and the cheerful tone of their voices, they apprehended no more danger than might accrue to a gauze or a ribbon from an overhanging branch or a stray bramble. The steepness of the ascent forced them occasionally to halt to take breath, but they stopped quite as frequently to gather the wild-flowers, and especially the sweet valley-lilies, there so abundant, — to look up at the time-stained ruin from a new point, or to comment on the beauties of the scenery.

The elder of the ladies spoke in English, to which her companion replied in the same language, but with a foreign accent, and occasional idioms, that belonged to another tongue. In fact, she was a native of Germany, whereas the other was one of those many thousands of British travellers whom the long peace, the steamboat, and the poetry of Byron had tempted to visit the "blue and arrowy" river. Both were young, handsome, and accomplished; but the Fraulein Von B. was unmarried; whilst Mrs. —— was a wife and a mother, and with her husband and her two children had occupied for some weeks a temporary home within the walls of Coblentz. It was in this city that a friendship had been formed between the German girl and the fair Islander, — the gentle pair who were now treading so freely and fearlessly under the walls of a castle where womanly beauty might formerly have ventured as safely as the doe near the den of the lion. But those days are happily gone by, — the dominion of brute force is over, — and the Wild Baron who doomed his victims to the treacherous abyss has dropped into an *Oubliette* as dark and as deep as his own.

At last the two ladies gained the summit of the mountain, and for some minutes stood still and silent, as if entranced by the beauty of the scene before them. There are elevations at which the mind loses breath as well as the body, — and pants too thickly with thought upon thought to find ready utterance. This was especially the case with the Englishwoman, whose cheek flushed, while her eyes glistened with tears; for the soul is touched by beauty as well as melted by kindness, and here nature was lavish of both, — at once charming, cheering, and refreshing her with a magnificent prospect, the brightest of sunshine, and the balmiest air. Her companion, in the mean time, was almost as taciturn, merely uttering the names of the places, — Ober-Lahnstein, Capellen, Stolzenfels, Nieder-Lahnstein, St. John's Church, — to which she successively pointed with her little white finger. Following its direction, the other lady slowly turned round, till her eyes rested on the castle itself, but she was too near to see the ruin to advantage, and her neck ached as she strained it to look up at the lofty tower which rose almost from her feet. Still she continued to gaze upward, till her indefinite thoughts grew into a wish that she could ascend to the top, and thence, as if suspended in air, enjoy an uninterrupted view of the whole horizon. It was with delight, therefore, that on turning an angle of the wall she discovered a low open arch which admitted her to the interior, where, after a little groping, she perceived a flight of stone steps, winding, as far as the eye could trace, up the massive walls.

The staircase, however, looked very dark, or rather dismal, after the bright sunshine she had just quitted, but the whim of the moment, the spirit of adventure and curiosity, induced her to proceed, although her companion, who was more phlegmatic, started several difficulties and doubts as to the practicability of the ascent. There were, however no obstacles to surmount beyond the gloom, some trifling heaps of rubbish, and the fatigue of mounting so many gigantic steps. But this weariness was richly repaid, whenever through an occasional loophole she caught a sample of the bright blue sky, and which like samples in general appeared of a far more intense and beautiful color than any she had ever seen in the whole piece. No, never had heaven seemed so heavenly, or earth so lovely, or water so clear and pure, as through those narrow apertures — never had she seen any views so charming as those exquisite snatches of landscape, framed by the massive masonry into little cabinet pictures, of a few inches square — so small, indeed, that the two friends, pressed cheek to cheek, could only behold them with one eye apiece! The Englishwoman knew at least a dozen of such tableaux, to be seen through particular loopholes in certain angles of the walls of Coblentz — but these "pictures of the Lahneck gallery," as she termed them, transcended them all! Nevertheless it cost her a sigh to reflect how many forlorn captives, languishing perhaps within those very walls, had been confined to such glimpses of the world without — nay, whose every prospect on this side the grave had been framed in stone. But such thoughts soon pass away from the minds of the young, the healthy, and the happy, and the next moment the fair moralist was challenging the echoes to join with her in a favorite air. Now and then indeed the song abruptly stopped, or the voice quavered on a wrong note, as a fragment of mortar rattled down to the basement, or a disturbed bat rustled from its lurking-place, or the air breathed through a crevice with a sound so like the human sigh, as to revive her melancholy fancies. But these were transient terrors, and only gave rise to peals of light-hearted merriment, that were mocked by laughing voices from each angle of the walls.

At last the toilsome ascent was safely accomplished, and the two friends stood together on the top of the tower, drawing a long, delicious breath of the fresh, free air. For a time they were both dazzled to blindness by the sudden change from gloom to sunshine, as well as dizzy from the unaccustomed height; but these effects soon wore off, and the whole splendid panorama, — variegated with mountains, valleys, rocks, castles, chapels, spires, towns, villages, vineyards, cornfields, forests, and rivers, was revealed to the delighted sense. As the Englishwoman had anticipated, her eye could now travel unimpeded round the entire horizon, which it did again and again and again, while her lips kept repeating all the superlatives of admiration.

"It is mine Faderland," murmured the German girl, with a natural tone of triumph in the beauty of her native country. "Speak — did I not well to persuade you to remain here, by little bits, and little bits, instead of a stop at Horcheim?"

"You did, indeed, my dear Amanda. Such a noble prospect would well repay a much longer walk."

"Look!—see—dere is Rhense—and de Marxberg"—but the finger was pointed in vain, for the eyes it would have guided continued to look in the opposite direction across the Lahn.

"Is it possible, from here," inquired the Englishwoman, "to see Coblentz?"

Instead of answering this question, the German girl looked up archly in the speaker's face, and then smiling and nodding her head, said slily, "Ah, you do think of a somebody at home!"

"I was thinking of him, indeed," replied the other, "and regretting that he is not at this moment by my side to enjoy—"

She stopped short—for at that instant a tremendous peal, as of the nearest thunder, shook the tower to its very foundation.   The German shrieked, and the ever-ready "Ach Gott!" burst from her quivering lips; but the Englishwoman neither stirred nor spoke, though her cheek turned of the hue of death. Some minds are much more apprehensive than others, and hers was unusually quick in its conclusions,—the thought passed from cause to consequence with the rapidity of the voltaic spark. Ere the sound had done rumbling, she knew the nature of the calamity as distinctly as if an evil spirit had whispered it in her ear. Nevertheless, an irresistible impulse, that dreadful attraction which draws us in spite of ourselves to look on what is horrible and approach to the very verge of danger, impelled her to seek the very sight she most feared to encounter. Her mind indeed recoiled, but her limbs, as by a volition superior to her own, dragged her to the brink of the abyss she had prophetically painted, where the reality presented itself with a startling resemblance to the ideal picture.

Yes, *there* yawned that dark chasm, unfathomable by the human eye, a great gulf fixed—perhaps eternally fixed—between herself and the earth, with all it contained of most dear and precious to the heart of a wife and a mother. Three—only the three uppermost steps of the gigantic staircase still remained in their place, and even these as she gazed at them suddenly plunged into the dreary void; and after an interval which indicated the frightful depth they had to plumb, reached the bottom with a crash that was followed by a roll of hollow echoes from the subterranean vaults!

As the sound ceased, the Englishwoman turned away, with a gasp and a visible shudder, from the horrid chasm. It was with the utmost difficulty that she had mastered a mechanical inclination to throw herself after the falling mass — an impulse very commonly induced by the unexpected descent of a large body from our own level. But what had she gained? Perhaps but a more lingering and horrible fate — a little more time to break her heart in — so many more wretched hours to lament for her lost treasures — her cheerful home — her married felicity — her maternal joys, and to look with unavailing yearnings towards Coblentz. But that sunny landscape had become intolerable; and she hastily closed her eyes and covered her face with her hands. Alas! she only beheld the more vividly the household images, and dear familiar faces that distractingly associated the happiness of the past with the misery of the present — for out of the very sweetness of her life came intenser bitterness, and from its brightest phases an extremer darkness, even as the smiling valley beneath her had changed into that of the Shadow of Death! The Destroyer had indeed assumed almost a visible presence, and like a poor trembling bird, conscious of the stooping falcon, the devoted victim sank down and cowered on the hard, cold, rugged roof of the fatal Tower!

The German girl, in the mean while, had thrown herself on her knees, and with her neck at full stretch over the low parapet, looked eagerly from east to west for succor, — but from the mill up the stream to the ferry down below, and along the road on either side of the river, she could not descry a living object. Yes — no — yes — there was one on the mountain itself, moving among the brushwood, and even approaching the castle; closer he came, — and closer yet, to the very base of the Tower. But his search, whatever it was, tended earthwards, for he never looked up.

"Here! — come! — gleich! — quick!" and the agitated speaker hurriedly beckoned to her companion in misfortune, — "we must make a cry both togeder, and so loud as we can," and setting the example she raised her voice to its utmost pitch; but the air was so rarefied that the sound seemed feeble even to herself.

At any rate it did not reach the figure below, — nor would a far louder alarm, for that figure was little Kranz, the deaf and dumb boy of Lahnstein, who was gathering bunches of the valley-lilies for sale to the company at the inn. Accordingly, after a desultory ramble round the ruins, he descended to the road, and slowly proceeded along the water-side towards the ferry, where he disappeared.

"Lieber Gott!" exclaimed the poor girl; "it is too far to make one hear!"

So saying, she sprang to her feet, and with her white handkerchief kept waving signals of distress, till from sheer exhaustion her arms refused their office. But not one of those pleasure-parties so frequent on fine summer days in that favorite valley had visited the spot. There was a Kirch-Weih at Neundorf, down the Rhine, and the holiday-makers had all proceeded with their characteristic uniformity in that direction.

"Dere is nobody at all," said the German, dropping her arms and head in utter despondence, — "not one to see us!"

"And if there were," added a hollow voice, " what human help could avail us at this dreadful height ? "

The truth of this reflection was awfully apparent; but who when life is at stake can resign hope, or its last, tearful contingency, though frail as a spider's thread encumbered with dew-drops ?

The German, in spite of her misgivings, resumed her watch; till after a long, weary, dreary hour, a solitary figure issued from a hut a little lower down on the opposite side of the Lahn, and stepping into a boat propelled it to the middle of the stream. It was one of the poor fishermen who rented the water, and rowing directly to the rapid, he made a cast or two with his net, immediately within the reflection of the castle. But he was too distant to hear the cry that appealed to him, and too much absorbed in the success or failure of his peculiar lottery to look aloft. Like the deaf and dumb boy, he passed on, but in the opposite direction, and gradually disappeared.

"It will never be seen!" ejaculated the German girl, again dropping her arm — a doubtful prophecy, however, for immediately afterwards the Rhenish steamboat crossed the mouth of the lesser river, and probably more than one telescope was pointed to the romantic ruin of Lahneck. But the distance was great, and even had it been less, the waving of a white handkerchief would have been taken for a merry or a friendly salute.

In the mean time the steamboat passed out of sight behind the high ground; but the long streamer of smoke was still visible, like a day-meteor, swiftly flying along, and in a direction that made the Englishwoman stretch out her arms after the fleeting vapor as if it had been a thing sensible to human supplication.

"It is gone also!" exclaimed her partner in misery. "And in a short while my liebe mutter will see it come to Coblentz!"

The Englishwoman groaned.

"It is *my* blame," continued the other, in an agony of self-reproach; "it was my blame to come so wide — not one can tell where. Nobody shall seek at Lahneck — dey will think we are dropped into de Rhine. Yes — we must die both! We must die of famishment — and de cornfields, and de vines is all round one!"

And thus hour passed after hour, still watching promises that budded and blossomed and withered — and still flowered again and again without fruition — till the shades of evening began to fall, and the prospect became in every sense darker and darker.

Barge after barge had floated down the river, but the steersman had been intent on keeping his craft in the middle of the current in the most difficult part of his navigation — the miller had passed along the road at the base of the mountain, but his thoughts were fixed on the home within his view — the female peasant drove her cows from the pasture — the truant children returned to the village, and the fisherman drifting down the stream, again landed, and after hanging his nets up to dry between the trees on the opposite meadows, re-entered his hut. But none saw the signal, none heard the cry, or if they did it was supposed to be the shrill squeak of the bat. There was even company at the inn, for the windows of Daquet's pavilion began to sparkle, but the enjoyments of the party had stopped short of the romantic and the picturesque — they were quaffing Rhein wein, and eating thick, sour cream, sweetened with sugar, and flavored with cinnamon.

"It is hard, mine friend," sobbed the German, "not one thinks but for themselves."

"It is unjust," might have retorted the wife and mother, "for *I* think of my husband and children, and *they* think of me."

Why else did her sobs so disturb the tranquil air, or wherefore did she paint her beloved Edward and her two fair-haired boys with their faces so distorted by grief? The present and the future — for time is nothing in such visions — were almost simultaneously before her, and the happy home of one moment was transfigured at the next instant into the house of mourning. The contrast was agonizing but unspeakable — one of those stupendous woes which stupefy the soul, as when the body is not pierced with a single wound, but mortally crushed. She was not merely stricken, but stunned.

"Mein Gott!" exclaimed the German girl, after a vain experiment on the passiveness of her companion, "why do you not speak something — what shall we do?"

"Nothing," answered a shuddering whisper, "except — die!"

A long pause ensued, during which the German girl more than once approached and looked down the pitch black orifice which had opened to the fallen stairs. Perhaps it looked less gloomy than by daylight in the full blaze of the sun, — perhaps she had read and adopted a melancholy, morbid tone of feeling too common to German works, when they treat of a voluntary death, or perhaps the Diabolical Prompter was himself at hand with the desperate suggestion, fatal alike to body and to soul, — but the wretched creature drew nearer and nearer to the dangerous verge.

Her purpose, however, was checked. Although the air was perfectly still, she heard a sudden rustle amongst the ivy on that side of the Tower, which, even while it made her start, had whispered a new hope in her ear. Was it possible that her signals had been observed — that her cries had been heard? And again the sound was audible, followed by a loud, harsh cry, and a large Owl, like a bird of ill omen, as it is, fluttered slowly over the heads of the devoted pair, and again it shrieked and flapped round them, as if to involve them in a magical circle, and then with a third and shriller screech sailed away like an Evil Spirit, in the direction of the Black Forest.

Nor was that boding fowl without its sinister influence on human destiny. The disappointment it caused to the victim was mortal. It was the drop that overbrimmed her cup.

"No," she muttered, "dere is no more hopes. For myself I will not starve up here, — I know my best friend, and will cast my troubles on the bosom of my mother earth."

Absorbed in her own grief the Englishwoman did not at first comprehend the import of these words; but all at once their meaning dawned on her with a dreadful significance. It was, however, too late. Her eye caught a glimpse of the skirt of a garment, her ear detected a momentary flutter, — and she was alone on that terrible tower !

*   *   *   *   *

And did she too perish? Alas ! ask the peasants and the fishermen who daily worked for their bread in that valley or on its river ; ask the ferryman who hourly passed to and fro, and the bargeman, who made the stream his thoroughfare, and they will tell you, one and all, that they heard nothing and saw nothing, for Labor looks downward and forward, and round about, but not upward. Nay, ask the angler himself, who withdrew his fly from the circling eddies of the rapids to look at the last beams of sunshine glowing on the lofty ruin, — and he answers that he never saw living creature on its summit, except once, when the crow and the raven were hovering about the building, and a screaming eagle, although it had no nest there, was perched on the Tower of Lahneck.

Note. — This story — which some hardy critic affirmed was "an old Legend of the Rhine, to be found in any Guide-book " — was suggested by the recital of two ladies, who attempted to ascend to the top of the Tower of Lahneck, but were deterred by the shaking of the stone stairs. They both consider, to this day, that they narrowly escaped a fate akin to the catastrophe of poor Amy Robsart; and have visible shudderings when they hear, or read, of old Rhenish castles and *oubliettes*.

THE SHORT PLEDGE.

"I 'LL tell you what it is," said the President of the Social Glassites, at the same time mixing a fresh tumbler of grog, — rather stiffer than the last, — for the subject of Temperance and Tea-totalism had turned up, and he could not discuss it with dry lips, — "I 'll tell you what it is: Temperance is all very well, provided it 's indulged in with moderation, and without injury to your health or business; but when it sets a man spouting, and swaggering, and flag-carrying, and tea-gardening, and dressing himself up like a play-actor, why he might as well have his mind unsobered with anything else."

"That's very true," said the Vice-President, — a gentleman with a remarkably red nose.

"I have seen many Teatotal Processions," continued the President, "and I don't hesitate to say, that every man and woman amongst them was more or less intoxicated — "

" Eh, what?" asked a member, hastily removing his cigar.

"Yes, intoxicated, I say, with pride and vanity — what with the bands of music, and the banners, and the ribbons, and maybe one of their top-sawyers, with his white wand, swaggering along at their head, and looking quite convinced that because he has n't made a Beast of himself he must be a Beauty. Instead of which, to my mind, there can't be a more pitiful sight than a great hulking fellow all covered with medals and orders, like a Lord Nelson, for only taking care of his own precious health, and trying to live long in the land; and particularly if he's got a short neck and a full habit. Why the Royal Humane Society might just as well make a procession of the people who don't drink water to excess, instead of those objects that do, and with ribbons and medals round their necks, for being their own life-preservers!"

"That's very true," said the Vice. "I've seen a Master Grand of a Teatotaller with as many ornaments about him as a foreign prince!"

"Why I once stopped my own grog," continued the President, "for twelve months together, of my own accord, because I was a little wheezy; and yet never stuck even a snip of ribbon at my buttonhole. But that's modest merit, — whereas a regular Temperance fellow would have put on a broad blue sash, as if he was a Knight of the Bath, and had drunk the bath all up instead of swimming in it."

"That's very true," repeated the Vice.

"Temperance is, no doubt, a virtue," said the President; "but is not the only one; though, to judge by some of their Tracts and Speeches, you would think that because a Totaller drinks Adam's ale he is as innocent as our first Parents in Paradise, which, begging their pardons, is altogether an error, and no mistake. Sin and strong drink are not born relations; though they often come together. The first murderer in the world was a water-drinker, and when he killed his poor brother, was as sober as a judge."

“If that arn’t true,” exclaimed the red-nosed Vice, “I ’ll be pounded ! ”

“It was intemperance, however,” said the President ; “because why? it was indulging in ardent passions and fermented feelings, agin which, in my humble opinion, we ought to take Long and Short Pledges, as much as agin spirituous liquors. Not to mention the strong things that come out of people’s mouths, and are quite as deleterious as any that go into them — for example, profane swearing, and lying, and slandering, and foul language, and which, not to name names, are dealt in by parties who would not even look at Fine Old Pineapple Rum, or Cream of the Valley.”

“That ’s correct, anyhow,” said the Vice ; and he replenished his tumbler.

“To be sure, Temperance has done wonders in Ireland,” continued the President, “and to my mind, little short of a miracle — namely, repealing the Old Union of Whiskey-and-Water, — and which would have seemed a much tougher job than O’Connell’s. However, Father Matthew has accomplished it, and instead of a Parliament in College Green we are likely to see a far stranger sight, and that ’s a whole County of Cork without a bottle to it.”

“Humph ! ” ejaculated the Vice, and took a liberal draught of his mixture. “But they ’ll take to party spirit in loo.”

“Like enough,” said the President ; “for when once we get accustomed to strong stimuluses, we find it hard to go without ’em ; and they do say, that many of those parties who have left off liquors, have taken to opium. But the greatest danger with new converts and *prostelytes,* is of their rushing into another extreme — and that reminds me of a story to the point.”

“Now then,” said the member with the cigar.

“It was last September,” said the President, “when I owned the Rose in June, and a sweet pretty craft she was. I had bought a lot of lines and a trawling net along with her ; and besides cruising for pleasure, we used now and then to cast about for a bit of fresh fish for my missus, or by way of present to a friend. Well, one day, just below Gravesend, we had fished all the morning, but without any luck at all, except one poor little skate that lay on the deck, making faces at us like a dying Christian, first pouting out its lips, and then drawing them in again with a long suck of its breath, for all the world like a fellow-creature with a stitch in the side, or a spasm in his chest. The next haul we got nothing but lots of mud, a bit of sea-weed, a lump of coal, a rotten bung, and an old shoe. However, the third time the net felt heavy enough for a porpus, and sure enough on hauling it up to the top of the water, we saw some very large fish a-flopping about in it, quite as big as a grampus, only nothing like the species. Well, we pulled and hauled, Jack and I — (you remember Jack) — till we got the creature aboard over the bulwarks, and there it rolled on the deck, such a Sea Monster as never was seen afore nor since. It was full six feet long, with a round head like a man's, but bald, — though it had a beard and whiskers of sandy-colored hair. We could not see the face, by reason of the creature always hiding it with its paws, which were like a man's hands, only with a sort of web between the fingers. All the upper part of the body was of a flesh or salmon color down to the middle, where the skin became first bluer, and then greener and greener, as well as more rough and scaly, till the body forked off into two distinct fish's tails.

"'I'll tell you what, master,' says Jack Rogers, after taking a good look at the monster, and poking it about a bit with a handspike, 'I'm blest if it is n't a Cock Mermaid!'"

"No doubt of it," said the Vice.

"To tell the truth," said the President, "I had the same thought in my head, but was afraid to name it, because such animals have been reckoned fabulous. However, there it was on the deck, as large as life, and a certain fortune to the owner, as an article for exhibition; and I won't deny that I began in my own mind a rough guess at the sum total of all the inhabitants of England, Scotland, Ireland, and Wales, at a shilling a head. Jack, too, seemed in a brown study, maybe settling what share, in right and justice, he ought to have of the profits, or perhaps wondering, and puzzled to make head or tail of the question, whether the creature was properly a beast or a fish. As for myself, I felt a little flustered, as you may suppose, not only by the strangeness of the phenomenon, but at the prospect of such a prodigious fortune. In point of fact, I was all in a tremor, like a steam-vessel with high-pressure engines, and accordingly sent Jack down below for my brandy-bottle out of the locker, just to steady my nerves.

'Here's to us both,' says I, nodding and winking at Jack, 'and to the Cock Mermaid into the bargain; for unless I'm mistaken, it'll prove a gold-fish in the end.' I was rather premature: for the noise of pulling out the cork made the creature look round, which was the first time we had caught a fair look at its face. When lo and behold! Jack no sooner clapped his eyes on the features, than he sings out again:

"'I'm blest,' says he — for I didn't allow swearing — 'I'm blest if it isn't Bob Bunce!'

"Well, the Merman gave a nod, as much as to say, 'You're right, I'm him;' and then scrambling up into a sitting posture, with his back agin the companion, made a sign to me for the bottle. So I handed him the flask, which he took a sup of through the net; but the liquor went against his fishified nature, and pulling a very wry face, he spirted it all out again, and gave me back the bottle. To my mind that settled the matter about his being a rational creature. It was *moral* impossible, though he might have an outside resemblance, like the apes and monkeys, to the human species. But I was premature again; for, after rolling about a bit, he took me all aback with an odd sort of a voice coming out of his mouth, which was as round as the hole of a flute.

"'Here,' says he, 'lend us a hand to get out of the net.'

"'It's Bob Bunce, sure enough,' cries Jack; 'that's his voice, I'll take my davit, howsomever he's got transmogrified.'

"And with that he stooped down and helped the creature, whatever it was, out of the net, and then popped him up on his two tails against the mast.

"'And now,' says he, 'if you're a Cock Mermaid, as master thinks, you may hold your tongue; but if so be you're Bob Bunce, as I suspects,' (and if Jack always used the solemn tone he did at that minute he'd make a first-rate popular preacher), 'why then don't renounce your godfathers and godmothers in your baptism, and your Christian religion, but say so at once like a man.'

"'I *ham* Bob Bunce, then,' said the creature, with a very strong emphasis, 'or rayther I *were*,' and along with the last word two great tears as big as swanshot sprang out of his pale blue eyes, and rolled down his flabby cheeks. 'Yes, I were Bob Bunce, and known by sight to every man, woman, and child in Deptford.'

"'That's true any how,' said Jack; 'cause why? You were so often a reeling drunk about the streets.'

"'There is no denying it,' said Bob, ' and plenty of contrary evidence if I did. But it warn't the strong liquors that ruined me, but quite the reverse; for you see, sir,' addressing me, 'one day after a drunken fit a she-teatotaller got hold of me while I was sick and sorry, and prevailed on me to join a temperance club, and take the long pledge, which I did.'

"'And now,' says she, ' you're nabb'd, and after that every drop of liquor you take will flare up agin you hereafter like blazes, and make a snap-dragon on you in the tother world.'

"'Well, being low and narvous, that scarified me at once into water-drinking, and I was fool enough to think, that the more water I drunk the more sober I should be ; whereby at last I reached the pint of taking above two or three gallons a-day. For all that I got no stronger or better, as the speeches and tracks had promised, but rather weaker and weaker; and instead of a fair complexion, began turning bluish and greenish, besides my body being covered, as they say, with gooseskin, and my legs of a scaly character. As for walking, I staggered worse than ever, through gettin' knockneed and splay-footed, which was the beginnin' of their transmogrification. The long and the short is, sir, though I didn't know it, that along o' so much water, I'd been drinkin' myself amphibbus.'

"'Well, that sounds like philosophy,' says Jack: 'but then, Bob, how come ye into the river?'

"'Ah!' says Bob, shaking his head, ' that's the sinful part o' the story. But between mortification, and the fear of being showed up for a mermaid, I resolved to put an end to myself, and so crawled down arter dark to Cole's wharf and flung myself into the river. But instead of drownding as I expected, the water that came into my mouth seemed to go out agin at my ears, and I found I could swim about and rise to the top or dive to the bottom as nat'ral as a fish. That gave me time to repent and reflect, and the consequence is, I've lived a wet life for above a week, and am almost reconciled to the same, only I don't take quite kindly yet to the raw dabs and flounders, and so was making my way down to the oyster-beds in the Medway, when your net come and ketch'd me up.'

19

"'But you would n't spend your days in the ocean, would you, Bob?' asked Jack, in a sort of coaxing tone that was meant to be very agreeable. 'As to hoysters, you may have 'em on dry land, real natives, and ready opened for you, and what 's more, pepper'd and vinegar'd, which you can't in the Medway. And in respect to walking, why, me and master would engage to purvide you with a carriage.'

"'A wan, you mean,' said the other, with a piercing look at Jack, and then another at me, that made me wince. 'A wan — and Bartlemy Fair — but I 'll die first!'

"And rising upright on his double tail, before we could lay hands on him, he threw a somerset over the bulwark, and disappeared."

"And was that the last of him?" said the Vice.

"It was, gentlemen," replied the President. "For Bunce, or Bounce, or Tea-totaller, or Sea-totaller, we never set eyes on him again."

"Well, that 's a warning anyhow," said the Vice, again helping himself from the bottle. "I 've heard political people talk of swamping the constitution, but never knew before that it was done with pump-water."

"Nor I neither," said the member with the cigar.

"Why you see," said the President, "Temperance is a very praiseworthy object to a proper extent; but a thing may be carried too far, as Sinbad said to the Old Man of the Sea. No doubt water-drinking is very wholesome while it 's indulged in with moderation, but when you come to take it to excess, why you may equally make a beast of yourself, like poor Bob Bunce, and be unable to *keep your legs*."

THE FATAL BATH.

IT is seldom that medical men are of accord in their theories: the differences of doctors have, indeed, passed into a proverb; but if there be any one point on which their opinions entirely harmonize, it is on the propriety of bathing with an empty stomach. The famous Doctor Krankengraber, in his most famous book, called "Immersion deeply Considered," forbids, under all kinds of corporeal pains and penalties, the use of the cold bath, after the midday meal. "Take it," he says emphatically, "as you value your life, health, and consequent peace, comfort, and happiness, by all means before, before, before dinner." It is a high authority to set up against; and yet if the pen were my professional implement instead of the sword, — could I write treatises as eloquently as the learned Esculapian, — I would cry to the ends of the earth, Bathe, as you love yourself, or love any one else, — as you love the precious meal itself, — bathe *after, after, after* dinner! Let the candid reader decide between us.

It is now nearly twenty years since I met the lovely and fascinating Christina F——, now, alas! Christina Von G——, at our Casino Ball. I had only the happiness of dancing one waltz with her — but what a waltz it was! It never left off! She had completely turned my head — not one turn from right to left, or otherwise; but she had set it spinning forever! Like the har-

HE-DIP-US, — TYRANNUS.

monious everlasting revolutions of the planets, was that dance with its music in my memory. All the rest of the night, or at least the few hours of morning slumber allowed me by my military duties, that ineffable whirl, with the same bright angel for my partner, went on in a dream.

Every one who happened, like myself, to be abroad in Coblentz, on the first of May, 1835, must recollect the remarkable whirlwind of that date, and its memorable effects. I saw it come down the Moselle, twirling round a jackdaw or two, some hides of leather, linen, and other articles caught up in its vortex; and then, passing over the Rhine towards Thal-Ehren-

breitstein, where I was then quartered, it disappeared in the
direction of Ems. But it left its mysterious influence behind.
After gazing for a moment at the place where it had vanished,
all of a sudden, striking up a popular air in a whistle, a coun-
tryman caught hold of a woman who happened to stand near
him, and compelled her, with gentle violence, to revolve with
him in the national dance. The hint took. A second pair
began to turn — a third — the infection spread — each caught
hold of a neighbor, male or female, — till in the space of a few
minutes, soldiers, officers, civilians, carmen, market-women,
ladies, maid-servants, barge-masters, peasants, old or young,
were all spinning. There was not an individual to be seen.
on either bank, or on the bridge, but was engaged in the universal waltz !

Alas ! the lovely Christina was to me as that tornado ! She
not only made me whirl myself, but everything else to whirl
round me. My thoughts flowed in circles; I could never project them in a straight line to any given point. I was a human humming-top, always humming that one dear air by Zir-
kel that I had danced to. My brain became dizzy and giddy,
the earth reeled beneath me. the sky spun round above me.
In short, I was eddying in endless circles in that Maelstrom of
Passion called Love.

The discovery of my state was no sooner made than I strove
to collect my senses, and soberly review the past, in order to
estimate my chance of eventual bliss. I recalled the affable
smile, the frank hand, the tender glance, of Christina; and especially her ready " Ja ! ja ! " to everything I said. I remembered the gracious expressions of her mother, with whom I
had also danced, even to the use of the affectionate " thou," as
though I were her son elect. I thought of the benevolent
smile of her father, as I touched glasses with him ; — and,
above all, I knew that I possessed more than that minimum
of revenue, without which officers of the Prussian army are forbidden to become Benedicts. Everything was in my favor.
Hope herself assumed the face and figure of Christina, and,
consenting to dance with me, I began spinning again worse
than ever. We waltzed now by wholesale, — Christina, myself, her mother and father, all her relations, and all mine,
in one great family circle !

In the mean time my military duties were not fulfilled in

the best manner for hastening my promotion; I became the standing joke of the standing army, at least of such part of it as garrisoned Coblentz. When the band struck up on the parade I began to revolve. I gave the word of command "Waltz!" instead of "Wheel!" On another occasion, when Captain Stumbké, at his rejoining the regiment, approached to embrace me, I seized him by the waist and actually turned him round in presence of the whole battalion! Never was such a delirium! But it was too sweet to last. One morning the telegraph on Ehrenbreitstein, with its arms all abroad, began to make signals; which my fond fancy merely converted into an invitation to the other telegraph on the top of the Palace, to come and waltz with it: there was, however, a darker purport in its motions. Our battalion was ordered to Posen!

I had danced into delight, and was now doomed to march out of it. On consideration, I determined to break my mind to Christina before I went; but no opportunity offered, and with my heart broken instead of my mind, I turned my back to Coblentz and the treasure it contained. My waltzing was over. One good turn deserves another, but, in doubt whether that good turn would ever come, I went on, without a single spin, to our journey's end.

I found the Polish city the same that I had left it; but every trace of gayety was gone. I still went, it is true, to balls where waltzes, gallopes, and mazurkas were danced; but I went in boots up to my knees. I had made a vow never to waltz again; and was keeping it better than vows are generally observed, when an event occurred that set me spinning again as fast as ever! — It was Christina herself, who entered the ball-room in the train of Princess L*****! I could have eaten my long boots without sauce! At any rate I wished them successively on the legs of every ugly villain that danced with her. To go the whole length of a confession, I almost wished her a mild sprained ankle herself! It went against me to look on: and as fast as the giddy pair whirled one way, as swiftly in mere contrariness I seemed to spin with a reverse motion. Formerly I was a happy humming-top;—I was now a whipping-top, lashed by the unsparing hand of jealousy till I reeled again! Possibly I should have ended, like certain rotary fireworks, with an explosion,—at all events I should have flown off to my quarters, when a few

gracious words from the Princess converted the centrifugal into a centripetal impulse. It was an invitation to a dinner and
ball on the succeeding Sunday, at which my former partner
would be present. Christina herself condescended to express
pleasure in the prospect of meeting me there; and when I
ventured to solicit her promise, engaged herself to dance with
me, as I fancied, with slight blush. Gracious heavens! how
I spun! — or else I had become conscious of the earth's revo-
lution! I whirled home without feeling my long boots, or
the legs that were in them. — I was a spirit, — something
ethereal — a zephyr waltzing with a zephyr, in a gentle
whirlwind, that carried us up, spirally, even into the seventh
heaven! Again Christina and Hope were one and the same
person. I went to bed, and dreamt that having offered in a
waltz, and been accepted in a waltz, we waltzed off to the altar
together.

Never were six such long days invented as ushered in the
blessed Sunday. However, they were so tedious that they
wore themselves out at last; and exactly as the clock struck
three, — lovers are never late, — I found myself at the Chateau,
or rather in its Park, in which, having come too early, I
preferred to amuse myself till the company arrived. I should
have been in time if my horse had walked; but he had gal-
loped: — I seemed destined to prove in my own person that
in much haste there is little speed.

The weather was warm, and I was still warmer; my face,
as I looked at it in a secluded lake to which I had sauntered,
was as hot and flushed as if I had just waltzed with a bear.
I looked at my watch, and then at the water, blue as the sky
itself, and studded with snow-white lilies; — the very reeds
bowed invitingly, and seemed to whisper, " Pray, walk in ! "
It was irresistible. In a trice, I was stripped, and luxuriating
in the cool element. After lingering a little at the brim to
enjoy an air-bath, I struck out towards the middle, now diving
like a wild duck, and then springing like a trout, or sailing
away after a prize lily. 'T was delicious! — Lovely nameless
Naiad! — thanks for that refreshing embrace! Thanks for
the present of those white porcelain lily-cups! Thanks for
the vocal melody of thy reeds! A thousand thanks for that
liquid, azure heaven! — but oh! — a thousand thousand, bil-
lions, trillions, quadrillions, quintillions, decillions of thanks

backwards — yea, hot, fervent, earnest, and bitter maledictions for all the rest!

"The Leech was sent, but not in mercy there!"

A BARE POSSIBILITY.

The first step I made out of the water disclosed my fate! Sharp as is the bite of the blut-egel, on land, when we are, perhaps, nervously expecting it, I had never noticed it in swimming; partly from a certain chilly numbness, partly from the constant muscular exertion, and partly from the frequent pricking of the broken reeds. A glance sufficed. There they were, a set of cuppers on each calf! As yet I could scarcely have lost a thimbleful of the vital fluid; but I felt as faint, as sick, and as ready to fall full length on the ground, as if I had lost quarts of it.

The first dinner-bell sounded. It was no time to be nice, and I tore off one or two of the bloodsuckers by force; but the flow of gore that followed proved to me that I had better have left them alone. Then I tried to shake them off by dancing, and had they been each a tarantula, they could not have bitten me into more frantic capering. But they held on like sailors in a storm. I looked at my legs and raved! I thought of Christina and groaned! In the folly of desperation I gnashed my teeth at the leeches, and shook my fist at them, and

A FINISHED DRAWING.

then, trying my very useless powers of persuasion, I apostrophized them, "Suck, suck, suck, ye vipers! — suck! suck! suck! suck!" But the vipers were in no such hurry as mine; — they pumped on quite composedly, and seemed only intent on filling out every wrinkle of their skins, in order that I might admire the detestably beautiful pattern down their abominable backs! I all but blasphemed! I cursed the weather, the water, the lilies, the leeches, — and then my own self for going in, — and still more for coming out. I never thought of the cramp, or I should have cursed it too for not seizing me in the middle of the lake!

The second bell sounded — like a death-bell: — and there was

I, as effectually pinioned and fastened to the spot by a few paltry vermin, as Gulliver by the Lilliputians. Methought I beheld my empty chair on one side of Christina, and on the other, a hatefully well-made fellow, with an odious handsome face, and a disgustingly sweet voice and manner, endeavoring to make amends for my absence. I stormed, raved, tore my hair, and even wept for vexation. In the paroxysm of my despair, I prayed for wooden legs!

Hitherto the sounds from the Chateau had nothing personal in their character; but now they pointedly addressed themselves to me. First I heard the clang of a gong; then the flourish of a hunting-horn; next the recall upon the bugle; and, finally, a general shout, in which my distempered fancy seemed to detect the clear, sweet voice of Christina above all the rest! I wonder, with water so handy, I did not commit suicide. But a sort of resignation, very different from the

"I WISH I COULD SELL OUT!"

marble Resignation which typified Count Pfefferheim leaning over his departed lady, had taken possession of me. It was grim and gloomy — I had resolved to try patience, a catholicon plaster, efficacious in every possible case, with the sole drawback, that nobody can get it to stick on. For my own part, I soon gave up the remedy. I happened to remember the trouble I endured, when I really wanted leeches, to make

them bite, and I could emulate Job no longer. I wished —
in such ecstasies we do not look before we leap in wishing —
that I had been affected with Hydrophobia, ere that fatal bath
— that I had been turned into a serpent at Schlangenbad, or
boiled to rags in the Kockbrunnen at Wiesbaden.

At last the clangor ceased ; but in lieu of it, I heard the servants running about and beating the wood for me, and calling
me by name. If I had been wise I should have answered ; —
but I was now worked up to the frenzy fit of nervousness ; I
felt my situation, except in my own eyes, sufficiently ludicrous ;
— and I dreaded lest some mischievous wag, or perhaps rival,
should delight to exhibit me in a ridiculous light to Christina.
In truth, I should have been, if discovered, a laughable figure
enough. To save time eventually, I had dressed myself so far
as I could — conceive, then, a gentleman, in full uniform above,
even to his cocked hat, but below, perfectly bare legged, with
three leeches hanging to one limb, and four to the other! I
should think no criminal ever felt more anxious of conceal-
ment than I did as I took refuge amongst the tallest reeds !

To pass the time, I had no better amusement than to watch
the leeches, how they swelled and filled, and, finally, rolled off,
gorged with my precious blood, a pailful of which I would
rather have shed for my country at any convenient time and
place ! And Christina — what could she think of my absence?
Why, she could only look upon me, as I looked on my leeches,
with aversion and disgust, — whilst her infernal neighbor, the
Colonel, in the splendid uniform of the Royal Guard, for such
I painted him, became every moment more agreeable. Of the
next five minutes I have no mental record ; my impression is,
that I was stark, staring, raving, rampant mad !

At length the last of my tormentors fell off, — and when
he touched the ground, as I had served all his fellows, I weaned
him with a stone from ever sucking again. It was a poor
revenge, for, after death, they bequeathed to me a new misery.
The blood would not cease flowing, even though I plucked all
the nap off one side of my hat to apply to the wounds. I
forgot how it would look afterwards stripped of its felt. I
was famished besides — but my cruellest hunger was in my
heart. O Christina ! It seemed an age, ere at last I dared
to creep gingerly into my white Kerseymeres ! My watch
marked it to have been but three hours !

I returned to the Chateau at the pace of a hearse; fearing

to put one foot before the other, and looking sharply every
other step at my legs.   As for the anticipated celestial
waltz — I seemed doomed to make one of that dreary corps of
long-visaged gentlemen who prefer to look on.   I arrived, however, stainless, spotless, — only I was obliged to keep one side
of my hat to myself.   An attempt was made to rally me on
my absence ; but my excuse of having lost myself in the forest passed off very currently ; and a tray was ordered for my
refreshment.   But I was unable to eat a morsel ; I could only
fill a glass of wine to pledge Christina, who had not shown any
sign of resentment ; on the contrary, she appeared to commis-
erate my wanderings in the wild woods.   In the mean time
the ball began.   As I entered the room, in a blaze of light, I
fancied that every eye was directed towards my legs : my head
swam, and for a minute I seemed waltzing with the whole assembly at once !   Christina looked twice reproachfully towards
me, ere with the air of a matrimonial martyr saluting his destined bride, I went up and claimed her hand.   The music
struck up ; we began to waltz, at least *she* did. turning me
round with her, as though she had been practising the dance
for the first time, with a lay-figure.   Stiffly and coldly as I
moved, methought I felt the circulation in every vein and ar-
tery becoming more and more rapid from even such gentle
exercise.   At last the whirl ceased, and we sat down again
side by side.   How I wished for the despised long boots up to
the knees, in which I might have chatted at my ease !   It was
impossible.   I never opened my lips except to say yes and no,
in the wrong place ; sometimes where I should have answered
I was mute.   One little stain of the slightest possible tinge of
crimson, which on eye but my own would have detected, absorbed my whole soul.   I was suffering the unspeakable tor-
tures of the murderer, conscious that his secret blood-guiltiness
was on the eve of coming to light !

The gentle Christina, after the first waltz, in consideration,
perhaps, of my supposed long ramble in the forest, had expressed
her intention of not dancing any more during the evening : a
little stir now made me look, and — the fiends seize him ! — a
tall, handsome Colonel, in the splendid dress uniform of the
Royal Guard, exactly such a figure as my jealous fancy had
formerly depicted, was leading her out to dance !   The music
played a waltz.   They turned, they spun, they flew round, in
each other's arms — giving me a turn also till my very soul

became sick and dizzy! My eyes grew dim,—I could no longer see—but I heard her frequent "ja! ja! ja!" and her light laugh!

I wish Doctor Krankengraber could have seen the plight I was in at that moment, merely through bathing, according to his detestable rule. O, that he could have felt my burning temples, my throbbing pulse, my palpitating heart! Had that floor before me been a pond, I verily believe I should have practically illustrated his "Immersion deeply Considered" with my pockets full of stones. I once or twice endeavored to catch the eye of Christina, but in vain. I addressed her, and she looked as coldly on me as one of our kachel-ofens* on a born Englishman!

I would fain have sought an explanation; but this haughty treatment sealed my lips. I no longer attributed her estrangement to any other cause than the imputed fickleness of the sex. Muttering something to the Princess about indisposition I left her ball, without blessing it, and flew home. Three days later I was again at her Chateau, determined to decide my fate. Christina had quitted Posen! In two short months afterwards the Berlin Gazette informed me that she was married to a Colonel of the Royal Guard.

I never beheld her again: but a she-cousin of mine, who was her bosom friend and confidant, in after years, thought proper, amongst other matters of feminine curiosity, to inquire on what grounds her unfortunate kinsman had been repelled. The answer she did me the favor to extract, and kindly sent it to me, by way of a correction, and a guide, probably, should I ever dream of addressing a lady again. The reader is welcome to partake of the document: it runs thus:—

"You ask me, dearest Bettine, why I did not like your cousin Albrecht? Under the seal of our sisterly confidence, I will frankly confess to you that it was through no fault of mine. I will even own to something like a preference, up to that memorable evening at the Princess L.'s. I had there determined to watch him narrowly, to observe every light and shade of his character—and you know the result. Did you ever hear of the young Count Schönborn; and the egregious personal vanity which brought him to his fate? Suspected of correspondence with the revolted Poles, he disappeared, and, according to the custom with deserters, a vilely daubed effigy,

* A German stove, cased with white tiles.

with his name at full length under it, was suspended on the public gallows.   He was still skulking in disguise at Berlin, and might doubtless have effected his escape — but shocked at the libellous picture that professed to represent him, he was actually arrested one morning, at the first dawn of light, brush and palate in hand, painting up the odious portrait to something more resembling the personal attractions of the original!   And now for our Albrecht.   Conceive him sitting languishingly — a Narcissus without his pond — seeing nothing, admiring nothing, but his own certainly well-turned legs! Fancy him stretching them, crossing them, ogling them in all possible attitudes, — taking back and front views of them, and along the outer or inner side.   Imagine him coquetting with them, carelessly dropping a handkerchief over them, as if to veil their beauties; sliding his enamored hand down them by turns, — and then, with great reluctance brought to dance on them, if dancing it might be called, so languidly, as if he feared to wear out the dear delicate limbs by the exertion.   Suppose him afterwards, relapsing into his former self-contemplation, so exclusively, as to neglect the common politeness of an answer even to a question from a lady — and a lady to whom he professed to show particular attention.   And now, dearest and best Bettine, you have my secret.   It is very well to marry a man with handsome legs, but one would not choose to have them always running in his head."

PALEY'S PHILOSOPHY.

THE CHARACTER.

" I would give ten thousand pounds for a character."
                                    COLONEL CHARTRES.

" IF you please, Ma'am," said Betty, wiping her steaming arms on her apron as she entered the room, — " if you please, Ma'am, here 's the lady for the character."

Mrs. Dowdum immediately jumped up from her chair, and with a little run, no faster than a walk, proceeded from the window to the fireplace, and consulted an old-fashioned watch which stood on the mantel-shelf.

" Bless me ! it *is* twelve o'clock, sure enough ! "

Now, considering that the visit was by appointment, and had been expected for the last hour, it will be thought remarkable that Mrs. Dowdum should be so apparently unprepared ; but persons who move in the higher circles within the vortex of what is called a perpetual round of pleasure, where visits, welcome or unwelcome, circulate with proportionate rapidity, can hardly estimate the importance of an interview in those lower spheres which, comparatively, scarcely revolve at all.   Thus for the last hour Mrs. Dowdum had been looking for the promised call, and listening with all her might for the sound of the knocker ; and yet when it did come, she was as much flurried as people commonly are by what is denominated a drop in.   Accordingly, after consulting the watch, she found it necessary to refer to the looking-glass which hung above it, and to make an extempore toilet.   First, she laid hold of her cap with both hands, and gave it — her flaxen wig following the impulse — what sailors term a half turn to the right, after which she repeated the same manœuvre towards the left ; and then, as if by this operation she had discovered the *juste milieu*, she left matters as they were.   Her shawl was next treated in the same fashion, first being lapped over one way, and then lapped over the other, and carefully pinned. Finally she gathered up a handful of the front of her gown below the waist, and gave it a smart tug downwards; and then having stroked it with both hands to make it "sit flat," if possible, instead of round, the costume was considered as quite correct. The truth is, the giving a character is an important business to all parties concerned: to the subject, who is about to be blazoned or branded as good for everything or good for nothing — to the inquirer, who is on the eve of adopting a Pamela or a Jezabel — and last, not least, to the referee herself, who must show that she has a character to preserve, as well as one to give away. There are certain standard questions always asked on such occasions, against one of which, " Is she clean and neat in her habits?" Mrs. Dowdum had already provided. " Is she sober?" and Mrs. Dowdum thrust a bottle of catsup, but which might have been taken for ratifia, into the corner cupboard. " Is she honest?" and Mrs. Dowdum poked the Newgate Calendar she had been reading under the sofa-bolster. An extra query will occasionally be put — " Is she decidedly pious?" and Mrs. Dowdum took up " Pilgrim's Progress." Lastly, two chairs were placed near the window, as chairs always are placed, when the respective sitters are to give and take a character. The reader will perhaps smile here; but in reality there is a great deal of expression about those rosewood or mahogany conveniences. A close observer who enters a parlor or drawing-room, and finds a parcel of empty seats away from the wall, can judge pretty shrewdly, from the area of the circle and other circumstances, of the nature of the foregone visit. Should the ring be large, and the seats far apart, the visit has been formal. A closer circuit implies familiarity. Two chairs side by side in front of the fender are strictly confidential — one on each side of the rug hints a *tête-à-tête* matrimonial. A chair which presents an angle to its companions has been occupied by a young lady from boarding-school, who always sits at one corner. Two chairs placed back to back need not speak — they are not upon speaking terms; and a chair thrown down, especially if broken, is equally significant. A creditor's seat is invariably beside the door; and should you meet with a chair which is neither near the fire, nor near the table, nor near any wooden companion, be sure that it has been the resting-place of a **poor** relation. In the present case, Mrs. Dowdum's two chairs were placed square, and dead opposite to each other, as if the parties who were to occupy them were expected to look straight into each other's faces. It might be called the categorical position.

"Now then, Betty, I am ready; show the lady up."

The lady was accordingly ushered up by Betty, who then retired, closing the door behind her, as slowly as servants always do, when they are shutting the curiosity without and the news within. After the usual compliments, the lady then opened the business, and the parties fell into dialogue.

"I am informed, Madam, by Ann Gale, that she lived with you three years?"

"Certainly, Ma'am — last Martinmas; which made it a month over, all but two days."

"She is sober, of course?"

"As a judge, Ma'am — would n't touch a drop of spirits for the world. Many's the good glass of g— I have offered her of a washer-day, for we washes at home, Ma'am; but she always declined."

"And she is steady otherwise — for instance, as to followers?"

"Followers, Ma'am! nothing in the shape, Ma'am; it would not be allowed *here;*" and Mrs. Dowdum drew herself up till her gown wanted smoothing down again.

"And her temper?"

"Remarkable mild, Ma'am. Can't be a sweeter. I've tried on purpose to try it, and could n't put her out."

"I beg pardon, Madam, for asking such a question in such a house; but she is clean in her habits of course?"

"Of course, as you say, Ma'am; else she would n't have stayed so long here;" and Mrs. Dowdum looked round her tidy apartments with great complacency.

"So far so good," said the lady, fixing her large, dark eyes intently on the little gray ones opposite. "And now, Madam, let me ask you the most important question of all. Is — SHE —HONEST?"

"As the day, Ma'am — you might trust her with untold goold!"

"Excuse me, Madam, but have you ever trusted her with it yourself?"

"Lord, Ma'am, scores and scores of times! She used to pay my bills, and always brought me the receipts as regular as clockwork."

A PART IS GREATER THAN THE HOLE.

"I am afraid, Madam, that circumstance is hardly decisive. Could she be trusted, do you think, in a house where there is a great deal of property — the mistress a little careless perhaps — and gold and bank-notes and loose change often lying about — to say nothing of the plate, and my own jewels?"

"All I can say is, Ma'am, I never missed anything — never! And not for want of opportunity — there's that watch, Ma'am, over the fireplace, it's a gold one and a repeater, Ma'am; she might have took it over and over, and me no wiser, for I'm apt to be absent. Then as for plate there's always my best silver teapot in that corner cupboard —"

“That may be all very true, Madam, and yet not very satisfactory. It’s the principle, Madam, it’s the principle. Have you never found her making free with trifles — tea, for instance, or your needles and pins?”

“Why, Ma’am, I can’t say exactly, not having watched such trifles on purpose — but certainly I have not lost more that way than by servants in general.”

“Ah, there it is!” exclaimed the lady, casting up her hands and eyes. “Nobody thinks of crime in its infancy — as if it would not grow up like everything else! We begin with pins and needles, and get on to brooches and rings. You will excuse, Madam, my being so particular, but nobody has suffered so much by dishonesty. I have been stripped three times.”

“You don’t say so!” exclaimed Mrs. Dowdum, with a motion of her chair towards the other, which telegraphically hinted a wish to know all the particulars.

“It is too true, indeed,” said the lady, with a profound sigh, “and always by means of servants. The first time all my plate went — 2,000 ounces, Madam, with the family crest, a boar’s-head, — Madam. Then they cleared off all the family linen, a beautiful stock, Madam, just renewed; and the third time I lost all my ornaments, pearls, Madam, emeralds — topazes — and diamonds, Madam, the diamonds I went to Court in.”

“It must have broke your heart, Ma’am,” observed Mrs. Dowdum, finishing with a prolonged and peculiar clucking with her tongue against the roof of her mouth.

“It nearly did, Madam,” said the lady, pulling out her handkerchief. “Not for my losses, however, although they were sufficiently considerable — but for the degradation of human nature. A girl too, that I had brought up under my own eye, and had impressed, as I thought, with the strictest principles of honesty. Morning, noon, and night, I impressed upon her the same lesson, — whatever you do, I used to say, be honest. It’s the fourth of the cardinal virtues — faith, hope, charity, honesty.”

“And the best policy besides,” said Mrs. Dowdum.

“The best policy, Madam! — the only policy, here or hereafter! It’s one of the first principles of our nature, Madam. The very savages acknowledge it, and recognize the

grand distinction of *meum* and *tuum*.   As Doctor Watts finely
says, —

> ' Why should I deprive my neighbor
> Of his goods against his will?
> Hands were made for honest labor,
> Not to plunder or to steal.' ''

"Yes, that's a truism indeed," said Mrs. Dowdum.   "And
pray what might become of the wicked hussy after all?"

"Ah! there's my trouble, Madam," said the lady, clasping
her hands together.   "With my own will she should have
lived a prey to her own reflections — but my husband would
not hear of it.   He could forgive anything, he said, but dishonesty.   So the Bow-Street runners were sent for, — the
unhappy girl was tried — I had to appear against her, and
she—she—she—oh, oh!" — and the lady, covering her face
with her hands, fell back in her chair.

"Be composed, Ma'am, — pray do — pray do — do, do, do,"
ejaculated the agitated Mrs. Dowdum.   "You must take a
sniff of something — or a glass of wine —"

"No — nothing — not for the world," sobbed the fainting
lady — "only water — a little water!"

The good-natured Mrs. Dowdum instantly jumped from her
chair, and ran down-stairs for a tumbler of the fluid — she
then rushed up-stairs for her own smelling-bottle; and then
she returned to the drawing-room, where she found her visitor, who eagerly took a long draught of the restorative.

"I am better — indeed I am — only a little faintness," —
murmured the reviving patient.   "But it is an awful thing —
a very awful thing, Madam, to conduce even indirectly to the
execution of a human being — for the poor creature was
hung."

"Ay, I guessed as much," said Mrs. Dowdum, with a
fresh clucking, and a grave shake of the head.   "Well, that's
just my own feeling to a T.   I don't think I could feel delighted at hanging any one, no, not even if they was to steal
the house over my head!"

"I honor you for your humanity, Madam," said the lady,
warmly pressing Mrs. Dowdum's little fat hand between both
her own.   "I hope you will never find occasion to revoke such
sentiments.   In the mean time I am extremely obliged — extremely.   Ann may come when she likes — and I have the
honor to wish you a very, very, good-morning."

"And I'm sure, Ma'am, I wish you the same," replied Mrs. Dowdum, endeavoring to imitate the profound courtesy with which she was favored, "and I hope and trust you will find poor Ann turn out everything that can be wished. I *do* think you may repose confidently on her honesty, I do indeed, Ma'am."

"We shall see, Madam, we shall see," repeated the Lady as she went down the stairs, whence she was ushered by Betty, who received a piece of money during the passage, to the street-door.

"What a nice woman!" soliloquized Mrs. Dowdum, as she watched her visitor across the street and round the corner. "What a *very* nice woman! Quite a lady too — and how she *have* suffered! I don't wonder she is so suspicious — but then she is so forgiving along with it! It was quite beautiful to hear her talk about honesty — Faith, Hope, and Honesty, —

> 'Why should I deprive my neighbor
> Of his goods against his will?' —

Why indeed! I could have listened to her — but — Mercy on us! Where *is* the goold watch as was on the mantel! — and — O Lord! where *is* the silver teapot I can't see in the cupboard? Thieves! Thieves! Thieves!"

*　　*　　*　　*　　*

"And to think," said Mrs. Dowdum, at her twentieth repetition of the story, — "to think that I've lost the family goold watch and my silver teapot, by letting of her in!"

"And to think," said Betty to herself, putting her hand in her pocket, — "to think that I only got a bad shilling for letting of her out!"

THE NEW LODGER.

POOR Miss Hopkinson! She had been ill for a fortnight, of a disorder which especially affected the nerves ; and quiet, as Dr. Boreham declared, was indispensably necessary for her recovery. So the servants wore list shoes, and the knocker was tied up, and the street in front of number four was covered with straw.

In the mean while, the invalid derived great comfort from the unremitting attentions of her friends and acquaintance ; but she was particularly gratified by the constant kind inquiries of Mr. Tweedy, the new lodger, who occupied the apartments immediately over her head.

"If you please, ma'am," said Mary, for the hundredth time. "it's Mr. Tweedy's compliments, and begs to know if you feel any better?"

"I am infinitely obliged to Mr. Tweedy, I 'm sure," whispered the sufferer, — "I am a leetle easier — with my best thanks and compliments."

Now, Miss Hopkinson was a spinster lady of a certain age, and she was not a little flattered by the uncommon interest the gentleman above stairs seemed to take in her state of health. She could not help recollecting that the new lodger and a very smart new cap had entered the house on the same day. She had fortunately worn the novel article on her accidental encounter with the stranger ; and, as she used to say, a great deal depended on first impressions.

"What a very nice gentleman!" remarked the nurse, as Mary closed the bed-room door.

"What an uncommon nice man !" cried Miss Filby, an old familiar gossip, who had come to cheer up the invalid with all the scandal of the neighborhood.

"And he will send, ma'am," said the nurse to the visitor, "to ask after us a matter of five or six times in a day."

"It is really extraordinary," said Miss Filby, "and especially in quite a stranger!"

"No, not quite," whispered the invalid. "I met him twice upon the stairs."

"Indeed!" said Miss Filby. "It 's like a little romance. Who knows what may come of it? I have known as sudden things come to pass before now !"

"There *is* summut in it sure*ly*," said the nurse; "I only wish, ma'am, you could hear how warm and pressing he is in asking after her, whoever comes in his way. There was this morning, on the landing —'Nurse,' says he, quite earnest-like, —'nurse, *do* tell me how she is.' 'Why then, sir," says I, 'she is as well as can be expected.' 'Ah !' said he, 'that 's, the old answer, but it won't satisfy *me*. Is she better or worse ?' 'Well then, sir,' says I, 'she 's much the same.' 'Ah,' says he, fetching sich a long-winded sigh, 'there 's where it is. She may linger in that way for months.' 'Let 's hope not,' says I. 'You 'll be pleased to hear as how she 's going to try to eat a bit o' chicking.' 'Chicking !' says he. saving your presence, ma'am, —'chicking be d——d to you know where — it's her nerves, nurse, her nerves, how are her nerves?' 'To be sure, sir,' says I, 'them's her weak pints, but Dr. Boreham do say, provided they're kept quiet, and not played upon, they'll come round agin in time.' 'Yes,' says he, 'in time, that's the divil on it; and you can't think how feeling he said it. — ' What a weary time,' says he, ' she have been!'"

"Well, upon my word!" exclaimed Miss Filby, "these are very like love symptoms indeed!   However, I'm not jealous, my dear," — and she shook her head waggishly at the invalid, who replied, with a faint smile, that she was a giddy creature, and quite forgot the weak state of her nerves. " But, to be sure, it is odd," said Miss Hopkinson to herself, and particularly in the present age, when polite gallantry to females is so much gone out of fashion." She then fell into a reverie, which her friend interpreted into an inclination to doze, and accordingly took her leave, with a promise of returning in the evening.

No sooner was her back turned, however, than the invalid called the nurse to her, and after giving sundry directions as to costume, intimated that she had an intention of trying to sit up a bit. So she was dressed and washed and bolstered up in a chair, and having put on a clean cap, she inquired of her attendant, rather anxiously, if she was not dreadfully altered and pulled down, and how she looked. To which the nurse answered, that " except looking a little delicate, she was really charming."

In the evening the doctor repeated his visit, and so did Miss Filby, who could not help rallying the invalid on the sudden recovery of her complexion.

"It's only hectic," said Miss Hopkinson, " the exertion of dressing has given me a color."

" And somebody else will have a color too," said the nurse, winking at Miss Filby, " when I tell him how very much some folks are improved."

"By the by," said Dr. Boreham, " it's only fair that people should know their well-wishers; and I ought to tell you, therefore, that the gentleman overhead is very friendly and frequent in his inquiries. We generally meet on the stairs, and I assure you he expresses very great solicitude — very much so indeed!"

Miss Hopkinson gave a short husky cough, and the nurse
and Miss Filby nodded significantly at each other.

"Ho! ho! the wind sits in that quarter, does it?" said the
doctor. "I may expect, then, to have another patient. 'He
grew sick as she grew well,' as the old song says," and chuck-
ling at the aptness of his own quotation, the facetious medi-
ciner took his leave.

CORNI OBLIGATO.

"There he is again, I declare," exclaimed the nurse, who
had listened as she closed the door. "He has cotched the
doctor on the stairs, and I'll warrant he'll have the whole
particulars before he lets him go."

"Very devoted, indeed!" said Miss Filby. "We must
make haste, and get you about again, my dear, for his poor
sake as well as your own."

At this juncture Mrs. Huckins, the landlady, entered the

room to ask after her lodger, and was not a little bewildered by a cross-fire of inuendoes from the nurse and the visitor. The strange behavior of the sick lady herself helped besides to disconcert the worthy woman, across whose mind a suspicion glanced that the nasty laudanum, or something, had made the patient a little off. her head. However, Mrs. Huckins got through her compliments and her courtesies, and would finally perhaps have tittered too, but that her attention was suddenly diverted by that most awful of intrusions, a troublesome child in a sick-room.

"Why, Billy, you little plague — why, Billy, what do you do in here? Where have you come from, sir? — I 've been looking for you this half-hour."

"I 've been up with Mr. Tweedy, the new lodger," said Billy, standing very erect, and speaking rather proudly. "We 've been a-playing the flute."

"The WHAT!" cried all the female voices in a breath.

"A-playing the flute," repeated the undaunted Billy. "Mr. Tweedy only whispers a toon into it now, but he says he 'll play out loud as soon as ever the old " — here Billy looked at the invalid, and then at his mother — "he says he 'll play out loud as soon as ever Miss Hopkinson is well, or else dead!"

*   *   *   *   *

"Pray, how did you leave Miss Hopkinson, ma'am." inquired Mr. Tweedy, about an hour afterwards, of a female whom he met at the foot of the stairs.

"Miss Hopkinson, sir! — oh, you horrid wicked wretch! you unfeeling monster!" — and totally forgetting the weak nerves of her friend, the indignant Miss Filby rushed past the New Lodger, darted along the passage, let herself out. and slammed the street-door behind her with a bang, that shook Miss Hopkinson in her chair.

PATRONAGE.

THE authenticity of the following letter will, probably, be disputed. The system of patronage to which it refers is one very likely to shock the prejudices of serious, sober-minded persons, who will naturally refuse to credit such practical anachronisms as the superannuation of sucklings. Goldsmith, it is true, has mentioned certain Fortunatuses as being born with silver ladles in their mouths; but it would be easier to suppose a child thus endowed with a whole service of plate, than to fancy one invested with a service of years. The most powerful imagination would be puzzled to reconcile an Ex-Speakership with an Infant untaught to lisp; or to recognize a retired Bow-Street runner in a nurseling unable to walk. The existence of such very advanced posts for the Infantry is, however, affirmed; but with what truth, from my total want of political experience, I am unable to judge. Mr. Wordsworth, indeed, who says that " the child is father of the man," seems to aim a quiz at the practice; and possibly the nautical phrase of " getting a good *birth*," may refer to such prosperous nativities. For the rest, grown gentlemen have unquestionably been thrust, sometimes, into public niches to which they were as ill adapted as Mr. D.; the measures taken by Patrons not leading invariably, like Stultz's, to admirable fits. But the lady waits to speak her mind.

(COPY.)

*To the Right Honorable Lord Viscount ***, &c., &c., &c., Whitehall.*

MAY IT PLEASE YOUR LORDSHIP,—
I humbly beg a thousand pardons and apologies for so great a liberty, and taking up time so valuable to the nation with

the present application.   Nothing short of absolute necessity could compel to such a course; but I make bold to say, a case of greater hardship never had the honor to be laid before official eyes.   My poor husband, however, is totally unaware of my writing; as he would certainly forbid any such epistolary step, whether on my part or his own; though in point of fact the shattered state of his nerves is such as to preclude putting pen to paper if ever so inclined.   But as a wife, and a mother, it would not become me to preserve silence, with my husband perishing by inches before my eyes; and particularly when a nobleman of your Lordship's rank would be sure to sympathize for an unfortunate gentleman, of birth and breeding, that after waiting above forty odd years for his rights, has only come at last into a public post that must, and will, be his death!

To favor with the particulars, my husband has the honor to be related very distantly to the Peerage; and as Your Lordship knows, it is the privilege of Aristocracy to provide for all their connections by comfortable public situations, which are sometimes enjoyed very early in life.   To such, Mr. D. had a hereditary right from his cradle, for his noble relative, the Duke of ——, was so condescending as to stand sponsor by proxy; and instead of the usual spoons, or a silver mug, made a promise to the Infant of some office suited to its tender age; for instance, a superannuation, or the like, where there is nothing to do, but the salary to receive.   In point of fact, the making the Baby a retired King's Messenger was verbally undertaken at the font: but before the child could come into office His Grace unfortunately went out of power, by dying of apoplexy, leaving nothing but a promise, which a new ministry was unjust and ungrateful enough not to make good. In this shocking manner, Your Lordship, was my husband thrown upon the world, without proper provision according to his station and prospects, and was degraded to the necessity of his own exertions for support, till his fortieth year, when the new Duke thought proper to stir in his behalf.   The truth is, a severe illness had left Mr. D.'s mind and nerves in such a pitiful shattered state, as to make him unfit for any business whatever, except public affairs; and accordingly it became the duty of his friends to procure him some post under government.   So a proper application was made to his Grace, and through his influence and the fortunate circumstance of an election at the time, Mr. D. was appointed to the dreadful situation he at present enjoys. Of course we entirely acquit His Grace, who never set eyes on my husband in his life, and therefore could not be expected to know the precise state of his constitution; but I appeal to Your Lordship, whether it was proper patronage for a man shattered in mind

"ONE BLACK BALL EXCLUDES."

and nerves, and subject to tremors, and palpitations, and bodily shocks of all sorts, to be made a Superintendent of Powder-Mills, with the condition of living attached to the works?

For my own part, Your Lordship, I looked on the Duke's letter of congratulations as neither more or less than my poor husband's death warrant. Indeed he was so dreadfully alarmed himself, as to be quite distressing to witness. He did nothing, the whole afternoon, but walk up and down the room, shaking his head at himself in the looking-glass, or looking up at the ceiling, and muttering, as if he was already exploding sky-high along with the Mills. But a refusal was out of the question, as it would have afforded his Grace too good an excuse for neglecting our interests for the future. To aggravate the case, the very day after our taking possession, there was what is called a blow at the works, and though so trifling as only to carry a roof off a shed, it struck a chord on Mr. D.'s nerves that has never done vibrating ever since. I do not exaggerate to say, that if he had been struck with the palsy and St. Vitus, both at once, he could not have showed more corporal agitation. He trembled in every limb like an aspen-tree; while his eyes rolled, and his head went from side to side, like the China Mandarin's; besides scouring up and down stairs, and rushing out of doors and in again, and trying all the chairs but could not sit anywhere, and stamping, and muttering, and dancing about, till I really expected he would scramble up the walls of the room, and fly across the ceiling, like our tortoise-shell cat in her fits. If I lived to Methusalem, Your Lordship, I should never forget it! Unluckily, being new to his office, a mistaken notion of duty possessed him that he ought not to quit the spot; indeed he solemnly declared, that if a blow was to take place in his absence, he would rather commit his own suicide than face the report of it in the newspapers, which had already indulged in some seditious sneers at his appointment. All that could be done, therefore, was to pack off Lucy, and Emily and Eliza, on week's visits among friends; myself remaining behind, as a wife's proper post, near my poor husband; but on the discomfortable condition of keeping under ground in the cellar, because gunpowder in convulsions always blasts upwards. What my feelings were, as we are troubled with rats, your Lordship may suppose; particularly when Mr. D. was officially called upon to inspect the damage; and never shall I forget his gashly appearance when he returned from his awful task! He was literally as white as a sheet; and totally incapable to get out a word, till he had swallowed three whole glasses of brandy! That settled his reason, but it was only to tell me that he had scraped and grazed the skin off every nubble of his backbone, by a bad fall from a ladder, which he had attempted to come down in wooden safety-shoes. Such, Your

Lordship, was our miserable day ; and it brought as wretched
a night.   Bed would not be heard of — and we set up in two
easy-chairs, shuddering with fright and cold, being December,
and every door and window thrown wide open, to give a
thorough vent through the house in case of another shock.
For Mr. D. was unfortunately possessed that one blow always

"FAITHFUL BELOW HE DID HIS DUTY,
BUT NOW HE'S GONE ALOFT!"

leads to another ; and what with fancying flying sparks, for it
was starlight, and sniffing fire, he had worked himself up, before morning, into a high fever and a light head.   The nearest
medical man was obliged to be called in — and he had to give
frightful doses of laudanum before Mr. D.'s nerves could be
lulled into a startlish sort of doze ; and at waking, he was
ordered to drink the strongest stimuluses ; as indeed are in
use to the present time.   But this continual brandy brandy,

brandy, as Your Lordship knows, is a dreadful remedy: though, as my poor husband says, he cannot fill up his place without its help. At times I could almost believe, tho' I would not breathe such a thing except to Your Lordship, that between the stimuluses, and the delirium, and the whole shock to the system, Mr. D. is a little beside his senses. The mad Doctors do say, that we are all, every one of us, crazy on a certain subject; and if such is the case, there can be no doubt that my husband's weak point is explosions, the extravagance of his precautions making him an everlasting torment to himself as well as to all about him. Of course it is to his disadvantage, and magnifies his terrors, not to have been brought regularly up to the business; not that he receives much comfort from those who have, for he says custom and habit have made them so daring and hardened, that they would not mind playing at snap-dragon in the Magazine, or grinding their knives on the millstone that crushes the gunpowder into grains.

Since the above accident we have had, thank goodness, no more blows; but, as Your Lordship is aware, a first impression will stick by us for all our lives to come. At the best of times, let my husband be reading, or writing, or eating his dinner, or in bed, or what not, the exploding notion will come across him like a flash of lightning; as for instance last Friday was a week. Mr. and Mrs. Trotter had dropped in to tea; after which we had a rubber; and were all very comfortable, my husband and me just in the nine-holes, when all of a sudden there was a fall of something and a scream. Up jumps Mr. D. of course, chucking his cards here, there, and everywhere, and calling a blow! a blow!—and as usual Emily and Lucy and Eliza and me rushed off to the coal-cellar, while Mrs. T. went into a fit. It is true, by the blessing of Providence, it was only the Housemaid letting her pail fall to screech at a bat; but what is very disagreeable, the Trotters are old friends, and have declined to set another foot within our doors. As for servants, it is next to impossible to keep one about me; and as Your Lordship's own Lady will confirm, there is nothing more unpleasant to a Mistress of a House than to be continually changing. But nine out of ten prefer giving warning, to attending to so many punctiliums as are laid down; and those that are willing to stay, break through so many of the rules, that I am obliged to discharge them, to prevent Mr. D. being ruffled by doing it himself. Besides it adds considerably to servants' works, to have chimneys swept as often as once a week, — and moreover, Mr. D.

BAT AND BAWL.

insists on keeping all flint and steels, and tinder, and matches, in his own bedroom, so that the housemaid has to go to him every morning for her lights. He is just as particular about extinguishing at night; and I lost the best cook I ever had, through her sitting up in her bedroom to mend her stays, though she might have known Mr. D. would come in to put her out — all of which is extremely unpleasant, and to me in particular.

These, Your Lordship, are serious domestic evils; and I wish I could say they were confined to the house. But the workmen at the Mills are so ungrateful as to hate my husband

for the over-care he obliges them to take of their own lives;
and make no secret of wanting his removal, by trying to torment him into resignation.   Not a day passes without squab-
bles about smoking, for Mr. D. is apt to sniff tobacco, and
insists on searching pockets for pipes, which the laborers one
and all decline; and besides scuffles, there have been several
pay-offs on the spot.   The consequence is ill-will and bad
blood to their superior, and it is become a standing practical
joke to play upon the family feelings and fears.   I have
twice suffered all the disagreeables of escaping from nothing
at all in my night-dress, exposed to rheumatism, and the natives of a low neighborhood; indeed only last Sunday the fire-
bell was rung by nobody, and no wind at all to speak of.
Another party at enmity is Doctor Worral and all his establishment; because Mr. D. felt it his public duty to have the
Doctor up before a Justice for allowing his Young Gentlemen
to send up fire-balloons.   We had one day of dreadful excitement on my husband's part, through a wicked little wretch of
a pupil flashing the sunshine into the Mill with a bit of looking-glass; and of course we are indebted for the Swing letters
we receive to the same juvenile quarters.   To make bad
worse, Mr. D. takes them all for Gospel, and the extra watch-
ings and patrollings, and precautions, after getting a threaten-
ing notice, are enough to wear out all our hearts.   As regards
the School, I am ready to agree that it is too near the Works;
and to tell the truth, I shake in my shoes as much as Mr. D.,
every fifth of November, at each squib and cracker that goes
off.   On the same score our own sons are an everlasting misery to us when they are at home: which they seldom are,
poor fellows, on that account.   But if there is one thing above
another that boys delight to play with, it is gunpowder; and
being at the very fountain-head, Your Lordship may conceive
the constant care it is to prevent their getting at it, and what
is worse, not always crowned with success.   Indeed even
more innocent playthings are obliged to be guarded against;
for, as their father says, "a little brat, just breeched, may strike
light enough to blow up a whole neighborhood, through only
spinning a peg-top in a paved yard."

Such, your Lordship, is our present melancholy state.   I
have not dwelt, as I might do, on expenses, such as the dresses
that are spoiled in the coal-cellar; the paying months' wages

instead of warnings; nor the trays upon trays of glass and china that are chucked down, as the way the servants always empty their hands when making their escapes from my husband's false alarms. Sometimes it's a chair falls overhead; or the wind slams the back-door; or a smell of burnt wood from the kitchen; or the ironing-blanket; or fat catched; or a fall of soot; or a candlesnuff; or a smoky coal; or, as I have known before now, only the smell of the drains; with a hundred other little things that will spring up in families, take what care you will. I ought not to forget thunder-storms, which are another source of trouble; for, besides seeing a dozen fanciful flashes for one real one, it is the misfortune of Mr. D. not to put faith in conductors, or, to use his own words, " in Franklin, philosophy, and fiddlesticks — and a birch rod as likely to frighten away lightning as an iron one." In the mean time, through the constant frights and flurries, I begin to find my own nerves infected by bad example, and getting into startlish habits; and my daughter Lucy, who was always delicate, seems actually going into a poor low way. Agreeable society might do much to enliven our spirits; but my husband is become very shy of visitors, ever since Captain Gower was so inconsiderate as to walk in, one foggy night, with a lighted cigar in his mouth. In fact he quite sets his face against the male sex; for, if they do not smoke cigars, he says, and carry lucifers, they strut on their iron heels, and flourish about with iron-pointed walking-sticks, and umbrellas. All which, Your Lordship, is extremely hard on myself and daughters, who, like all young people, are fond of a little gayety; but the very utmost they are allowed, is a single quadrille party at Christmas, and then they are all obliged to dance in list shoes.

I humbly trust to Your Lordship's liberality, and goodness of heart, to view the particulars of the above melancholy statement with attentive consideration. As it may occur to inquire how we have suffered so long without complaining, I beg to inform your Lordship, that, being such a time of profound peace, we have lived on from year to year in the hope that no more ammunition would be required; and consequently the place would become a comfortable sinecure. But it appears that Spain and Portugal, and other countries, have gone to war on condition of being supplied with gunpowder;

and accordingly, to our bitter disappointment, the works are as vigorous as ever. Your Lordship will admit the hardship of such a cruel position to a man of Mr. D.'s very peculiar constitution; and I do hope and trust will also regard his interests with a favorable eye, in consideration of his long-standing claims upon the country. What his friends most desire for him is some official situation, — of course with a sufficient income to support his consequence, and a numerous family, — but without any business attached to it, or only so much as might help to amuse his mind for one or two hours in the day. Such a removal, considering my husband's unfitness for anything else, could occasion no sort of injury to the public service; particularly as his vacancy would be so easy to fill up. There are hundreds and thousands of land and sea officers on half-pay, who have been used to popping, and banging, and blowing up rockets and bomb-shells, all their lives; and would, therefore not object to the Powder Mills; especially as the salary is handsome, with a rent-free house and garden, coal and candles, and all the other little perquisites that belong to public posts. As regards ourselves, on the contrary, any interest is preferable to the gunpowder interest; and I take upon myself to say, that Mr. D. would be most proud and happy to receive any favor from your Lordship's administration; as well as answering for his pursuing any line of political principles, conservative or unconservative, that might be chalked out. Any such act of patronage would command the eternal gratitude of Mr. D., self, and family; and, repeating a thousand apologies for thus addressing, I beg leave to remain

Your Lordship's most humble, obedient,
and devoted servant,
LUCY EMILY DEXTER.

P. S. — Since writing the above, I am sorry to inform your Lordship, that we have had another little blow, and Mr. D.'s state is indescribable. He is more shaken than ever, and particularly through going all down the stairs in three jumps. He was sitting reading at the time, and, as he thinks, in his spectacles; but as they are not to be found, he is possessed that they have been driven into his head.

MRS. GARDINER.

A HORTICULTURAL ROMANCE.

CHAPTER I.

> " What sweet thoughts she thinks
>   Of violets and pinks."
>
> L. Hunt.

> " Each flower of tender stalk whose head, though gay
>   Carnation, purple, azure, or specked with gold,
>   Hung drooping, unsustained, them she upstays."
>
> Milton.

> " How does my lady's garden grow? "
>
> Old Ballad.

> " Her knots disordered, and her wholesome herbs
>   Swarming with caterpillars."
>
> Richard II.

I love a Garden!

" And so do I, and I, and I," exclaim in chorus all the he and she Fellows of the Horticultural Society.

" And I," whispers the philosophical Ghost of Lord Bacon.

" And I," sings the poetical Spirit of Andrew Marvel.

" Et moi aussi," chimes in the Shade of Delille.

" And I," says the Spectre of Sir William Temple, echoed by Pope, and Darwin, and a host of the English Poets, the sonorous voice of Milton resounding above them all.

" And I," murmurs the Apparition of Boccaccio.

" And I, and I," sob two Invisibles, remembering Eden.

" And I," shouts Mr. George Robins, thinking of Covent Garden.

" And I," says Mr. Simpson, — formerly of Vauxhall.

" And I," sing ten thousand female voices, all in unison, as if drilled by Hullah, — but really, thinking in concert of the Gardens of Gul.

[What a string I have touched!]

"We all love a Garden!" shout millions of human voices, male, female, and juvenile, bass, tenor, and treble. From the East, the West, the North, and the South, the universal burden swells on the wind, as if declaring in a roll of thunder that we all love a Garden.

But no,—one solitary voice,—that of Hamlet's Ghostly Father, exclaims in a sepulchral tone, "I don't!"

No matter,—we are all but unanimous; and so, Gentle Readers, I will at once introduce to you my Heroine,—a woman after your own hearts,—for she is a Gardiner by name and a Gardener by nature.

CHAPTER II.

AT Number Nine, Paradise Place, so called probably because every house stands in the middle of a little garden, lives Mrs. Gardiner. I will not describe her, for looking through the green rails in front of her premises, or over the dwarf wall at the back, you may see her any day, in an old poke bonnet, expanded into a gypsy-hat, and a pair of man's gloves, tea-green at top, but mouldy-brown in the fingers, raking, digging, hoeing, rolling, trowelling, pruning, nailing, watering, or otherwise employed in her horticultural and flori-cultural pursuits. Perhaps, as a neighbor, or acquaintance, you have already seen her, or conversed with her, over the wooden or brick-fence, and have learned in answer to your kind inquiries about her health, that she was pretty well, only sadly in want of rain, or quite charming, but almost eaten up by vermin. For Mrs. Gardiner speaks the true "Language of Flowers," not using their buds and blossoms as symbols of her own passions and sentiments, according to the Greek fashion, but lending words to the wants and affections of her plants. Thus, when she says that she is "dreadful dry," and longs for a good soaking, it refers not to a defect of moisture in her own clay, but to the parched condition of the soil in her parterres: or if she wishes for a regular smoking, it is not from any unfeminine partiality to tobacco, but in behalf of her blighted geraniums. In like manner she sometimes confesses herself a little backward, without allusion to any particular branch, or twig, of her education, or admits herself to be rather forward, quite irrelevantly to her behavior with the other sex. Without this key her expressions would often be unintelligible to the hearer, and sometimes indecorous, as when she told her neighbor, the bachelor at Number Eight, *à propos* of a plum-tree, that "she was growing quite wild, and should come some day over his wall." Others again, unaware of her peculiar phraseology, would give her credit, or discredit, for an undue share of female vanity, as well as the most extraordinary notions of personal beauty.

"Well," she said one day, "what do you think of Mrs. Mapleson?" meaning that lady's hydrangea. "Her head is the biggest, — but I look the bluest."

In a similar style she delivered herself as to certain other subjects of the rivalry that is universal amongst the suburban votaries of Flora: converting common blowing and growing substantives into horticultural verbs, as thus: —

"Miss Sharp crocussed before me, — but I snow-dropped sooner than any one in the Row."

But this identification of herself with the objects of her love was not confined to her plants. It extended to everything that was connected with her hobby, — her gardening implements, her garden-rails, and her garden-wall. For example, she complained once that she could not rake, she had lost so many of her teeth, — she told the carpenter the boys climbed over her so, that he should stick her all over tenter-hooks, — and sent word to her landlord, a builder, the snails bred so between her bricks that he must positively come and new-point her.

"Phoo! phoo!" exclaims an incredulous, Gentle Reader, — "she is all a phantom!"

Quite the reverse, sir. She is as real and as substantial as Mrs. Baines. Ask Mr. Cherry, the newsman, or his boy, John Loder, either of whom will tell you, — on oath if you require it, — that he serves her every Saturday with the *Gardener's Chronicle.*

CHAPTER III.

My first acquaintance with Mrs. Gardiner was formed when she was " in populous city pent," and resided in a street in the very heart of the city. In fact in Bucklersbury. But even there her future bent developed itself as far as her limited ways and means permitted. On the leads over the back warehouse, she had what she delighted to call a shrubbery, viz. : —

> A Persian Lilac in a tea-chest,
> A Guelder Rose in a washing-tub,
> A Laurustinus in a butter-tub,
> A Monthly Rose in a Portugal grape-jar,

and about a score of geraniums, fuchsias, and similar plants in pots. But besides shrubs and flowers, she cultivated a few vegetables, — that is to say, she grew her own sallads of " mustard and cress " in a brown pan ; and in sundry crockery vessels that would hold earth, but not water, she reared some half-dozen of Scarlet Runners, which, in the proper season, you might see climbing up a series of string-ladders, against the back of the house, as if to elope with the Mignionette from its box in the second-floor window. Then indoors, on her mantel-shelf, she had hyacinths and other bulbs in glasses, — and from a hook in the ceiling, in lieu of a chandelier, there was suspended a wicker-basket, containing a white biscuit-ware garden-pot, with one of those pendent plants, which, as she described their habits and sustenance, are " fond of hanging themselves, and living on hare." But these experiments rather tantalized than satisfied her passion. Warehouse-leads, she confessed, made but indifferent gardens or shrubberies, whilst the London smoke was fatal to the complexion of her mop-rose and the fragrance of her southernwood, or in her own words, —

" I blow dingy — and my old man smells sutty."

Once, indeed, she pictured to me her *beau ideal* of " a little Paradise," the main features of which I forget, except that with reference to a cottage *ornée*, she was to have " a jessamy in front, and a creeper up her back." As to the garden, it was to have walks and a lawn of course, with plenty of rich loam, that she might lay herself out in squares, and ovals, and diamonds — butter-tubs and tea-chests were very well for town, but she longed for elbow-room, and earth to dig, to rake, to hoe, and trowel-up, — in short, she declared, if she was her own missis, she would not sleep another night before she had a bed of her own, — not with any reference to her connubial partner, but she longed, she did, for a bit of ground, she did not care how small. A wish that her husband at last gratified by taking a bit of ground, *he* did not care how small, in Bunhill Fields.

The widow, selling off the town house, immediately retired to a villa in the country, and I had lost sight of her for some months, when one May morning taking a walk in the suburbs, whilst passing in front of Number Nine, Paradise Place, I overheard a rather harsh voice exclaiming, as if in expostulation with a refractory donkey, —

"Come up! Why don't you come up?"

It was Mrs. Gardiner, reproaching the tardiness of her seeds.

I immediately accosted her, but as she did not recognize me, determined to preserve my incognito, till I had drawn her out a little to exhibit her hobby.

"Rather a late spring, ma'am!"

"Wery, sir, — werry much so indeed. Lord knows when I shall be out of the earth, I almost think I'm rotted in the ground."

"The flowers are backward indeed, ma'am. I have hardly seen any except some wall-flowers farther down the row."

"Ah, at Number Two — Miss Sharp's. She's poor and single — but I'm double and bloody."

"You seem to have some fine stocks."

"Well, and so I have, though I say it myself. I'm the real Brompton — with a stronger blow than any one in the place, and as to sweetness, nobody can come nigh me. Would you like to walk in, sir, and smell me?"

Accepting the polite invitation, I stepped in through the little wicket, and in another moment was rapturously sniffing at her stocks, and the flower with the sanguinary name. From the walls I turned off to a rose-bush, remarking that there was a very fine show of buds.

"Yes, but I want sun to make me bust. You should have seen me last June, sir, when I was in my full bloom. None of your wishy-washy pale sorts (this was a fling at the white roses at the next door) — none of your Provincials, or pale pinks. There's no maiden blushes about me. I'm the regular old red cabbage!"

And she was right, for after all that hearty, glowing, fragrant rose is the best of the species — the queen of flowers, with a ruddy *embonpoint*, reminding one of the goddesses of Rubens. Well, next to the rose-bush there was a clump of Polyanthus, from which, by a natural transition, we come to discourse of Auriculas. This was delicate ground, for it appeared there was rivalry between Number Nine and Number Four, as to that mealiness which in the eye of a fancier is the chief beauty of the flower. However, having assured her, in answer to her appeal, that she was "quite as powdery as Mr. Miller," we went on very smoothly through Jonquils, and Narcissuses, and Ranunculus, and were about to enter on "Anymonies," when Mrs. Gardiner suddenly stopped short, and with a loud "whist!" pitched her trowel at the head of an old horse, which had thrust itself over the wooden fence.

"Drat the animals! I might as well try flowering in the Zoölogical, with the beasts all let loose! It's very hard, sir, but I can't grow nothing tall near them front rails. There was last year — only just fancy me, sir — with the most beautiful Crown Imperial you ever saw — when up comes a stupid hass and crops off my head."

I condoled with her of course on so cruel a decapitation, and recovered her trowel for her, in return for which civility she plucked and presented to me a bunch of Heartsease, apologizing that "she was not Bazaar (pro Bizarre), but a very good sort."

"It's along of living so near the road," she added, recurring to the late invasion. "Yesterday I was bullocked, and to-morrow I suppose . I shall be pigged. Then there's the blaggard men and boys, picking and stealing as they go by. I really expect that some day or other they'll walk in and strip me!"

I sympathized again; but before the condolence was well finished, there was another "whist!" and another cast of the missile.

"That's a dog! They're always rampaging at my front, and there goes the cat to my back, and she'll claw all my

bark off in scrambling out of reach! Howsomever that's a
fine lupin, ain't it?"

I assured her that it deserved to be exhibited to the Horticultural Society.

"What, to the flower show? No thankee. Miss Sharp
did, and made sure of a Bankside Medal, and what do you
think they gave her? Only a cerkittifit!"

"Shameful!" I ejaculated, "why it was giving her nothing
at all," and once more I restored the trowel, which, however,
had hardly settled in its owner's hand, than with a third
"whist!" off it flew again like a rocket, with a descriptive
announcement of the enemy.

"Them horrid poultry! Will you believe it, sir, that 'ere
cock flew over, and gobbled up my Hen-and-Chickens!"

"What! '*all your pretty chickens and their dam*'?"

"Yes, *all my Daisy.*"

[Reader! — if ever there was a verbal step from the Sublime to the Ridiculous — *that* was it.]

CHAPTER IV.

My mask fell off. That destructive cock was as fatal to my
incognito as to the widow's flowers: for coming after the cat
and the dog, and the possible pigs, and the positive bullock,
and the men, and the boys, and the horse, and the ass, I could
not help observing that my quondam acquaintance would have
been better off in Bucklersbury.

"Lord! and is it you?" she exclaimed with almost a scream;
"well, I had a misgiving as to your woice;" and with a rapid
volley of semi-articulate sounds the Widow seized my right
hand in one of her own, whilst with the other she groped hurriedly in her pocket. It was to search for her handkerchief,
but the cambric was absent, and she was obliged to wipe off
the gushing tears with her gardening glove. The rich loam
on the fingers, thus irrigated, ran off in muddy rivulets down
her furrowed cheeks, but in spite of her ludicrous appearance
I could not help sympathizing with her natural feelings, however oddly expressed.

"She could not help it," she sobbed — "the sight of mo
overcame her. When she last saw me, — *He* was alive —

who had always been a kind and devoted husband — as never
grudged her nothing — and had given her that beautiful butter-tub for her laurustiny. She often thought of him — yes,
often and often — while she was gardening — as if she saw
his poor, dear bones under the mould — and then to think that
she came up, year after year — " flourishing in all her beauty
and flagrance " — and *he* did n't. " But look there ; " and
smiling through her tears, she pointed towards the house, and
told me a tale, that vividly reminded me of her old contrivances
in Bucklersbury.

" It 's a table-beer barrel. I had it sawed in half, and there
it is, holding them two hallows, on each side of the door. But
I shan't blow, you know, for a sentry ! "

Very handsome indeed !

" Ain't they ? And there 's my American Creeper. Miss
Sharp pretends to creep, but Lor bless ye, afore ever she gets
up to her first-floor window, I shall be running all over the
roof of the willa. You see I 'm over the portico already."

A compliment to her climbing powers was due of course,
and I paid it on the spot; but we were not yet done with
creepers. All at once the Widow plucked off her garden-
bonnet, and dashing it on the gravel, began dancing on it like a
mad woman, or like a Scotch lassie tramping her dirty linen.
At last when it was quite flat, she picked the bonnet up again,
and carefully opening it, explained the matter in two words.

" A near-wig ! "

And then she went on to declare to me that they were the
plagues of her life — and there was no destroying them.

" It 's unknown the crabs and lobsters I 've eaten on purpose, but the nasty insects won't creep into my claws. And
in course you know what enemies they are to carnations. Last
year they ruined my Prince Albert, and this year I suppose
they 'll spoil the Prince of Wales ! "

CHAPTER V.

A propos of names.

I do wish that our Botanists, Conchologists, and Entomolo-
gists, and the rest of our scientifical Godfathers and Godmothers would sit soberly down, a little below the clouds, and

revise their classical, scholastical, and polyglottical nomenclatures. Yea, that our Gardeners and Florists especially would take their watering-pots and rebaptize all those pretty plants, whose bombastical and pedantical titles are enough to make them blush, and droop their modest heads for shame.

The Fly-flapper is bad enough, with his Agamemnon butterfly and Cassandra moth, —

"What 's Hecuba to him or he to Hecuba?"

but it is abominable to label our Flowers with antiquated, outlandish, and barbarous flowers of speech. Let the Horticulturists hunt through their Dictionaries, Greek and Latin, and Lempriere's Mythology to boot, and they will never invent such apt and pleasant names as the old English ones, to be found in Chaucer, Spenser, and Shakespeare.

O, how sweetly they sound, look, and smell in verse — charming the eye and the nose, according to the Rosicrucian theory, through the ear! But what is a Scutellaria Macrantha to either sense? Day's Eyes, Oxeyes, and Lippes of Cowes have a pastoral relish and a poetical significance — but what song or sonnet would be the sweeter for a Brunsvigia?

There is a meaning in Windflowers, and Cuckoo-buds, and Shepherd's Clocks, whilst the Hare-bell is at once associated with the breezy heath and the leporine animal that frequents it. When it is named, Puss and the blue-bell spring up in the mind's eye together — but what image is suggested by hearing of a Schizanthus retusus?

Then, again, Forget-me-Not sounds like a short quotation from Rogers's "Pleasures of Memory," Love-lies-Bleeding contains a whole tragedy in its title — and even Pick-your-Mother's-heart-out involves a tale for the novelist. But what story, with or without a moral, can be picked out of a Dendrobium, even if it were surnamed Clutterbuckii, after the egotistical or sycophantical fashion of the present day?

There was a jockey once who complained bitterly of the sale of a race-horse, just when he had learned to pronounce its name properly — Roncesvalles; but what was that hardship, to the misfortune of a petty nurseryman, perhaps, losing his Passion-Flower, when he had just got by heart Tacksonia Pinnatistipula?

"Reform it altogether!"

It looks selfish, in the learned, to invent such difficult no-menclatures, as if they wished to keep the character, habits, origin, and properties of new plants to themselves. Nay, more, it implies a want of affection for their professed favorites — the very objects of their attentions.

"How — a want of affection, sir?"

Yes — even so, my worthy Adam! For, mark me — if you really loved your plants and flowers —

"Well, sir?"

Why, then, you would n't call them such *hard names*.

CHAPTER VI.

To return to Mrs. Gardiner.

The Widow having described the ravages of the earwigs beckoned me towards her wall, and was apparently about to introduce me to a peach-tree, when abruptly turning round to me, she inquired if I knew anything of chemicals; and without giving time to reply, added her reason to the question.

"Cos I want you to pison my Hants."

Your aunts!

"Yes, the hemmets. As to Dr. Watts, he don't know nothing about 'em. They won't collect into troops to be trod into dust, they know better. So I was thinking if you could mix up summut luscious and dillyterious —"

She stopped, for a man's head suddenly appeared above the dwarf wall, and after a nod and a smile at the widow, saluted her with a good morning. He was her neighbor — the little old bachelor at Number Eight. As he was rather hard of hearing, my companion was obliged to raise her voice in addressing him, and indeed aggravated it so much that it might have been heard at the end of the row.

"Well, and how are *you*, Mr. Burrel, after them East winds?"

"Very bad, very bad indeed," replied Mr. Burrel, thinking only of his rheumatics.

"And so am I," said Mrs. Gardiner, remembering nothing but her blight: "I 'm thinking of trying tobacco-water and a squiringe."

"Is that good for it?" asked Mr. B., with a tone of doubt and surprise.

"So they say: but you must mix it strong, and squirt it as hard as ever you can over your affected parts."

" What, my lower limbs ? "

" Yes, and your upper ones too. Wherever you 're maggotty."

"Oh !" grunted the old gentleman, "you mean vermin."

" As for me." bawled Mrs. G., " I 'm swarming ! And Miss Sharp is wus than I am."

" The more 's the pity." said the old gentleman, " we shall have no apples and pears."

" No, not to signify. How 's your peaches ? "

" Why, they set kindly enough, ma'am, but they all dropped off in the last frosty nights."

"Ah, it ain't the frost," roared Mrs. G. " You 've got down to the gravel — I know you have — you look so rusty and scrubby ! "

" I wish you good morning, ma'am," said the little old bachelor, turning very red in the face, and making rather a precipitate retreat from the dwarf wall — as who would n't, thus attacked at once in his person and his peach-trees?

"To be sure, he was dreadful unproductive," the Widow said ; " but a good sort of body, and ten times pleasanter than her next-door neighbor at Number Ten, who would keep coming over her wall, till she cut off his pumpkin."

She now led me round the house to her " back," where she showed me her grassplot, wishing she was greener, and asking if she ought not to have a roll. I longed to say, on Greenwich authority, that about Easter Monday was the proper season for the operation, but the joke might have led to a check in her horticultural confidences. In the centre of the lawn there was an oval bed. with a stunted shrub in the middle, showing some three or four clusters of purple blossoms, which the Widow regarded with intense admiration.

" You have heard, I suppose, of a mashy soil for roddydandums ? Well, look at my bloom, — quite as luxurus as if I 'd been stuck in a bog ! "

There was no disputing this assertion ; and so she led me off to her vegetables, halting at last at her peas, some few rows of Blue Prussians, which she had probably obtained from Waterloo, they were so long in coming up.

" Backard, an't I ? "

Yes, rather.

"Wery—but Miss Sharp is backarder than me. She's hardly out of the ground yet—and please God, in another fortnight I shall want sticking."

There was something so comic in the last equivoque, that I was forced to slur over a laugh as a sneeze, and then contrived to ask her if she had no assistance in her labors.

"What, a gardener? Never! I did once have a daily jobber, and he jobbed away all my dahlias. I declare I could have cried! But it's very hard to think you're a valuable bulb, and when summer comes, you're nothing but a stick and a label."

Very provoking indeed!

"Talk of transplanting, they do nothing else but transplant you from one house to another, till you don't know where you are. There was I, thinking I was safe and sound in my own bed, and all the while I was in Mr. Jones's."

It's scandalous!

"It *is*. And then in winter when they're friz out, they come round to one a beggin' for money. But they don't freeze any charity out of me."

All ladies, however, are not so obdurate to the poor Gardeners in winter—or even in summer, in witness whereof here follows a story.

CHAPTER VII.

An elderly gentlewoman of my acquaintance, on a visit at a country house in Northamptonshire, chanced one fine morning to look from her bedchamber, on the second story, into the pleasure-ground, where Adam, the Gardener, was at work at a flower-border, directly under her window. It was a cloudless day in July, and the sun shone fervidly on the old man's bald, glossy pate, from which it reflected again in a number of rays, as shining and pointed as so many new pins and needles.

"Bless me!" ejaculated the old lady, "it's enough to broil all the brains in his head;" and unable to bear the sight, she withdrew from the casement. But her concern and her curiosity were too much excited to allow her to remain in peace.

Again and again she took a peep, and whenever she looked, there, two stories below, shone the same bare round cranium, supernaturally red, and almost intolerably bright, as if it had been in the very focus of a burning-glass. It made her head ache to think of it!

Nevertheless she could not long remove her eyes, she was fascinated towards that glowing sconce, as larks are said to be by the dazzling of a mirror.

In the mean time, to her over-heated fancy, the bald pate appeared to grow redder and redder, till it actually seemed red-hot. It would have hardly surprised her if the blood, boiling a gallop, had gushed out of the two ears, or if the head, after smoking a little, had burst into a flame by spontaneous combustion. It would never have astonished her had he danced off in a frenzy of brain-fever, or suddenly dropped down dead from a stroke of the sun. However he did neither, but still kept work, work, working on in the blazing heat, like a salamander.

"It don't signify," muttered the old lady, "if he can stand it I can't." and again she withdrew from the spectacle. But it was only for a minute. She returned to the window, and fixing her eyes on the bald, shining, glowing object, considerately pitched on it a cool pot of beer — not literally, indeed, but in the shape of five penny pieces, screwed up tight in brown paper.

MORAL. — There is nothing like *well-directed* benevolence!

CHAPTER VIII.

"YES, all gardeners is thieves!"

As I could not dispute the truth of this sweeping proposition from practical experience, I passed it over in silence, and contented myself with asking the Widow whence she acquired all her horticultural knowledge, which she informed me came "out of her Mawe."

"It was *him* as give me that, too," she whimpered, "for he always humored my flowering; and if ever a grave deserved a strewing over it's his'n — There's a noble old helm."

Very, indeed.

"Yes, quite an old antique, and would be beautiful if I could only hang a few parachutes from its branches."

I presume you allude to the parasites?

"Well, I suppose I do. And look there's my harbor. By and by, when I'm more honeysuckled I shall be water-proof, but I ain't quite growed over enough yet to sit in without an umbrella."

As I had now pretty well inspected her back, including one warm corner, in which she told me she had a good mind to cow-cumber — we turned toward the house, the Widow leading the way, when wheeling sharply round, she popped a new question.

"What do you think of my walk?"

Why that is kept very clean and neat.

"Ah, I don't mean my gravel, but my walk. At present you see I go in a pretty straight line, but suppose I went a little more serpentiny — more zigzaggy — and praps deviating about among the clumps — don't you think I might look more picturesque?"

I ventured to tell her, at the risk of sending her ideas to her front, that if she meant her *gait*, it was best as it was; but that if she alluded to her path, a straight one was still the best, considering the size of her grounds.

"Well, I dare say you're right," she replied, "for I'm only a quarter of a haker if you measure me all round."

By this time we were close to the house, where the appearance of a vine suggested to me the query whether the proprietor ever gathered any grapes.

"Ah my wine, my wine," replied the Widow, with as grave a shake of the head, and as melancholy a tone as if she had really drunk to fatal excess of the ruby juice. "That wine will be the death of me, if somebody don't nail me up. My poor head won't bear ladder-work; and so all training or pruning myself is out of the question. Howsomever, Miss Sharp is just as bad, and so I'm not the only one whose wine goes where it should n't."

Not by hundreds of dozens, thought I, but there was no time allowed for musing over my own loss by waste and leakage: I was roused by a "now come here," and lugged round the corner of the house to an adjacent building, which bore about the same proportion to the villa as a calf to a cow.

"This here's the washus."

So I should have conjectured.

"Yes, it's the washus now — but it's to be a greenus. I intend to have a glazed roof let into it for a conservatory, in the winter, when I can't be stood out in the open air. They've a greenus at Number Five, and a hottus besides — and thinks I, if so be I do want to force a little, I can force myself in the copper!"

The Copper!

"Yes. I'm uncommon partial to foreign outlandish plants — and if I'm an African, you know, or any of them tropicals, I shall almost want baking."

These schemes and contrivances were so whimsical, and at the same time so Bucklersburyish, that in spite of myself, my risible muscles began to twitch, and I felt that peculiar internal quiver about the diaphragm which results from suppressed laughter. Accordingly, not to offend the Widow, I hurried to take my leave, but she was not disposed to part with me so easily.

"Now come, be candid, and tell me before you go, what you think of me altogether. Am I shrubby enough? I fancy sometimes that I ought to be more deciduous."

Not at all. You are just what you ought to be — shrubby and flowery, and gravelly and grassy — and in summer you must be a perfect nosegay.

"Well — so I ham. But in winter, now, — do you really think I am green enough to go through the winter?"

Quite. Plenty of yews, hollies, box, and lots of horticultural laurals.

[I thought now that I was off — but it was a mistake.]

"Well, but — if you really must go — only one more question — and it's to beg a favor. You know last autumn we went steaming up to Twitnam?"

Yes — well?

"Well, and we went all over Mr. What's-his-name's Willa."

Pope's — well?

"Well then, somebody told us as how Mr. Pope was very famous for his Quincunx. Could you get one a slip of it?"

CHAPTER IX.

" WELL, for my part," exclaims Fashion, " those who please may garden; but I shall be quite satisfied with what I get from my Fruiterer, and my Greengrocer, and my bouquets. For it seems to me, sir, according to your description of that Widow, and her operations, that gardening must be more of a trouble than a pleasure. To think of toiling in a most unfashionable bonnet and filthy gloves, for the sake of a few flowers, that one may buy as good or better, and made artificially by the first hands in Paris! Not to name the vulgarity of their breeding. Why I should faint if I thought my orange flowers came out of a grocer's tea-chest, or my camelia out of the butter-tub!"

No doubt of it, madam, and that you would never come to if sprinkled with common water instead of Eau de Cologne.

" Of course not. I loathe pure water — ever since I have heard that all London bathes in it — the lower classes and all. If *that* is what one waters with, I could never garden. And then those nasty creeping things, and the earwigs! I really believe that one of them crawling into my head, would be enough to drive out all my intellects!"

Beyond question, madam.

" I did once see a Lady gardening, and it struck me with horror! How she endured that odious caterpillar on her clothes without screaming, surpasses my comprehension. No, no — it is not Lady's work, and I should say not even Gentleman's, though some profess to be very fond of it."

Why as to that, madam, there is a style of gardening that might even be called aristocratical, and might be indulged in by the very first Exquisite in your own circle.

" Indeed, sir ? "

Yes, in the mode, madam, that was practised in his own garden by the Poet Thomson, the Author of the " Seasons."

" And pray how was that, sir ? "

Why by eating the peaches off the wall, with his hands in his pockets ; or in other words, gobbling up the fruits of industry, without sharing in the labor of production.

" O, fie! that's Radical! What do you say, my Lord ? "

" Why, 'pon honor, your ladyship, it does n't touch me —

for I only eat other people's peaches — and without putting my hands in my pockets at all."

CHAPTER X.

"But do you really think, sir," asks Chronic Hypochondriasis, "that gardening is such a healthy occupation?"

"I do. But better than my own opinion, I will give you the sentiments of a celebrated but eccentric Physician on the subject, when he was consulted by a Patient afflicted with your own disease.

"Well, sir, what's the matter with you?" said the bluff Doctor.

"Why nothing particular, Doctor, if you mean any decided complaint. Only I can't eat, and I can't drink, and I can't sleep, and I can't walk — in short, I can't enjoy anything except being completely miserable."

It was a clear case of Hypochondriasis, and so the Physician merely laid down the ordinary sanitary rules.

"But you have n't prescribed, Doctor," objected the Patient. "You have n't told me what I am to take."

"Take exercise."

"Well, but in what shape, Doctor?"

"In the shape of a spade."

"What — dig like a horse?"

"No — like a man."

"And no physic?"

"No. You don't want draughts, or pills, or powders. Take a garden — and a Sabine farm after it — if you like."

"But it is such hard work?"

"Phoo, phoo. Begin with crushing your caterpillars — that's soft work enough. After that you can kill snails, they 're harder — and mind, before breakfast."

"I shall never eat any!"

"Yes you will, when you have earned your grub. Or hoe, and rake, and make yourself useful on the face of the earth."

"But I get so soon fatigued."

"Yes, because you are never tired of being tired. Mere indolence. Commit yourself to hard labor. It's pleasanter than having it done by a Magistrate, and better in private grounds than on public ones."

"Then you seriously suppose, Doctor, that gardening is good for the constitution?"

"I do. For King, Lords, and Commons. Grow your own cabbages. Sow your own turnips, — and if you wish for a gray head, cultivate carrots."

"Well, Doctor, if I thought —"

"Don't think, but do it. Take a garden and dig away as if you were going to bury all your care in it. When you're tired of digging, you can roll — or go to your walls, and set to work at your fruit-trees, like the Devil and the Bag of Nails."

"Well, at all events, it is worth trying; but I am sadly afraid that so much stooping —"

"Phoo, phoo! The more pain in your back, the more you'll forget your *hyps*. Sow a bed with thistles, and then weed it. And don't forget cucumbers."

"Cucumbers!"

"Yes, unwholesome to eat, but healthy to grow, for then you can have your *frame* as strong as you please, and regulate your own *lights*. Melons still better. Only give your melon to the melon-bed, and your colly to the collyflowers, and your Melancholy's at an end."

"Ah! you're joking, Doctor!"

"No matter. Many a true word is said in jest. I'm the only physician, I know, who prescribes it, but take a garden — *first remedy in the world* — for when Adam was put into one he was *quite a new man!*"

But, Mrs. Gardiner.

I had taken leave of her, as I thought, by the wash-house door, and was hurrying towards the wicket-gate, when her voice apprised me that she was still following me.

"There is one thing that *you* ought to see at any rate, if nobody else does."

And with gentle violence she drew me into a nook behind a privet hedge, and with some emotion asked me if I knew where I was. My answer of course was in the negative.

"It's Bucklersbury."

The words operated like a spell on my memory, and I immediately recognized the old civic shrubbery. Yes, there they were, the Persian Lilac, the Guelder Rose, the Monthly Rose, and the Laurustinus, but looking so fresh and flourishing, that it was no wonder I had not known them ; and besides the chests and tubs were either gone, or plunged in the earth.

"Not quite so grubby as I were in town," said the Widow, "but the same plants. Old friends like, with new faces. Just take a sniff of my laylock — it's the same smell as I had when in London, except the smoke. And there's my monthly rose — look at my complexion now. You remember how smudgy I was afore. Perhaps you'd like a little of me for old acquaintance," and plucking from each, she thrust into my hand a bouquet big enough for the Lord Mayor's coachman on the Ninth of November.

"Yes, we've all grown and blown together," she continued, looking from shrub to shrub, with great affection. "We've withered and budded, and withered and budded, and blossomed and sweetened the air. We're interesting, ain't we?"

O very — there's a sentiment in every leaf.

"Yes, that's exactly what I mean. I often come here to enjoy 'em, and have a cry — for you know *he* smelt 'em and admired 'em as well as us," and the mouldy glove might again have had to wipe a moistened eye, but for an alarm familiar to her ear, though not to mine, except through her interpretation.

"My peas! my peas! old Jones's pigeons!"

And rushing off to the defence of her Blue Prussians, she gave me an opportunity of which I availed myself by retreating in the opposite direction, and through the wicket. It troubles me to this day that I cannot remember the shutting it; my mind misgives me that in my haste to escape it was most probably left open, like Abou Hassan's door, and with as unlucky consequences.

Even as I write, distressing images of a ruined Eden rise up before my fancy — cocks and hens scratching in flower borders — pigs routing up stocks or rolling in tulips — a horse cropping rose-buds, and a bullock in Bucklersbury! and all this perhaps not a mere vision! That woeful figure with starting tears and clasped hands contemplating the scene of havoc, not altogether a fiction!

Under this doubt, it will be no wonder that I have never revisited the Widow, or that when I stroll in the suburbs my steps invariably lead me in any other direction than towards Paradise Place.

CHAPTER XII.

I HAVE told a lie!

I have written the thing that is not, and the truth came not from my pen. There was deceit in my ink, and my paper is stained with a falsehood. Nevertheless, it was in ignorance that I erred, and consequently the lie is white.

When I told you, Gentle Reader, that any day you pleased you might behold my heroine, Mrs. Gardiner, I was not aware that Mrs. Gardiner was no more.

"No more!"

No — for by advices just received, she is now Mrs. Burrel, the wife of the quondam little old Bachelor at Number Eight.

"What!—married! Why then she did go over the wall to him as she promised."

No, miss — he came over to her.

"What!—By a rope ladder."

No — there was no need for so romantic an apparatus. The wall, as already described, was a dwarf one, about breast high, over which an active man, putting one hand on the top, might have vaulted with ease. How Mr. Burrel, unused to such gymnastics, contrived to scramble over it, he did not know himself; but as he had scraped the square toes of each shoe — damaged each drab knee — frayed the front of his satin waistcoat — and scratched his face, the probability is, that after clambering to the summit, he rolled over, and pitched headlong into the scrubby holly-bush on the other side.

For a long time it appears, without giving utterance to the slightest sentiment of an amorous nature, he had made himself particular, by constantly haunting the dwarf wall that divided him from the widow, — overlooking her indeed more than was proper or pleasant. For once, however, he happened to look at the right moment, for casting his eyes towards Number Nine, he saw that his fair neighbor was in a very disagreeable and dangerous predicament — in short, that she was in her own water-butt, heels upwards.

He immediately jumped over the brick partition, and bellowing for help, succeeded, he knew not how, in hauling the unfortunate lady from her involuntary bath.

" Then it was not a suicide ? "

By no means, madam. It was simply from taking her hobby to water. In plainer phrase, whilst endeavoring to establish an aquatic lily in her waterbutt, she overbalanced herself and fell in.

The rest may be guessed. Before the Widow was dry, Mr. Burrel had declared his passion — Gratitude whispered that without him she would have been " no better than a dead lignum vitæ " — and she gave him her hand.

The marriage day, however, was not fixed. At the desire of the bride, it was left to a contingency, which was resolved by her " orange-flowering " last Wednesday — and so ended the " Horticultural Romance " of Mrs. Gardiner.

A TALE OF TERROR.

The following story I had from the lips of a well-known Aeronaut, and nearly in the same words.

It was on one of my ascents from Vauxhall, and a gentleman of the name of Mavor had engaged himself as a companion in my aerial excursion. But when the time came his nerves failed him, and I looked vainly around for the person who was to occupy the vacant seat in the car. Having waited for him till the last possible moment, and the crowd in the gardens becoming impatient, I prepared to ascend alone; and the last cord that attached me to the earth was about to be cast off, when suddenly a strange gentleman pushed forward and volunteered to go up with me into the clouds. He pressed the request with so much earnestness, that having satisfied myself by a few questions of his respectability, and received his promise to submit in every point to my directions, I consented to receive him in lieu of the absentee; whereupon he stepped with evident eagerness and alacrity into the machine. In another minute we were rising above the trees: and in justice to my companion, I must say, that in all my experience, no person at a first ascent had ever shown such perfect coolness and self-possession. The sudden rise of the machine, the novelty of the situation, the real and exaggerated dangers of the voyage, and the cheering of the spectators, are apt to cause some trepidation, or at any rate excitement in the boldest individuals; whereas the stranger was as composed and comfortable as if he had been sitting quite at home in his own library-chair. A bird could not have seemed more at ease, or more in its element, and yet he solemnly assured me upon his honor, that he had never been up before in his life. Instead of exhibiting any alarm at our great height from the earth, he evinced the liveliest pleasure whenever I emptied one of my bags of sand, and even once or twice urged me to part with

more of the ballast.   In the mean time, the wind, which was
very light, carried us gently along in a northeast direction,
and the day being particularly bright and clear, we enjoyed a
delightful bird's-eye view of the great metropolis, and the sur-
rounding country.   My companion listened with great interest,
while I pointed out to him the various objects over which we
passed, till I happened casually to observe that the balloon
must be directly over Hoxton.   My fellow-traveller then for
the first time betrayed some uneasiness, and anxiously inquired
whether I thought he could be recognized by any one at our
then distance from the earth.   It was, I told him, quite impossible.   Nevertheless he continued very uneasy, frequently
repeating, "I hope they don't see me," and entreating me earnestly to discharge more ballast.   It then flashed upon me for
the first time that his offer to ascend with me had been a whim
of the moment, and that he feared the being seen at that perilous elevation by any member of his own family.   I therefore
asked him if he resided at Hoxton, to which he replied in the
affirmative;   urging again, and with great vehemence, the
emptying of the remaining sand-bags.

This, however, was out of the question, considering the altitude of the balloon, the course of the wind, and the proximity
of the sea-coast.   But my comrade was deaf to these reasons
— he insisted on going higher;   and on my refusal to discharge
more ballast, deliberately pulled off and threw his hat, coat,
and waistcoat overboard.

"Hurrah, that lightened her!" he shouted; "but it's not
enough yet," and he began unloosening his cravat.

"Nonsense," said I; " my good fellow, nobody can recognize
you at this distance, even with a telescope."

"Don't be too sure of that," he retorted rather simply;
"they have sharp eyes at Miles's."

"At where?"

"At Miles's Madhouse!"

Gracious Heaven!—the truth flashed upon me in an instant.   I was sitting in the frail car of a balloon, at least a mile
above the earth, with a Lunatic.   The horrors of the situation,
for a minute, seemed to deprive me of my own senses.   A
sudden freak of a distempered fancy — a transient fury — the
slightest struggle might send us both, at a moment's notice,
into eternity!   In the mean time, the Maniac, still repeating

his insane cry of "higher, higher, higher," divested himself, successively, of every remaining article of clothing, throwing each portion, as soon as taken off, to the winds. The inutility of remonstrance, or rather the probability of its producing a fatal irritation, kept me silent during these operations: but judge of my terror, when having thrown his stockings overboard, I heard him say, "We are not yet high enough by ten thousand miles — one of us must throw out the other."

To describe my feelings at this speech is impossible. Not only the awfulness of my position, but its novelty, conspired to bewilder me — for certainly no flight of imagination — no, not the wildest nightmare-dream, had ever placed me in so desperate and forlorn a situation. It was horrible! — horrible! Words, pleadings, remonstrances were useless, and resistance would be certain destruction. I had better have been unarmed, in an American wilderness, at the mercy of a savage Indian! And now, without daring to stir a hand in opposition, I saw the Lunatic deliberately heave first one, and then the other bag of ballast from the car, the balloon of course rising with proportionate rapidity. Up, up, up it soared — to an altitude I had never even dared to contemplate — the earth was lost to my eyes, and nothing but the huge clouds rolled beneath us! The world was gone I felt forever! The Maniac, however, was still dissatisfied with our ascent, and again began to mutter.

"Have you a wife and children?" he asked, abruptly.

Prompted by a natural instinct, and with a pardonable deviation from truth, I replied that I was married, and had fourteen young ones who depended on me for their bread.

"Ha! ha! ha!" laughed the Maniac, with a sparkling of his eyes that chilled my very marrow. "I have three hundred wives, and five thousand children; and if the balloon had not been so heavy by carrying double, I should have been home to them by this time."

"And where do they live?" I asked, anxious to gain time by any question that first occurred to me.

"In the moon," replied the Maniac; "and when I have lightened the car I shall be there in no time."

I heard no more, for suddenly approaching me, and throwing his arms around my body —

*   *   *   *   *   *

MR. CHUBB.

A PISCATORY ROMANCE.

CHAPTER I.

> " Let me live harmlessly, and near the brink
> Of Trent or Avon have a dwelling-place,
> Where I may see my quill or cork down sink
> With eager bite of Perch, or Bleak, or Dace."
>
> J. DAVORS.

> " I care not, I, to fish in seas,
> Fresh rivers best my mind do please,
> Whose sweet, calm course I contemplate,
> And seek in life to imitate."
>
> PISCATOR'S SONG.

> " The ladies, angling in the crystal lake,
> Feast on the waters with the prey they take,
> At once victorious with their lines and eyes,
> They make the fishes and the men their prize."
>
> WALLER.

MR. CHUBB was not, by habit and repute, a fisherman. Angling had never been practically his hobby. He was none of those enthusiasts in the gentle craft, who as soon as close time comes to an end, are sure to be seen in a punt at Hampton Deeps, under the arches of Kew Bridge, or on the banks of the New. River, or the Lea, trolling for jack, ledgering for barbel, spinning for trout, roving for perch, dapping for chub, angling for gudgeon, or whipping for bleak. He had never fished but once in his life, on a chance holiday, and then caught but one bream, but that once sufficed to attach him to the pastime ; it was so still, so quiet, so lonely ; the very thing for a shy, bashful, nervous man, as taciturn as a post, as formal as a yew hedge, and as sedate as a quaker. Nevertheless he did not fall in love with fishing, as some do, rashly and madly, but as became his character, discreetly and with deliberation.

It was not a nasty passion, but a sober preference founded on esteem, and accordingly instead of plunging at once into the connection, he merely resolved, in his heart, that at some future time he would retire from the hosiery line and take to one of gut, horsehair, or silk.

In pursuance of this scheme, whilst he steadily amassed the necessary competence, he quietly accumulated the other requisites; from time to time investing a few more hundreds in the funds, and occasionally adding a fresh article to his tackle, or a new guide, or treatise to his books on the art. Into these volumes, at his leisure, he dipped, gradually storing his mind with the piscatory rules, " line upon line, and precept upon precept," till in theory he was a respectable proficient. And in his Sunday walks, he commonly sought the banks of one or other of our Middlesex rivers, where, glancing at sky and water, with a speculative eye, he would whisper to himself— " a fine day for the perch," or " a likely hole for a chub;" but from all actual practise he religiously abstained, carefully hoarding it up, like his money, at compound interest, for that delicious Otium-and-Water, which, sooner or later, Hope promised he should enjoy.

In the mean time, during one of these suburban rambles, he observed, near Enfield Chase, a certain row of snug little villas, each with its own garden, and its own share of the New River, which flowed between the said pleasure-grounds on one side, and a series of private meadows on the other. The houses, indeed, were in pairs, two under one roof, but each garden was divided from the next one by an evergreen fence, tall and thick enough to screen the proprietor from neighborly observation; whilst the absence of any public foot-path along the fields equally secured the residents from popular curiosity. A great consideration with an angler, who, near the metropolis, is too liable to be accosted by some confounded hulking fellow with " What sport, — how do they bite?" — or annoyed by some pestilent little boy, who will intrude in his swim.

" Yes, *that's* the place for me," thought Mr. Chubb, especially alluding to a green lawn which extended to the water's edge — not forgetting a tall lignum-vitæ tree, against which, seated in an ideal arm-chair, he beheld his own Eidolon, in the very act of pulling out an imaginary fish, as big and bright as a fresh herring.

“Yes, that *is* the place for me!” muttered Mr. Chubb: “so snug — so retired — so all to one’s self!   Nobody to overlook, nothing to interrupt one! — No towing-path — no barges — no thoroughfare — Bless my soul! it’s a perfect little Paradise!”

And it was the place for him indeed — for some ten years afterwards the occupant died suddenly of apoplexy — whereupon Mr. Chubb bought the property, sold off his business, and retiring to the villa, which he christened “ Walton Cottage,” prepared to realize the long water-souchyish dream of his middle age.

“And did he catch anything?”

My dear Miss Hastie — do, pray, allow the poor gentleman a few moments to remove, and settle himself in his new abode, and in the mean while, let me recommend you to the care of that allegorical Job in petticoats, who is popularly supposed to recreate herself, when she is not smiling on a monument, by fishing in a pool.

CHAPTER II.

Eureka!

The day, the happy day is come at last, and no bride, in her pearl silk and orange flowers, after a protracted courtship, ever felt a more blissful flutter of spirits than Mr. Chubb, as in a bran-new white hat, fustian jacket, and drab leggings, he stands on the margin of the New River, about to become an angler for better or worse.

The morning is propitious.   The sky is slightly clouded, and a gentle southerly zephyr just breathes, here and there, on the gray water, which is thickly studded with little dimples that dilate into rings, — signs, as sure as those in the zodiac, of Aquarius and Pisces.   A comfortable arm-chair is planted in the shadow of the tall lignum-vitæ — to the right, on the grass, lies a landing-net, and on the left, a basket big enough to receive a salmon.   Mr. Chubb, himself, stands in front of the chair; and having satisfied his mind, by a panoramic glance, of his complete solitude, begins precipitately to prepare his tackle, by drawing the strings of a long brown holland case into a hard double knot.   But he is too happy to swear, so he only blesses his soul, patiently unravels the knot, and complacently allows the rod to glide out of the linen cover. With deliberate care he fits each joint in its socket, — from the butt glittering with bright brass, to the tapering top — and then with supple wrist, proves the beautiful pliancy of the " complete thing." Next from the black leather pocketbook he selects a line of exquisite fineness, and attaches it by the loop to the small brazen wire ring at the point of the whale-bone. The fine gut, still retaining its angles from the reel, like a long zigzag of gossamer, vibrates to the elastic rod, which in turn quivers to the agitated hand, tremulous with excitement. But what ails Mr. Chubb? All at once he starts off into the strangest and wildest vagaries, — now clutching like Macbeth at the air-drawn dagger, and then suddenly wheeling round like a dog trying to catch his own tail — now snatching at some invisible blue-bottle buzzing about his nose, — next flea-hunting about his clothes, and then staring sky-wards with goggle eyes, and round open mouth, as if he would take a minnow! A few bars rest — and off he goes again, — jumping, — spinning, — skipping right and left — no urchin striving to apprehend Jack O'Lantern ever cut more capers.

He is endeavoring to catch his line that he may bait the hook ; but the breeze carries it far a-field, and the spring of the rod jerks it to and fro, here and there and everywhere but into his eager hand. Sometimes the shot swing into his eye, sometimes the float bounces into his mouth or bobs against his nose, and then, half caught, they spring up perpendicularly, and fall down again, with the clatter of hail, on the crown of his white beaver. At last he succeeds — at least the hook anchors in the skirts of his jacket. But he is in too good humor to curse. Propping the rod upright against the tall lignum-vitæ, he applies both hands to the rescue, and has just released the hook from the fustian, when down drops the rod, with a terrible lash of its top-joint in the startled stream, — whilst the barbed steel, escaping from his right finger and thumb, flies off like a living insect, and fastens its sting in the cuff of his left sleeve with such good will, that it must be cut out with a penknife. Still he does not blaspheme. At some damage to the cloth, the Kirby is set free — and the line is safe in hand. A little more cautiously he picks up the dripping rod, and proceeds to bait the hook — not without great difficulty and delay, for a worm is a wriggling slippery thing, with a natural aversion to being lined with wire, and when the fingers are tremulous besides — the job is a stiff one. Nevertheless he contrives, ill or well, to impale a small brandling; but remembering that he ought first to have plumbed the depth of the water removes the worm and substitutes a roll of thin lead. Afterwards he adjusts the float to the proper soundings, and then there is all the wriggling, slippery, nervous process to be gone through over again. But Patience, the angler's virtue, still supports him. The hook is baited once more, — he draws a long, deep sigh of satisfaction, and warily poising his rod, lets the virgin line drop gently into the rippling stream !

Now then all is right ! Alas, no ! The float instead of swimming erect, sinks down on its side for want of sufficient ballast ; a trying dilemma, for the cure requires a rather delicate operation. In fact, six split shot successively escape from his trembling fingers — a seventh he succeeds in adjusting to the line, on which he rashly attempts to close the gaping lead with his teeth ; but unluckily his incisors slip beside the leaden pellet, and with a horrid cranch go clean through the crisp gut !

Still he does not blaspheme ; but blessing his body, this time, as well as his soul, carefully fits a new bottom on the line, and closes the cleft shot with the proper instrument, a pair of pliers. Then he baits again, and tries the float, which swims with the correct cock — and all is right at last ! The dreams, the schemes, the hopes, the wishes of a dozen long years are realized ; and if there be a little pain at one end of the line, what enormous pleasure at the other !

Merrily the float trips, again and again, from end to end of the swim, and is once more gliding down with the current, when suddenly the quill stops — slowly revolves — bobs — bobs again — and dives under the water.

The Angler strikes convulsively — extravagantly — insanely ; and something swift and silvery as a shooting-star flies over his head. It should, by rights, be a fish — yet there is none on his hook ; but searching farther and farther, all up the lawn, to the back-door, there certainly lies something bright and quivering on the stone step — something living, scaly, and about an inch long — in short, Mr. Chubb's first bleak !

23

CHAPTER III.

HAPPY Mr. Chubb! Happy on Thursday, happier on Friday, and happiest on Saturday!

For three delightful days he had angled, each time with better success, and increasing love for the art, when Sunday intervened — the longest *dry* Sunday he had ever spent in his life. This short fast, however, only served to whet his appetite for the sport, and to send him the earlier on Monday to the river's edge, not without some dim superstitious notion of catching the fine hog-backed perch he had hooked in a dream over night.

By this time practice had made him perfect in his manipulations. His rod was put together in a crack — the line attached to it in a jiffy, the hook baited in a twinkling, and all ready to begin. But first he took his customary survey, to assure him that his solitude was inviolate — that there was no eye to startle his *mauvaise honte*, for he was as sensitive to observation, as some skins to new flannel: but all was safe. There was not a horse or cow even to stare at him from the opposite meadow — no human creature within ken, to censure his performance or criticise his appearance. He might have fished, if he had pleased, in his nightcap, dressing-gown, and slippers.

The ineffable value of such a privacy is only appreciable by shy, sensitive men, who ride hobbies. But Toby Shandy knew it when he gave *a peep over the horn-beam hedge* before he took a first whiff of the ivory pipe attached to his smoking artillery. And so did Mr. Chubb, as after a preliminary pinch of snuff, and an ecstatic rub of his hands, he gently swung the varnished float, shotted line, and baited hook, from his own freehold lawn, into the exclusive water.

The weather was lovely, the sky of an unclouded blue, and the whole landscape flooded with sunshine, which would have been too bright but that a westerly breeze swept the gloss off the river, and allowed the Angler to watch, undazzled, his neat tip-capped float. Thrice the buoyant quill had travelled from end to end of the property, and was midway on its fourth voyage, when — without the least hint of bite or nibble — it was violently twitched up, and left to dangle in the air, whilst Mr. Chubb distractedly stared on a new object in the stream.

A strange float had come into his swim !

And such a float ! — A great green and white pear-shaped thing — of an extra size, expressly manufactured for the most turbulent waters ; but magnified, by the enormity of the trespass, into a ship's buoy !

Yes — there it was in his own private fishing-place, down which it drifted five or six good yards before it brought up, on its side, when the force of the current driving the lower part of the line towards the surface, disclosed a perfect necklace of large swanshot, and the shank of a No. 1 hook, baited, as it seemed, with a small hard dumpling !

Mr. Chubb was petrified — Gorgonized — basilisked! His heart and his legs gave way together, and he sank into the elbow-chair ; his jaw locked. his eyes protruding in a fixed stare, and altogether in physiognomy extremely like the fish called a Pope or Ruff, which, on being hooked, is said to go into a sort of spasmodic fit, through surprise and alarm.

However, disappointment and vexation gradually gave way to indignation, and planting the chair against the evergreen hedge, he mounted on the seat, with a brace of objurgations on his lips — the one adapted to a great hulking fellow, the other for an infernal little boy ; but before either found vent, down he scrambled again, with breakneck precipitation, and dropped into the seat. To swear was impossible — to threaten or vituperate quite out of the question, or even to remonstrate. He who had not the courage to be polite to a lady, to be rude or harsh to one? — never ! What then could he do ? Nothing, but sit staring at the green and white float, as it lay on its side, making a fussy ripple in the water, till SHE chose to withdraw it.

At last, after a very tedious interval, the obnoxious object suddenly began to scud up the stream, and then rising, with almost as much splutter as a wild duck, flew into the neighboring garden. The swanshot and the hook flew after it, but the little dumpling, parting asunder, had escaped from the steel, and the halves separately drifted down with the current, each nibbled at by its own circle of New River bleak.

Mr. Chubb waited a minute, and then fell to angling again ; but as silently, stealthily, and sneakingly, as if instead of fish-

ing in his own waters he had been poaching in those of Cashio-
bury, —

> " Because Lord Essex would n't give him leave."

But even this faint enjoyment was shortlived. All at once
he heard, to the left, a plash as if a bullfrog or water-rat had
plumped into the river, and down came the great green and
white nuisance, again dancing past the private hedge, and
waltzing with every little eddy that came in its way. Of
course it would stop at the old spot — but no, its tether had
been indefinitely prolonged, and on it came, bobbing and beck-
ing, till within a foot of the little slim tip-capped quill of our
Fisherman. He instantly pulled up, but too late — the bottoms of the two lines had already grappled. There was a
hitch and then a jerk — the swanshot with a centrifugal impulse went spinning round and round the other tackle, till silk
and gut were complicated in an inveterate tangle. The Unknown, feeling the resistance, immediately struck, and began
to haul in. The perplexed Bachelor, incapable of a " Hallo ! "
only blessed his own soul in a whisper, and opposed a faint
resistance. The strain increased ; and he held more firmly,
deperately hoping that his own line would give way : but instead of any such breakage, as if instinct with the very spirit
of mischief, the top-joint of his rod suddenly sprang out of its
socket, and went flying, as the other lithe top seemed to beckon
it — into HER garden !

It was gone, of course, forever. As to applying for it,
little Smith would as soon have asked for the ball that he had
pitched through a pane of plate-glass into Mrs. Jones's drawing-room.

All fishing was over for the day ; and the discomfited Angler
was about to unscrew his rod and pack up, when a loud
" hem ! " made him start and look towards the sound — and
lo ! the unknown Lady, having mounted a chair of her own,
was looking over the evergreen hedge and holding out the
truant top-joint to its owner. The little shy bashful Bachelor,
still in a nervous agony, would fain have been blind to this civility ; but the cough became too importunate to be shirked, and
blushing till his very hair and whiskers seemed to redden
into carotty, he contrived to stumble up to the fence and stam-
mer out a jumble of thanks and apologies.

" Really, ma'am — I 'm extremely sorry — you 're too good,
— so very awkward — quite distressing — I 'm exceedingly
obliged I 'm sure — very warm, indeed," — and seizing the
top-joint he attempted to retreat with it, but he was not to
escape so easily.

" Stop, sir ! " cried one of the sweetest voices in the world,
" the lines are entangled."

" Pray don't mention it," said the agitated Mr. Chubb, vainly
fumbling in the wrong waistcoat-pocket for his penknife. " I 'll
cut it, ma'am — I 'll bite it off."

" O, pray don't ! " exclaimed the lady ; " it would be a sin
and a shame to spoil such a beautiful line. Pray, what do
you call it ? "

What an unlucky question. For the whole world Mr.
Chubb would not have named the material — which he at
last contrived to describe as " a very fine sort of fiddle-
string."

" O, I understand," said the Lady. " How fine it is — and
yet how strong. What a pity it is in such a tangle ! But I
think with a little time and patience I can unravel it ! "

" Really, ma'am, I 'm quite ashamed — so much trouble —
allow *me*, ma'am." And the little Bachelor climbed up into
his elbow-chair, where he stood tottering with agitation, and
as red in the face, and as hot all over, as a boiling lobster.

" I think, sir," suggested the Lady, " if you would just have
the goodness to hold these loops open while I pass the other
line through them — "

" Yes, ma'am, yes — exactly — by all means — " and he
endeavored to follow her instructions, by plunging the short,
thick fingers of each hand into the hank ; the Lady meanwhile poking her float, like a shuttle, up and down, to and fro,
through the intricacies of the tangled lines.

" Bless my soul ! " thought Mr. Chubb, " what a singular
situation ! A lady I never saw before — a perfect stranger !
— and here I am face to face with her — across a hedge —
with our fingers twisting in and out of the same line, as if we
were playing at cat's-cradle ! "

CHAPTER IV.

" HEYDAY ! It is a long job !" exclaimed the Lady, with a gentle sigh.

" It is indeed, ma'am," said Mr. Chubb, with a puff of breath as if he had been holding it the whole time of the operation.

" My fingers quite ache," said the Lady.

" I'm sure — I'm very sorry — I beg them a thousand pardons," said Mr. Chubb, with a bow to the hand before him. And what a hand it was ! So white and so plump, with little dimples on the knuckles, — and then such long taper fingers, and filbert-like nails.

" Are you fond of fishing, sir ? " asked the Lady, with a full look in his face for the answer.

" O, very, ma'am — very partial, indeed ! "

" So am I, sir. It's a taste derived, I believe, from my reading."

" Then mayhap, ma'am," said Mr. Chubb, his voice quavering at his own boldness, " if it is n't too great a liberty — you have read the ' Complete Angler ' ? "

" What, Izaak Walton's ? O, I dote on it ! The nice, dear old man ! So pious, and so sentimental ! "

" Certainly, ma'am — as you observe — and so uncommonly skilful."

" O, and so natural ! and so rural ! Such sweet green meadows, with honeysuckle hedges ; and the birds, and the innocent lambs, and the cows, and that pretty song of the milk-maid's ! "

" Yes, ma'am, yes," said Mr. Chubb, rather hastily, as if afraid she would quote it ; and blushing up to his crown, as though she had actually invited him to " live with her and be her love."

" There was an answer written to it, I believe, by Sir Walter Raleigh ? "

" There was, ma'am — or Sir Walter Scott — I really forget which," stammered the bewildered Bachelor, with whom the present tense had completely obliterated the past. As to the future, nothing it might produce would surprise him.

" Now, then, sir, we will try again ! " And the Lady

sumed her task, in which Mr. Chubb assisted her so effectually, that at length one line obtained its liberty, and by a
spring so sudden, as to excite a faint scream.

"Gracious powers!" exclaimed the horrified little man,
almost falling from his chair, and clasping his hands.

"I thought the hook was in my eye," said the Lady; "but
it is only in my hair." From which she forthwith endeavored
to disentangle it, but with so little success, that in common
politeness Mr. Chubb felt bound to tender his assistance. It
was gratefully accepted; and in a moment the most bashful
of bachelors found himself in a more singular position than
ever — namely, with his short thick fingers entwined with a
braid of the glossiest, finest, softest auburn hair that ever
grew on a female head.

"Bless my soul and body!" said Mr. Chubb to himself;
"the job with the gut and silk lines was nothing to this!"

CHAPTER V.

THAT wearisome hook! It clung to the tress in which it had
fastened itself with lover-like pertinacity! In the mean time the
Lady, to favor the operation, necessarily inclined her head a little downwards and sideways, so that when she looked at Mr.
Chubb, she was obliged to glance at him from the corners of her
eyes — as coquettish a position as female artifice, instead of accident, could have produced. Nothing, indeed, could be more
bewitching! Nothing so disconcerting! It was a wonder
the short thick fingers ever brought their task to an end, they
fumbled so abominably — the poor man forgot what he was
about so frequently! At last the soft glossy braid, sadly
disarranged, dropped again on the fair smooth cheek.

"Is the hook out?" asked the Lady.

"It *is*, ma'am — thank God!" replied the little Bachelor,
with extraordinary emphasis and fervor; but the next moment making a grimace widely at variance with the implied
pleasure.

"Why, it's in your own thumb!" screamed the Lady, forgetting in her fright that it was a strange gentleman's hand
she caught hold of so unceremoniously.

"It's nothing, ma'am — don't be alarmed; — nothing at all
— only — bless my soul, — how very ridiculous!"

"But it must hurt you, sir."

"Not at all, ma'am — quite the reverse. I don't feel it — I don't indeed! — Merely through the skin, ma'am, — and if I could only get at my penknife —"

"Where is it, sir?"

"Stop, ma'am — here — I've got it," said Mr. Chubb, his heart beating violently at the mere idea of the long taper fingers in his left waistcoat-pocket — "But unluckily it's my right hand!"

"How very distressing!" exclaimed the lady; "and all through extricating me!"

"Don't mention it, ma'am, pray don't — you're perfectly welcome."

"If I thought," said the lady, "that it *was* only through the skin — I had once to cut one out for poor dear Mr. Hooker," and she averted her head as if to hide a tear.

"She's a widow, then!" thought Mr. Chubb to himself. "But what does that signify to me — and as to her cutting out the hook, it's a mere act of common charity."

And so, no doubt, it was; for no sooner was the operation performed, than dropping his hand as if it had been a stone, or a brick, or a lump of clay, she restored the penknife, and cutting short his acknowledgments with a grave "Good morning, sir," skipped down from her chair, and walked off, rod in hand, to her house.

Mr. Chubb watched her till she disappeared, and then getting down from his own chair, took a seat in it, and fell into a reverie, from which he was only roused by putting his thumb and finger into the wrong box, and feeling a pinch of gentles, instead of snuff.

CHAPTER VI.

The next day Mr. Chubb angled as usual; but with abated pleasure. His fishery had been disturbed; his solitude invaded — he was no longer Walton and Zimmerman rolled into one. From certain prophetic misgivings he had even abandoned the costume of the craft, — and appeared in a dress more suited to a public dinner than his private recreation — a blue coat and black kerseymere trousers — instead of the fustian jacket, shorts, and leathern gaiters.

The weather was still propitious, but he could neither confine his eye to his quill nor his thoughts to the pastime. Every moment he expected to hear the splash of the great green and white float, — and to see it come sailing into his swim. But he watched and listened in vain. Nothing drifted down with the current but small sticks and straws or a stray weed, — nothing disturbed the calm surface of the river, except the bleak, occasionally rising at a fly. A furtive glance assured him that nobody was looking at him over the evergreen fence — for that day, at least, he had the fishery all to himself, and he was beginning, heart and soul, to enjoy the sport, — when, from up the stream, he heard a startling plunge, enough to frighten all the fish up to London or down to Ware! The flop of the great green and white float was a whisper to it — but before he could frame a guess at the cause, a ball of something, as big as his own head, plumped into his swim, with a splash that sent up the water into his very face! The next moment a sweet low voice called to him by his name.

It was the Widow! He knew it without turning his head. By a sort of mental clairvoyance he saw her distinctly looking at him, with her soft liquid hazel eyes, over the privet hedge. He immediately fixed his gaze more resolutely on his float, and determined to be stone-deaf. But the manœuvre was of no avail. Another ball flew bomb-like through the air, and narrowly missing his rod, dashed — saluting him with a fresh sprinkle — into the river!

"Bless my soul," thought Mr. Chubb, carefully laying his rod across the arms of his elbow-chair, "when shall I get any fishing!"

"A fine morning, Mr. Chubb."

"Very, ma'am — very, indeed — quite remarkable," stammered Mr. Chubb, bowing as he spoke, plucking off his hat, and taking two or three unsteady steps towards the fence.

"My gardener has made me some ground bait, Mr. Chubb, and I told him to throw the surplus towards your part of the river."

"You're very good, ma'am, — I'm vastly obliged, I'm sure," said the little Bachelor, quite overwhelmed by the kindness, and wiping his face with his silk handkerchief, as if it had just received the favor of another sprinkle. "Charming weather, ma'am!"

"O, delightful!—It's quite a pleasure to be out of doors. By the by, Mr. Chubb, I'm thinking of strolling—do you ever stroll. sir?"

"Ever what?" asked the astounded Mr. Chubb, his blood suddenly boiling up to Fever Heat.

"For jack and pike, sir—I've just been reading about it in the Complete Angler."

"O, she means *trolling*," thought Mr. Chubb, his blood as rapidly cooling down to temperate. "Why, no, ma'am—no. The truth is,—asking your pardon,—there are no jack or pike, I believe, in this water."

"Indeed! That's a pity. And yet, after all. I don't think I could put the poor frog on the hook—and then sew up his mouth,—I'm sure I couldn't!"

"Of course not, ma'am—of course not," said the little Bachelor, with unusual warmth of manner,—"you have too much sensibility."

"Do you think, then, sir, that angling is cruel?"

"Why really, ma'am"—but the poor man had entangled himself in a dilemma, and could get no further.

"Some persons say it is," continued the Lady,—"and really to think of the agonies of the poor worm on the hook—but for my part I always fish with paste."

"Yes—I know it," thought Mr. Chubb,—"with a little hard dumpling."

"And then it is so much cleaner," said the lady.

"Certainly, ma'am, certainly," replied Mr. Chubb, with a particular reference to a certain very white hand with long taper fingers. "Nothing like paste, ma'am—or a fly—if it was not a liberty, ma'am, I should think you would prefer an artificial fly."

"An artificial one!—O, of all things in the world!" exclaimed the Lady with great animation. "*That* cannot feel! —But then"—and she shook her beautiful head despondingly—"they are so hard to make. I have read the rules for artificial flies in the book,—and what with badger's hair, and cock's cackles (she meant hackles), and whipping your shanks (she meant the hook's), and then drubbing your fur (she meant dubbing with fur), O, I never could do it!"

Mr. Chubb was silent. He had artificial flies in his pocketbook, and yearned to offer one — but, deterred by certain recollections, he shrank from the task of affixing it to her line. And yet to oblige a lady — and such a fine woman too — and besides the light fall of a fly on the water would be so much better than the flopping of that abominable great green and white float! — Yes, he would make the offer of it, and he did. It was graciously accepted, — the rod was handed over the hedge, and the little Bachelor, — at a safe distance, — took off, with secret satisfaction, the silk line, its great green and white float, its swanshot, the No. 1 hook and its little hard dumpling. He then substituted a fine fly-line, with a small black ant-fly, and when all was ready, presented the apparatus to the lovely Widow, who was profuse in her acknowledgments. "There never was such a beautiful fly," she said, "but the difficulty was how to throw it. She was only a Tryo (she meant a Tyro), and as such must throw herself on his neighborly kindness, for a little instruction."

This information, as well as he could by precept and example, with a hedge between, the little Bachelor contrived to give; and then dismissed his fair pupil to whip for bleak; whilst with an internal "Thank Heaven!" he resumed his own apparatus, and began to angle for perch, roach, dace, gudgeons, — or anything else.

But his gratitude was premature — his float had barely completed two turns, when he heard himself hailed again from the privet hedge.

"Mr. Chubb! Mr. Chubb!"

"At your service, ma'am."

"Mr. Chubb, you will think me shockingly awkward, but I've switched off the fly, — your beautiful fly, — somewhere among the evergreens."

Slowly the Angler pulled up his line — at the sacrifice of what seemed a very promising nibble — and carefully deposited his rod again across the arms of the elbow-chair.

"Bless my soul and body!" muttered Mr. Chubb, as he selected another fly from his pocketbook, — "when shall I ever get any fishing!"

CHAPTER VII.

Poor Mr. Chubb!

How little he dreamt — in all his twelve years dreaming, of ever retiring from trade into such a pretty business as that in which he found himself involved! How little he thought, whilst studying the instructive dialogues of Venator and Viator with Piscator, that he should ever have a pupil in petticoats hanging on his own lips for lessons in the gentle art! Nor was it seldom that she required his counsel or assistance. Scarcely had his own line settled in the water, when he was summoned by an irresistible voice to the evergreen fence, and requested to perform some trivial office for a fair Neophyte, with the prettiest white hand, the softest hazel eyes, and the silkiest auburn hair he had ever seen. Sometimes it was to put a bait on her hook — sometimes to take off a fish — now to rectify her float — and now to screw or unscrew her rod. Not a day passed but the little Bachelor found himself *tête-à-tête* with the lovely Widow, across the privet hedge.

Little he thought, the while, that she was fishing for him, and that he was pouching the bait! But so it was: — for exactly six weeks from the day when Mr. Chubb caught his first Bleak — Mrs. Hooker beheld at her feet her first Chubb!

What she did with him needs not to be told. Of course she did not give him away, like Venator's chub, to some poor body; or baste him, as Piscator recommends, with vinegar or verjuice. The probability is that she blushed, smiled, and gave him her hand; for if you walk, Gentle Reader to Enfield, and inquire concerning a certain row of snug little villas, with pleasure-grounds bounded by the New River, you will learn that two of the houses, and two of the gardens, and two of the proprietors have been " thrown into one."

" And did they fish together, sir, after their marriage ? "

Never! Mr. Chubb, indeed, often angled from morning till night, but Mrs. C. never wetted a line from one year's end to another.

THE HAPPIEST MAN IN ENGLAND.

A SKETCH ON THE ROAD.

> "It is the Soul that sees; the outward eyes
> Present the object; but the Mind descries,
> And thence delight, disgust, and cool indifference rise."
>
> CRABBE.

"A CHARMING morning, sir," remarked my only fellow-passenger in the Comet, as soon as I had settled myself in the opposite corner of the coach.

As a matter of course and courtesy I assented; though I had certainly seen better days. It did not rain; but the weather was gloomy, and the air felt raw, as it well might with a pale, dim sun overhead, that seemed to have lost all power of roasting.

"Quite an Italian sky," added the stranger, looking up at a sort of French gray coverlet that would have given a Neapolitan fancy the ague.

However, I acquiesced again, but was obliged to protest against the letting down of both windows in order to admit what was called the "fresh, invigorating breeze from the Surrey Hills."

To atone for this objection, however, I agreed that the coach was the best, easiest, safest, and fastest in England, and the road the most picturesque out of London. Complaisance apart, we were passing between two vegetable screens, of a color converted by dust to a really "invisible green," and so high that they excluded any prospect as effectually as if they had been Venetian blinds. The stranger, nevertheless, watched the monotonous fence with evident satisfaction.

"No such hedges, sir, out of England."

"I believe not, sir!"

"No, sir, quite a national feature. They are peculiar to the enclosures of our highly cultivated island. You may travel from Calais to Constantinople without the eye reposing on a similar spectacle."

"So I have understood, sir."

"Fact, sir: they are unique. And yonder is another rural picture unparalleled, I may say, in Continental Europe, — a meadow of rich pasture, enamelled with the indigenous daisy and a multiplicity of buttercups!"

The oddity of the phraseology made·me look curiously at the speaker. A pastoral poet, thought I — but no — he was too plump and florid to belong to that famishing fraternity, and in his dress, as well as in his person, had every appearance of a man well to do in the world. He was more probably a gentleman farmer, an admirer of fine grazing-land, and perhaps delighted in a well-dressed paddock and genteel haystack of his own. But I did him injustice, or rather to his taste — which was far less exclusive — for the next scene to which he invited my attention was of a totally different character — a vast, bleak, scurfy-looking common, too barren to afford even a picking to any living creatures, except a few crows. The view, however, elicited a note of admiration from my companion : —

"What an extensive prospect! Genuine, uncultivated nature — and studded with rooks!"

The stranger had now furnished me with a clew to his character; which he afterwards more amusingly unravelled. He was an Optimist ; — one of those blessed beings (for they are blessed) who think that whatever is, is beautiful as well as right : — practical philosophers, who make the best of everything ; imaginative painters, who draw each object *en beau*, and deal plentifully in *couleur de rose*. And they are right. To be good — in spite of all the old story-books, and all their old morals — is not to be happy. Still less does it result from Rank, Power, Learning, or Riches ; from the single state or a double one, or even from good health or a clean conscience. The source of felicity, as the poet truly declares, is in the Mind — for like my fellow-traveller, the man who has a mind to be happy will be so, on the plainest commons that nature can set before him — with or without the rooks.

The reader of Crabbe will remember how graphically he

has described, in his "Lover's Journey," the different aspects of the same landscape to the same individual, under different moods — on his outward road, an Optimist, like my fellow-traveller, but on his return a malecontent like myself.

In the mean time, the coach stopped — and opposite to what many a person, if seated in one of its right-hand corners, would have considered a very bad lookout, — a muddy square space, bounded on three sides by plain brick stabling and wooden barns, with a dwarf wall, and a gate, for a foreground to the picture. In fact, a straw-yard, but untenanted by any live-stock, as if an Owenite plan amongst the brute creation, for living in a social parallelogram, had been abandoned. There seemed no peg here on which to hang any eulogium; but the eye of the Optimist detected one in a moment: —

"What a desirable Pond for Ducks!"

He then shifted his position to the opposite window, and with equal celerity discovered "a capital Pump! with oceans of excellent Spring Water, and a commodious handle within reach of the smallest Child!"

I wondered to myself how he would have described the foreign Fountains, where the sparkling fluid gushes from groups of Sculpture into marble basins, and without the trouble of pumping at all, ministers to the thirst and cleanliness of half a city. And yet I had seen some of our Travellers pass such a superb Water-work with scarcely a glance, and certainly without a syllable of notice! It is such Headless Tourists, by the way, who throng to the German Baths, and consider themselves Bubbled, because, without any mind's eye at all, they do not see all the pleasant things which were so graphically described by the Old Man of the Brunnens. For my own part I could not help thinking that I must have lost some pleasure in my own progress through life by being difficult to please.

For example, even during the present journey, whilst I had been inwardly grumbling at the weather, and yawning at the road, my fellow-traveller had been revelling in Italian skies, salubrious breezes, verdant enclosures, pastoral pictures, sympathizing with wet habits and dry, and enjoying desirable duck-ponds, and parochial Pumps!

What a contrast, methought, between the cheerful, contented spirit of my present companion, and the dissatisfied temper and tone of Sir W. W., with whom I once had the uncomfortable honor of travelling *tête-à-tête* from Leipzig to Berlin. The road, it is true, was none of the most interesting, but even the tame and flat scenery of the Lincolnshire Fens may be rendered still more wearisome by sulkily throwing yourself back in your carriage and talking of Switzerland! But Sir W. W. was far too nice to be wise — too fastidious to be happy — too critical to be contented. Whereas my present coach-fellow was not afraid to admire a commonplace inn — I forget its exact locality — but he described it as "superior to any Oriental Caravansery — and with a Sign that, in the Infancy of The Art, might have passed for a *Chef d' Œuvre.*"

Happy Man! How he must have enjoyed the Exhibitions of the Royal Academy, whereas to judge by our periodical critiques on such Works of Modern Art, there are scarcely a score out of a thousand annual Pictures that ought to give pleasure to a Connoisseur. Nay, even the Louvre has failed to satisfy some of its visitants, on the same principle that a matchless collection of Titians has been condemned for the want of a good Teniers.

But my fellow-traveller was none of that breed: he had nothing in common with a certain Lady, who with half London, or at least its Londoners, had inspected Wanstead House, prior to its demolition, and on being asked for her opinion of that princely mansion, replied that it was "short of cupboards."

In fact, he soon had an opportunity of pronouncing on a Country Seat — far, very, very far inferior to the House just mentioned, and declared it to be one which " Adam himself would have chosen for a Family Residence, if Domestic Architecture had flourished in the primeval Ages."

Happy Man, again! for with what joy, and comfort, and cheerfulness, for his co-tenants, would he have inhabited the enviable dwelling; and yet, to my private knowledge, the Proprietor was one of the most miserable of his species, simply because he chose to go through life like a pug-dog — with his nose turned up at everything in the world. And, truly flesh is grass, and beauty is dust, and gold is dross, nay, life itself but a vapor; but instead of dwelling on such disparagements, it is far wiser and happier, like the florid gentleman in one corner of the Comet, to remember that one is not a Sworn Appraiser, nor bound by oath like an Ale-Conner to think small beer of small beer.

From these reflections I was suddenly roused by the Optimist, who earnestly begged me to look out of the Window at a prospect which, though pleasing, was far from a fine one, for either variety or extent.

"There, sir,—there's a Panorama! A perfect circle of enchantment! realizing the Arabia Felix of Fairy Land in the County of Kent!"

"Very pretty, indeed."

"It's a gem, sir, even in our Land of Oaks—and may challenge a comparison with the most luxuriant Specimens of what the Great Gilpin calls Forest Scenery!"

"I think it may."

"By the by, did you ever see Scrublands, sir, in Sussex?"

"Never, sir."

"Then, sir, you have yet to enjoy a romantic scene of the Sylvan Character, not to be paralleled within the limits of Geography! To describe it would require one to soar into the regions of Poetry, but I do not hesitate to say, that if the celebrated Robinson Crusoe were placed within sight of it, he would exclaim in a transport, 'Juan Fernandez!'"

"I do not doubt it, sir."

"Perhaps, sir, you have been in Derbyshire?"

"No, sir."

"Then, sir, you have another splendid treat *in futuro*—Braggins—a delicious amalgamation of Art and Nature,—a perfect Eden, sir,—and the very spot, if there be one on the Terrestrial Globe, for the famous Milton to have realized his own 'Paradise Regained'!"

In this glowing style, waxing warmer and warmer with his own descriptions, the florid gentleman painted for me a series of highly-colored sketches of the places he had visited; each a retreat that would wonderfully have broken the fall of our first Parents, and so thickly scattered throughout the counties, that by a moderate computation our Fortunate Island contained at least a thousand "Perfect Paradises," copyhold or freehold. A pleasant contrast to the gloomy pictures which are drawn by certain desponding and agriculturally-depressed Spirits who cannot find a single Elysian Field, pasture or arable, in the same country!

In the mean time, such is the force of sympathy, the Optimist had gradually inspired me with something of his own spirit, and I began to look out for and detect unrivalled forest scenery, and perfect panoramas, and little Edens, and might in time have picked out a romantic pump, or a picturesque post, — but, alas! in the very middle of my course of Beau Idealism, the coach stopped, the door opened, and with a hurried good-morning, the florid gentleman stepped out of the stage and into a gig which had been waiting for him at the end of a cross-road, and in another minute was driving down the lane between two of those hedges that are only to be seen in England.

"Well, go where thou wilt," thought I, as he disappeared behind the fence, "thou art certainly the Happiest Man in England!"

Yes — he was gone; and a light and a glory had departed with him. The air again felt raw, the sky seemed duller, the sun more dim and pale, and the road more heavy. The scenery appeared to become tamer and tamer, the inns more undesirable, and their signs were mere daubs. At the first opportunity I obtained a glass of sherry, but its taste was vapid; everything in short appeared "flat, stale, and unprofitable." Like a *Bull* in the Alley, whose flattering rumors hoist up the public funds, the high, sanguine tone of the Optimist had raised my spirits considerably above par; but now his operations had ceased, and by the usual reaction my mind sank again even below its natural level. My short-lived enthusiasm was gone, and instead of the cheerful, fertile country through which I had been journeying, I seemed to be travelling that memorable long stage between Dan and Beersheba where "all was barren."

Some months afterwards I was tempted to go into Essex to inspect a small Freehold Property which was advertised for sale in that county. It was described, in large and small print, as "a delightful Swiss Villa, the prettiest thing in Europe, and enjoying a boundless prospect over a country proverbial for Fertility, and resembling that Traditional Land of Promise described metaphorically in Holy Writ as overflowing with Milk and Honey."

Making all due allowance, however, for such professional flourishes, this very Desirable Investment deviated in its features even more than usual from its portrait in the prospectus.

The Villa turned out to be little better than an ornamented Barn, and the Promised Land was some of the worst land in England, and overflowed occasionally by the neighboring river. An Optimist could hardly have discovered a single merit on the estate; but he did; for whilst I was gazing in blank disappointment at the uncultivated nature before me, not even studded with rooks, I heard his familiar voice at my elbow: —

" Rather a small property, sir — but amply secured by ten solid miles of Terra Firma from the encroachments of the German Ocean."

" And if the sea could," I retorted, "it seems to me very doubtful whether it would care to enter on the premises."

" Perhaps not as a matter of marine taste," said the Optimist. " Perhaps not, sir. And yet, in my pensive moments, I have fancied that a place like this with a sombre interest about it, would be a desirable sort of Wilderness, and more in unison with an Il Penseroso cast of feelings than the laughing beauties of a Villa in the Regent's Park, the Cynosure of Fashion and Gayety, enlivened by an infinity of equipages. But excuse me, sir, I perceive that I am wanted elsewhere," and the florid gentleman went off at a trot towards a little man in black, who was beckoning to him from the door of the Swiss Villa.

" Yes," was my reflection as he turned away from me, if he can find in such a swamp as this a Fancy Wilderness, a sort of Shenstonian Solitude for a sentimental fit to evaporate in, he must certainly be the Happiest Man in England."

As to his pensive moments, the mere idea of them sufficed to set my risible muscles in a quiver. But as if to prove how he would have comported himself in the Slough of Despond, during a subsequent ramble of exploration round the estate, he actually plumped up to his middle in a bog; — an accident which only drew from him the remark that the place afforded " a capital opportunity for a spirited proprietor to establish a Splendid Mud Bath, like the ones so much in vogue at the German Spaws !"

" If that gentleman takes a fancy to the place," I remarked to the person who was showing me round the property, " he will be a determined bidder."

"Him bid!" exclaimed the man, with an accent of the utmost astonishment — "Him bid! — why he's the Auctioneer that's to sell us!   I thought you would have remarked that in his speech, for he imitates in his talk the advertisements of the famous Mr. Robins.   He's called the Old Gentleman."

"Old! why he appears to be in the prime of life."

"Yes, sir, — but it's the other Old Gentleman — "

"What! the Devil?"

"Yes, sir, — because you see, he's always *a knocking down of somebody's little Paradise.*"

SPECIMEN OF THE COCK AND BULL GENUS.